Caroline James always wanted to write but instead of taking a literary route, she followed a career in the hospitality industry, which included owning a pub and a beautiful country house hotel. She was also a media agent representing many celebrity chefs.

When she's not writing, Caroline likes to go wild water swimming or walk with Fred, her Westie.

www.carolinejamesauthor.co.uk

T0337133

THE FRENCH COOKERY SCHOOL

CAROLINE JAMES

One More Chapter
a division of HarperCollins*Publishers* Ltd
1 London Bridge Street
London SE1 9GF
www.harpercollins.co.uk
HarperCollins*Publishers*
Macken House, 39/40 Mayor Street Upper,
Dublin 1, D01 C9W8

This paperback edition 2024
1
First published in Great Britain in ebook format
by HarperCollins*Publishers* 2024
Copyright © Caroline James 2024
Caroline James asserts the moral right to be identified
as the author of this work

A catalogue record of this book is available from the British Library

ISBN: 978-0-00-866979-9

Printed and bound in the UK using 100% Renewable Electricity
by CPI Group (UK) Ltd

For Willow
Our precious sunflower
and the sunshine in my life.

Prologue

In the tiny village of Poutaloux-Beauvoir, in the medieval municipality of Chauvigny in Western France, the run-down estate of La Maison du Paradis, once vibrant and meticulously tended, bore the mark of neglect. The eighteenth-century garden appeared abandoned, and hedges, no longer neatly trimmed, tangled with wild rambling roses as overgrown grasses swayed lazily in a warm summer breeze.

On a pathway leading to the main house, Waltho Williams, tall and handsome, held a large wooden trug. The oblong container overflowed with lavender plants, their young stems slender, the silvery-green leaves lengthy and linear.

'There are dozens more like this,' Waltho called out to a woman kneeling beside him.

Lauren Dubois caught her long silken hair, the colour of spun gold, and twisted it into a knot at the base of her neck.

She shaded her cornflower-blue eyes with delicate fingers and smiled at Waltho.

'I'll plant lavender along all the pathways,' Lauren said as a bee, drawn to the lavender's nectar, buzzed nearby. 'In time, it will flourish, and as we restore the garden, delicate blossoms will form a sea of purple and blue, and it will be filled with a wonderful perfume.'

Waltho's gaze fell on Lauren. Her loveliness never ceased to amaze him, and his heart swelled as he watched the love of his life dig gently into the soil to anchor her favourite plants. They both knew that in the years to come, the lavender would flourish and provide a magnificent welcome for visitors to their home. Waltho watched a tabby cat slowly approach, and a rhythmic purr emanated from the furry companion, a mixture of stripes and swirls. The cat sat in the sunshine beside Lauren, its bond evident as she reached out to absently stroke her pet.

Waltho sighed with contentment. His life was complete in this French idyll with the woman he'd joyously spend the rest of his days. Staring beyond the estate, Waltho smiled as he saw a carpet of gold dance in a gentle breeze. Fields of sunflowers held brilliant yellow petals to the sun, their sensory symphony enveloping the entire landscape, casting a warm and inviting glow. Time stood still, and, closing his eyes, Waltho silently thanked whatever god had brought them here.

Chapter One

Three years later

O n a hot and sultry day in early July, Waltho Williams stood on the terrace of a shaded corner of his home, La Maison du Paradis, and posed a question. Would today, with the opening of the French Cookery School, mark the first day of the rest of his life?

Waltho raised his chin and thoughtfully stroked the newly grey tinge of neatly shaved stubble, a sharp contrast to his skin, the colour of night. Looking out to the garden, he filled his lungs with the sweet smell of wildflowers from a nearby border and watched the colourful heads sway in the warm breeze. Each petal created a carnival of colour against the rich soil, and his artist's eye admired their fluidity and beauty. Reaching out, he picked a sprig of lavender from wands planted deep in an old terracotta pot. The intense, heady scent, pinched between his fingers, jogged his memory, and a sharp pain stabbed in his chest.

'Oh, Lauren.' Waltho sighed. 'If only you had lived to see what you created.' His eyes were misty as the years dissolved, and he remembered the journey that had led him to this place.

Three years ago, with Lauren by his side, Waltho had wandered through the streets of Chauvigny, huddled tight under the ruins of a medieval castle. Climbing steep winding alleys, they'd marvelled at monuments and been fascinated by pretty houses displaying window boxes abundant with fragrant lavender. It felt a million miles from the hustle and bustle of London with its overcrowded streets and rushed commuters. City life no longer felt attractive, and as their visits increased, the slower pace of life in France became appealing.

The sale of a two-bedroomed apartment in Gipsy Hill and Waltho's studio in Crystal Palace provided funds, and Waltho remembered Lauren's joy of discovering La Maison du Paradis, which sat in an enviable countryside position. Tired and run-down, the building was crying out to be loved and restored, and Lauren, a reputable dealer in antiques, convinced Waltho that they had found their dream home. A place where they could create a business, too, and guests could enjoy a holiday and learn something new. Taking a leap of faith and trusting in his beloved Lauren's instincts, they moved life in its entirety to Poutaloux-Beauvoir, and their labour of love began.

Waltho stroked the warm stone of a smooth white wall typical of buildings in the area and looked up at the rustic roof that had been replaced. The new ochre tiles had been exorbitant, as had the many window shutters, freshly painted the palest blue. Neat pathways boasted flourishing lavender bushes, creating welcoming routes to the house.

A vivid memory of Lauren planting the young stems was haunting. Waltho rubbed a hand over his smooth bald head and clenched his fists. 'Lauren,' he whispered, 'if only you were here.' Despite the day's heat, Waltho felt an involuntary shiver, and a chill ran down his spine. Her death was still crystal clear in his mind.

Biting on his lip, Waltho closed his eyes, almost feeling Lauren's emancipated frame, held gently in his arms throughout the agony of her illness. Her cancer was a one-way ticket to eternity, deadly and swift. No matter how much Waltho willed strength from his body into Lauren's frail and diminished figure, Lauren soon gave up the fight. Waltho shook his head to rid himself of memories etched deep.

In the years that followed, knowing that Lauren had insisted Waltho carry on, it was with a heavy heart that he set to. But La Maison du Paradis had broken the budget and the property needed to generate an income.

Now, he was ready.

Waltho took a deep and steadying breath, then set off to walk through a courtyard. He paused to study a plant climbing lazily over a gazebo and plucked several straggling leaves from the woody stem with nimble fingers. A long oak table was positioned beneath the gazebo and as Waltho traced the grain, he considered the fingerprint of nature.

'If only humans could so lovingly be brought back to life,' he whispered and remembered endless hours spent sanding and restoring the aged piece of furniture.

Gazing out to the garden, Waltho glimpsed a swimming pool. The surface water, unmoving, lay like a mirror beneath the sunny sky. His artist's eye considered the subtle light that changed during the day, creating an evolving palate of colour. It looked so cool and inviting that Waltho was tempted to strip off and plunge in.

But there was no time to swim. A phone rang within the house, and moments later, Waltho heard footsteps crunching across a gravelled path.

'Hey!' a voice called. 'Tomas has left the airport and is on his way.'

Waltho walked towards the woman who approached. 'Merci, Angelique,' he replied. 'Everyone will soon be here. Are we ready?'

'As ready as we will ever be. Housekeeping has finished preparing the guests' rooms.'

Angelique wore a lime-green kaftan and inches of silver bangles on each wrist. They jingled as she moved. Her fiery red hair hung in long silky tresses, clipped back with two tortoiseshell combs, and her fingers gripped a mobile phone, the case encrusted with sparkling bling.

Waltho reached out to take Angelique by the shoulders and, leaning down, kissed each of her rouged cheeks. 'I couldn't have done this without you,' he said.

'Nonsense.' She dismissed his words with a shake of her head but smiled with pleasure, touching her fingers to her hair. 'La Maison du Paradis needed a loving owner, and I needed a job,' she added. 'Your hard work has paid off.'

Waltho nodded and thought of the website created to promote La Maison du Paradis. Themed with sunflowers throughout, the home page announced:

The French Cookery School

Immerse yourself in the French countryside and enjoy a week's cookery holiday at La Maison du Paradis. Relax in our elegant residence surrounded by picturesque countryside and relish outdoor dining and cooling swims in our pool.

Your host welcomes you to his home and is proud to engage the services of a Michelin-starred chef who will guide you through the secrets of his kitchen.

Daily excursions will explore the beauty and history of the area. Leave with new skills, new friends and a feeling of well-being.

La Maison du Paradis awaits!

The description had worked and the course that was about to begin was full. Waltho anxiously looked at his watch. Tomas would leave Bordeaux Airport and arrive in less than two hours if the roads were clear.

'Let's have a cool drink,' Angelique said, 'before the party begins.' She reached out and linked her arm through Waltho's to lead him along the pathway towards the house.

Waltho paused and patted Angelique's hand then took one last long lingering glance at his surroundings. Finally, after difficult years, his home was ready to welcome the first guests to La Maison du Paradis.

Chapter Two

Bordeaux Airport was busy. School vacations had begun, and the race to get to France's holiday homes, gites and hotels was underway. In the bustling arrivals terminal, travellers waited to collect luggage and pass through immigration. Weary from their journey, they were suddenly energised by the mechanical sound of the luggage carousel beginning to rotate.

Caroline Carrington felt that she was melting. There had been no breeze when she'd left her Kensington home in the early hours, and the oppressive heat that hung like a cloud over the streets of London felt even hotter on her arrival in France. She fanned her face, hoping that the coming week was worth the expense and remembered the previous day when Stanley, her soon-to-be ex-husband, had yelled at her.

'Dear Lord, Caro!' Stanley exploded as he stared at the banking app on his phone, eyes wide. 'A luxury holiday at Quinta do Lago would be far less than the price of this wretched cookery course you insist on joining.' Stanley's complexion was puce as he shook his unruly mop of thick blond hair.

Caroline ignored Stanley's rant. There was no likelihood of them ever taking a holiday together again. 'Do calm down,' she told him. 'You'll have heartburn if you carry on.'

'Heartburn is the least of my worries if you insist on spending money we simply do not have.' Stanley grunted. He reached into their wine fridge to uncork a Chateau Montelena Cabernet Sauvignon 2015 and, pouring a large glass, guzzled it down.

Caroline refrained from reminding Stanley that a regular delivery of expensive Napa Valley wines was one of the reasons that their bank account was constantly overdrawn.

Now, as she waited for her luggage, Bordeaux Airport felt hot and uncomfortable and she mopped her brow, shaking her head to rid all thoughts of Stanley. Pleased to be out of the poisonous atmosphere at home, Caroline watched cases of all shapes and sizes teeter precariously on the moving carousel. Remembering how carefully she'd packed for this trip, she wondered if her broken heart was parcelled into the tissued layers of designer clothing. She certainly hadn't left it in Kensington, just anger and confusion in her wake. Unable to live up to her husband's expectations over the years, the end of her marriage was painful and Caroline needed space to think.

Stanley hadn't stirred when she moved noisily around the house, slamming cupboards, and raising the volume on the kitchen radio. His snores rumbled from behind the door of his bedroom. At least he was home, she thought as she saw her Samsonite suitcase burst onto the carousel, and not out till all hours doing goodness knows what. Securing her Louis Vuitton monogrammed bag onto her shoulder, Caroline braced herself and reached out to grab the handle of her case.

'Don't mind me, dear!' a voice called out.

Caroline felt a hot hand on her arm, causing her to stumble and let go of her case. 'Really!' she exclaimed in frustration and, as her luggage was transported away, she turned to see who the voice belonged to.

'Ah, that's a shame. You'll get it next time round.' A rotund woman in orange slacks and a matching T-shirt stood before Caroline. Her lips were as orange as her outfit, and Caroline noticed lipstick staining her teeth.

'Be a darlin' and grab my holdall.' The woman nudged Caroline and nodded as a vast canvas bag that had seen better days wobbled towards them.

Caroline gritted her teeth and was tempted to move away, but remembering her manners bent forward and, with considerable effort, grabbed the woman's heavy bag and heaved it off the moving belt.

'Thank you, duckie,' the woman said, 'that's very kind, and I'm sure your bag will be along soon. Now, where's the lav? I'm desperate to spend a penny.'

'Duckie?' Caroline muttered, clenching her jaw as she watched the orange vision trudge away.

A short while later, with her case by her side, Caroline left the arrivals hall and headed out to Bordeaux's brilliant sunshine. Squinting through Dior sunglasses, she searched for her transport to La Maison du Paradis.

A young man stepped forward and held out a sign. 'Bonjour. Hello? Are you going to Poutaloux-Beauvoir to the cookery school at La Maison du Paradis?' he asked and beamed when Caroline nodded her head. He held a clipboard and ticked her name from a list, then took her case. 'Please, this way.'

Caroline followed and soon stepped into an air-conditioned minibus. She sighed with relief as she chose a seat and sat down on the soft upholstery. Escorted by the young man, other guests emerged from arrivals and joined Caroline. Polite nods were exchanged as everyone made themselves comfortable in readiness for the journey ahead.

Caroline noted two identical women travelling together and a woman on her own. The latter had a page-boy hairstyle, the locks dark and shiny. Short and well-padded in stature, she was emphatic that the driver was careful with her cases.

'Last one!' the young man called out and turned to assist the final passenger who lumbered into the vehicle and levered themselves onto a seat beside Caroline.

Caroline froze. Her travel companion was the woman who'd barged into her at the airport! Tensing, she gripped her bag to her knee.

'Hello.' The woman grinned and wriggled her bulk alongside Caroline's knees. 'We meet again.'

'How. Do. You. Do.' Caroline stared straight ahead. Had she travelled all this way and spent an astronomical amount on a cookery holiday, only to be imprisoned with this wretched woman, who smelt of cheap perfume and whose body heat seared the skin beneath Caroline's immaculately cut linen trousers. She grimaced at the woman's tawdry outfit and tacky bag, then stared out of the window at the crowds setting off on excursions to make memories of their own. She took a deep breath and remembered her mindfulness class, mentally removing herself from the situation. Exhaling slowly, she closed her eyes.

'Care for a jelly baby?'

A podgy elbow nudged Caroline's toned arm. Opening her eyes, she saw a fist hovering over her lap, gripping a bag of sticky sweets.

'No, thank you.'

'Oh, go on.' The elbow nudged again. 'One of these will stop you feeling sick.'

Caroline's fingers tentatively dipped into the bag. If she went along with the woman, it might silence her for the rest of the journey.

'You must have been up early like me?' the woman asked. 'I travelled from Manchester, did you?'

'Gatwick.' Caroline was curt.

'Fancy the flights arriving together.' She chuckled. 'Do you think the cookery school fixed it so that guests got here at the same time?'

'It would be a sensible arrangement.' The jelly baby had begun to soften, and as the first taste of sugar melted in a mouth that hadn't chewed a sweet in forty years, Caroline shuddered.

'Sticky little buggers, aren't they?' the woman continued. Her tongue rolled around the inside of her cheek, and Caroline winced as she heard sucking noises.

Shuffling in her seat, the woman looked around at the other passengers. 'I do hope that it's not just us girls on the course.' She lowered her voice and tilted her head. 'We need a few fellas to keep us in line.' She thrust out her hand. 'I'm Francesca, by the way. A posh name for a Lancashire lass born and bred in Blackpool. My mam thought it might make me better myself.'

'Caroline.' Caroline's reply was brusque. She wanted to add that Francesca's mother had been overly optimistic.

'Oh, that's a lovely name, can I shorten it to Caro? You can call me Fran, everyone else does.'

'I prefer Caroline, thank you.' Caroline stared out of the window. Only Stanley called her Caro, and she hated it.

As their transport left the city and took the slip road heading north to join the autoroute, the driver announced that his name was Tomas, and he estimated that they would arrive at La Maison du Paradis by mid-afternoon.

'Toe-mah,' Fran said and nudged Caroline again. 'I love his accent, and he's a handsome young man.'

'Tomas,' Caroline corrected. 'He's French.'

'Get away.' Fran folded her arms. 'I'd never have guessed.' She smiled and closed her eyes.

In moments, to Caroline's relief, Fran was sound asleep.

Caroline watched the rolling French countryside speed by as they drove past characterful villages and towns. As

Fran's snores rumbled, Caroline stared at an opulent Baroque chateau and admired the architectural style. The building was magnificent with its high slate roof and central dome. It was set back from the road, and she studied the sunny terraces that led down to acres of manicured gardens, wondering if the holiday would include visiting such a chateau. The brochure had promised outings to local places of interest. Caroline thought how much Stanley would enjoy being in an area surrounded by vineyards, especially Saint-Émilion and the grand crus that he adored. But it was no use thinking of Stanley. Her husband had made it clear that there was no hope of a future together and as the miles sped on, she wondered what on her earth was in store in the weeks and months to come.

The jelly baby dissolved, and Caroline longed to scrub the sugary substance from her brilliant white implants. Taking a small canister from her bag, she sprayed her mouth with peppermint freshener. She found hand gel and rubbed it over her fingers. Fran had slumped to one side. Brassy auburn hair fell from a clip and to Caroline's dismay, Fran heaved a sigh, and her head rolled onto Caroline's shoulder. She tried to push her off, but Fran was too heavy and released a loud snore. Horrified, Caroline glanced around, praying other passengers didn't think the wheeze was hers.

In the opposite seat, the identical ladies, clearly twin sisters, sat forward and smiled. 'Bless her,' they said, their grey heads bobbing in unison.

Bless her? Caroline was incredulous. *I'd like to throttle her*, she thought. But, assuming it would take a bomb under the unconscious body to wake her sleeping companion, she gave up. If she couldn't move Fran, she might as well join her. Closing her eyes, Caroline began to count imaginary chateaus.

In no time, she was sound asleep too.

Chapter Three

Daniel Douglas de Beers stood in the kitchen at La
Maison du Paradis and studied his workspace for
the coming days. More familiar with the clinical
surroundings of glass and chrome at his own establishment,
the rustic environment reminded him of the pages of a rural
French cookery book where geese gobbled over a stable
door and warm, freshly baked baguettes lay in a hand-
woven reed basket, beside a wood-burning stove.

In this kitchen, a sturdy farmhouse table took centre
stage. Daniel imagined it as a gathering place over the years
where family and friends shared the simple pleasure of food
harvested from the walled vegetable garden. La Maison du
Paradis was a far cry from the tourist-filled Cotswolds,
where his restaurant was a magnet for rich city folk, who
sped through country lanes in their Porsches and Ferraris.
Gastronomy came alive in his honey-hued house, and the
charismatic chef charmed everyone who entered the gates.
Daniel was proud that in his formative years, he'd

developed his expertise in renowned establishments worldwide, including The Ritz in London and Sandy Lane in Barbados.

As he admired the homely French kitchen and ran his fingers over a butcher's block resting on a cool granite surface, Daniel thought of all the places he'd travelled to. When his marriage broke down, to avoid an angry wife and her lawyers, he'd spent a year at Tokyo's prestigious Nihonryori Ryugin, which enabled him to include Eastern flavours to the eclectic range of global cuisine that he now served at Dining at Daniel De Beers.

Daniel cocked his head to one side and smiled as he remembered that his time in Toyko had diluted press interest when, to his horror, his wife sold her story. But to his surprise, on his return, the bad-boy reputation that she'd exploited, only enhanced his career.

Daniel began to pace the kitchen. It was a carefully thought-out, durable workspace, and he liked the style, nodding approval. It would function well.

His staff had questioned why he would leave his business for a week. His answer had been that he was treating it as a holiday, combined with his desire to give back to the industry by sharing his knowledge. In truth, Daniel didn't give a toss for the wealthy, fee-paying students. He'd jumped at the opportunity to get his hands on the generous sum that Waltho offered, for he was sorely in need of funds to pay off a gambling debt. Daniel sighed as he ran his fingers over hand-painted ceramic tiles in soft, muted colours. One day he would stop. His gambling habit had been born in a pub, where the young

Danny Beers had fought hard to earn enough to work his way from pot-washing to manipulating his way into famous kitchens. Learning everything he could about cooking, wins on the tables had supplemented his meagre income.

Ah, but the wins are few and far between these days, Daniel thought as he stared at gleaming copper pots and pans hooked on an overhead rack.

Reaching up to pluck a leaf from a bunch of herbs hanging from the ceiling, he tasted tangy thyme and, despite the uncomplicated surroundings, suddenly felt at home in this kitchen. It might not have the modern equipment expected of a Michelin-starred chef, but it was the perfect environment to guide a group through some of the secrets of his culinary repertoire.

He'd come a long way from the tenements of Glasgow, where he'd been raised. Never in his wildest dreams had Daniel imagined ending up where he was. Changing his name and eradicating his past had helped the chef reinvent himself, and he was proud of all he'd achieved. But disowning his inebriated parents had come at a cost. Devoid of family to share his success, an emotional void had widened and only the buzz of gambling seemed to fill it.

Daniel heard a knock on an inner door, and turning, he saw through the glass panelling the smiling face of Tomas, his sous chef for the week. Tomas was employed at a nearby chateau, famous for fine dining, and he'd taken a week's leave to work with the English chef.

Raising his hand, Daniel beckoned Tomas in.

'Hey, Tomas, did you have a good drive?' Daniel asked and cuffed Tomas on the shoulder.

'Oui. Everyone on time and no traffic delays.' Tomas rolled the sleeves of his T-shirt over tattooed muscles, then tucked the hem into the narrow waist of his faded blue jeans. He sat down on one of the mismatched pastel-painted chairs.

'What sort of group are they?'

'Personnes d'âge.' Tomas shrugged. 'Mature, mostly asleep all the way,' he added.

'Are you sure there's no eye candy likely to be strutting around the pool?'

'Absolument pas!' Tomas shook his head, and a thick blonde fringe flopped over his tanned face. Flicking it away, he added, 'Best not to be distracted.'

'I'm not so sure, but I agree we have work to do.' Daniel dragged a chair over the terracotta tiled floor and pulled a file across the table.

For the next fifteen minutes, the two men studied the paperwork. They stood when they were happy that everything was in order, and both knew what was expected of the other. In a room to one side of the kitchen, uniforms, newly ordered and neatly pressed, hung by a locker, and the chefs hurriedly changed.

'Waltho has asked for refreshments in the house at four o'clock,' Daniel said as he buttoned his jacket. 'There's a welcoming reception, and the guests will need nourishment.'

'I have everything ready,' Tomas replied and went to a

preparation room where two large fridges were heavily stocked and cupboards groaned with ingredients.

Daniel stared at his rugged reflection in a mirror beside the locker. Blue eyes that still held a twinkle stared back. His tinted hair was thick and dark. Years ago, he'd been compared to a young Elvis and his looks, though fading, enticed females of all ages. He touched his fingers to his face and examined the lines around his eyes and the slightly sagging skin beneath a finely chiselled jawline. *'You've still got it.'* He confidently nodded. *'Even if you won't see fifty again,'* he added with a sigh.

Smoothing the crisp cotton jacket over a slight paunch, Daniel rolled his shoulders and joined his outstretched fingers. Cracking his knuckles, he winked at his reflection.

'Are you ready to rock?' Daniel asked Tomas.

'Mais bien sûr,' Tomas replied and, taking a tray laden with refreshments, led the way through the house.

Caroline stood in her room on the first floor of La Maison du Paradis. Her fingers traced the pale blue shutters as she stared out at the cameo scene ahead. Pale muslin drapes fluttered in a cooling breeze that whispered from the garden below, where the view beyond was idyllic. The soft fabric caressed her arm like a lover's kiss, and Caroline sighed and rubbed her skin. She could hardly remember what a kiss felt like, nor the last time Stanley had shown her any affection.

Years ago, he'd been discreet and Caroline had ignored

Stanley's extra-marital affairs. She'd moved into a separate bedroom, choosing lifestyle over emotions, for living in Kensington suited her well. If he decided to play away, she'd been happy to overlook it. But as she kicked off her jewelled white sandals, she sighed and wondered if she would have continued the farcical marriage had Stanley not wanted out.

Stepping barefoot across lime-washed pine flooring, Caroline stood on a balcony, where a wrought iron table and matching chairs, covered with pale pink cushions, sat in one corner. A pretty pottery vase had been placed in the centre of the table, filled with sweet-smelling lavender. Caroline sat down and, raising her sunglasses, studied a field of sunflowers. Mesmerised by the blanket of gold swaying gently, she watched the sturdy stalks reach towards the sky. Their energy was almost tangible, and she considered the wonder of nature that created something so beautiful.

'If only that simple, transformative state could work for me,' she sighed.

Caroline's shoulders relaxed for the first time in what felt like forever. The balmy air and heady scent from the garden were hypnotic, and it was all she could do to stay awake. How wonderful it would be to lie down, pillowed by feather down, on the deep mattress of the carved bed in her room and let her cares drift away. Caroline's lids felt heavy, and her head slumped forward.

No more anxiety over her errant husband, no more financial difficulties and no business worries to disturb her sleep. Her eyes closed, and Caroline snoozed, vaguely aware of distant sparrows chirping in the hedgerows.

As the birds dive-bombed across the pool's surface, an elderly cat lay in the hot sunshine on a pathway beneath Caroline's balcony. Its body lazily stretched, old bones benefitting from the warm sun and fur glistening as it soaked up the sun. An occasional twitch of a tabby tail was the only acknowledgement of its presence. Under a cloudless sky, the garden shimmered in the heat, and the humid air almost vibrated with untapped energy as though waiting for La Maison du Paradis to come to life.

'Cooee, Caro! Hello, duckie!'

Caroline's head jerked up at the sound of Fran's loud voice. Disorientated, she blinked as she looked around.

'Over here!' Fran called out. She flapped her hands and waved.

Grabbing the table, Caroline steadied herself. She realised that Fran was standing on an adjacent balcony.

'What's your room like?' Fran called out. 'Mine's got a fancy roll-top bath!'

Caroline's fingers smoothed her blonde bob, cut stylishly to enhance high cheekbones, and highlighted to remove any traces of grey. 'It's very nice,' she snapped.

Damnation! The irritating woman was on the other side of the wall. Rigid with anger, Caroline stepped into her room, turning away from Fran. Her case sat on a luggage rack, and flinging it open, she began to unpack. As Caroline smoothed and hung her outfits in a pine armoire, she wondered if Fran would hound her throughout their stay. It felt alien to be with someone so upbeat. How would she avoid Fran if they shared almost every waking hour together in the kitchen or during activities and meals?

The woman might be nosey and if Caroline wasn't careful, she would face intrusive questions that demanded humiliating answers.

Caroline sighed. Despite the beautiful surroundings, her holiday hadn't begun as planned. But, she reasoned, there were others on the course, and if she ignored Fran, the woman would be drawn to someone else.

Tidying her carefully chosen outfits, Caroline vowed not to let a singular person spoil her experience. She'd paid through the nose to momentarily escape her situation and was determined to learn as much as possible from a Michelin-starred chef. God knows her business needed a lift. Caroline's Catering had suffered horribly during the pandemic, being unable to trade, and it had been in poor financial health before then. Her divorce was hurtling along, and she knew that if she ever got back to work she'd need skilful commercial planning in the months ahead.

Opening a drawer with lavender-scented lining, Caroline neatly placed her underwear. She mustn't think about all that now. La Maison du Paradis was meeting all her expectations. Her room was delightful, the house looked charming, and she couldn't wait to meet the host and the celebrity chef.

Caroline's face lit up when she stepped into the bathroom. A chandelier hung above the marble-tiled floor, and a gilded French mirror had been placed above an antique wooden table stacked with soft, fluffy towels and expensive toiletries. Wall sconces matched brass taps, and bright white tiling gave a fresh, modern twist. She thought that the person who'd designed this room had a great deal of flair as she removed her clothes and stepped into the shower.

A short while later, Caroline was ready for the welcome reception.

With immaculate hair and fresh makeup, she smiled and sprayed a generous amount of Dioriviera; the floral perfume was pleasing and reminded her of old-fashioned roses. Picking up her St Marc clutch bag, she slid the silver chain over her shoulder, locked the room and placed the key in the pocket of her white linen dress.

Gripping the rail of a sweeping staircase that led to the ground floor, Caroline descended into a hallway, where stained glass above an oak door shone shafts of colourful light. She could hear chattering voices beyond the double doors to her left, and she reached out to turn the handles. Caroline was used to elegance and good taste, and her Kensington home reflected this, as did the many homes she visited when catering for high-profile dinner parties and events. But the salon that she entered took her breath away.

Huge windows highlighted a light and spacious area. Adding to the room's symmetry, they made the plastered walls appear taller, creating the perfect canvas for art displays. A myriad of soft colours in throws and drapes seemed inspired by the beauty of the countryside beyond open patio doors. Parquet flooring, in a herringbone pattern, was covered in antique rugs. As Caroline moved forward, she stared at the slightly distressed furniture, which, together with valuable antique pieces, added to the comfort of the room.

An arrangement of sunflowers stood in a tall vase on a console table where a silver bowl held ice and chilled bottles, and Caroline realised she was thirsty.

'Mrs Carrington.' A man appeared and held out his hand. 'My name is Waltho Williams, and I welcome you to my home.'

'I'm very pleased to be here,' Caroline replied, noting that her handsome host was dressed conservatively in chinos and a short-sleeved shirt. He oozed grace and good manners. 'Do call me Caroline,' she said and shook his hand.

'May I offer you some refreshment?' he asked. 'A soft drink, wine, champagne?'

'Champagne would be perfect.'

'I trust your journey wasn't too tiring?' Waltho handed her a tall flute.

'Hot and humid in London and busy at the airports.' Caroline took a sip of the deliciously chilled drink.

'I'm afraid that the weather isn't much cooler here. We've had a heatwave for several weeks with no sign of it abating.'

'I hope your kitchen has air-conditioning; it will be unbearable without it.'

'Sadly, this old property lacks such modern installations.' Waltho smiled. 'But we've fitted many fans and will do our best to ensure you are comfortable.'

Caroline wanted to say it was the very least he could do for the exorbitant price she'd paid, but she was taken aback.

There was something about Waltho's eyes, where gold flecks sparkled from endless depths of amber. Used only to Stanley's deep pools of blue, which were mostly cold and unwelcoming, Caroline was mesmerised. She hardly noticed a woman dressed in a vibrant lime-green kaftan who joined them.

'Hello, I'm Angelique,' the woman announced as she refreshed Caroline's glass. 'I'm your hostess during your stay,' she added.

Caroline turned to observe the jangling silver bangles covering Angelique's arms. Large ruby drops hung from her ears, and her red hair was swept into a heavy pleat with a diamante comb. As the hostess poured, Caroline's gaze noted Angelique's fingernails, painted individually in the colours of the rainbow. Suddenly feeling frumpy, Caroline adjusted the strap of her bag and quickly dismissed the thought as she smoothed her fingers over her designer dress. Angelique asked about her journey, and Caroline muttered a reply before querying Angelique's accent, which she couldn't place.

'I'm Dutch, with an English mother,' Angelique explained.

As they conversed politely and Waltho stood alongside, Caroline studied Angelique's pale, freckled complexion, contrasting starkly with Waltho's rich brown skin. They made a striking couple.

Suddenly, the salon doors burst open, and Fran entered the room. Caroline had almost forgotten about her travelling companion and sighed as she watched Fran's entrance.

'So sorry, me darlings,' Fran laughed, 'I fell asleep in the bath and got my bum wedged in. It's taken me forever to climb out.'

Fran grinned, and Caroline noted that lipstick smeared on her teeth was now a bright shade of cerise. Her tight-fitting, animal-print jumpsuit was adorned with chunky, tacky jewellery that seemed to cover every spare inch of Fran's flesh.

'Hello, Caro!' Fran called out and, helping herself to a cordial, bustled over to join them.

Caroline took a step back. What on earth was the woman thinking? Fran's outfit would be better suited to an afternoon in a gaming arcade at the end of a seaside pier. Not the refinement of a French manor house.

Moving away from Fran, Caroline's eyes were drawn to an unsigned painting in the middle of the wall. Shades of purple and hues of blue framed the face of a woman, turned upward as though looking at an unseen moon, her eyes a cornflower blue and her expression serene. Long golden hair cascaded down her back, merging with a border of lavender blooms.

'This artwork is exceptional,' Caroline said, 'who's the artist?'

Waltho coughed. Gripping his glass, he stepped back.

Before Caroline could repeat her question, Angelique moved to the centre of the room and announced. 'I would like to introduce your host for this holiday,' Angelique said. 'Please, everyone, meet Waltho Williams.'

Waltho smiled shyly as polite applause rippled. 'Ladies and gentlemen,' he said, 'it is my pleasure to welcome you to La Maison du Paradis for what I hope will be an informative, rewarding and joyful week of gastronomy, relaxation and making new friends.'

Heads nodded as guests looked around to study the people they would soon get to know.

'There are a few housekeeping rules, and Angelique will explain. I look forward to acquainting myself with you all when we meet for dinner.' Waltho smiled again as the door to the salon opened. 'Your meal this evening is being prepared by a talented chef eager to meet you. Let me introduce your tutor.' Waltho swept out an arm. 'Daniel Douglas de Beers.'

Daniel entered the room, and everyone turned. The chef made the most of his entrance and circled the guests, shaking outstretched hands.

When Caroline's hand was pumped, she was blinded by a set of molars straighter and brighter than her own. Staring at his nut-brown face, which contrasted starkly against the white of a logoed jacket, Caroline wondered how many hours he'd spent sunbathing by the pool. But, to his credit, she found Daniel as charming as his many guest appearances on TV cookery shows.

Fran lumbered across the room and kissed the chef's cheek, 'Hello, duckie!' she said, leaving a sizeable cerise imprint. 'I must have your autograph,' she babbled, whipping a folding fan out of her cleavage. 'Gawd, it's hot.' Fran waved the fan across her face. 'My Sid watches all your shows; he thinks I'll be able to cook like you by the time I get home.'

'I will endeavour to please both you and your husband.'

Daniel raised his hand to flick back a thick lock of hair that had slipped from his carefully arranged coiffure. 'Now, please enjoy the refreshments,' he instructed, waving Tomas forward.

'Don't mind if I do,' Fran said as Tomas produced a tray of tiny entrees. She grabbed a plate and tucked into a miniature whirl.

'Really!' Caroline whispered as Fran brushed puff pastry flakes from her chin. She was fed up with Fran and stared as her bulging mouth moved robotically. *It's enough to put one off food forever*, she thought.

Caroline decided she needed some air and, ignoring Fran, deposited her empty glass on the console. Marching through the room to the open doors, she vanished into the garden.

Chapter Four

F ran watched Caroline leave the room. With a superior air, she reached into a posh leather bag and placed enormous sunglasses on the bridge of her perfect nose before disappearing outside. As Fran ate a salmon savoury, she sat down and wondered if Caroline had eaten. Her rake-thin figure suggested it unlikely and, licking mayonnaise from her lips, Fran considered why someone so svelte would choose to spend a week at a cookery school, where guests would be encouraged to indulge each day.

Maybe she has a speedy metabolism, Fran thought. Perhaps Caroline was one of those athletic types who could eat whatever they liked and never put a pound on. She wore her clothes well on her slim body, and her gorgeous white jewelled sandals were obviously very expensive. Fran bit into a blini with cream cheese and chuckled. She only had to look at a cupcake and she went up a dress size.

'Would you like a confection?' Tomas appeared and held out a porcelain platter.

Fran stared at the assortment of delicate treats. She dabbed at her mouth with a napkin, leaving a faint pink blot. 'These look lovely,' Fran said, 'what have we here?'

'These are macarons.' Tomas smiled. 'A type of almond meringue.'

'Yummy,' Fran replied and picked out a strawberry flavour.

'They are sandwiched together with a filling, and I am sure Chef will instruct, in a lesson, this week.'

'Smashing.' Fran smiled and bit into the smooth exterior. The slightly crisp texture melted on her tongue.

'You notice the lightness and délicatesse?' Tomas asked.

'Oh, yes,' Fran sighed, 'bloody lovely.' She spied a chocolate macaron and reached out. 'But if I eat too many of these, you'll have to hoist me onto the bus to go back home.'

'Life is like chocolate, savour it before it melts.'

'I like that expression.' Fran smiled again. 'I like these too, they are gorgeous.'

'C'est bien, faites-vous plaisir.'

Fran had no idea what Tomas had said, but her eyes studied his luscious lips and his velvety words sounded like the purr of a satisfied cat.

'I could listen to you all day,' Fran giggled. 'Has anyone ever told you that you are handsome and have a very sexy voice?'

'Mais, oui.' Tomas's grin was wicked. 'And I cook how I look.'

Fran almost choked on her chocolate macaron. 'Get away with you.' She playfully slapped Tomas on his arm.

Laughing, Tomas turned away.

Taking a sip of her cordial, Fran watched the young man glide across the room. She thought being young, naturally charming and drop-dead gorgeous would ease Tomas through life and she silently wished him well. But what would Sid think if he saw his wife of forty years going weak at the knee? At least she still had a romantic pulse, and there was nothing wrong with admiring the beauty of youth.

'Oh Sid,' Fran sighed as she watched Tomas offer his plate to the twin sisters who giggled like schoolgirls as they accepted a macaron. 'What am I doing on a cookery course like this?'

Daniel Douglas De Beers had his back to Fran and was surrounded. As she watched him meet and greet the sisters, she remembered why she'd made this trip to France.

Her husband idolised Daniel.

Sid considered the chef one of the most skilled on the culinary scene. He always made sure that he watched Daniel's shows and said that the chef was "a man's man" who liked a drink and was often seen at rugby matches and horse racing meetings. But as Fran heard Daniel charm the pants off the two sisters she thought he was very much a ladies' man.

Fran suddenly felt very tired; it had been such an early start. Placing her drink down, she yawned, ruminating on her husband's plans. Her head fell forward, and closing her eyes, she began to daydream. In moments, Fran was asleep.

'You could cook like that,' Sid had told Fran when they sat with supper on trays on their knees at home in Dunromin, their house in a cul-de-sac at Blackpool's North Shore. A popular cookery show was on TV and Sid waved his fork at the screen to study Daniel Douglas De Beers whipping up a few simple ingredients to produce a delectable dish.

'Posh food made simple,' Sid added as he forked a sausage. 'Just imagine if you knew how to knock out a menu that would have folks queuing at the door,' Sid said as he noted the ingredients Daniel used in his recipe. 'That chef makes everything look easy. You'd pick it up in no time. Just think, lass,' Sid said wistfully, 'we could transform our café into a posh restaurant.'

For weeks, Fran had wondered if Sid was taking some hallucinatory drug and had kept an eye on the post for suspicious parcels or surreptitious knocks on the door. She knew that she was a dab hand at the fryer and made the best batter in Blackpool. Fran's Fish 'n' Chips were notorious, and folk queued out of the door for a Friday Night Special. But fine dining was never on the menu at their café and Fran doubted that her cooking could ever live up to Sid's expectations.

Not to be deterred, Sid was persistent. He'd always dreamt of putting their hometown of Blackpool on the culinary map. 'You've got to have a dream, to make your dream come true,' Sid often told Fran.

During the dark days of the pandemic, their takeaway business had soared, and their bank balance reached a level they'd never imagined. 'Let's give a fancy restaurant a go, lass,' Sid pleaded. 'If it doesn't work out, we can always go back to selling fish and chips.'

'Why don't we buy a place in Spain?' Fran asked, still reluctant to commit and conscious that they had money to afford a nice villa.

But Sid's dream had been one he'd talked of since the first day they'd met.

'I want to serve the best food in Blackpool.' Sid was emphatic when, as innocent teenagers, they'd sat on the prom in deckchairs overlooking the crowded beach. 'Look at all these folk.' He spread out an arm and pointed to holidaymakers enjoying donkey rides and Mr Whippy ice creams. Straightening his button-down Ben Sherman shirt, Sid fiddled with braces supporting two-toned trousers.

At the same time, Fran thoughtfully dunked a straw in her bottle of Babycham. 'The best grub is fish and chips,' Fran replied, 'that's what Blackpool is known for.'

Sid had lit a Woodbine and offered it to Fran. 'Alright,' he'd agreed, 'I know you're right, but no one can take a dream away, and it's my dream that one day Sid and Fran Cartwright will have foodies flocking to our door.'

Working two jobs each, the ambitious young couple soon saved enough for a lease on a shack on the Golden Mile. Selling candy floss and burgers, in time, they rented a fish and chip café by the central pier, which they eventually purchased. But Sid never lost sight of his dream, and as the years rolled by, Fran anxiously kept a silent counsel, knowing that it would take great courage to change course from the life that they knew.

'Wake up, sleepy head.'

Fran felt a hand on her arm and opened her eyes to see Angelique standing before her. 'Oh heck, I must have dozed off.' Fran rolled her shoulders and wriggled her bottom until she was upright in her chair.

'Can I get anything for you?' Angelique asked.

'No, I'll be as right as rain, just a power nap,' Fran grinned, 'you look after the others.' She reached for her cordial, and as she slowly sipped, her daydream re-surfaced, and she thought more about her husband.

Sid was the best husband she could ever have wished for, and she loved him with all her heart. The balding man with a paunch, who'd stood by her side since schooldays, had supported her through thick and thin, every trial and tribulation and, Fran sighed, there had been plenty of those.

Fran smiled, and as she noted Waltho discuss a painting with a guest, she thought of Sid searching the internet in his endless quest to research cookery schools. How he'd jumped for joy when he discovered Daniel was hosting a week's tuition in France!

And now, here she was. Intoxicated by Sid's excitement, she'd given in and gone along with the idea. After all, her old man was right. If their restaurant failed, they could always return to serving fish and chips. A staple diet in Blackpool.

Fran thought France was the stuff of dreams as she stared at the lovely antiques and elegant surroundings, and she determined, somehow, she'd soak up every bit of knowledge from the celebrity chef. Fran knew that she'd have to work as hard as possible to discover fine dining secrets. Sid was keen to open the doors of Fran's Finest Fare, and she prayed they'd made the right decision. But at sixty-one, was Fran up to the challenge?

'Girl power for the over-sixties!' Fran nervously giggled out loud.

'I'm pleased to see that you are amused.'

Fran looked up to see Daniel standing before her. For a moment, she thought Elvis had entered the building as the sun streamed into the room and silhouetted the chef. 'Has anyone ever told you that you look like Elvis?' Fran asked and patted the seat next to her.

'It has been mentioned that I resemble the famous man in his younger days.' Daniel sat down. He ran his fingers through his hair, unconsciously creating a quiff.

'Aye, I can see that,' Fran smiled. She thought Daniel looked like Elvis at the end of his career but considered it impolite to comment. 'I'm very pleased to meet you,' she said, 'you've got a great deal to teach me.'

'I'll certainly do my best,' Daniel assured.

'Your best won't be good enough. I want a cast-iron guarantee that I will leave here capable of cooking and creating dishes just like you.'

Daniel did a double take as he studied the middle-aged woman dressed like a soap opera barmaid.

'Aye, I know I don't look like a chef.' Fran realised she still held a sticky chocolate macaron in one hand. She popped it in her mouth and munched. 'But with your help, that has to change.'

'Then I warn you, we have much work to do.'

'I've never shied away from hard work,' Fran replied, and with a knowing smile, she nodded and confidently patted Daniel's thigh.

As buzzing cicadas provided a background melody to the sultry summer evening, Waltho stood by a serving counter in the courtyard and watched Angelique move around the long oak table beneath the gazebo. Every few steps, she stopped to check a place setting and adjust the position of a knife or glass. The table looked inviting as warm rays of end-of-day sunshine cast a golden glow. Wildflowers placed in jars and tied with ribbon were centred on a runner, giving colour to the stark white of porcelain plates and linen napkins.

Reaching for a corkscrew, Waltho popped the corks from bottles of wine as Angelique placed menus, and as she passed, she held one out.

'Tonight, they eat like kings,' she said, 'Daniel and Tomas have prepared a delicious dinner.'

Waltho smiled. 'Tomorrow, guests will dine on the fruits of their labours in the kitchen.' Picking up a menu, he read out loud.

La Maison du Paradis presents…
Warm chicken livers and chanterelles on toast
Steak au poivre with wilted spinach
Baked custard tart with strawberries.

Cheese from the region

The menu was deliberately English enough to suit their guests on the first night. Waltho had been surprised that no one expressed concerns over dietary needs. These days, everyone seemed fixated on intolerance to staples such as wheat, nuts, shellfish or dairy. And with no vegetarians, Chef's extensive recipes could be enjoyed by all.

'Almost time,' Angelique said and lit the candles.

For the dinner service, Angelique wore white with jewels bordering the collar and cuffs of her gown. It was a striking contrast to her red hair, loosely piled into a chignon with tendrils escaping and falling to her shoulders.

'You look delightful,' Waltho said.

Angelique turned and smiled.

'Ah, here they come.' Waltho moved forward to welcome guests who slowly appeared from different sections of the house to assemble on the terrace.

'Good evening, Jeanette and Pearl,' Waltho greeted the Bournemouth sisters. 'I hope you have everything you need?'

'Yes, we do,' they chimed as they took an aperitif, 'and our room is lovely.'

'And which of you is Jeanette?' Waltho asked, looking from one to the other.

The identical sisters giggled. 'Jeanette always wears a turquoise necklace, and my necklace is pearl,' Pearl informed him.

'Ah, that helps,' Waltho laughed.

Turning his head, he saw Caroline. She wore a peach-coloured dress that hugged her body and swirled at the knee. Waltho thought how lovely she looked as he handed her a drink and watched Caroline turn to talk to the sisters.

Next came a slim, smartly dressed man. Joining Caroline's group, he rubbed at heavily rimmed spectacles with a clean white handkerchief and bowed slightly.

'Hello, everyone,' the man said, 'my name is Ahmed Singh.' Placing the spectacles on his nose and running fingers through thick dark hair, he explained that he'd also travelled from London. Cautious of flying, he preferred travelling by train.

Ahmed was interrupted when the short, bossy woman with a sharply cut, jet-black bob, who'd travelled in the minibus, appeared.

'Good evening,' she said, 'I'm Bridgette Haworth from Lancashire.'

Guests gazed at Bridgette's flower-embellished headband and ankle-length tube dress patterned with leaves. Once seated, Bridgette would merge into the foliage around the gazebo.

Meanwhile, at the rear of the house, newcomers climbed out of taxis, and Angelique welcomed three locals. Well-known to each other, the expats had purchased properties in and around Poitiers in the days when fifty thousand euros would buy a mansion. Now, with their French citizenship, retired and often bored, they were keen to dig into their gilt-edged pensions for the novelty of an English man cooking in France and had enrolled to join the course each day.

Waltho and Angelique handed out olives and tiny

cheese puffs, and both looked up when Fran, almost running, hurried across the courtyard. Still wearing her animal-print jumpsuit, she'd added a matching scarf that scooped her hair into a turban style.

'Oh heck!' Fran said, 'So sorry, I got talking to Sid and couldn't get him off the phone.' She breathed as Waltho handed her a drink. 'He's keen to hear my news.'

'How agreeable that he is so interested,' Angelique offered Fran a cheese puff.

'Yes, he wants to know everything about everyone,' Fran laughed. 'You'd think he was on this holiday with me.'

Guests were wide-eyed as they watched a cheese puff slip from Fran's fingers and disappear down her cleavage.

'That's a goner,' Fran laughed. 'It will take a brave man to fish that one out. Any offers?'

Tomas appeared and announced that dinner was ready. Angelique guided guests to the table, and Caroline took Ahmed's arm. 'Rescued!' she whispered to a bemused Ahmed.

Everyone shook out napkins as Waltho poured wine. The sun had begun to dip, creating a glow across the sky, and suddenly, a myriad of twinkling lanterns draped around the courtyard came alight, creating a magical atmosphere that embraced the oncoming night.

'Bob appetite!' The guests raised glasses. 'Here's to a wonderful holiday!'

Chapter Five

S ally Parker-Brown was exhausted. The drive had been busy after disembarking from the Brittany Ferry at St Malo. Despite using toll roads, which were usually clear, she'd been frustrated by holiday traffic, motorhomes and caravans all heading south for the summer. School was out, and most of France appeared to be on vacation. Was it her imagination, or did truck drivers enjoy taunting Sally in her Mercedes-Benz? It was terribly distracting when horns hooted and speed limits were ignored as Sally sailed along the autoroutes, passing everything ahead. As she negotiated the busy streets of Le Mans, Sally, who was thirsty, hot and hungry, looked forward to a pit stop.

She needed strong coffee and something substantial to eat.

The car park at Hotel Le Prince was full, but to her relief, a Renault with a family on board was pulling out, and Sally smoothly manoeuvred into the parking space. She yawned as she turned off the ignition and, lifting her arms, stretched wide. For the umpteenth time that day, Sally wondered if it would have been easier to fly to France and take the cookery school transport to La Maison du Paradis. She could have relaxed and even enjoyed a few glasses of wine during the journey, watching the world pass by at someone else's pace.

But one of Sally's passions in life was her car and Romeo, her beloved Mercedes-Benz SL class two-door coupé, was Sally's pride and joy. Her heart lurched whenever she looked at the brilliant white paintwork and soft leather interior in the boldest shade of red. Romeo was a high-powered sports car who never let her down. He never broke her heart, and time spent in his company was the highlight of Sally's day.

When she'd received Waltho's invitation for a complimentary place at the cookery school in return for publicity wherever she could place an article, the journalist had jumped at the chance. It was also the perfect opportunity to put Romeo on the road and enjoy a lovely drive through France.

Sally grabbed her oversized tote bag and checked the passenger seat to ensure she'd not left anything of value. Then, easing herself out, she straightened her crumpled shorts, smoothed her T-shirt and locked her car.

She winced when, at the hotel reception desk, she learned that the parking charge was now twenty euros. It had been half the price the last time she'd arrived here. Taking her receipt, she thanked the receptionist and made her way out through a cobblestone passage to a large courtyard at the side of the hotel. The atmosphere was buzzing with laughter and chinking glasses against a background of modern music. Sipping and smiling, an eclectic mix of people sat in chic, colourful clothes beneath bright-coloured canopies. Pendant lights and strings of lanterns created ambient light as diners hustled for space at the different outlets serving food and wine.

'Déjà vu...' Sally whispered, and, for a moment, the previous year dissolved, and she saw herself sitting at a table in the busy wine bar attached to the hotel. A bottle of Beau Joie champagne brut sat in an ice bucket. Halfway down her third glass, Sally was holding the hand of a dark-haired man, staring into the deep pool of his aqua-blue eyes and drowning in the depths.

Ross Briscoe. The love of her life. The man who'd broken her heart into a thousand little pieces and, as fast as the speed he drove, had tossed them into the wind.

Sally shook her head. It was no use trawling over old times, she told herself. She'd stopped here to erase the memory and by following previous footsteps, finally bury her lover's ghost.

The wine bar was full, and an oppressive heat hung like a curtain. Sally squeezed through groups of friends, families and couples and found a stool where she perched herself at a high-top table. Catching the waiter's attention, she ordered water and a glass of Ross's favourite champagne. To hell with the cost, and one glass of bubbles with food wouldn't affect her driving. She remembered the last meal they'd shared here and studied the menu. Her mouth watered as she decided between a charcuterie board, pâté and cornichons, or a cheese platter. When the waiter returned, she closed the menu and asked for a plate of grenouille au beurre à l'ail.

Raising her champagne, Sally called out, 'To hell with you, Ross Briscoe!'

Nearby diners turned to stare with curiosity at the dishevelled English woman with vivid pink hair who was talking to herself.

Sally's food arrived, and as she tucked in, she grinned. Ross had been horrified when he realised that the food he'd ordered was, in fact, frog in garlic butter and not the tender chicken breast he'd expected. He explained that, as a kid, he'd had a pet frog named Fred in the pond at his parent's home. Eating a French Fred, he said as his handsome face twisted into a scowl, would make him feel like a cannibal.

'That will teach you to learn a bit of the language,' Sally muttered as she chewed a chunk of French Fred, dipped bread and licked warm, garlicky sauce from her lips. 'You can't depend on me anymore to translate your menu choice.'

'L'anglais…' hissed a haughty-looking woman sitting at the adjacent table with a long, angular nose. Cradling a small dog, she held a smouldering cigarette in a holder. She shook her head as she listened to Sally reason with herself. The dog began to yap, and stroking fur bunched in a tiny red ribbon, the woman rolled her eyes and turned away.

Sally pushed her plate to one side and asked for a café noir with an extra shot. She needed the caffeine to keep her awake for the final part of her journey. As Sally sipped the strong coffee, the memory of her time with Ross seeped back. A vintage sports car enthusiast, he'd been racing at Le Mans Classic, and they'd booked their accommodation at Hotel Le Prince. On the last night, Ross gave Sally a ring as they sat in this same wine bar.

A silver band with three embedded emeralds.

'Like the colour of your eyes,' Ross said as Sally stroked the tiny green jewels.

She'd forced a smile when he told her it was a friendship ring, a sign of how well their relationship worked. She'd hoped for more in her besotted state, but as she slipped the ring onto her right hand, she was confident that an engagement ring would soon follow.

'Désirez-vous autre chose?' the waiter asked as he whipped Sally's empty coffee cup from the table.

'No, thanks,' Sally replied. She felt elated as she thrust enough euros to cover her bill into his outstretched hand. The visit had been cathartic. 'I won't require anything else from this establishment.' Slipping off her stool, Sally addressed the surrounding diners. 'In fact, this is the last time you will see me. My days here are done.'

Grabbing her bag, she flung it onto her shoulder. As she passed the woman with the dog, Sally ruffled the animal's fur. 'Woof, woof!' she called out and marched away.

'Mon Dieu…' The woman took a deep drag on her cigarette, closed her eyes and covered the dog's ears. 'The crazy English…' she sighed.

On the first day of the cookery course, breakfast at La Maison du Paradis was a lively affair. Following a good night's sleep, guests were up early and eager to enjoy a sumptuous buffet in the salon. Angelique busied herself as she encouraged people to help themselves to the tempting display of cold meats, a variety of cheese, fruit, bread and pastries.

Caroline spooned a slice of nectarine into a bowl, then added a teaspoon of natural yoghurt and a drizzle of honey. Looking around at the tables that had been arranged, she decided to sit outside on the terrace, where a canopy created shade. The temperature felt warm despite the early hour, and another blistering hot day lay ahead.

As she sipped iced water and ate slowly, Caroline thought of the previous night. The conversation had been animated as guests got to know each other, and Angelique asked everyone to introduce themselves.

'More wine!' Bridgette, tucking into her dinner, held up her glass for Waltho to refill. Turning to the guests, the bossy little woman announced, 'I'm an expert gardener, a recipient of the Chelsea Flower Show gold award multiple times, and am the owner of Flaxby Manor.' Bridgette paused to take a sip. 'I've been married to Hugo for most of my life but am now widowed. I'm the youngest seventy-something I know and searching for new experiences.'

Heads nodded with interest, but before questions could be asked, Angelique asked Ahmed to introduce himself.

Pushing his chair back and standing, Ahmed gave a little bow and began shyly, 'Hello,' he began, 'I'm Ahmed Singh, and I'm a retired dentist from Solihull.'

'Anything to add to that?' Bridgette asked as she picked a strand of wilted spinach from a front tooth.

Caroline watched Ahmed shake his head and return to his seat, suddenly fascinated with his spectacles as though reluctant to share more. She turned to the sisters as Angelique invited them to speak.

'Jeanette and Pearl, we're obviously twins,' they laughed. 'I wear a pearl necklace, and Jeanette's is turquoise,' Pearl added, 'so you can tell us apart.' They stroked the rope of gems at their throats. 'We have a bustling gift shop in Bath by Pulteney Bridge.'

'Bath is a marvellous city,' Bridgette butted in. 'Parade Gardens are a horticultural heaven.'

'Yes, Bath has some beautiful, landscaped areas.' Pearl agreed. 'We thought this holiday would be fun as we love France and enjoy cooking.'

Caroline's response had been short when it came to her own turn.

'My name is Caroline Carrington, and I am the proprietor of Caroline's Catering in Kensington,' she informed everyone before abruptly turning to her dinner.

'Thank you.' Angelique smiled and indicated that Fran should go next.

'Well, you've probably guessed that I'm a Lancashire lass,' Fran beamed.

Caroline shuddered. A layer of cerise gloss coated Fran's teeth.

'Sid and me have a fish and chip café by the central pier in Blackpool,' Fran ploughed on, 'and it's always been Sid's dream to have a fancy restaurant.' She picked a peppercorn from her tongue and nudged Bridgette. 'Eh, that steak is lovely, isn't it?'

Bridgette, who was still grappling with wilted spinach, nodded her head.

'Anyway,' Fran said, 'when the pandemic happened, our business went through the roof with takeaways because everywhere was closed. Folk on the Fylde Coast love their fish and chips,' she added. 'Sid invested in a couple of delivery vans, and we were swamped with orders from noon till night. So, with tons of money swimming about in our bank accounts, Sid says now is the time to take a leap of faith and live his dream of opening a fancy restaurant.'

Intrigued, Caroline sat up. How she wished that her bank account was swimming about with money and how odd it was to hear someone being so open about their finances. In her Kensington circle, everyone had sealed lips where incomes were concerned.

'And here you are, Fran,' Angelique concluded and turned to other guests, nodding approval.

Now, as Caroline sat in the morning sunshine and finished her breakfast, she tore her thoughts away from the previous evening.

In the garden, Sally Parker-Brown was strolling along the lavender path. Her journalistic eyes took in neatly trimmed boxwood hedges and tall cypress trees casting shadows, reflected on the surface of the swimming pool. Fluffy puffs of cloud drifted overhead and a scorching sun bathed a quaint stone fountain where crystal clear water cascaded in a graceful arc, rippling into circles in the basin below.

'What a setting,' Sally breathed and thought of the articles that would soon spring from her keyboard.

Sally's late arrival had surprised everyone when she'd driven her gorgeous sports car onto the drive as guests bid each other goodnight. With only a brief introduction, they'd been interested to learn that Sally was a food writer and here to take notes on the course.

'Good morning!' Caroline looked up and called out to Sally.

Sally, who'd been for a swim, wore a pretty polka-dot bikini that matched her pale pink hair. She carried a towel and held up her hand to wave.

'Are you joining us for breakfast?' Caroline asked.

'No thanks, I rarely eat at this time of day,' Sally replied, patting her stomach. 'I try to keep the pounds off but don't have much luck.'

Caroline watched Sally head to her room on the other side of the house and thought the journalist had a perfect hourglass figure. But she was sympathetic to anyone who wished to stay slim. After all, she'd been on a diet all her life and working with the constant temptation of food needed great discipline.

An aroma of patchouli wafted by, and Caroline noticed Angelique. Elegant in an embroidered cheesecloth kaftan, she moved gracefully amongst the guests, offering more coffee while advising that class would begin at nine o'clock. Chef liked his students to be punctual.

From beyond the salon doors, Fran's voice boomed. 'Best get ready!' she called out.

Caroline sighed. The woman was like a foghorn, constantly alerting anyone in her vicinity to the sound of her voice.

'There you are, Caro.' Fran appeared on the terrace. 'Hiding away by yourself. You should have let me know, and I would have joined you for breakfast.'

'What a shame I missed you.' Caroline folded her napkin and, placing it on the table, pushed back her chair.

'Did you sleep well?' Fran asked. She was nibbling a pain au chocolat and holding a glass of apple juice.

'Not as well as I might,' Caroline said. In truth, she'd spent most of the night with earplugs and a pillow moulded around her head to drown out the snores coming from the other side of her bedroom wall.

'I slept like a baby,' Fran replied, glugging back her juice. 'Must be something in the air.' She placed the empty glass on the table and dabbed at the pastry flakes around her mouth.

'Yes, I believe you did.' Caroline resisted the urge to tell her neighbour that she'd slept the sleep of the dead, which kept Caroline awake for hours.

There was no point in starting the day on a sour note.

'Oh, look.' Fran ran forward. 'There's a pussy!' She bent down to stroke the sizeable tabby that circled her legs.

Caroline was allergic to cats and didn't appreciate Fran's sudden display of adoration. Shaking her head and moving away, she replied, 'I'd prefer it if you kept your pussy well away from me.'

Fran, who'd scooped the fluffy creature into her arms, stifled a laugh. 'Don't worry, duckie, there's no danger of that!'

Chapter Six

Ten Perspex folders had been neatly placed around the long farmhouse table in the centre of the room in the main kitchen of La Maison du Paradis. They held typed recipes and a blank notebook alongside pencils and pens. Beside each was a folded apron, and as the hands of a country wall clock ticked towards nine o'clock, excited guests entered the kitchen.

'Should we sit anywhere?' Jeanette and Pearl asked as they positioned themselves behind a pair of pastel-painted chairs.

'No point in dawdling about.' Bridgette pulled out a chair and sat down.

As Fran settled beside Ahmed, Caroline moved to the opposite end of the table.

The expat guests had also arrived and politely greeted everyone by enquiring about their night's rest. As the hands on the clock reached the hour, Daniel and Tomas came into the kitchen. Both wore white jackets and checked cotton trousers. Daniel picked up a small brass bell. Shaking it, he called the class to order.

'One person appears to be missing?' Daniel raised an eyebrow and pointed to an empty space beside Fran. He turned as a door suddenly burst open, and Sally rushed in.

'Sorry, sorry!' she exclaimed breathlessly. 'My hair straighteners have gone on the blink, and I had to find Angelique, and then she couldn't get hers to work and insisted that we find Waltho, who would know how to mend them...' Sally paused and took a gulp of air. 'I hope I haven't missed anything?' she asked, glancing at the clock.

'Not at all. Daniel acknowledged the latecomer. 'Are you Sally Parker-Brown, the journalist?' he asked.

'That's me.' Sally stroked the strap of a camera hanging around her neck. 'I'm not a great timekeeper, I'm afraid,' she added, 'but I'll do my best.'

'That's all we ask.' Daniel waved his hand towards the empty chair.

'Hello, dear,' Fran whispered as Sally sat down, 'I saw you in the pool. You cut quite a dash in that striking bikini.'

'But I got my hair wet, and now it looks a sight.' Sally pulled at the frizzy pink mop that fell over her forehead. She touched the back of her head, where the cut was neatly shaved.

'You look like a candyfloss, and I love it,' Fran giggled.

'Ladies.' Daniel shook his bell. 'May we start?'

'Oh er, sorry, boss,' Fran said.

'Chef,' Daniel corrected.

'Sorry, Chef.' Fran nodded.

'Welcome, everyone.' Daniel looked at each guest in

turn. 'Your culinary journey begins today, and I hope that it will be the beginning of a gastronomic experience, leaving you with unforgettable memories.'

Fran sat up, agog with interest and tried not to watch Tomas, who looked like he'd stepped straight from the glamour pages of a lad's mag. She put aside her unforgettable memory of the young man taking an early dip that morning. Fran had always been an early riser, and her sunrise walk through the adjacent field of cheerful sunflowers had been the perfect start to her day. Now, she gripped her pen and focused on Daniel.

'Although you are in France, this course isn't about French gastronomy,' Daniel said, studying the eager faces. 'This may surprise you, but French cooking invariably involves elaborate preparation. Chefs in professional kitchens work endlessly to produce foams and quenelles, blanching, braising, sautéing, and simmering stocks for hours.' He studied the guest's faces. 'French specialities are eaten repeatedly and these days are more for tourists on holiday. You are not here to learn about these,' he said.

'This is beginning to sound like a lecture,' Fran whispered to Ahmed.

'Did you know that the French eat fast food just like the rest of us?' Daniel asked.

Caroline shuddered. 'Don't include me,' she said, 'I've never had fast food in my life.'

'You don't know what you're missing,' Fran laughed.

'I must inform you that there are currently more McDonald's in France than elsewhere in Europe. But I digress,' Daniel said brightly. 'This week, I hope you will be inspired and learn some of the rudiments of cookery and discover time-saving tips from myself and Tomas that will be helpful in your culinary journey.'

Daniel instructed Tomas to explain the necessary housekeeping rules. When the guests were thoroughly acquainted with fire exits, bathroom facilities and emergency procedures, Daniel thanked his sous chef and walked around the kitchen.

'So, we begin,' he said and paused at one end of the table. 'Cooking is an art, and patience a virtue.' He raised his hands and placed his fingers in a pyramid under his chin. 'All good cooks require the attribute of patience.'

Guests opened their folders, and one or two started to write in their notebooks. 'You must have the ability to shop well,' he emphasised. 'This will decide what dish to cook, and your menus will depend on the season, the availability and ultimately – the cost.' He held his palms up. 'There is no mystery. Fresh ingredients and a systematic approach are the keys to a good dish.'

Fran was thoughtful as she listened. Beside her, Ahmed scribbled away.

'However,' Daniel continued, 'there is one ingredient you cannot buy, and this is the most important of all.'

As guests looked up, some frowned, others were puzzled with pens poised above part-filled pages.

'The most important component that you can bring to the table is... love.' Daniel touched his heart and smiled. 'Love for food and love for those you cook for.'

Heads dipped, and pens began to move once more.

'There is no mystery. With love, you can become like Van

Gogh, Monet or Degas and create artistry on the plate, a palette of colour that tastes of sunshine, joy and… love.'

Fran was beginning to wonder if she'd enrolled in the right class, and as she reached into her folder, she expected to pull out a paintbrush.

'You will learn to understand your own expertise.' Daniel began to stride again. 'Trust in yourself at the cookery altar and be grateful for the gospel of knowledge that I am about to hand to you.'

Fran scratched her head. She hadn't expected Daniel to come over all religious, but if that's how he wanted things, she'd join him on the journey. She wondered if they would say the Lord's Prayer before they got cracking, or perhaps sing a hymn? Subconsciously, Fran clasped her hands together and half-closed her eyes.

But, to her relief, prayers were ignored, and the kitchen soon swung into action.

Guests were moved to sit together on one side of the table. On the other, Tomas placed trays of ingredients, knives, spoons and spatulas before Daniel, who tied a crisp white apron around his waist.

'Stocks and sauces,' Daniel announced. 'A good sauce will lift an ordinary dish into something quite exceptional.' He reached for a mound of fish trimmings while Tomas poured a litre of water into a large pan, placed it on the stove behind Daniel and brought it to a boil.

Daniel chopped onions, carrots, celery and leeks. He demonstrated chopping techniques and told the guests to invest in a good set of knives and keep them razor-sharp. 'A sharp knife will cut, but a blunt knife will cause injury by slipping.' He added the ingredients to the pan. Placing fresh herbs in muslin, he tied them into a bouquet garni and added this with peppercorns and a good slosh of white wine.

'In thirty minutes, we will strain the ingredients, et voila! Our fish stock is ready.'

Daniel watched Sally remove the lens cover from her camera to take photos as the chefs worked. Conscious of the camera, he smiled and held himself in a sultry pose. At the same time, Tomas showed the guests how to make a variety of sauces from stocks he'd previously prepared.

'Now, it is *your* turn. Aprons on!' Daniel said. 'Remember, ladies and gentlemen, the fruits of your labours will be served at dinner tonight.'

Splitting the group into two, Tomas led his group into the adjacent kitchen, and the remaining guests stayed with Daniel. Each was given a sauce to make, and everyone got to work by referring to the recipe sheets in their folders.

Fran's pen hovered over her recipe for a velouté sauce, and noting the three essential ingredients of butter, flour and fish stock, she reached for a saucepan and wooden spoon.

'What have you got?' Fran called out to Sally.

'Béchamel,' Sally replied. She was several steps ahead of Fran and pulled a face as her spoon dipped into her sauce, and she stirred a lumpy, gloopy mess.

'Oh heck,' Fran laughed as she ran a finger over Sally's spoon and tasted the over-seasoned, clumpy concoction. 'That's horrible!'

'I've not got off to a very good start,' Sally grimaced.

'I've never been able to cook; beans on toast are the best I can manage.'

The two women giggled as they huddled over the saucepan.

'What's going on here?' Daniel suddenly materialised and, peering into the pan, scrutinised Sally's sauce.

To Sally's surprise, the chef smiled and touched her shoulder. 'It's my fault,' he said, 'I didn't spend enough time with you, showing you the basics.' He reached for the pan and thrust it into Fran's hand, indicating that she should empty the contents and take the pan to the sink. Locating clean utensils, Daniel began again.

Fran felt like a kitchen porter as she moved through the kitchen. She was tempted to gather dirty dishes and plates from the other guests. But remembering how much she'd paid for the course, she deposited the pan in the sink and returned to her station. Passing Caroline, she paused to ask what she was making.

'Hollandaise,' Caroline replied as she lifted a double boiler from the heat and, taking the upper pan, poured a perfectly emulsified sauce, creamy and velvety in texture, into a clean bowl. She handed Fran a teaspoon. 'Would you like to taste it?'

Fran dunked her spoon into the mixture.

She was tempted to close her eyes as the silky sauce caressed her tongue, and her taste buds savoured the richness of the ingredients. No curdling mess or over-cooked eggs for Caroline. It was ten out of ten for her hollandaise.

'It's absolutely bloody lovely,' Fran said, 'I've never tasted anything like it, well done.'

Fran noted Caroline's smug expression. She took her teaspoon to the sink and deposited it in Sally's sullied pan.

The temperature in the kitchen had risen, and despite the whirring of several fans, Fran's face was flushed, and her clothes clung to her hot body. She reached into a fridge for a bottle of iced water.

'How's it going, Ahmed?' Fran asked as she took a slug of her drink and returned to her velouté. The dentist appeared hot and nervous. His spectacles were misty as he leaned over his recipe sheet with a perplexed frown.

'Not so well,' Ahmed replied, taking a handkerchief to clean his lens. 'Can you help?'

'Aye, of course, what have you got?'

'Aioli.'

'Oh heck, sounds like a flower. Just stick "glad" in front of it.'

Fifteen minutes later, Ahmed was as proud as punch as he sat before a pretty pottery bowl containing a rich, thick, garlicky aioli. 'Thank you, my friend!' he called out to Fran.

'My pleasure,' Fran replied, wiping her brow. She was acutely aware that the guests in this kitchen had all made their sauces, and she was way behind.

As Fran stirred flour into her melted butter, Daniel clapped his hands and told everyone to stop what they were doing.

'You've all done very well,' Daniel said. 'Caroline, your hollandaise is restaurant worthy and Ahmed, I will be first to eat your delicious aioli tonight at dinner.' He praised

Sally for mastering her béchamel and said he was proud of her persistence. It was the sign of a great cook. Turning to Fran, Daniel sighed. 'I'm afraid you need to talk less and cook more,' he admonished. 'We won't be sampling your efforts tonight.'

Fran was tempted to lift the wooden spoon from her pan and flick floury balls in Daniel's face, but with all eyes staring in her direction, she smiled and nodded and told Daniel that she would try harder in the next session.

Instructing everyone to take a break, Daniel left the group to head into the adjacent kitchen and check on guests working with Tomas. Fran almost gave him the finger as she watched the chef saunter away and flick the quiff of hair covering his forehead. She was glad that Elvis had almost left the building.

'I thought he was a bit harsh on you.' Sally touched Fran's arm.

'Yeah, me too,' Fran sighed. She pulled on the strings of her apron and tossed it onto a chair. 'But he's the professional. He probably thinks I am messing about on this course and will never have what it takes to open a fancy restaurant.' Fran shrugged. 'But my moaning won't enable me to learn anything, and that's what I'm here for.'

Sally linked her arm through Fran's. 'Come on, I know where the bar is. Let's grab a drink.'

'Sounds like a good idea.' Fran patted Sally's hand. 'I'll probably cook better if I'm sozzled.'

'We've got to be back in half an hour, so there's time before the next tuition,' Sally said as they left the kitchen.

'I wonder where our outing will be this afternoon?'

'I heard Angelique say we are having a picnic lunch by the river.'

'By heck, that sounds grand.'

'A great photo opportunity.'

'Of course, I'd almost forgotten you're here to write about the course.' Fran followed Sally into the salon and watched as Sally found ice and two glasses. 'On second thoughts, just a soft drink for me,' she said, 'I'll have a tipple later.'

'Yes, I'd better stick to juice too.' Sally reached into a fridge to pour fresh apple juice.

'Cheers,' Fran said, stepping out to the terrace to sit under the canopy. 'Now tell me about this article you're writing.'

Sally sat down and explained to Fran that she would make prolific notes and take umpteen photographs during the week. She hoped to spend time with Waltho to understand the ideology behind his La Maison du Paradis plans. Sally also wanted to spend time with Daniel to gather as much information as possible on the chef to help promote the course. Readers loved celebrities, and juicy titbits sold stories.

'Have you always been a journalist?' Fran asked.

'Yes, I'm afraid so.'

'Don't you like your job?'

'On the contrary, I love it, but it gets harder as you get older with someone younger and keener, always ready to pounce and take your place.'

'I'm sure you're terrific.' Fran nodded.

'I grew up in Cheshire and worked for a local paper

when I left school. The *Congleton Express* was snatched up by Congletonians when it went to print each Thursday. It taught me a lot about writing mundane reports of stolen bicycles, county shows and even murder.'

'Murder?'

Sally laughed. 'Yes, murder too, but food was always my biggest interest and I suggested a weekly column covering restaurants in the area.'

'So, what happened?'

'It was successful, and I've worked my way up to being the food and drink reporter for the *Manchester Daily News*. I work remotely and do a lot of freelance work for the nationals.'

'So, once you've got all the information on this course, you'll write it up and sell an article?' Fran asked.

'Probably several,' Sally replied. 'There are many approaches I can take to place the articles, from the cookery glossies, Sunday supplements about food and travel and many online opportunities.'

'Blimey, does it pay well?'

'It keeps Romeo topped up with gas,' Sally grinned.

'Romeo?'

'My car.'

'Ah, that gorgeous vehicle parked up on the drive.' Fran nodded. 'She's a beauty.'

'He,' Sally corrected. 'Romeo is male. The only male that's ever been good for me.'

'It sounds like a love story?'

'How much time do you have?' Sally shook her head.

'My love life is a disaster. I never thought I'd be sad and single at fifty.'

'Sad? No one should be sad in such a beautiful place as this.' Fran stood up, 'Come on, you can tell me all about it in due course. I'll take you for a walk in the sunflowers later. That will put sunshine and happiness in your life.'

'Sounds perfect,' Sally said and stood too. 'I suppose we should get back to class?'

'Aye, I'm in enough trouble with Elvis. Better not be late.' Fran picked up her pace, and as they hurried back to the kitchen, she began to sing, *'A little less conversation, a little more action!'*

Chapter Seven

A n enticing aroma of fresh herbs and spices greeted
the guests as they returned to the kitchen following
the break. Bridgette and Ahmed, who'd enjoyed coffee,
sitting companionably together in the sunshine on a garden
swing beside the vegetable garden, pulled out chairs and
sat down. Bridgette pulled her face into a scowl as Daniel
rang his bell and explained that the session would cover the
art of preserving.

As the chef described the need for a steriliser in good
condition and Tomas placed clean glass jars on the table,
Bridgette held up her hand.

'Excuse me for interrupting, Chef,' Bridgette began, 'but
I am perfectly capable of making jam at home and know
how to sterilise a bottle.' She looked around at the group. 'I
am sure others will join me in saying that we are here to
learn clever cooking tips from a Michelin-starred chef, not
make marmalade?'

No one spoke, and heads bowed as Daniel looked up from his steriliser.

'So, you know how to do this?' His lip curled as he stared at Bridgette and pointed to the ingredients on the table. 'You can make a perfect tomato sauce from scratch or a wonderful mushroom and olive paste?'

'Well, I am sure...' Bridgette stuttered.

'And you know how to preserve the lemons used in Moroccan cookery or make a flawless herb oil and perfectly pickled cherries?' Daniel's eyes blazed. The chef, unused to having his skills questioned, was livid. 'Perhaps you will explain how to pot pork or preserve goose,' Daniel reasoned, 'and I would be most interested to hear your thoughts on brawn.'

'No one eats brawn these days,' Bridgette retaliated, but her face was flushed, and she was already regretting her question.

Daniel pulled a tray of ingredients towards him and held up a pig's tail, part of the animal's head and a trotter. 'Brawn is a delicacy on many fine-dining menus today and takes great skill to prepare.'

Jeanette and Pearl held their pens in the air and piped up, 'We would like to know how to make brawn,' they chimed.

'Can't beat a bit of brawn,' Fran added, 'lovely with a slice of gherkin.'

Daniel turned away from Bridgette and, smiling at the rest of the group, proceeded with his preserving master class.

Two hours later, Fran held a bottle of tomato sauce in her hand and turned to Ahmed, 'Who knew that you could add onions, mustard powder, paprika, cloves, garlic, peppers and oil to tomatoes and make the most delicious sauce I have ever tasted?' Fran licked her lips, which were stained dark with her concoction. 'This will be better than ketchup on my chips.'

'Ah, but you have forgotten one ingredient,' Ahmed warned, shaking his head.

'I don't think so.' Fran looked puzzled and picked up her recipe sheet to study it. 'What have I forgotten?' she asked.

'LOVE!' Ahmed called out and began to laugh.

'Oh, there's plenty of that in here.' Fran laughed too, then grabbed her pen to write a fancy label. *Fran's Fantastic Tomato Sauce*, she wrote in her best handwriting.

'Made with love,' Ahmed replied as he fashioned a label for his jar of quince jelly. 'Look out, Chef is heading our way with his tasting spoons.'

Fran looked up as Daniel bore down and dipped a long-handled spoon in Ahmed's quince jelly. 'Superb!' he said and touched a finger to his thumb. 'Magnifique, Ahmed.' Taking another spoon, Daniel tasted Fran's tomato sauce. 'No, far too seasoned.'

Daniel dramatically winced as though he'd been stung by a bee and Fran thought he was overplaying his reaction. Was it his intention to put her through her paces if she was to fulfil her dream?

'Focus more, Fran,' Daniel added before moving away.

Fran was stunned and turned to shield her face from the group.

'Oh, Fran.' Ahmed put an arm on Fran's shoulder. 'Don't get upset; I think your sauce is delicious.'

'Thanks, Ahmed,' Fran sniffed. 'I'm a silly old mare. It's just that I thought I'd got it spot on. Chef is right, I need to listen more.'

Tomas clapped his hands, and everyone stopped what they were doing.

'Angelique has instructed me to tell you to meet at the front of the house in ten minutes, where transport awaits,' Tomas announced, 'I will be driving you to a surprise destination.'

Sliding paperwork into folders, the group packed up and headed off.

'Blimey, not much time for a wash,' Fran muttered as she flapped her blouse with her fingers to cool her skin. Catching up with Sally, they hurried to their rooms.

'Nor any time to sort my hair.' Sally ruffled her frizzy hair.

'You look grand, lass, don't worry about it.'

Caroline was ahead of them, and Fran called, 'Oi, Caro! Save us a seat on the bus!'

On the edge of the village Poutaloux-Beauvoir, a bridge made of golden bricks formed a welcoming arch over the river Vienne. In one direction lay a cluster of houses adorned with cascading baskets of colourful blossoms and overflowing window boxes. Various businesses traded their wares nearby, including a bakery, bar and hair salon. Beside the bridge, a winding path led down to grassy riverbanks where locals and visitors often gathered to bathe in the cool, clear water on hot days, picnic under the trees, or sit and admire the peaceful countryside.

Waltho and Angelique had travelled ahead of the guests to park near the bridge, lay out blankets and chairs and erect a long table in a quiet, shady spot beside the river. They carried baskets from Waltho's car and set out a picnic lunch.

'Tomas is on the way,' Angelique said. She closed her phone and slid it into the pocket of her kaftan. After carefully placing glasses beside jugs of local wine, she reached into a canvas bag and took out a bouquet of lavender from the garden at La Maison du Paradis. Waltho filled a vase with water from the river, and Angelique arranged the blooms and moved them to the centre of the table.

Standing back to admire their efforts, Angelique asked, 'So what are your thoughts on our guests?'

Waltho tilted his head to one side. 'An interesting group,' he replied.

'Is that all?'

'It's too early to make assumptions or reason why people have travelled here.' Waltho paused. 'Everyone has a motive. Caroline is wealthy and bored, Fran is eager to learn, and the sisters want a relaxing holiday.'

'Bridgette?' Angelique raised an eyebrow.

'Who knows.'

'Ahmed?'

'Angelique, you are too curious. It is not our place to judge the guests.'

'I can't help it.' A slow smile formed on her face. She took a tortoiseshell clip from her pocket, and as she lifted her wrist to clip it into her hair, her bangles jingled.

'Your hair is almost titian in the sunlight,' Waltho said, 'it's quite beautiful.'

'Don't change the subject.' Angelique poured them both a glass of wine and handed one to Waltho.

'These are not questions I can answer; I don't know these people, but perhaps in a few days, we will know more.' Waltho sipped his wine. 'They seem like a decent bunch, and I am happy they are providing me with the funds to continue this lifestyle.'

'Don't you mean so that you can start painting again?'

Waltho frowned. Angelique had a point. Lauren had been his driving force and delighted in his work. He knew in that moment, she'd have insisted that he spontaneously capture the image of Angelique's halo of hair and commit the image to canvas. But Waltho hadn't lifted a brush, opened his paints or set up his easel since Lauren's death and hadn't the slightest desire to do so.

'You are one of the best artists in this area of France,' Angelique persisted.

'The area is full of artists.'

'Not as good as you. If you painted again, you wouldn't need cookery school guests; you could do what you originally planned and run art classes. Host painting courses in your beautiful home with like-minded people.'

'I am happy with the way things are.' Waltho put down his glass.

'But you wouldn't be paying a huge fee to a celebrity chef.'

Waltho looked towards the bridge. 'Just leave it,' he sighed. 'I want this week to be successful and hope that by bringing a journalist here, we can plan and fill many more courses.'

Angelique knew better than to push Waltho further. He was a closed book. Not to be opened anytime soon.

'Our guests have arrived,' Waltho said, raising his hand to show Tomas where they were.

'Let's enjoy the afternoon,' Angelique said, waving at the guests.

Waltho's handsome face turned towards her, and he smiled. 'Mais bien sûr,' he replied, 'but of course.'

They could see Fran marching ahead of the pack, heading down the pathway. Dressed in Lycra shorts, pink trainers and a racing-style vest, she wore huge pink sunglasses and held up both hands when she spotted Waltho and Angelique.

'Yoo-hoo!' Fran called out. 'Here we are!'

Sally followed, wearing jogging shorts, a T-shirt, and plimsols. She held her camera and pointed it towards the river to get a shot of the bridge.

Caroline, neat in white capri pants and a cotton blouse, was heard to call out to Sally, 'I'll get out of the way,' she said, as though fearing to be caught in the photo.

'I do love a picnic.' Ahmed rubbed his hands together as he accompanied the expats and Bridgette.

In matching straw bonnets and summery dresses, Jeanette and Pearl agreed, 'So do we!'

As they all arrived at the shady hollow, their eyes were wide when they saw the picnic that had been prepared.

'Come, find a place to rest and help yourselves to food.' Angelique handed out drinks, and Waltho asked if anyone needed insect repellent.

'Over here!' Fran yelled as she sprawled on a blanket. 'The little blighters are nipping already.' She lifted a leg and sprayed liberally.

Caroline sipped a glass of iced water. She watched as Sally helped herself to a crisp baguette and fill her plate with a selection of cheese.

'Are you going to eat?' Sally asked as she spooned soft Camembert onto the bread and took a bite. 'This cheese is gorgeous.'

Caroline put her glass down and forked salad into a bowl. The mixed greens were tossed with herb oil, made in the morning class, and combined with Niçoise olives and tomatoes.

'Crikey, you won't last long on that,' Sally said as she sipped wine, then scooped pâté and ham onto her plate.

'There's so much food,' Caroline replied, 'and I ate far too much at dinner last night. It's very tempting to indulge and overeat.'

'Isn't that what we're here for?' Sally asked. 'It's a holiday too.' Her journalist's brain was whirring. Studying the type of people who paid for expensive courses like this made sense. Alluding to different characters in her writing spiced things up.

'I don't want to put on any weight.' Caroline nibbled on a rocket leaf.

'Why, have you got a weight problem?' Sally swigged her wine. Her dart landed on the bull's eye, and she saw Caroline shudder.

Quickly composing herself, Caroline replied, 'No, I certainly haven't.' She was dismissive. 'I've always kept in shape.'

Sally's sixth sense told her that Caroline wasn't being honest, and as she watched the woman move away, she wondered if she should follow up on the conversation. After all, weight loss stories sold too.

Waltho had placed folding chairs at the edge of the blankets, and glancing around to ensure she was alone, Caroline sat down. She didn't feel like company. Peering over her sunglasses, Caroline bit into an olive. She studied the group, where Sally was chatting to the sisters, jotting down their remarks.

Biting into a vine tomato next, Caroline savoured the sweet, fruity flesh that had ripened under a warm Mediterranean sun. It was heaven and she knew she'd eat the lot if a bowl was before her. The cheese Sally was gorging was equally as tempting, and Caroline resisted the urge to leap up and fill her plate.

She had to stay strong.

The afternoon heat made Caroline drowsy, and her mind wandered to days long gone, when she'd first met Stanley. She'd been several sizes bigger, and a drunken tryst at university in Durham had ended with Caroline becoming pregnant.

One of the conditions you made when you reluctantly agreed to marry me was that I lose weight, Caroline thought. She knew that Stanley would never have agreed to marry her had her father not threatened to dismember him and throw him into the pit where he'd spent his entire working life at the coal face.

'I'm going places, Caro,' Stanley pleaded as he stood in the tiny bedroom at her parents' home, 'the last thing I need, as well as a child, is an overweight wife on my arm.'

Without sparing her a glance nor noting the tears that trickled down her plump cheeks, Stanley had run his fingers through his hair and admired his reflection. 'I'm going into journalism and ultimately politics and need to be taken seriously. If you can't take control of your weight, we'll be a laughingstock.'

Caroline sighed as she opened her eyes and watched Sally pose the guests for a group photo. She'd tried to live up to Stanley's expectations throughout her married life, but following their wedding, not only had she dramatically lost weight, she'd also lost the baby.

Caroline bit on her lip and felt a heaviness in her chest. A stillborn birth was in nature's hands, the midwife had told her. She'd assured the bereft mother there was plenty of time for more children. In her heart, Caroline convinced herself that to become thin and not gain pregnancy weight, she'd denied her baby vital nutrition. This must have been the real cause of the stillbirth.

But by then, she was married to Stanley and living in

London. Stanley had begun work as a reporter for *The Times*, and Caroline became the stay-at-home wife who tended to her husband's every need. In time, she became pregnant again, and, despite Stanley's, 'Watch your weight, old gal, we don't want you bloating up again,' she'd had a healthy pregnancy.

Leo was a bouncing eight-pound baby.

Caroline finished her salad and resisted the urge to turn from the guests and lick the bowl clean of the delicious herb oil that shimmered on the surface. She was about to go for a stroll when she saw Waltho approaching.

'May I?' Waltho asked. He held a dish in his hands.

'Yes, of course, do sit down.'

Caroline caught the sparkling glimmer in Waltho's delicious eyes and felt a strange flutter. Was the man aware of his appeal, she wondered. Nervously, she sat straighter and crossed her legs.

'I thought you might like some fruit.' Waltho produced a linen napkin and held it out. 'You've eaten very little?'

'I've had sufficient, thank you.' Caroline twisted the watch on her wrist and anxiously stared at the fruit. 'Perhaps a slice of melon,' she conceded, not wishing to offend.

'The river is shallow.' Waltho glanced towards the water. 'The locals are worried about the fish.'

'Hmm,' Caroline licked her lips. The melon was sweet, the cold flesh refreshing.

'So many months of hardly any rain,' Waltho added as they watched a listless stream flow gently over rock and stones. 'The riverbank is wilted and brown, and no one seems to know when the weather will break. It is the hottest July on record.' He indicated for Caroline to eat more. 'The berries are fresh, picked from the garden this morning.'

'They're perfect,' Caroline agreed and nibbled on a blueberry.

'I trust that the kitchen wasn't too hot earlier?'

'Surprisingly, the fans are effective; I was comfortable, thank you.'

Suddenly, Angelique clapped her hands. They glanced up as she announced their departure in fifteen minutes.

Caroline began to fold her napkin.

'It's a short lesson when you return,' Waltho said, 'and I hope the classes won't be too tiring in the heat.'

'We're here to work, and the fans are coping,' Caroline replied. 'I see from our notes that we're making pastry, no doubt we will enjoy some of these delicious berries in a tart with dinner.'

'But make sure you relax after class,' Waltho was insistent, 'I want my guests to enjoy the house, gardens, and, of course, the pool.'

'Not for me,' Caroline winced, 'I can't swim.'

A memory flashed of a drunken Stanley playfully pushing Caroline into a pool at Quinta do Logo. The Portuguese lifeguard had scolded Stanley after rescuing Caroline, choking and terrified from the deep water and she'd never been near water again.

Before Waltho could ask why Caroline couldn't swim, Sally let out a cheer and several guests began to clap.

'What on earth…' Caroline turned to see what was causing all the commotion, and to her horror, she saw Fran striding barefoot across the grass in a baby-pink tankini. Her hair was soaking wet, and her skin glistened.

'Sid wanted a picture of me posing by the water,' Fran giggled as she got closer, 'I had a hell of a job keeping my phone steady and not slipping off a rock.'

'Looks like you fell in?' Sally laughed and held out a towel.

'No, dear, I put my bits and pieces on the bank, then had a good old splash about to cool me down.' Fran had drawn level with Caroline, and droplets sprayed onto Caroline's Capri pants as she towelled her hair.

'Oh, really!' Caroline exclaimed.

'Keep your hair on, Caro, the water is clean.' Fran gave a beaming smile, then patted the bulge of white tummy peeping out of her tankini. 'You should try it.'

'No. Thank you.'

Caroline stepped back and rubbed her fingers on her trousers as though ridding them of debris. Moving away from Waltho without glancing in anyone's direction, she picked up her pace and made her way to the bridge, where the cool air of the air-conditioned minibus welcomed her. Settling comfortably into her seat, Caroline stared out of the window. The guests had clustered into groups, happily chatting as they returned.

'They all have such confidence,' Caroline whispered, and closing her eyes to block the image, she turned her head away.

Chapter Eight

The heat was oppressive late afternoon as Daniel lay by the swimming pool. Stark naked, he stretched out on an old-fashioned steamer chair. He enjoyed exposing his flesh to the sun and considered an all-over tan made his wobbly bits more attractive. Reaching the age of fifty was depressing, and it felt like the declining years had begun. He was determined to hang on for as long as he could; creams for his skin, potions for his hair and even a touch of liposuction kept Daniel sculpted into a shape he was happy with.

Comfortably padded by the mattress covering the old-fashioned sunbed, Daniel idly watched birds soaring above and thought about the many attractive antique and vintage pieces placed throughout La Maison du Paradis. Waltho had great taste in furniture, and Daniel wondered how long the artist had taken to acquire such an impressive collection.

He held the cold bottle of beer to his hot skin. Taking a

long drink, he smiled. 'That's so good,' he said. The malty draught was refreshing, and Daniel remembered how guests had been drowsy when they'd returned for the pastry class. But he'd robustly shown them the skill of rough puff and soon put life back into the eager cooks.

Adjusting his sunglasses, Daniel thought of Sally. Conscious of her photography, he was keen to make a good impression.

'Such an attractive woman…' Daniel took another sip of beer.

As he'd demonstrated the art of bringing flour and butter together, he'd glanced at Sally, his fingers caressing the dough like a shapely woman's body. He remembered their eyes meeting and grinned. Her cheeks had turned pink, almost matching her hair.

Looking around at the deserted pool, Daniel watched a tabby cat appear.

It sauntered along the pathway, limbs glossy with precision movements and tail held high. Despite the cat's age, the creature had character. Once-sharp eyes, though cloudy, held a glint of curiosity and, noticing Daniel, the cat paused. She studied the prone body, baking in the sunshine as though assessing the human for feline gain. Apparently deciding that Daniel wasn't worthy of a purr or a pause to wrap itself around an outstretched hand, the cat promenaded past to sit in the shade of a lavender bush.

'Here, puss, puss,' Daniel called out, rubbing his fingers together to encourage the cat. But his appeal was in vain. The cat wasn't to be disturbed and replied with a hiss.

'Stuff you,' Daniel mumbled and, closing his eyes again, leaned back.

He wondered what a stuffed cat might taste like and let his recipe bank filter through stocks and sauces, deciding which would suit roast tabby best. But before Daniel could enter culinary dreamland, he heard voices heading towards the pool. Reaching for his shorts, he hurriedly slipped them on.

'I'm first in!' Daniel heard Fran call out. She gripped a pink pelican-style inflatable that matched the gloss on her lips, and he noted that she was accompanied by Sally.

'Not a chance,' Sally replied.

To Daniel's delight, Sally threw a towel on an adjacent recliner and slipped out of her shorts and T-shirt. He studied Sally's lithe and pleasing body, in prime condition for her age. Lightly tanned limbs, a flat stomach and a brief bikini were a satisfying sight. Daniel smiled as Sally stood by the side of the pool to raise her arms and then, with a heel kick, dived elegantly into the water, hardly raising a ripple.

As he contemplated ordering a bottle of cold white wine, he decided that he'd ask Sally to join him. Daniel was so fixated that he hadn't noticed Fran pulling a sarong from her rounded body and throwing her inflatable into the pool.

Holding her nose and closing her eyes, Fran suddenly dive-bombed into the pool. Like a tsunami, the water rose in a tidal wave and splashed all over the chef, soaking his hair and ruining his quiff.

'Bloody hell!' Daniel cried out as Fran surfaced and came up smiling.

'Oh, sorry!' Fran said. 'I didn't see you there.' She turned her back and murmured to Sally, 'That'll teach him to find fault with my tomato sauce.'

Giggling, Fran reached for the pelican inflatable and slipped it over her head. In moments, she was bobbing about on the water.

Furious, Daniel stood and gathered his towel. What was Fran playing at? She was on a cookery course to improve her skills with a Michelin-starred chef, and here she was, ruining his afternoon, upsetting the man who could change her life.

Daniel finger-combed his wet, floppy fringe, slipped into a pair of sliders, and walked away. His anticipated chat with Sally would have to wait until he'd groomed his hair.

Splashing about in the water, Fran and Sally chuckled.

'Was it something I said?' Fran asked.

'You're impossible,' Sally laughed. 'He'll probably poison your dinner.' She lay on her back and spread out her arms. 'You nearly drowned me too.'

'I love swimming and am trained as a deep-water lifeguard. I help at our local pool. The lad's there say I remind them of Pamela Anderson.' Fran giggled.

'You amaze me,' Sally giggled too as she envisaged Fran in a red skimpy one-piece, walking around with purpose, chatting happily to the swimmers.

'But don't worry, my lifeguard's uniform is more *Carry On Camping* than *Baywatch*.'

Sally smiled and closed her eyes, 'This weather is wonderful,' she said.

'Bit too hot for me, but the water is lovely.' Fran let her fingers drift along the water's surface, trailing them gently.

'So, tell me more about life in Blackpool,' Sally asked as she swished about.

'Well, it's a grand place, bustling in high season with many folks travelling from all over to enjoy the Golden Mile and Pleasure Beach.'

'Pleasure Beach?'

'Aye, it's like a fancy funfair with thrilling rides and a roller coaster called the Big One.'

'Do you indulge?'

'It's not my cup of tea, but I like to watch the kiddies, and there's lots for them to do.'

'Blackpool sounds like a wonderful place for families.' Sally turned on her tummy to doggy paddle beside Fran. 'Do you have any children?'

'Children?' Fran raised her head from the pelican and puffed out her cheeks. 'We were never blessed, dear,' she quietly replied.

'Oh Fran, I'm so sorry.' Sally touched Fran's arm. 'I didn't mean to put my foot in it.'

'Don't worry, it wasn't meant to be, though it wasn't through lack of trying.' Fran gave a wistful smile. 'Such a shame. I think Sid and I would have made good parents.'

'Did you never think to adopt?'

'Oh, I lost so many babies, and adoption was a consideration for a while, but our families made up for it, and we have nephews and nieces galore to spoil.' Kicking her legs, Fran began to circle. 'I love them all, and they call me their Number Two Mum.'

'I feel guilty to tell you that I never wanted kids.' Sally raised a hand and ran her fingers through the wet mop of hair.

'Don't feel guilty. We all have different dreams. What did you dream of?'

'My career. It was too important, and I've never been in a relationship that felt right for babies.'

'As long as you're happy, no one should judge you.'

'My mother does, for one,' Sally rolled her eyes. 'She's horrified that I've reached the age of fifty with no ring on my finger and no miniature Sallys doing wonderful worldly things to make a grandmother proud.'

'I'm sure she wants the best for you.'

'Who knows? Mother spends her life in Spain with husband number three, wining and dining on the Costas.'

'Bargain Brits Abroad?'

'Hardly bargain; her husband is loaded. Something to do with owning a property company.'

'Very nice. Tell me, who was the rotter who broke your heart?'

'His name was Ross Briscoe. Remind me to tell you about it over a large glass of Waltho's delicious wine.'

'Aye, I will.'

Fran looked up to see Angelique approach. She carried a tray with drinks.

'Refreshment, ladies?' Angelique called out.

In her wake came Bridgette, Ahmed, Jeanette and Pearl.

Dressed for the pool, they made a colourful sight. Bridgette wore a poppy-patterned, skirted swimsuit and a large straw hat. Ahmed was modest in a peaked cap, knee-length shorts and a polo shirt covering his slim frame. Jeanette and Pearl wore turquoise and silver-coloured suits and, after placing towels and totes on an empty steamer chair, tugged flower-covered rubber hats over their heads.

'Lovely.' Fran turned to Sally. 'I can feel a party starting,' she said. Dipping her head, she lifted the pelican away and swam to the side of the pool. 'Wine for me!' Fran called out.

'And me,' Sally said and adeptly raised her body out of the water.

Fran scaled the steps, and water pooled as she joined Angelique and raised a beaker of cold chardonnay. 'Cheers, everyone, and here's to all our clever concoctions today, especially my tomato sauce!'

In the corner of her balcony, Caroline sat in the shade. She could hear laughter from the other side of the garden, where guests gathered around the pool. Fran's voice was the loudest, and Caroline imagined the tone of the conversation. The fish and chip queen would hold court, regaling the guests with northern tales. Fran had easily made friends with Sally, and Caroline considered them an unlikely pair.

What made a friendship, Caroline pondered as she sipped an iced water. Since the pandemic, friendships seem thin on the ground. There were times when Caroline longed to gossip, to let off steam about Stanley and vent her feelings. But she had no one she could turn to. No one would understand.

Caroline gazed beyond the garden, and her eyes fell on the field of swaying sunflowers, their petals a carpet of gold under the rays of the early evening sun. Suddenly, she felt every one of her sixty-one years and realised she was terribly lonely.

But it hadn't always been that way.

When Leo was young, Caroline had made friends through his playgroup and school. During his university years, she became a lady who lunched and got involved in charities Stanley supported. But with an empty nest and Stanley rarely at home, so-called friends drifted away, and Caroline was bored. It had been an impulsive decision to start her own little business, catering for dinner parties and elegant events, and, to her shame, she realised that it was something she should never have begun.

Caroline sighed and took another sip of water.

The pandemic had increased the business debt she'd accumulated in a short space of time. Caroline's Catering was only two years old when bookings dried up, and the country went into isolation. After which, it pained her to sit down with their accountant and hear the reality of the situation.

Richard was a family friend. Mature and kindly, his words were soft. 'You've spent too much and poorly invested in equipment and staff, and your costings have been unrealistic,' he'd said as he showed her the figures. 'If you restart, you will need an injection of capital. Otherwise, I suggest you pay off the debts and wrap the company up.'

Stanley was silent as he'd listened to Richard's advice.

Caroline had crossed her fingers and prayed that her husband wouldn't embarrass her. But she was wrong, and when Stanley began, he let rip with such force that his verbal blast echoed throughout the house.

'Dear Lord, Caro!' Stanley's face was as purple as the merlot he favoured and veins popped as he threw his chair back and lumbered to his feet. 'Why didn't you tell me?'

'Why didn't you ask?' she'd responded.

'I should have guessed that a housewife could never run a business,' Stanley seethed. 'You might have served a decent supper, but professional cooking is hardly your forte. Don't think for one moment that I am about to inject any capital into Caroline's Catering to prop it up.'

Still staring at the sunflowers, Caroline remembered, at that point, she'd seen red.

Months of frustration and being cooped up with a drunken Stanley, between bouts of him breaking lockdown to sneak out, came to a boil. With the country back at work, she'd hardly seen him, yet had evidence of his philandering: the scent of perfume on his suit and traces of makeup on his shirts. Refusing to rise to the bait before Richard, she'd taken the full force of Stanley's wrath. When Richard left, and Stanley stormed out, in frustration and exasperation, she'd drunk a bottle of her husband's most expensive wine.

Caroline touched her forehead and groaned as she thought of the massive hangover she'd endured, made worse by news the following day, when Stanley announced that he was divorcing her.

Though he refused to admit to an affair, Caroline secretly knew that he must have landed on his feet when, by chance, she discovered his relationship with a wealthy widow.

'Celia sodding Ackland,' Caroline muttered through gritted teeth and drummed her fingers on the pretty wrought iron table.

She remembered glancing through the window of the River Café one lunchtime while walking through Hammersmith. Shocked, Caroline saw Stanley and Celia sitting together on the terrace, and Caroline recognised the rake-thin woman. A bottle of Krug sat by their table and Caroline wanted to rush in and pour it over Celia's perfectly groomed head. But as she walked away, Caroline knew that all was lost.

Her marriage was over.

'And here I am,' Caroline told herself as a tiny bird fluttered down and perched on the balcony railing to pause in its busy avian life. Its little claws gripped tightly, and Caroline stared at the soft brown feathers and thought of the simple beauty of life in France – a stark comparison to her own.

Caroline sighed as the bird flew away. She had no one she could talk to. No one would understand her shame in losing her husband and inevitably, her business. Even Leo was difficult. But perhaps Caroline had failed to understand her son? Leo, who'd flitted from one job to another before finding an enviable position in the Foreign Office.

Caroline had considered getting out of her marriage when Leo left home, but the thought of being on her own, unable to finance herself, had been daunting, and she'd stayed put.

The air was still hot, and Caroline ran a hand across her brow. She wondered if Leo was stifling, too, in his London office. She longed to have a caring relationship with her son, but other than birthdays and Christmas get-togethers and occasional meals in town, they didn't have a lot in common.

Leo disliked his father almost as much as Caroline.

'Dad ambles through life by the seat of his pants,' Leo said, 'and I don't want to be like you, Mum. You should have left Dad years ago when you were young enough to make a new life.'

Leo's comments were hurtful and added to Caroline's dismay.

As Caroline reflected on her surroundings, she had no idea what life held in store once the house was sold, debts repaid and Stanley had disappeared into the sunset with Celia. She prayed there was sufficient for her to streamline her business and keep going, then set up home, perhaps in an apartment. It would have to be small, but at least she'd have something of her own.

'Stop feeling sorry for yourself,' Caroline tutted and leaned her elbows on the table. She told herself that she must enjoy her time in France. Who knew if she'd ever have funds for such indulgence again?

Caroline's stomach rumbled, and she realised she was

hungry, having eaten sparsely all day. She wondered what was on the menu tonight and thought about Daniel and Tomas whipping up something delicious with stocks and sauces to accompany the guests' efforts.

'Yoo-hoo! Caro!'

Caroline inwardly groaned. Fran had appeared beneath her balcony, and as she peered through the railing, Caroline could see that Sally was with her, their arms tightly linked.

'We know you're up there,' Fran persisted. 'Join us in the salon if you fancy a livener?'

It was no use. Fran would carry on all night if she didn't get an answer. Gripping the table, Caroline forced a smile and leaned over the balcony.

'Hello,' Caroline said, 'it looks like you've had a refreshing swim.'

The pair resembled two drowned rats, and Caroline wondered how on earth they would be ready for dinner.

'Aye, the water was heaven; you must try it,' Fran beamed. 'Shall we see you in ten minutes?'

'Very well.'

'Too-de-loo then, tart yourself up!'

Caroline stepped back into her room. 'Tart yourself up?' she angrily asked her reflection. What drugs was Fran taking? Opening the doors to the armoire, Caroline reached for a silk dress in vivid shades of blue. Short-sleeved and falling to a tulip-shaped hem, it was stylish, elegant, and as far removed from a tart as possible.

As Caroline lay the gown on her bed, she wondered what outfit Fran would be flaunting. Would they be subjected to yet another body-hugging jumpsuit, or was there a range of equally vile dresses to come out of Fran's vast holdall?

Determined to stay calm and enjoy everyone's company, Caroline headed to the bathroom to prepare for the evening ahead.

Chapter Nine

The shade in the courtyard was a luxury after the day's heat, despite humid air which hung oppressively as fading light cast shadows in the pink and purple sky. Guests had gathered around the table, and as they took their seats, their conversation merged with the chirping of crickets and the sounds of the oncoming night. In the distance, an owl hooted, and candles flickered in tall glass holders as the lanterns and fairy lights cast dancing shadows on sun-tinged skin.

'How lovely it all looks,' Jeanette and Pearl cooed as they drew back chairs to sit beside Bridgette and Ahmed. Dressed in matching sheath dresses, they had pretty combs in their hair.

'I wonder what we are going to eat?' Ahmed asked.

'Your aioli with the appetisers was delicious.' The sisters nodded.

'I thought it was rather good, myself.' Ahmed removed

his spectacles to polish them, and his eyes sparkled with pride.

'Divine with the prawn blinis,' Bridgette agreed. 'They whetted my appetite.' She smoothed her poppy-printed skirt and spread a napkin across her knees.

'Be heck, it's hot!' Fran sat beside Sally. 'I almost kept my cozzie on to keep cool,' she said as she fanned her face. 'My skin perspires too much to apply makeup, and there's no chance of slapping on any pan stick; the best I can manage is lippie.'

Caroline, on the other side of Sally, gazed at Fran. True to form, Fran's teeth were covered in pink gloss. At least the guests hadn't been subjected to animal print and deep cleavage, and she noted that Fran's outfit was relatively modest. A plain knee-length shift that she'd over-embellished with layers of chunky jewellery.

On the other hand, Sally had scrubbed up well from her crumpled shorts and T-shirt. Caroline leaned back to read the label poking out of the back of Sally's gorgeous cut-out jumpsuit by Halpern. In shades of aquamarine, shoestring straps supported two triangles of fabric attached by ties to the trousers, exposing expanses of Sally's back and tummy. Her pale pink hair had been tamed into a sleek style, the fringe sweeping low on one side.

'I do admire your adventurous haircut,' Caroline said as she studied Sally's partially shaved style. 'Your outfit is courageous too.'

As soon as she'd spoken, Caroline realised that her words might be wrongly interpreted. She watched Sally reach into a basket of freshly baked bread, then look up to study Caroline's blonde hair.

'My hairdresser says I should stay away from a bob-cut. It can be so ageing,' Sally replied to Caroline's veiled insult and broke a piece of bread. 'This jumpsuit was a Harrods designer room sale bargain.' Sally paused and stared at Caroline's dress. 'That's an excellent Donna Karan. I saw something similar on eBay. Did you find it there?'

Caroline flushed. She unconsciously touched her hair and let her fingers drift over her dress, aware that Sally was studying her.

'I... I... haven't ever shopped on eBay,' Caroline stuttered, as Sally picked up the breadbasket again and turned to Ahmed.

'Do try this bread,' Sally said, 'it's delicious.'

Aware that she'd been snubbed, Caroline could have kicked herself. She hadn't meant to insult Sally. Why was it so difficult to engage in a simple conversation? Was Leo right – had she failed to seize the opportunity to leave Stanley when she could have propelled herself back into society and gained confidence? Perhaps her business would have fared better had she not been so aloof with customers, too?

'Penny for your thoughts?' Waltho asked and pulled out a chair beside Caroline.

Caroline felt relieved. Surely, she couldn't upset this caring man who generously opened his home to guests.

'Oh, I was thinking about the day,' Caroline muttered.

'Did you enjoy it?' he asked.

'Yes, thank you.'

'I hope you managed a siesta after class?'

'Well, I sat quietly in my room,' Caroline replied.

'You must rest when you can. This heat is draining.'

'No sign of it abating?'

'The forecasters say it will break with a storm, but there are no predictions when that might happen.'

'Global warming.'

'Without a doubt. We're simply not used to it being so hot in summer.'

'The view from my balcony is wonderful. All those sunflowers in the surrounding fields and the acres of lavender next door are breathtaking.'

'One of the reasons I came to live here,' Waltho smiled. 'I never tire of the landscape.'

'I can understand that. I notice that you've planted lavender all over the garden,' Caroline said, 'and there are displays throughout the house. Is there a reason? Does it encourage bees or something else?'

Waltho looked down, and Caroline noticed his hand gripping his wine glass. When he looked up, he seemed distracted by the sight of Tomas and Daniel's arrival with the first course.

'Ah, dinner has begun,' he said as Angelique placed their appetiser before them. 'Bon appetit.'

Caroline turned from Waltho and wondered if she'd put her foot in it, again. She let her question go unanswered as she stared at her beautifully arranged plate. Trout pâté, wrapped in a light, flaky pastry and served with hollandaise sauce.

At the end of the table, Daniel announced, 'Tomas has

prepared pâté de truite as your appetiser, but before we begin, let me explain that cooking should not be a chore.'

Eyes looked up. Hungry guests held knives and forks poised.

'When you entertain, consider making at least one course of the meal a day ahead.' Daniel pointed to the pâté. 'Tomas made this yesterday, and today, it is perfect; the flavours have improved by infusing overnight.'

Heads bowed to study layers of pink and green wrapped in a golden frame. Ravenous tummies rumbled, and mouths salivated.

'Try to enjoy yourself if you are planning a dinner party. If one course is complicated, ensure the next is easy, and don't forget to balance your menu.'

'May we know the ingredients of this appetiser?' Bridgette called out.

'Yes, of course,' Daniel replied, 'the trout has been filleted and lightly blended, marinated in Moselle with garlic, fresh herbs, morels, and shallots, then strained.' Daniel paused and turned to Fran. 'Using a smooth and creamy velouté sauce,' he said, 'which some of you still need to master, remove the salmon from the marinade and mix with eggs, morels and seasoning.'

'Oh heck, I've got Chef's scowl. I'll have to brush up on my velouté,' Fran whispered to Sally, 'it needs to be as good as your béchamel.'

'Bollocks to my béchamel.' Sally giggled.

'Line a terrine with flaky pastry, layer the ingredients and cover with more pastry.' Daniel studied the faces to find Caroline. 'Bake in a hot oven and then serve with a rich, smooth, perfectly blended hollandaise sauce. Tonight, we can thank Caroline for her wonderful effort.'

Placing their cutlery down, everyone politely applauded Caroline for her delicious hollandaise.

'Now, please begin.' Daniel took his seat and toasted the guests, raising a glass of wine as everyone attacked the starter.

'He made that sound very simple,' Brigette said to Ahmed. 'I think there's a lot more to the recipe.'

'The secrets of a Michelin-starred chef are never fully uncovered.' Ahmed forked terrine into his mouth. 'But this is wonderful!'

'I hope enough secrets will be shared to justify the cost of the course,' Bridgette chuntered as she licked her lips and nodded approval, agreeing that the terrine was sublime.

Fran ran a finger over the last residue of sauce on her empty plate. 'Caro, that sauce is blinding!' she called out. Not waiting for a reply, she turned to Bridgette. 'Now, tell us why a talented landscape gardening expert would come on a course like this?'

Bridgette finished her appetiser and pushed her plate away. 'Quite simple, really,' she sighed. 'Boredom.'

Bridgette had indulged in several pre-dinner drinks, which loosened her tongue.

'Boredom?'

'Yes, since my Hugo popped his clogs, I've felt bored and have lost interest in life.'

'But your gardens are open to the public. Surely that keeps you busy?' Fran asked.

'Not so much these days. I have a team of gardeners

who know what they are doing.' Bridgette slumped in her chair. 'They can manage perfectly well without me.'

Ahmed said, 'I heard someone say you are a cruise ship speaker?'

'Yes, I was, once or twice a year,' Bridgette said. 'I lectured on board. It was fun.' She tapped her fingers on the table and frowned. 'Hugo often used to accompany me, but he's ruined that by dying.' She pushed her plate away and tugged at her hair, tucking it behind her ears. 'I *have* been on a cruise since his death, but a dear friend died while we were in the Caribbean and with so much death in the air, I simply can't bring myself to do any more at the moment.'

'But you have a busy life with your gardening awards?' Fran remembered Bridgette telling everyone she was a multiple gold award winner at the Chelsea Flower Show.

'I've stopped all that, such hard work.' Bridgette's voice began to break. 'I no longer have any friends. People have died or gone gaga and ended up in old folk's homes.' She stared at the wrinkles and fine lines on the skin of her hands and poked at a dark-pigmented area. With a sniff, she sighed. 'Once you hit a certain age, like me, you become invisible. One tends to be ignored. I know that every generation has its day, but our day seems to have faded and the grim reaper is fast approaching.'

'You are very young at heart.' Fran reached for a tissue and held it out. Her voice was gentle, and she touched Bridgette's arm. 'You're so confident.'

'Oh, my dear,' Bridgette patted Fran's hand, then dabbed at her eyes with the tissue, 'that's all for show. You have no idea how I had to steel myself to make this trip. My confidence has suddenly gone, buried with Hugo and all my friends.' Bridgette shuddered, and her eyes misted over again.

Fran studied Bridgette and thought that the woman was still going through the stages of grief following the death of her husband. Fran had seen it before with her own pals. It affected everyone at different times. Bridgette was feeling depressed and convinced that she had no friends. She was in denial about her talents and even felt angry with Hugo for leaving her.

'Well, I want to be your friend,' Fran announced, 'and I think you are lovely.'

'And me,' Ahmed said, 'I would like the honour of being your friend too.'

'Can I be included on the friendship list?' Sally asked.

'Bridgette dear, we will be your friends. Come and stay with us in Bath,' the twins joined in.

'There's always room for you at our homes.' The expats held up their glasses.

'Dear, wonderful people, I think I might cry.' Brigette reached out and wrapped her arms around Ahmed and Fran.

Fran returned the hug and gave Ahmed a wink. 'Well, that's sorted then. Now, before you soak our second course with your tears,' she dabbed a tissue under Brigette's eyes, 'let's find out what Chef has in store for us.'

Their next course arrived.

Confit of duck served with bean stew. Daniel, at great length, explained that the dish was originally a speciality of Gascony, and this recipe was centuries old. He was patient with guests who wished to know the secrets of curing and slowly cooking the duck, and politely answered their questions.

————————

Caroline picked at her meat and spooned a tiny amount into her mouth with two beans and a slither of tomato. As she slowly chewed, she watched Fran chat with Bridgette and Ahmed. She wondered what it was about Fran that enabled her to easily socialise. Caroline couldn't stomach Fran's coarseness, but it didn't seem to stop others from enjoying her company.

As Caroline reluctantly began to eat, she heard Daniel explain that the fat from the duck was perfect for roasting potatoes and if combined with the shredded leftovers, created delicious rillettes that would go well with Ahmed's quince jelly.

Determined to make amends with Sally, Caroline turned and started a conversation. 'Are you enjoying your meal?' she asked.

'Yes, it's delicious,' Sally replied.

'I notice that you chat with everyone. Will you include the guests in your articles?'

'Well, I would need everyone's permission if I use their images or mention them by name,' Sally said, holding her fork aloft and staring at Caroline. 'Would you be willing?'

'I, er, I'm not sure.' Flustered, Caroline knew she would refuse the request, not wanting publicity, which might ultimately highlight her problems. She felt Sally staring at her plate, and knowing she'd barely touched her meal, Caroline rumpled her napkin to cover her food before pushing it to one side. The journalist might have a nose for weight-related articles and would suss out a binge eater who lived perpetually with a war against food.

Caroline intended to keep details of her life strictly off-limits.

Their main course was followed by a summer tarte with crème patisserie and topped with fresh berries from the garden. Daniel explained that the pastry was made with the finest butter from Poitou-Charentes, and the creamy unsalted product was perfect for cooking because it contained a high percentage of fat.

'I thought too much fat was bad for you?' Bridgette asked.

'Did you?' Daniel shrugged. 'It is the fat that gives such a wonderful flavour.'

'Everything in moderation,' Bridgette conceded.

Everyone agreed that dinner was delicious, and more wine flowed. Cognac was offered with coffee, and Waltho announced that guests were to set their alarms early for the following day. He explained that Daniel and Tomas were escorting the group to the market in Chauvigny. They would be given ten euros each to shop for something they would later prepare in class.

Caroline saw Jeanette and Pearl clap their hands.

'Oh, how exciting!' the twins said. 'We mustn't have a late night. We don't want to miss anything.' Linking arms, the twins left for bed.

The expats, glancing at their watches, said it was getting

late, and they must go too. Waltho stood to see them on their way while Angelique poured more drinks.

Caroline, who declined anything further, also decided to retire. 'Goodnight, everyone,' she said, 'I hope you all sleep well.'

'Like a baby,' Bridgette slurred, 'beddy-byes for me.' She rose unsteadily. Too much wine, followed by Waltho's fine cognac, had left her wobbly. Rushing to assist, Fran and Ahmed stood on either side and took hold of Bridgette's arms. Angelique, concerned for the guest, went to help.

'We'll make sure she's all tucked up,' Fran said, 'won't we, Ahmed?'

'Most definitely,' the retired dentist replied, 'and I'll make sure that I knock her up in the morning.'

The guests retired and Sally giggled at Ahmed's slip of the tongue, as she watched Bridgette being assisted from the courtyard. Alone at the table, she saw Daniel approach with a decanter in his hand.

'A little more cognac?' he asked and poured a generous measure.

'I shouldn't really, it's getting late.'

'Sit for a while and share a drink with me; the moonlight is lovely.'

Sally felt his eyes travel from her face to the smooth skin of her shoulders before coming to rest on her breasts, which were barely concealed by her jumpsuit.

'I often skinny-dip when everyone is in bed,' he added as he pulled out a chair and sat down.

'A bit silly when you've been drinking all evening.'

'You're on holiday. Relax,' Daniel soothed.

'No, I'm not. This is work.'

'Nice work if you can get it.'

'But this is a working week for you too.' Sally watched the chef lean back and puff out his chest.

'I'm here because I love to share my knowledge.' Daniel held his glass to the light to swirl the rich amber liquid. 'It is my mission in life to help people.'

'Especially wealthy middle-agers and the boomer generation who seem to be the majority of folk on this course.'

'That's a cynical opinion. Everyone has a right to fill in the culinary gaps they missed when they were younger.'

'Like Fran?' Sally asked.

'Fran has much to learn. Her dream of opening a restaurant is ambitious.'

'You must have had the same dream, too?'

'Indeed, but no one helped me. I had a tough road to travel.'

'Tell me about it.' Sally's curiosity was piqued, and she smelt an exciting story.

'Perhaps, another time.' Daniel was vague. Sitting forward, he turned to stare at Sally. 'Has anyone ever told you that your eyes shine like emeralds?'

Sally took a sip of her drink and laughed.

'You look even prettier when you smile. Your green eyes sparkle.'

As he moved closer, Sally felt Daniel's warm breath on her neck. Suddenly, she was back in the wine bar in Le Mans, and Ross was presenting her with a cheap emerald ring as he, too, compared her eyes to the precious jewel. Sally felt her body tense as she fought back feelings of anger.

Are all men the same? Pushing her chair back, Sally stood.

'Did I say something wrong?'

Sally watched Daniel's mouth fall open. 'Nothing more than you probably parrot out to any female with a pulse.'

'But…'

'Goodnight, Daniel,' Sally called out as she sauntered away. 'Don't forget to set your alarm. You don't want to be late for culinary gap-filling in the morning.'

As Sally left, Daniel tried to determine what he'd done to upset her. Emptying his glass, he reached out to drain her unfinished drink. The brandy was soothing, and soon, he began to plan his advance. Some women like to be chased. Given that they had less than a week, he had his work cut out but was confident that Sally would submit to his advances both in and out of the bedroom. Her notebook would be filled with a glowing account of Daniel's unlimited talent, and he visualised the Sunday supplement feature.

Tomas and Angelique appeared, and Tomas sighed as he cleared the table. 'So much mess…' he muttered while Angelique collected glasses and placed them on a tray.

'We have an early start.' Angelique's eyes rested on Daniel, encouraging him to help. 'Let's get cleaned up here as fast as we can.'

But Daniel's mind was elsewhere, and, placing his empty glass on Angelique's tray, he stood, tucked his hands in his pockets and strolled away to fantasise about Sally.

Chapter Ten

The following morning, guests were up and about early. After breakfast, they gathered belongings and assembled at the front of La Maison du Paradis. Tomas, looking slightly bleary-eyed, sat behind the wheel of the minibus. At the same time, Angelique indicated that guests take their seats.

As everyone climbed on board, she handed out bottles of water. 'It's going to be hot again. Please remember to keep hydrated,' she said.

Taking a seat at the front alongside Tomas, Angelique waved to Waltho, who was at the wheel of his bright red Citroën with Daniel in the passenger seat.

'Everyone ready?' Angelique asked as bodies and bags were secured.

They set off with Waltho following close behind.

At the back of the bus, Fran sat beside Brigette. 'How are you feeling today?' she asked, patting Bridgette's hand.

'A bit foolish, if I'm honest,' Bridgette replied. 'I think I had one too many last night. I apologise if I was morbid.'

'Don't be so daft,' Fran said, 'sometimes it is good to say how we feel and not bottle things up.'

'I'm sure you're right.' Bridgette nodded. 'After Hugo died, I felt that I could carry on as normal, but it's only now, sometime later, that I am realising he really *has* gone.'

'Aye, he's not just popped out to the shops or disappeared to mow the lawn.'

'Oh, my dear, Hugo would never have done that; he'd have been at the golf club, spending hours on the nineteenth hole with his cronies.'

'Be kind to yourself,' Fran said, smiling, 'that's what my Sid always says.'

'Sid is a very wise man.'

'Sid is the salt of the earth, and don't think I don't know how you must be feeling because I can't imagine my life without him.'

'I've never really understood grief like this,' Bridgette said. 'I thought I was coping, but here, in this wonderful place, it all seems to have caught up with me.'

'That's because La Maison du Paradis is working its magic, and you don't have to pretend to anyone, and here, you can be yourself.'

'How true.' Bridgette had a far-off look.

On a seat in front of Fran and Bridgette, Caroline couldn't help but overhear their conversation. She marvelled at the friendship that had sparked between two women, poles apart. Caroline had never had a close friend – acquaintances perhaps, but no one she could trust or pour her heart out to.

As Fran and Bridgette discussed the longevity of marriage and living with a soulmate, Caroline stared out at the sunflower fields. She remembered Waltho telling her that the government had encouraged farmers to plant crops to provide oil. It was healthier than the rich, creamy butter much loved by the nation.

Now, she heard Fran regale Bridgette with a tale of a holiday in Benidorm, where Sid's dream of having a fancy restaurant had first begun.

Caroline sighed.

She knew Benidorm from TV trailers that advertised the programme named after the Spanish town, and she'd skimmed past them as fast as her fingers could reach the remote. Caroline couldn't imagine culinary inspiration coming from the cafés and bars in Benidorm and thought that Fran and Sid should stick to fish and chips.

But as she listened to the two women talk fondly about their partners, Caroline felt envious. Fran and Bridgette would never know what it felt like to be rejected. To feel crushed and belittled in love.

Caroline had spent her married life trying to live up to Stanley's unreal expectations of how a wife should be. With no financial worries, Fran and Bridgette would never know the anxiety of failure in business nor the fear Caroline faced for her future years.

As the drive took in the splendour of the lush

countryside and she stared at the pretty villages they passed through, she wondered what Stanley was doing. As a speechwriter to a popular conservative MP, he was probably at the House, conjuring up words that had little depth or meaning but would roll off the tongue of his eloquent employer.

For all his arrogance and ambition, Caroline knew that Stanley hadn't really amounted to much. Speechwriters weren't the best paid in politics, and she thought he should have progressed further up the career ladder. But Stanley's freelance work had supplemented their income, combined with a healthy cash sum from his deceased parents and the inheritance of the family home. This kept Stanley in some style, but conscious of his level of spending, she wondered how much of the house was now mortgaged. Caroline had never had the luxury of inheriting from her parents, whose terraced cottage in the Northeast had been rented until their deaths.

Caroline glanced at her phone and reminded herself that her solicitor had promised that he would call mid-week with a clear picture of the financial state of their affairs. She prayed that it wasn't as bad as she feared.

Distracted from her gloom, Caroline raised her head to listen to Angelique, who'd begun to speak.

'We are arriving in Chauvigny,' Angelique called out. 'Please look ahead, and you will see the remains of five elevated medieval castles that provided a strategic location during the Middle Ages.'

Guests nudged each other, and eyes were alight. Perched high above the town, amidst green hills on a spur of rock, they could see the magnificent historical buildings as they came into view.

'Chauvigny was a crossroad for important trade routes, and today is a popular tourist destination,' Angelique explained. 'There will be time to explore the castles. For those of you who wish to, please let Tomas or myself know.'

'Are the castles worth a look?' Sally asked. She sat behind Angelique with her camera poised.

'Absolutely,' Angelique replied, 'the oldest is at the top above the newer parts of the city. I recommend the medieval centre where you will see narrow streets and old half-timbered houses. There are craft shops and restaurants, too.'

'Don't forget the church of Saint-Pierre,' one of the expats reminded Angelique. 'It's the main church of Chauvigny and is world famous for its sculptures and painted columns.'

Angelique suggested that their purchases in the market should be a priority if they wished to sightsee later. 'We are about to cross a bridge over the magnificent Vienne,' she continued, 'and will soon arrive at our destination.'

Bodies leaned forward to peer out the windows to catch sight of the crystal-clear water flowing lazily downstream. The bridge was lined with troughs of trailing flowers, and as they crossed, Jeanette and Pearl pointed to the colourful blossoms in full summer bloom.

Tomas carefully negotiated the narrow streets until they arrived at an area reserved for coaches. The pavements were packed with older people, homemakers, families and tourists heading to the market. As Tomas manoeuvred the minibus into place, everyone unbuckled seat belts and reached for their bags.

Angelique turned to the guests. 'Remember, take your time here. Enjoy the atmosphere. People have been coming to this market for more than a thousand years. It is a place to pause, gossip, and learn about the latest scandals, births and deaths. Talk to the stallholders and try their produce. Most of all, enjoy this wonderful place.'

Angelique handed each person a ten-euro note as everyone piled off the minibus. 'Whatever you purchase, you will cook later,' she said. 'If you need assistance, Tomas, Waltho, Daniel and I will help. Please meet back here in an hour.'

At this point, Waltho and Daniel appeared. Both wore Panama hats and looked comfortable in cool cotton shirts. Daniel wore red shorts with a Valentino belt and Tom Ford Aviator sunglasses. He made a beeline for Sally, who hitched a rucksack to her back and slung her camera around her neck.

'Hello, would you like some assistance?' Daniel's words were smooth as he eased alongside the journalist. 'You look lovely today.' His gaze travelled over Sally's tanned legs. She wore shorts, a sleeveless pink vest, and glittery trainers.

Sally looked at Daniel and smiled. 'No thanks,' she said, 'I'm fine, but I think that Jeanette and Pearl here would love you to accompany them through the market.' She saw Daniel roll his eyes, but with the twins bearing down, he soon regained his charm.

'Of course,' he replied, 'perhaps we can share a pastis later?'

'Perhaps we can,' Sally replied and, turning her back, moved forward to catch up with Fran and Bridgette, who'd hijacked the company of Tomas.

The expats were familiar with the market and, in the company of Angelique, set off for their favourite stalls. Delicious smells filled the air, and there was an excited buzz as the crowds conversed and stallholders called out.

Caroline, who was left with Ahmed and Waltho, felt pleased to be in their company. The market was thick with people, and nervously, she clutched her bag. 'Will you lead?' she asked Waltho.

'But of course,' he replied.

Waltho was the perfect guide. He came to the market weekly and knew many stallholders who greeted him warm-heartedly from beneath colourful canopies. They offered local cheeses, fresh fruits, vegetables, breads and pastries, and counters piled high with ice displayed every variety of fish.

At a meat stall, they stopped to watch an elderly woman select her choice. With eyes narrowed and thin lips pursed, she sniffed, prodded and poked at fleshy joints and fatty loins with the intensity of a diamond dealer. The butcher bellowed out and flashed the steel of his knife.

As customers surged forward, arms raised and hands pointing, Ahmed shrank back and clutched his ten euros.

Caroline stopped at a long trestle table where oysters, stacked in colourful buckets, were graded and priced by the dozen.

'I haven't had an oyster for years,' she said as she

watched a woman wearing a short leather skirt haggling with the oyster seller.

'Would you like to try one now?' Waltho asked.

'Oh, goodness, no thanks,' Caroline replied, mentally calculating her calorie count for the day.

Caroline watched the woman, who held a pocket-sized pooch in her arms and tapped a pointed high heel as she demanded a deal on her purchase. With much waving of hands, shrugs and sighs, the order was complete, and the woman's crimson lips broke into a beatific smile. 'Bien,' the woman said and teetered away.

'I would like to try the oysters,' Ahmed announced, digging into his pocket for his wallet.

'Please,' Waltho dismissed Ahmed's wallet, 'allow me.'

Moments later, Waltho held a platter of six oysters, liberally dressed with mignonette sauce. 'We have two each,' Waltho said.

Ahmed grinned and gave a little bow, then took an oyster, tossed back his head and devoured his first.

'Oh...' Caroline was hesitant, 'if you insist.'

She took an oyster, held it gingerly and closed her eyes. Conscious of Waltho close by, Caroline slowly raised the shell to her lips.

For a moment, she was a carefree girl, standing by a shack on a northeast beach. She could almost smell the sea and hear her dad encouraging her to indulge as the salty taste of the oyster awakened her taste buds. The piquant sauce hit the back of Caroline's throat, and the combination of vinegar and shallots almost made her eyes water.

The oyster was the most delicious thing she'd tasted in ages!

As she swallowed, Caroline opened her eyes and realised she was smiling.

Smiling back, Waltho held out the platter. 'Have more,' he encouraged as Caroline eagerly took another.

'Lovely,' Ahmed laughed, dabbing his mouth, 'that was a first for me.'

'Let it be the first of many new tastes.'

Waltho thanked the stallholder and moved his guests forward into the market which was a mix of everything one could wish to purchase. As well as produce and flowers, people jostled for bargains in clothes or studied tools of every description. Hand-crafted pottery, porcelain and artworks were laid out under the blazing sun, surrounded by children playing and dogs tied on long leads.

While Tomas sat in a café to enjoy coffee, his charges, Fran and Bridgette, had wandered away to a fruit stall. The vendor had become animated when the two prodded and poked her nectarines.

'I didn't want to buy her fruit anyway,' an affronted Bridgette murmured. 'Did you see the price of her peaches? Daylight robbery,' she chuntered.

Sally, who had caught up with them, clicked away with her camera. 'You almost wore a peach on the back of your head,' she giggled.

They stopped beside a long table where vegetables of

every colour, shape and size were stacked in wooden crates.

'I think I'll make some soup,' Fran said. 'These broad beans will do,' she pointed to the large, flattish objects and held out her ten-euro note. 'Por favor, amigo!' she called to an old man, who looked as wizened as the stack of sweet potatoes he stood before.

'Quoi?' he pulled a face.

'Nous voudrions dix euros de fèvres, s'il vous plaît.' Sally hastily stepped in and explained Fran's request.

Bridgette turned to Sally. 'And I'd like a ten-euro selection for a roasted vegetable side dish,' she said. 'Please convey this to our friend.' She nodded at the old man, who returned her smile with a toothy grin.

After bagging the vegetables, he took Bridgette's hand and raised it to his lips. He kissed her skin with cracked dry lips and a dip of his head, then winked as she snatched it back.

'Good heavens!' Bridgette exclaimed, her cheeks turning pink.

'You see,' Fran laughed, linking Bridgette's arm as they set off, bags bulging with their purchases, 'you're making new friends already.'

They passed a stall where cages held rabbits and chickens, and a long queue had formed.

'Surely not?' Bridgette closed her eyes as images of bunnies being slaughtered for the pot came to mind.

'They must be keeping them for pets,' Fran said as she trailed her fingers through the bars to stroke a silky bunny.

Sally clicked her camera to capture the moment and smiled at Fran's naivety.

After an hour, hot and happy, the trio joined the guests who'd reassembled at Angelique's meeting point.

'We've got ripe pears and some delicious red wine,' Jeanette and Pearl said, and they dug into a bag to hold up their purchases.

'I have cheese from a local goat farm.' Ahmed gripped a package wrapped in greaseproof paper and tied with string. 'Two cousins make the cheese from the goat's milk, and they feed the goats on fodder that they grow on the farm.' He breathed deeply. 'The hay and clover give it a wonderful aroma and flavour.'

Everyone moved back as a strong, unpalatable smell oozed from the packaging.

Caroline had purchased fresh hens' eggs and thick, double cream and intended to make a crème brûlée.

The expats had bought mussels and shrimp. Tomas placed them in a cooler box alongside Sally's local sausages and Caroline's eggs and cream.

Angelique checked everyone back onto the minibus, and they set off for the castles.

Fran reached into a paper bag and pulled out a blackened bun. 'Anyone fancy a bite?' she asked, passing the bulging bag to Ahmed. 'I can't pronounce the name of these, but they are supposed to have a cheesy filling.' Fran bit into the bun and tasted the burned topping.

Ahmed tentatively broke off a piece and placed it in his mouth.

'It's called a tourteaux fromage,' Angelique explained,

'originally left in the oven too long by a baker.' Fran pulled a face and returned the half-eaten tourteaux to its bag.

———————

A short while later, having ascended a steep hill, the guests piled out of the minibus again. Angelique told them they had two hours to take in the history of the monuments, not forgetting the ancient church.

'There are many cafés in the village centre if you wish to take refreshments,' Waltho added as the group set off across the cobbles.

Soon, their eyes were wide as the years rolled away to centuries past. Classed as one of the most beautiful sights in France, five fortified castles, in excellent condition, provided walkways and ramparts for visitors to gaze at panoramic views of the Vienne, the water glistening in the hazy heat of the day. Alleyways led to half-timbered buildings housing craft shops selling leather goods, pottery, and porcelain, where some of the guests chose souvenirs to take home.

Bridgette was fascinated by the church of Saint-Pierre, described by her guidebook as a jewel of Romanesque art. 'I've never seen anything like it,' she breathed as she stepped into the vast nave with its elevated vaulted ceiling, 'and it's so light everywhere.' Staring at the twelfth-century columns painted in bright colours, she turned to her guidebook. 'Redone in 1857, these colours have been faithfully copied from those used in the Middle Ages.' She looked in awe at the abundant decorations depicting monsters and scenes from hell, besides dragons and the Archangel Michael weighing the souls of the dead. 'Macabre but mesmerising...'

Angelique had reserved a shady spot at a restaurant named La Bigorne. With tables on a terrace, it stood in the centre of the medieval village.

The guests, now hot and thirsty, gratefully sat down and ordered refreshments.

'La Bigorne is famous for galettes,' Angelique said, 'you might like to try one.'

Fran held a menu and studied the selection. She chose a Galette d'Harcourt and Sally and Bridgette decide to share a Galette Kookabuffa. Caroline, sitting alongside, declined and ordered sparkling water.

'Blimey, it's a feast!' Fan exclaimed as a crusty cake-like dish was placed before her. 'Come on, Caro, why don't you have half of this.' Fran reached for a plate and began to slice through the galette.

'No ... no, I'm fine, thank you.' Caroline, most insistent, held up her hand and shook her head.

'You'll waste away if you don't eat,' Fran said, forking a slice wobbling with ham, cheese, and potato. 'It's scrummy,' she mumbled as melted cheese dripped from the corner of her mouth.

Caroline turned away as Ahmed leaned in. 'May I?' he asked, reaching for the portion Fran placed on the plate.

'Fill your boots,' Fran beamed. She glanced at Sally and

Bridgette, munching happily, too. 'How's your Kookabuffy thingy?'

'Very good,' Bridgette replied, 'rather like a pancake with folded edges, the mozzarella with tomato and pesto works well.'

Nearby, Daniel stood in the shade. He was enjoying a pastis as he watched the guests, his eyes lingering on Sally. Unaware that Waltho was behind him, he almost choked when Waltho suddenly patted him on the back.

'Are you joining the group?' Waltho asked and smiled at the chef.

'Yes, of course.' Daniel scowled. The aniseed-flavoured liquid had spilt onto his shorts. Taking a napkin, he pulled out a chair and came to sit by Sally.

'Had an accident?'

Daniel felt a damp patch slowly spread across his crotch. He dabbed at the stain and ignored Sally's remark. But his eyes, shaded by sunglasses, studied her from top to toe.

'Aren't you eating?' Sally licked pesto from her lips.

I'd like to be eating you... Daniel thought and decided that Sally had very kissable lips. 'I've had an omelette champignon. It was delicious.'

He watched her push her empty plate away.

'I wondered when a good time would be to chat about the course?' she asked.

'You'd like to interview me?' Daniel resisted the urge to punch the air.

'Yes. I want to get as much information as possible while we have the opportunity.'

'The opportunity for what exactly?' Daniel raised an eyebrow.

'Oh please… Be professional,' Sally said, frowning.

'I'll be delighted to assist you to ensure you get as much as you need for your article.'

'Isn't it more about me assisting you?' Sally raised an eyebrow. 'A spread in one of the weekend supplements or a glossy foodie magazine will fill your restaurant for months, and online content will reap the rewards indefinitely.'

'I'm pleased that you will have so much to write about.' Daniel kept his tone neutral. He didn't like Sally being in control but knew she held the trump card. 'Why don't we begin with an hour by the pool after class this afternoon?'

'Perfect.' Sally nodded.

Angelique was on her feet. Clapping her hands together, she told the guests that it was time to make their way back to the minibus.

'Wagons roll!' Fran called out, and the party set off.

Chapter Eleven

The kitchen in La Maison du Paradis was hot. Tomas propped the doors open, hoping for cooler air to waft in, but the air that blew through the fans was heavy and muggy. The guests, weary from their morning excursion, felt lethargic as Tomas and Daniel began class. But as Daniel shook his bell, they were jolted to attention.

'Unfortunately, we have very high temperatures to deal with,' Daniel said and mopped his brow, 'but this afternoon, you only have two hours of work, and then you can relax by the pool and cool down. If you finish before, you can leave earlier.'

Fran, perched on a stool, fanned her face. At least it wouldn't take long to knock up her soup. She felt smug as she looked at the ingredients placed before the guests. Some of their purchases would take ages to prepare, but her bag of broad beans would be a piece of cake. Boil a few beans in a bit of stock with onions, season and liquidise and hey presto – Bob's your uncle! Job done. She'd be out by the pool faster than it took to peel a sprout.

Fran noted that Daniel had begun his usual pre-class lecture, and many guests were yawning.

'In a professional kitchen, when I started, we worked eighteen-hour shifts in furnace-like conditions,' Daniel said. He searched the weary faces to drive home his point. 'To learn at the table of some of the finest chefs in the world is considered part of a young person's training. Heat can be a job hazard; you must ignore it.'

Fran looked quizzical and wondered why Daniel referred to a young person. There wasn't a soul under sixty on the course except for Sally.

'So, a little heat, a couple of hours, is nothing,' Daniel continued. 'A chef's life is tough. If you want to succeed, you will learn to endure difficult conditions, knowing that in time, with practice and discipline, you will become the creator of culinary dreams beyond your wildest imagination.'

'Good grief,' Fran whispered as Daniel turned to Tomas to discuss ingredients, 'I hadn't realised that we must all aspire to be Gordon Ramsey.'

'I've only come on the course to cook a decent meal for my partner,' Ahmed replied.

'We just want to host lovely dinner parties,' Jeanette and Pearl joined in.

'Chef has never stood for ten hours cooking fish and chips beside a boiling-hot fat fryer.' Fran laughed. 'But as me and Sid want to open an upmarket restaurant, I'd better pay attention.' She blotted her forehead and turned to

Caroline. 'What about you, Caro?' Fran asked, 'What do you hope to gain from the course?'

At the end of the table, Caroline shrank back.

She hadn't expected to be included in the conversation and had no intention of discussing her personal life. In truth, she'd come on the course to get away from Stanley while their finances were being worked out. If she learned something new, it would be a bonus and inspire her in whatever work she needed to do next to make ends meet in her soon-to-be-single life.

But Caroline was saved when Daniel shook his bell. 'Let's get to work!' he said.

With Tomas, he split the group between the two kitchens. He told the guests to ask for advice to ensure their dishes exceeded their expectations. After all, he grinned, everyone would taste them at dinner that night.

Tomas suggested that Sally serve her spicy Chauvigny sausages with chicory and a brioche salad and advised her on a dressing by whisking together mustard, vinegar, and oil, seasoned to taste. She sliced the sausages and sautéed them until they were as golden as Tomas' tan. Tearing the brioche into bite-sized pieces, she pan-fried it in the cooking juice, adding capers, lemon juice and parsley.

'This is delicious,' Sally said to Tomas as she munched on a bite of brioche, 'I've never thought of serving a salad this way.

'We can finish by caramelising the chicory before serving.'

'Yippee!' Sally smiled. 'Am I done?'

'Mais oui, to the pool you go.' Tomas grinned as he packed Sally's salad into a fridge.

Ahmed was delighted with his goat's cheese soufflé and the trick Tomas taught him about preparing in advance and reheating later. At the same time, Bridgette kept busy prepping her Mediterranean vegetables.

Daniel guided Caroline through the rudiments of the perfect crème brûlée. He showed her how to ensure that the mixture didn't curdle and was impressed that she'd chosen thick yellow cream and the freshest farm eggs, explaining that baked in the oven, in ramekins partially immersed in a water bath, gave a better, creamier texture.

Beside an oak dresser stacked with cookery books, the expats poured over recipes for their mussels and shrimps. At the same time, Jeannette and Pearl used Daniel's steriliser and, with his help, learned how to poach pears in a rich red wine sauce.

———————————

In one corner of the kitchen, Daniel ambled over to Fran and asked what she was making.

'Broad bean soup,' Fran proudly replied. 'Fresh and tasty and served chilled.'

'Excellent. Perfect for such a hot day,' Daniel agreed. 'But you seem to be behind,' he commented as he watched Fran busily rinse her beans.

'Oh, I'm not worried. I'll soon be on a sunbed.' Fran popped the beans out of their shells and into a colander. 'And I can't wait for a refreshing swim.'

Daniel frowned and picked up a single bean.

'But I fear you won't finish in time for dinner,' he said.

'There's plenty of time. I've only got to rinse the beans, boil them in stock, season and liquidise, add a splodge of cream and the job is as good as done.'

'There are at least five kilos of beans.'

'Yep, it's going to be tasty.'

'You must first blanche the beans in boiling water.'

Fran looked puzzled. She would be boiling the little buggers, so why bother with blanching?

Daniel rubbed the bean pod between his fingers. After a few moments, he cracked it open to reveal a sizeable, flattish bean. He held it up and stared at Fran. 'Broad beans have a tough and bitter casing,' he said, 'it is the bright green inner bean that is edible.'

'Eh?' Fran frowned, her gaze falling between Daniel's single bean and the mountain of beans in her colander.

'You must double pod each bean by hand to remove the tough skin. Only then will you be able to make your soup.'

'But I'll be here all afternoon!' Fran exclaimed.

'Dinner isn't until nine. You have time.' Daniel shrugged. 'Don't forget to add onions and garlic,' he added, and, with no offer of help or further assistance, Daniel wandered away.

As Elvis left the building, Fran gritted her teeth and picked up a knife. She attacked the beans. She was the only one left in the kitchen, and had a long afternoon ahead.

'Oh Sid, what have I done?' Fran sighed and stared in dismay at the clock. 'There's goes my swim and sunbathe!'

In the garden, the tabby cat strolled lazily along the lavender-lined path leading to the pool. Self-confident and aware of her feline beauty, the tabby searched for a place to lie down. Her ears, which had weathered many battles, swivelled to catch human sound.

'Here, puss, puss,' Daniel called, reaching out as the cat approached him.

The tabby stopped, and her yellow eyes, like lasers, flashed a warning to Daniel.

'Who's a pretty pussy?' Daniel persevered, noting her upright tail like a probe, deciding which way to go.

Sally sat beside Daniel at a canopied table and watched the chef encourage the cat.

'Are you fond of cats?' she asked.

'I love them,' Daniel replied.

He'd read somewhere that women melted when they saw a man being kind to animals. But this old tabby was tricky, and Daniel had his work cut out.

'Puss, puss, puss.' Daniel rubbed his fingers in an endearing movement, expecting the cat to give in and curl its ageing body around them.

Hiss! Claws splayed, the cat lashed out and almost sliced Daniel's skin.

'You little wretch!' Daniel snatched his hand back and, glaring at the creature, wondered again what pot roast pussy would taste like.

Sally laughed and scooped the cat onto her lap. 'I don't think she likes you,' she said, and as she stroked the tabby's sagging tummy, it purred. 'They say that cats have a sixth sense.'

'Or no sense at all,' Daniel muttered, glaring at the smug animal nestling on Sally's naked knees. 'Shall we carry on with the interview?'

On the other side of the pool, Angelique had set up a bar. Shaded by a vast umbrella, cold drinks chilled on ice. 'Everyone, please, help yourselves,' she called out. 'No more work today.'

Ahmed lay on a lilo in the pool, eyes closed, fingers trailing in the water, as he lazily floated about on his back. At the same time, Jeanette and Pearl tossed a ball to each other. The expats were sipping wine and playing cards in a shady corner while Bridgette and Caroline sat under a canopy.

In a wispy white cover-up, Caroline was slathering her skin with factor fifty. Turning to Bridgette, she asked, 'What are you reading?'

Bridgette, in her poppy-print swimsuit, held an unopened book on her lap.

'A mystery, it's supposed to be a page-turning thriller,' she replied, 'but I don't seem to be able to get into the story.'

'Perhaps it's too hot to read?'

'Perhaps it is,' Bridgette sighed. She felt lethargic and was tempted to go inside and put her feet up, but there was no air in her room. It was cooler out here.

In the sky, the sun was still high. A golden fire against a brilliant blue.

Staring at the pool, Bridgette saw the sun's rays reflected like a mirror, the surface rippling around Ahmed's Lilo. She noted Jeanette and Pearl looking relaxed as they sat on the side, their toes splashing gently.

'Are you enjoying your holiday?' Bridgette asked.

'It's been interesting,' Caroline replied, 'what about you?'

'I think it's doing me good. I needed some space and thought I wanted to be on my own while I was here.' Bridgette removed her sunglasses. 'But talking to Fran has proved helpful. That woman has a heart of gold.'

'Yes, everyone seems to like Fran,' Caroline said through gritted teeth and wondered why she found it so difficult to bond with the woman.

'What do you think of Waltho's way of running things?' Bridgette continued.

'I think the set-up is perfect.'

'It's a magical place, isn't it?'

'Like stepping into another world.'

'This is the first cookery course he's held.' Bridgette rubbed her eyes.

'Oh? I didn't know that.'

'Yes, we are the newbies on whom the rest of the summer depends.'

'Because of Sally's articles?'

'That and our own personal recommendations. Once word of mouth gets out, things tend to take off.' Bridgette shrugged. 'My landscaped gardens are open to the public, and I've never had to advertise. Visitors soon spread the word.'

'I wonder why he doesn't run art classes,' Caroline commented, 'Angelique says art is Waltho's passion, and this is the perfect place for artists to be inspired.'

'It's a question to be asked.'

'Angelique is an asset too and so helpful in ensuring that everything runs smoothly.'

'Yes, she's very efficient,' Bridgette agreed as she stared over to the other side of the pool, where she could see Daniel and Sally deep in discussion. 'I'd say that Chef has a roving eye for Sally, wouldn't you?'

Caroline followed Bridgette's gaze and saw that the pair were laughing and giggling, and Daniel had his arm snaked around the back of Sally's chair. 'I thought she was supposed to be working?'

'If that's work, good luck to her.' Bridgette smiled. 'I wonder where Fran has got to?' Bridgette sat up and peered over her sunglasses. Fran was nowhere to be seen. 'I heard her say that she couldn't wait to have a swim and cool off.'

'Probably gone for a lie-down, no wonder it's so quiet,' Caroline murmured and closed her eyes. She was sleepy and hoped Bridgette wouldn't send out a search party. It was so peaceful and relaxing in the shade without Fran's excitable voice playing on a constant loop.

Suddenly, Bridgette shouted across the pool, 'I SAY! DANIEL!'

Caroline almost vaulted out of her seat as Bridgette's voice cut through the afternoon's peace. It caused Ahmed to unexpectedly fall off his lilo and into the water, showering Jeanette and Pearl.

The expats, eyes wide, spun around from their card game as Ahmed surfaced, coughing and spluttering.

'Have you seen Fran?' Bridgette yelled.

Daniel smirked. 'Yes, of course,' he said, 'she's in the kitchen.'

'What on earth is she still doing in there?'

'Making bean soup.' Daniel shrugged.

'But she can't possibly take so long, and she wanted a swim so badly.'

'Then she should have chosen a dish that doesn't require individual peeling of hundreds of broad beans.'

Daniel was smiling.

'We can't possibly leave her to do all that work alone,' Bridgette said, pushing her feet into her shoes and grabbing her hat. She glared at Daniel as the expats pushed back their chairs, and Jeanette and Pearl hauled Ahmed from the pool.

Leading the charge for the kitchen, Bridgette marched away.

'Did I do something wrong? If Fran wants to have a professional kitchen, she must learn...' Daniel turned to Sally and held up his hands.

But Sally was on her feet and thrust the cat on Daniels's lap before he had time to finish.

'Ow!' Daniel cried out as claws as sharp as a scalpel scraped across his naked knees.

'I'm going to help.' Sally picked up her notebook. 'We'll finish this another time.'

'But what about the interview?' he called after Sally's retreating back.

In frustration, Daniel held the tabby by the scruff of her neck and was tempted to hurl her into the pool. But suddenly, he realised he wasn't alone.

Caroline was staring at him.

Very gently, Daniel placed the tabby on the ground. 'Who's a pretty pussy?' he said.

Gritting his teeth, Daniel watched the animal wander away. Then, thrusting his arms into his shirt and dabbing at his sorely scratched skin, Daniel realised he'd better help with the beans, too. The wrath of the class so early in the course was not what Daniel had planned.

Chapter Twelve

D aniel and Tomas stood side by side in the kitchen and put the finishing touches to the evening meal. Mussels and shrimp in a cream sauce required a certain amount of preparation just before serving, and Daniel could have kicked himself for letting the expats off with so little to do that afternoon. He sautéed the shrimp and poached mussels in cider and wine with the expats' prepared shallots, bouquet garni, parsley and garlic. Then he flamed them in Calvados to be thickened with cream.

Tomas ladled broad bean soup into dishes. 'This soup is delicious,' he commented, taking a spoon and dipping it in. 'Fran has achieved the consistency à la perfection. It's like a fine gazpacho.'

Making a ring with his thumb and forefinger, Tomas touched them to his lips.

Daniel barely looked up. Earlier, he'd survived the bean incident by heading back into the kitchen and graciously reaching out to Fran.

'Congratulations Fran,' he'd said. 'I gave you a little test to see if you would complain, but no...' Daniel smiled as though he'd seen an angel. 'You put your head down and uncomplainingly got on with the job.' He'd taken a handful of beans and concluded, 'Now, as a team, we are all here to help.'

Guests, at first judgemental of Daniel, began to smile too, and Daniel realised that he shouldn't have left Fran on her own. The task was soon completed with all hands on deck, and Fran had made her soup. Grateful for their help, she'd followed fellow guests to the pool.

Angelique came into the kitchen. She wore a kimono of rainbow colours, and her bangles jingled as she moved.

'Are you ready?' Angelique asked.

'Certainement.' Tomas looked at Daniel, who nodded. 'Let's go.'

In the courtyard, everyone sat at the table. Refreshed after showers and aperitifs, the guests looked forward to their dinner.

'What a wonderful time we had in Chauvigny,' Jeanette and Pearl said to Ahmed, who agreed that the market was memorable and the castles a sight to see.

'I enjoyed the church of Saint-Pierre,' Bridgette commented and tucked a napkin into the collar of her floral print dress. 'I've never seen paintings and sculptures quite like it,' she added.

The expats who'd stayed by the pool all afternoon and continued with the card game were boisterous after several bottles of wine. They applauded as Daniel and Tomas appeared with the starter.

'I'm never buying beans again,' Fran said as the soup was placed before everyone.

'Three cheers for the broad bean queen!' the expats called out.

'This is very good.' Bridgette dipped her spoon into the chilled soup. 'So tasty and flavoursome.'

Sally turned to Fran. 'You've excelled yourself.' She smiled at Fran, who'd turned red like a rooster.

As Fran sipped her soup, she felt humbled. Everyone had been so kind that day, rushing to assist when they heard she was struggling with the beans.

Everyone but Caroline.

Fran peered above her spoon, looking over to where Caroline was sitting. In a cucumber-coloured slip, the woman looked as cool as the shade of her dress. Listening attentively to Waltho's conversation, Caroline barely touched her soup. At the same time, she toyed with a small wedge of bread, and Fran wondered why Caroline was on a course celebrating the love of food when she barely ate a morsel.

Plates were cleared, and the next course presented.

Ahmed's goat cheese soufflé was a resounding hit. Served in tiny, fluted dishes, the light and airy texture melted in the mouth.

'A taste sensation,' the expats agreed, leading another round of applause.

Sally's salad course followed, and opinions on serving warm chicory were exchanged.

'These sausages have got quite a kick,' Fran told Sally, tucking into the salad.

'It's the peri peri,' Sally replied, 'the stall holder said it's a Mozambique blend.'

'Well, the peri is very … hot!' Gasping, Fran reached for a glass of water, 'Tasty though,' she added and fanned her face with her napkin.

The mussel and shrimp dish came next, and everyone praised the expats. Daniel gave a special mention to Bridgette's beautifully prepared Mediterranean roast vegetables. Doubting they could eat another mouthful, the guests sighed as Jeanette and Pearl's pears were placed beside tiny ramekins of Caroline's crème brûlée.

'I didn't think I could manage another bite,' Fran said as she pushed her empty dessert plate away and rubbed her belly. 'That was a feast, and those pears were perfect with the red wine sauce.' She looked around the table. When her eyes met Caroline's, she said, 'Caro, you knocked it out of the park with your crème brûlée. It was heaven.'

In return, Caroline politely nodded.

Waltho rattled a spoon against a glass and stood to make an announcement. 'I hope everyone has enjoyed their day,' he began as the guests sat up to listen. 'Tomorrow, Daniel will be hosting a class on one of France's finest delicacies, and you will master the art of making macarons.'

'Bravo!' Bridgette spoke up. 'My favourites.'

'We have arranged a special treat in the afternoon in Montmorillon, known as the city of writing and book professions.'

'I thought this was a cookery course,' Ahmed whispered to Bridgette, 'although I am sure it will be interesting.'

'There will be a reason for the visit,' Bridgette whispered back.

'During your visit,' Waltho said as he looked at the expectant faces, 'we have arranged a tour of a macaron museum. The family-owned and run Maison Rannou-Métivier is a macaron bakery operating for over one hundred years.'

'Bingo!' Bridgette nudged Ahmed. 'I told you there was method in Waltho's madness.'

Ahmed plunged his spoon into Caroline's crème brûlée; he was in taste heaven and oblivious to Bridgette.

'Will we be sampling the macarons?' Bridgette asked.

'Yes, of course. A tasting tour has been arranged,' Waltho said as he sat down.

After desserts, Angelique served coffee and placed limoncello on the table.

Sally pointed to the pretty glass bottle and poured a measure for Fran. 'Try one of these,' she said, 'Daniel has his own recipe, and it's a smashing digestive.'

'By heck, that's good!' Fran licked creamy yellow liqueur from her glossy pink lips. 'I hear that you are getting on very well with our Elvis look-a-like?' she asked.

'Elvis?'

'Aye, don't you think Daniel has a look of the rock and roller?'

'I hadn't given it any thought,' Sally replied, 'but his hair is similar, and he perfects that smouldering eye look and maybe does have a bit of a swagger...'

'I rest my case. But you're probably too young to

remember Elvis in his heyday. He was the sexiest man alive.'

'Do you think Daniel is sexy?'

'Yes, I do.' Fran had a far-off look. 'A bit like my Sid. Before he lost most of his hair and developed a pot belly.'

Sally turned to look at Fran.

'Sid is my Blackpool Babe.'

'Aw, I hope I meet him one day.'

'You're always welcome at Dunromin; our home is yours.'

'Maybe I'll visit when you open your new restaurant.'

'Now that would be something to look forward to.' Fran touched Sally's arm. She felt an affinity with the woman sitting alongside her. They seemed to gel whenever they were together, and Fran felt their blossoming friendship might be long-term.

'Now tell me about you and Daniel,' Fran said. 'Were you doing more than interviewing him? I heard that you were flirting?'

'Let me guess, Bridgette has been gossiping.' Sally rolled her eyes. 'She must have been eavesdropping by the pool this afternoon.'

'Don't wriggle away from the question.'

'He's not my type,' Sally began, 'and I've always been attracted to the wrong sort of men. Daniel would be too much trouble.' She shrugged. 'But guess what…'

'What?'

'He says he likes to go skinny-dipping in the pool at night when everyone is in bed.'

'Oh, heck, the naked chef!'

Sally giggled again. 'I never thought of that.'

'Perhaps we should join him one night and see what lies beneath the celebrity chef apron?' Fran giggled, too. 'Nakedness aside, do you get on with him?'

'Our conversation was easy, and he made me laugh. From a work perspective, he's a talented chef.'

'But do you fancy the pants off him?'

'Oh, Fran, what a question,' Sally sighed, 'I don't think I'll ever fancy anyone again after Ross.'

'Ah, yes, you were going to tell me about him.'

'He was the love of my life, but he broke my heart.'

'Do you want to talk about it?'

'I've never really told anyone.' Sally looked down at her hands and rubbed the skin of her wedding finger. 'My friends thought he was just another passing relationship, and it turns out he was.'

'But you thought it was more.' Fran's voice was soft.

Sally began, and once she started, she poured out her heart to Fran. She explained how she'd been invited to spend a weekend with friends to watch the biannual vintage sports car event in Le Mans. Ross, paid to drive classic cars and race them worldwide, was competing. It was a fun event, and the fun carried over when he was introduced to Sally at a post-event party.

'I felt an instant attraction,' Sally explained, 'suddenly my whole being came alive in his presence, and we had so much in common too.'

She told Fran that Ross wrote about his obsession in various motor magazines, and, with a shared passion for journalism, they'd hit it off instantly.

'Our relationship deepened, I adored Ross and travelled with him. I loved the excitement of the trips and the thrill of racing.' Sally stared into the distance, deep in thought. 'He gave me a ring,' she said. 'I thought it was an engagement ring until he told me it was to celebrate our friendship.'

'Friendship?' Fran raised her eyebrows.

Sally nodded. 'The next day, I discovered he had another "friendship" with a much younger model. A Barbie look-alike who turned up at the track at Le Mans in ridiculous high-heels and a skirt no more than a frill. She made a terrible scene.'

'Oh dear, what did you do?'

'I pulled the ring off my finger, flung it at Barbie and screamed that I hoped his friendship with her lasted longer than it had with me.'

'Barbie got off lightly. Did you see him again?'

'No. I returned to our room at Hotel Le Prince, and after flinging all his stuff out of the second-floor window, I jumped into Romeo and drove home.'

'It's a shame you didn't keep the ring.' Fran was practical.

'Not really. It was a cheap piece of bling and a bit of an insult.' Sally sighed. 'Ross cleaned me out emotionally and financially.'

'Financially?'

'Oh yes, he was always the big spender, full of promises, but my money paid for everything. He'd got himself into debt, and I helped him. It was a stupid thing to do.'

'No wonder you feel so angry.'

'No, Fran. It's not just anger. I feel used. It was my

chance at love, and I lost it through being deceived.' Sally folded her arms and turned away, unable to look at Fran. 'And I'd saved for a deposit and was about to buy a house, but Ross, the bastard, blew it.' There were tears in Sally's eyes. 'The pain I felt has been horrible because Ross really did break me both emotionally and financially.'

'Oh, love, I'm so sorry you feel like that.' Fran squeezed Sally's arm. 'It's probably none of my business,' her tone was soft, 'but I always think we don't progress until we've felt pain. As hard as it sounds, the bad times make the good times great.'

'So, what are you saying?'

'You are a beautiful woman, and you deserve to be loved. Have fun and enjoy life; don't let the past ruin the future.'

'Then you think that I should give Daniel a chance?' Sally sat up.

'A fling with no strings might do you good, be it with Daniel or someone else.'

'This week is supposed to be all about work.'

'It shouldn't be all work and no play, and there might be a kind heart beneath Daniel's celebrity apron.' Fran grinned.

They both looked up as Daniel appeared. His exertions for the day were over, and it was time to relax. He'd changed from his chef's whites and was now dressed in shorts and a shirt. He'd slipped his bare feet into soft suede loafers.

'Another limoncello?' Daniel asked and leaned in.

Almost a caress, he brushed Sally's naked shoulder with his hand and reached across the table for the bottle.

'Not for me, thanks,' Fran said. 'It's time I hit the hay, or I'll be knackered in the morning.'

'I'd love one,' Sally said, holding up her empty glass and glancing at Fran.

'Are you sure you won't have one *before you go*?' Daniel emphasised.

Fran knew she'd been dismissed and pushed back her chair. 'Mustn't be late for macaron class, eh Chef?' She nodded towards Daniel as Sally looked up, 'Goodnight to you both.' Fran grinned and gave her new friend a wink. 'Sleep tight.'

Chapter Thirteen

Caroline had hardly slept. There wasn't a breath of air in her room, and despite the luxurious cotton sheet that she lay under, she'd felt hot and anxious for most of the night. Flinging the sheet to one side, she'd reached for the hem of her La Perla nightgown and pulled it over her head. Lying naked in the dark, with her windows open wide, the sounds of the night seemed amplified, making sleep impossible.

Cicadas buzzed in the backdrop of darkness, and an owl gave a long, loud hoot, perched on a branch overlooking its domain. Caroline wondered if the creature was signalling the presence of a predator or communicating with a mate.

Whatever it was up to, she wished it would stop.

Next door, Fran's snores almost made the wall between them shudder, and if that wasn't bad enough, a cat was yowling beneath her window, and another had joined in. If only the moggies would move on and sort out their territorial dispute somewhere else!

It was no use. Trying to sleep was hopeless, and Caroline slipped out of bed and reached for her dressing gown. The silk felt wonderfully cool on her skin, and, taking a bottle of water from her bedside, she stepped barefoot onto the balcony.

Outside, the air was oppressive. Despite a clear, starry sky, the night hung like a heavy cloak, almost suffocating the world below. The cats had started up again, and Caroline moved to the railing. She held the bottle and was about to shower the noisy creatures when she realised that a figure was walking through the garden.

Caroline squinted and tilted her head to get a better look.

It was a man. Soundless, his steps were deliberate until he came to the lavender-lined path. She watched as he crouched down, then, breaking a sprig, held it to his face.

'How strange,' Caroline whispered as the moon appeared from behind a cloud and lit up the stranger. 'Waltho!' Caroline gasped.

Waltho straightened but still held the lavender; his head was bent, and Caroline felt sure she could see his shoulders shaking. After a few moments, she saw him reach into a pocket. A sudden flash of white and Waltho wiped his eyes with a handkerchief. Then, as the moon disappeared, he vanished into the darkness.

Caroline was mystified. She'd forgotten all about the yowling cats and noisy night creatures and, sitting down, held the water to her lips and took a long drink. She remembered her dinner conversation with Waltho. He was a charming host and made excellent conversation, and she'd learned that he'd studied at the Royal College of Art in the seventies, in London, when the style was still in the Hockney era. Caroline was fascinated and, during the meal, learned that Waltho's parents were from the Caribbean, of the Windrush generation, and he'd grown up in the East End.

Caroline instantly understood his working-class roots but didn't reveal her own humble beginnings as a miner's daughter in a pit village in the Northeast.

That was a fact she never revealed.

Waltho was proud of his parents and their determination that he should have a better life. His mother sketched scenes of the island, and when she saw that her young son's drawings were better than her own, she encouraged his talent and pushed him to do well.

Caroline was fascinated as she listened to Waltho.

'My parents worked around the clock to finance my education,' he told her. 'When I graduated from the Royal College of Art, I knew all my hard work had been worth it.'

'Why was that?' she'd asked.

'They said that it was the proudest day of their lives.'

Waltho's eyes had softened, and Caroline remembered how his lips had fallen into a warm smile as he reminisced.

Caroline loved art. She'd spent many solitary hours in galleries and at exhibitions over the years as a distraction from her day-to-day. She'd been keen to know why Waltho's style was more classical when he must have been learning at the start of the Young British Artists Movement.

His reply had been simple.

'I never got involved in the wild partying then, and I

suppose I didn't hold with the artist's use of shock tactics in their work.' Waltho explained that he'd taken the contemporary route out of respect for his parents.

She learned that he'd achieved moderate recognition in his gallery and shown many artists' works over the years, including a collection of vases inspired by the young and exciting Grayson Perry. Waltho spoke of fellow students and name-dropped those who'd climbed the art world ladder to international success.

'I was lucky,' Waltho said. 'I enjoyed doing something I loved.'

Caroline remembered questioning Waltho about La Maison du Paradis and why he'd upped sticks and moved to France. Now, as she sat, listening to the sounds of the night, Caroline sensed that Waltho was carrying a hidden sadness.

A burden seemed to weigh him down, and, at the time he'd merely smiled and diverted the conversation. The man's personal life felt almost as private as her own.

'But what about you?' he'd asked. 'Tell me about your life and why you decided to come on this course?'

Caroline grimaced. She knew that she'd waffled worthlessly about life in Kensington with Stanley, and made pointless small talk without giving away the reality of her current position nor the anxieties that plagued her.

Some things were not for sharing.

A cockerel crowed far away and the blackness was lifting. Light slowly appeared in rays of pink and purple, and Caroline realised that dawn was approaching. That special moment when a new day feels like a gift. The creatures were quiet, and the atmosphere felt serene. Trance-like, Caroline stared as the scene unfolded before her eyes.

'By heck, Caro – what a sunrise, it's a blinder!'

Caroline almost leapt from her chair as Fran's voice boomed out.

'Couldn't you sleep?' Fran asked.

Stepping onto her balcony, she was inches away.

'Hardly,' Caroline snapped.

'Aye, it was hot, wasn't it? I've got a pillow spray that helps me; you can have a squirt if you like?'

'No, thank you.' Caroline's nostrils flared as she grabbed her water bottle. The last thing she needed was a squirt of whatever horrible concoction Fran used to ease insomnia.

Caroline was angry.

Her moment of calm had been interrupted, and this wretched woman even plagued the early hours. Before she could stop herself, she lashed out. 'It was your snores that kept me awake,' Caroline hissed, 'and I've not had a wink of sleep since I've been here!'

Not waiting for a response, Caroline gathered her gown and swept past Fran, whose mouth had fallen open.

'I'm s— so sorry,' Fran muttered.

But Caroline had gone.

The kitchen at La Maison du Paradis sparkled in the daylight. With the door open and sunlight streaming in, surfaces shone, and pots and pans shimmered. Clean white aprons lay in place settings alongside carefully measured ingredients in pottery containers and precisely laid-out equipment.

'Have you seen Daniel?' Angelique asked Tomas as she checked that everything was ready. With her vigilant eyes, she straightened a knife and polished a spoon.

'Non,' Tomas yawned, 'maybe the heat is getting to him. Il fait déjà tellement chaud.'

'Yes, I know it is very hot already, but if the guests can put up with it, so can you and Daniel.' Angelique glanced at the clock on the wall. 'Now, please, go and find him; we can't have Chef turning up late.'

Tomas shrugged and rolled his eyes as he walked away. It seemed he wasn't the only one to have had a late night and he wondered where Chef had gotten to. He certainly hadn't gone with Tomas to a bar in the village where drinks and music had lasted until the early hours.

Waltho came into the kitchen and looked around. Walking to the door, he asked, 'Is there a problem?' Tilting his head to investigate the garden, he expected to see Tomas and Daniel picking herbs.

'I hope not.' Angelique stared at the clock again. 'But Chef is on the missing list, and I've sent Tomas to find him.'

'I'm sure he's on his way,' Waltho said. He watched Angelique scrutinise everything on the table, ready for the guests. 'Day three of the course, how do you think it's going?'

'Okay, the guests seem happy and I am sure they are learning from Daniel.'

'Do you think they are enjoying the activities?'

'Probably more than the cooking.' Angelique smiled.

'The trip today will be interesting.' Waltho leaned on a counter. 'Montmorillon is such a special place.'

'The macaron shop and patisserie are favourites for me. Perhaps you will buy me chocolates?'

Waltho chuckled. 'Perhaps I will. You work so hard and deserve a treat.'

They looked up as guests arrived, and Angelique indicated for everyone to take their place. 'Make yourselves comfortable,' she said, 'Chef will be along presently.'

Bridgette plonked herself beside Fran and placed her folder on the table. Reaching for her pen, she opened her notebook. 'This should be good,' Bridgette said, 'have you made macarons before?'

'I'd never heard of them until I came here.' Fran looked around the kitchen. 'I thought they were a fancy by Mr Kipling.'

Bridgette noted that Fran seemed distracted and wasn't her usual cheery self. In a plain navy dress, even her clothing seemed subdued, with not a trace of animal print nor cerise in sight.

'Is everything alright, my dear?' Bridgette asked.

Fran sighed, 'Not really. I seem to have kept half the house awake with my snoring last night.'

'Really?' Bridgette looked puzzled, 'I didn't hear anything and slept like a baby. Who've you upset?'

'Oh … no one in particular.'

'Let me guess.' Bridgette nodded. 'Caroline, by any chance?'

'Well, yes. Caroline says she hasn't had a wink of sleep since she arrived because of me. I feel terrible about it.'

'What nonsense, the woman has a tongue in her head. She has only to ask Angelique for earplugs or an herbal knock-out tablet; she's sure to keep a supply.'

'I can't continue to keep her awake and think I'd better sleep in the garden tonight.'

'You certainly will not. Don't worry, we'll find a solution as the day goes on.' Bridgette tugged on Fran's dress and lowered her voice, 'And for goodness' sake, get changed before we go on our trip. Your wonderful flamboyant outfits are the highlight of everyone's day.'

Before Fran could reply, Tomas entered the kitchen, followed by a bleary-eyed Daniel.

'Another one who looks like they didn't get any sleep,' Bridgette whispered.

'Oh heck, did I keep Chef awake too?'

Bridgette patted Fran's knee, and as Daniel rang his bell, they both sat up to attention.

'Good morning, everyone,' Daniel began. His hair was damp, and he looked tired as he ran his fingers through the thick black fringe, pushing it away from his face. 'Today, we learn about French macarons. A great delicacy in this country. In England, they are mistaken for a *macaroon*.' He emphasised the word, and his eyes travelled the length of the table, studying faces to ensure he had everyone's attention. 'A macaroon is a dense coconut-flavoured mixture, but more of that later.'

'Where's Sally?' Fran whispered and nudged Bridgette, who shrugged.

Before Bridgette could reply, Daniel shot Fran an angry glance. He'd heard her whisper. Not wishing to get in any more trouble, Fran held a finger to her lips and nodded.

'Unlike the macarons we will sample this afternoon, we will begin with the better-known Paris macaron.' Daniel picked up a water bottle and drank the contents as though he'd been parched in a desert for days.

'Hangover,' Bridgette muttered with a firm nod of her head.

Tomas held out a serving dish, and Daniel selected a macaron.

'Look at this,' he said, holding the macaron high for everyone to see. 'In various pastel colours and flavours, it is a perfectly formed almond meringue disc, uniform in size and sandwiched with a ganache filling.' With a finger, he circled the smooth surface. 'This is strawberry in flavour, but you will make many different types today.'

Tomas held out another dish and selected a tiny almond cookie.

'As you can see, Tomas is showing us a version of an almond pastry, baked until pale brown and resembling a small cookie. Many patisseries in France serve this style of macaron, and the recipe is a closely guarded secret.' Daniel reached out. He picked one up, studied it and took a bite. 'Delicious,' he announced. 'The recipe is never written down but passed on by word of mouth from generation to generation.'

'Blimey, gawd knows what my recipe would end up as,' Fran giggled, 'I'd never remember the ingredients.'

Daniel flashed another look that could kill, and Fran

replaced her finger to zip her lips. Picking up her pencil, she made notes.

With his hands behind his back, Daniel started to pace the length of the room.

'Here we go…' Bridgette whispered.

'Catherine de Medici's chef was said to have introduced the macaron to France, but I think this is a myth.'

'What are your own thoughts?' Ahmed piped up.

Daniel stopped his pacing. 'A good question; someone is paying attention.' He smiled at Ahmed. 'In the 1700s, two Carmelite nuns sought asylum during the French Revolution, and to pay for their housing, they baked macarons and sold them. They were known as the "Macaron Sisters."'

'Sounds like a pop group,' Fran whispered.

'I'm sure the Nolan Sisters have nothing to worry about,' Bridgette replied.

Daniel glared at Fran again. 'In these times, the macarons were plain with no filling or flavouring.' Daniel ran his eyes along the line of guests. 'But, in the 1930s, pastry chefs began to add fillings and spice, sometimes liqueurs.'

'Now we're talking.' Bridgette glanced at a bottle of Crème de Cassis alongside Cointreau and green Chartreuse.

'Many famous bakers have claimed to have invented the macaron,' Daniel said, 'and later, we will visit the oldest macaron bakery in Montmorillon. Their traditional family recipe has remained unchanged for over one hundred and fifty years.'

'Let's hope they wrote the recipe down,' Bridgette commented.

'It is a recipe that they will never divulge,' Daniel said, 'but I am sure you will find the visit interesting.' He stopped and picked up his bell. 'Now, you have many macarons to make before we leave. Let's bake!'

Chapter Fourteen

F or their excursion that afternoon, as promised, the guests were taken to Montmorillon. The town lay on both sides of the river Gartempe, offering a unique medieval heritage, and many buildings in an area known as the City of Writing and Book Professions had been lovingly restored.

After their early macaron class, where everyone mastered the techniques required to bake the perfect confection, Angelique and Tomas assisted the guests onto the minibus and drove them through the countryside. Waltho chugged ahead in his ancient Citroën with a somewhat worse-for-wear, Daniel, sitting alongside.

As Tomas drove slowly through the town, the guests stared expectedly through the window. They people-watched tourists, who'd flocked to enjoy the ancient setting and discover old houses and twelfth-century monuments, plus the Notre Dame Church, quaint booksellers and craft shops in abundance.

Sally was missing from the party, but Fran, concerned for her new friend's wellbeing, had tracked the journalist down before they left. She'd found Sally creeping along the corridor from a section of the house reserved for the staff.

'Bloody hell,' Fran exclaimed, 'you look like you've been pulled through a hedge backwards.' She noted Sally's frizzy pink hair, puffy eyes and unkempt appearance. Peering closely, Fran saw a hint of a bruise on Sally's neck. 'Are there vampires in Daniel's room?' she asked. 'Have you slept in that dress?'

'Very funny,' Sally muttered as she hurried along, 'I blame you.'

'Me? Why, what have I done?' Fran was breathless as she tried to keep up.

'All that talk about the past not ruining the future.'

'So, nothing to do with the strongest limoncello on the planet and a horny chef?'

'Shush…' Sally looked anxiously around as she placed her key in the lock of her bedroom door. 'Someone might hear.'

'Nothing wrong with a bit of fun, as long as there are no Barbies in the background,' Fran said. 'Tell me, what happened after I went to bed last night?'

Sally grabbed Fran's arm and bundled her into the room.

'I can't believe it,' Sally began, 'there must have been something in the limoncello.'

'Did he drug you?' Fran was affronted, her nostrils suddenly flaring.

'God no, calm down,' Sally said and, taking Fran's hand,

they sat on her bed. 'It must have been something about the twinkling stars, moonlight and heady night air.'

'Go on…'

'Well, Daniel suggested a swim, and recklessly I thought, "Why not?"'

'You went swimming with him?' Fran's eyes were wide.

'Yes. I thought I'd keep to one end of the pool and paddle about under the stars, but as we slipped out of our clothes…'

'You saw how aroused he was?'

'He was like a magnet that I couldn't resist.'

'I see.'

'Oh Fran, it's been so long, and it was so good. La Maison du Paradis is such a magical place. I never thought about the possibility of being hurt again and just gave in to the moment.'

Behind her smudged mascara, Sally's eyes were dreamy, and Fran felt her friend's body relax as she spoke of her night's passion with Daniel.

'Well, I'm happy for you,' Fran said, 'we all need a bit of excitement in our lives from time to time, even us old ones.' She nudged Sally and grinned. 'But we'll miss the bus if you don't get a move on.'

'I can't go like this; it will take me ages to sort myself out,' Sally glanced at her crumpled dress and ran her fingers through her frazzled hair.

'But you've already missed the macaron class. You can't miss any more of the day.'

'I can use your notes to catch up.' Sally leapt to her feet.

'Tell them I had an urgent call from an editor and had to do some work.'

'I can do that, but will you join us?'

'Yes, I'll give Romeo a spin as soon as I shower and sort myself out.'

'Alright. I'll meet you in Montmorillon.'

Now, as Fran crossed an old Gothic bridge and leaned over the side to look at the shallow river, she was confident that Sally was on her way. Everyone was under the assumption that an important call had held her up.

'Just look at these magnificent buildings,' Bridgette called out.

Striding ahead, she wore walking shorts to her knees, an Aertex shirt and hiking boots. She'd placed a Tilley hat on her head, and a rucksack sat firmly on her back. Fran thought Bridgette resembled Brown Owl and felt sure she must have been a leader in the Brownies.

Everyone else had dressed in sensible, comfortable clothing, having been advised by Angelique that the afternoon would involve a fair amount of walking if they wanted to take in the sights of Montmorillon, where the alleys and pathways were steep in places.

Fran felt out of place in a silver-shaded jumpsuit, animal-print headband and sparkly trainers.

'We're heading to the medieval quarter, where booksellers, calligraphers, painters and potters share the space,' Angelique announced.

'Don't forget to visit the museum of typewriters,' Waltho added as he strolled along, Panama in place, looking relaxed and comfortable in chinos and a cotton Nehru shirt.

'I wonder if they've replaced the timber in those old houses?' Fran queried. She tugged her headband away from her hot brow as she stared at the misshapen medieval dwellings that lined their route. 'They'd fall down if there was a plague of woodworm,' she added.

'Timber is one of the longest-standing building materials ever used by man and has been used for over ten thousand years,' Bridgette informed, and, reaching into her rucksack, handed Fran a bottle of water. 'The wood will be treated for worm.'

Fran, grateful for the cooling drink, took a long sip.

Together with Waltho, they paused by a bookshop named L'artisan du Livre, painted in a vibrant orange with pretty pots of flaming flowers. An old man with a straggly grey beard sat on a wobbly chair, one leg crossed over the other as he gripped a foot and, with a large pair of scissors, began to clip his toenails.

'Bonjour,' Bridgette nodded, unconcerned as a jagged ridge of moon-shaped nail flew past.

The old man stared at Bridgette with piercing blue eyes from a face suggesting a well-lived life. He shrugged and nodded towards a table piled high with books. Bridgette picked up an ancient map book while Waltho reached for a coffee table tome – a biography of a female French artist.

'That looks interesting,' Bridgette commented as she watched Waltho turn the pages.

'Yes, doesn't it?' He paused and stared at a sepia image and felt a sudden reconnection with art. For a moment, he wondered if Caroline's questions about his background had sparked this.

'This book is about Camille Claude, one of my favourite sculptors,' Waltho said. 'She was best known for her work in marble and bronze and in 1871, at the age of seventeen, she enrolled in art college, which was very progressive at the time. She worked with Rodin for a portion of her career.' His finger traced the image which depicted the sculptor's Bust of Rodin. 'They were more than tutor and pupil though,' Waltho added thoughtfully, 'and engaged in a passionate affair.'

'Something that still happens today,' Fran murmured. She was miles away and wondered where Sally had got to. As she idly fingered the pages of the book she'd picked up, she looked around and saw Daniel sitting in a corner café by a cobbled square.

'What have you got there?' Bridgette asked, nudging Fran from her daydream.

'Oh, it's just a book called *Motel Models*. I think it's about drive-in accommodation.' Fran glanced down and noted photographs of different roadhouses and hostelries, but her eyes were wide. 'Blimey, remind me never to book in there,' she said as images of scantily clad models in athletic poses on beds and banquettes filled the glossy pages. 'These girls are contortionists!'

'Interesting outfits,' Brigette noted and raised her eyebrows, turning the book to get a better look. 'I like the studded neck collar with matching cuffs, and the peek-a-boo bra with a leather thong looks comfortable.'

Fran jerked her head back and gave Bridgette a dazed look, but before she had time to reply, a car roared into the square and stopped outside the café.

'Oh, look, it's Sally and Romeo!' Fran called out. 'Shall we wait for her?'

Waltho handed the old man ten euros, and as Bridgette and Fran put down their books, they stared at the scene unfolding on the cobbles. Sally wore dark glasses and a silk square knotted over her hair. Her lips, matching Romeo's interior, were a bold red. As she flung the Mercedes door open, her long, slim legs elegantly swung from the driver's seat, and she stepped out.

'Hello, everyone,' Sally said and untied her scarf to flick her beautifully styled hair into place. Dressed in a pretty playsuit that would have befitted a teenager, she looked years younger than her actual age and, hoisting her camera bag onto her shoulder, stopped by Daniel and gave him a knowing smile.

Taking the camera, she removed the lens and clicked away. 'Chef at work?' she commented.

Daniel, sipping a medicinal pastis, studied Sally from top to toe then raised one eyebrow and nodded. 'Just enjoying a little pick-me-up, I didn't get much sleep,' he grinned. 'Care to join me?'

'No thanks, I need to catch up with my friends,' Sally replied. 'But you can keep an eye on Romeo,' she added.

'Throw me the keys,' Daniel called out.

'Are you mad?' Sally laughed and patted her pocket where Romeo's keys were safely secured. She turned to join Fran and Bridgette.

'My word, you look like a film star in that getup,' Fran said as she linked Sally's arm.

'Nice wheels,' Bridgette added and strolled ahead.

Sally stared at Bridgette and whispered to Fran, 'What on earth is Brigette wearing?'

'Aye, well, I think she must have been in the Brownies or the Girl Guides,' Fran replied, staring at Bridgette's unflattering shorts. 'At least she's comfortable. This jumpsuit is playing havoc with my hot thighs.' She reached for the clingy fabric and pulled it away from her legs.

'You look lovely, a silver splash of radiance against these beige walls.'

Together, they strolled along the cobbles, staring at a tower built on a rocky outcrop overlooking the town.

'What is the statue on the top of the tower?' Fran asked, craning her neck to look up.

'It looks like the Virgin Mary.' Sally squinted into the sun.

'Blimey, there are Virgin Marys around every corner in France, and I've never seen so many churches.' Fran glanced at an information map that Angelique had given everyone. 'There's four churches within throwing distance and an octagon chapel on the hill.' Fran pointed to an eight-sided building that had stone arches inset with ornate sculptures. 'It says here that the basement is a sacred place to bury bones.'

'I'll swerve that, thank you,' Sally said, holding her camera and clicking away.

'Do we need a church visit?' Fran asked Sally. 'Have you got any sins you want to confess.'

Sally giggled. 'None that I can repeat in a church,' she said.

'Don't get too carried away with the naked chef.' Fran

frowned. She thought of Daniel's short temper in the kitchen and his annoyance towards her when she got things wrong.

'It was just sex, a holiday fling, Fran, nothing more.'

'Aye, that's what they all say…' Fran sighed.

Gripping Sally's arm, they set off to explore.

Waltho stood by the bridge and checked his watch. The guests would return from the old town at any moment, and together, make their way to the macaron museum. He looked at the sky and felt the day was hotter than ever. The extreme temperature didn't seem to be lessening, and conscious of the guest's ages, he wanted to get them out of the blazing sun.

Daniel's course wasn't for lightweights and the chefs kept their students hard at work during class. With the additional activities, Waltho was aware that there wasn't much time to relax. Still, as he watched Jeanette and Pearl appear from a café, he was confident that everyone was enjoying themselves.

The only person that gave him concern was Caroline.

Caroline didn't mix, and he'd discussed this with Angelique, who said he worried too much. There would always be an odd one out, she'd assured him.

But Waltho *was* worried.

Caroline was a closed book and beneath her brittle exterior he sensed a deep sadness, much like his own. It pained him to be aware of such unhappiness, and he wondered if he could help her in some way.

Over dinner the previous evening, he'd attempted to engage her in conversation about her life and gleaned that she was married to Stanley, a former journalist. Now a speechwriter for a conservative MP, he worked in the House of Commons. From what little she told him, Waltho intuitively thought that Stanley was rarely at home and was probably something of a party animal. She'd said little, other than that she'd run a catering company before the pandemic.

The woman oozed anxiety despite her aloof outer shell. Waltho also noticed that she rarely put more than a morsel of food in her mouth, and he wondered why she'd chosen to spend a week on a cookery course. As he watched everyone gather, Caroline appeared isolated from the group and Waltho resisted an urge to go over and give her a reassuring cuddle.

But it was time to move on.

Angelique was conducting a head count. Catching her eye as she held up two fingers to indicate that two guests were missing, Waltho nodded in understanding. Then, suddenly, before Angelique had time to express her concern further, a car roared around a corner and screeched to a halt before the group.

It was Sally arriving in Romeo. Daniel, sitting alongside, was braced and gripping the dashboard. White-faced, his fringe was at right angles, and his eyes were wide with fear.

'I'll walk the rest of the way,' Daniel was heard to say as he swung his legs out of the vehicle. His knees almost buckled as he straightened up and frantically flattened his hair.

Chuckling, Waltho gave Angelique a thumbs-up, then went over to Caroline to walk beside her.

'Did you enjoy the sights of Montmorillon?' he asked.

Caroline was wearing an enormous, wide-brimmed hat which appeared to shade her whole body. Underneath, dark glasses made it impossible to read her expression.

'Yes, thank you,' she replied.

'Do you like historical monuments?'

'Well, I'm married to one, so I must.' Caroline removed her glasses. She didn't laugh, nor did her face crack a smile.

Determined to lighten the mood, Waltho continued. 'There were some wonderfully interesting books in the shops; I found this at L'artisan du Livre.' Waltho held up the book he'd been perusing. 'It's about the sculptor Camille Claudel.'

'I'm sure you'll find that most informative.' Caroline clutched her bag, turning her head as though studying every building they passed in detail.

Waltho felt a tension between them and attempted to lighten the mood.

'Fran picked up a book that turned out to be full of erotica,' he said with a smile.

'Well, she would.' Caroline turned to Waltho. 'Wouldn't she?'

Waltho stared at Caroline's fretful face. If only he could think of something to say that would put her at ease. 'She wasn't sure Sid would approve and didn't make the purchase,' he stumbled on.

'Then we are all relieved of the book being passed around the dinner table tonight.'

They'd reached the museum, and an employee hurried forward to greet Waltho.

Stepping away from Caroline, Waltho glanced back. For a moment, their eyes met and she seemed to implore him to stay with her. But in a flash, she lowered the brim of her hat and turned away.

With a sigh, Waltho shook the employee's hand. 'This way, everyone!' he called out.

Inside the museum, Caroline placed headphones over her ears and adjusted the commentary to English. As she followed the group on their tour, she could have kicked herself for being so dismissive of Waltho. What on earth was the matter with her? The man was polite and kind and did all he could to make the guests comfortable.

As she fiddled with the volume on the headset, Caroline sighed. Why did she feel so awkward with others? Had Stanley drained every last bit of confidence from his wife, leaving her terrified of forming any friendship? There was no doubt that what was left of her self-assurance had set sail for sunnier seas when Stanley filed for divorce.

Caroline sat on a bench. Lost in her thoughts, she was vaguely aware of the commentary explaining the history of almonds. She wondered if she was so brow beaten by Stanley that she misread any kind act or thoughtful gesture. Her inner demon was active, and no matter how hard she tried to overcome it, Caroline was uncomfortable in the company of a man so attractive as Waltho, even though she knew he was just being kind.

It wasn't as though she craved male attention.

Stanley had seen to that; for years, he'd put her down and made her feel unwanted. It had taken all her courage to stand up for herself and start her little business in a defiant gesture of independence. But, like her marriage, even that looked doomed to fail.

Caroline noticed that Fran was standing nearby.

Waving an arm, Fran gestured to a wall covered with framed information about almonds, their heritage and their journey to being made into macarons. At least the headphones drowned out Fran's voice, Caroline thought miserably, and she didn't have to listen to the woman prattle on. She was probably regaling the others with Sid's love of the little brown nut.

The tour was moving, and with a sigh, Caroline stood and followed the others.

A little while later everyone took seats in the tasting room. Caroline removed her headphones to hear Daniel explain that the macarons they were about to taste were made using a secret recipe.

'The museum, as you now know, is called Rannou-Métivier,' he said. 'They have been baking macarons here for more than a hundred and fifty years, and the origins of the company date back to the seventeenth century.'

'Blimey, let's hope that these folk had good memories. He'll tell us next that the recipes were never written down,' Fran commented to Bridgette.

'Two sisters developed a secret recipe and bequeathed it to their servant, Marie Bugeaud, who married Auguste Métivier, and he created the brand. The recipe was never written down but passed verbally through the family, over the generations.'

'Told you.' Fran nudged Bridgette.

Before them lay individual tasting plates, and as Caroline watched guests select their first bite, she sipped an accompanying almond cordial. Then, when no one was looking, she took a tissue from her bag and deposited most of the delicacies. She noticed that the twins were swapping macarons, and Sally had arranged her samples into a tempting photographic image and was clicking away. Further down the table, Fran ate macarons like candies, cheeks bulging and crumbs flying.

Bewildered by Fran's appetite, Caroline considered that the team would require a forklift truck to get her on the minibus by the end of the week. With a sigh, she pushed her plate away.

'If everyone is ready,' Angelique said, 'we will make our way out through the shop, where you will find wonderful gifts and the most delicious chocolates and macarons.'

'Treat yourselves,' Waltho added as he ushered the guests. 'Don't forget to take something home for your loved ones.'

'Sid would enjoy munching on a macaron,' Fran said as she paused by a glass-covered counter. 'I'll treat him to a box of these lovelies too.' She smiled at an assistant and pointed to a box of chocolates with a sliding drawer wrapped with gold ribbon.

'My goodness,' Bridgette said, 'have you seen the prices? We'll need a bank loan to buy a box of these.' She stood back to watch Waltho select a four-drawer box of liqueur chocolates. He handed them to Angelique, who kissed him fondly on each cheek when they were wrapped. 'No wonder the course is so expensive if he can splash out like that,' Bridgette added.

'Don't be such a spoilsport,' Fran laughed, 'treat yourself.'

'I'm not sure I'd ever spend so much on chocolates,' Bridgette replied as she looked around. She raised her eyebrows when she saw Ahmed, chatting to an assistant and pointing to a heart-shaped box of chocolates. He ordered four, and the assistant packed them into a gold-embossed carrier.

Outside the shop, as guests waited for Tomas to appear with the minibus, Ahmed reached into the carrier and handed Fran, Bridgette and Sally each a box.

'To thank you for your company, and remind you to always cook with love,' Ahmed smiled.

Bridgette's mouth fell open, and her eyes were wide. 'A — Ahmed,' she stuttered, 'you really shouldn't. They are so expensive and such an extravagance.'

'No expense spared for you, dear lady.' Ahmed bowed slightly.

Sally enveloped Ahmed in an enormous bear hug. 'That's the nicest thing anyone has done for me in a long time,' she said. 'Thank you so much.'

Fran held the heart-shaped box to her chest and beamed. 'I knew you were a good 'un,' she said, 'but as we will all need a dentist after chomping on this lot, perhaps there is a method in your madness?'

Everyone laughed, and Ahmed shook his head. 'My dentistry days are over,' he said.

'But you've one box left,' Fran said, 'is it for someone special at home?'

'No, my partner likes savouries. He never eats chocolates.' Ahmed was thoughtful, 'These are for someone who I think needs a little love in her life too.'

Ahmed walked over to Caroline, who stood alone. He took the box from the carrier and handed her the gift, then gave his customary bow, and, with the minibus parked nearby, followed the expats as they climbed aboard.

Fran watched Caroline stare at the chocolates in her hand, and momentarily, Fran was sure she saw Caroline's shoulders quiver. But in seconds, Caroline had pushed the gift deep into her bag and hurried to take her seat.

'I think Ahmed may have wasted his money with that one,' Fran whispered and stroked the scarlet bow on her box of chocolates.

'Who agrees that we should share these out on the minibus and let everyone have a treat?' Bridgette called out.

'Yes, let's share some of Ahmed's love.' Sally was already unwrapping her ribbon as they all clambered aboard.

'Chocs away!' Fran said, and, parting glossy lips, her eyes sparkled as they began to share Ahmed's love and hand out their chocolates.

Chapter Fifteen

Many guests slept on the return journey from Montmorillon. Despite air-conditioning on the minibus, the day's heat had worn everyone out, and a bleary-eyed party disembarked when they arrived at the front of the house.

'Too much chocolate,' Bridgette said and set off for the swimming pool. 'I need to work it off.' She held her walking boots by the laces and swung them in one hand as she unbuttoned her shorts and stepped out. Revealing her poppy-printed swimsuit beneath, she cast off her shirt and stood beneath the shower.

'Anyone joining me?' she called out, and Ahmed said that he would be with her as soon as he'd changed.

'Not for us.' The twins both yawned. 'We're going to put our feet up.'

Fran longed to lie down, but knowing that her snores would disturb Caroline, who'd gone to her room, she sighed and resigned herself to a sunbed in the shade by the pool.

'You looked tired,' Sally said, 'why don't you go and rest?'

'Better not. I'm out of favour with my neighbour. Not just with my daily comments, but my snoring keeps her awake all night.

'Oh, don't worry about that,' Sally smiled. 'Bridgette and I have it all sorted.'

'Eh? What do you mean?'

'Bridgette mentioned that Caroline was being difficult, so I'm moving into your room, and you're moving into mine.'

'B... but?'

'Come on, it won't take an instant. I'll help you pack up.' Sally reached for Fran's bag and began to walk beside her.

'But your room is at the back of the house, miles away.'

'Yes,' Sally interrupted, 'it's lovely and quiet and remote from anyone else.' She chuckled. 'You can snore as loud as you like.'

'But it's too much trouble to ask you to move into my room, and besides, you'll have to sit on the balcony next to Caroline; there'll be no escape.'

'I'll manage.' Sally paused and peered at Fran over her sunglasses. 'I might sneak out occasionally.'

'Oh, of course, I'd forgotten about Chef.'

'Daniel has a lovely two-roomed suite above the kitchen.'

'That sounds cosy.'

'Don't worry, Fran, I'm using him just as much as he may be using me. It's just sex.'

'Fair play.' Fran nodded. 'If you have any lingering feelings for Ross, the only way to get rid of them is to get back on the horse, so to speak. So, I hope you have a good old gallop.'

'Well, a canter, at least.' Sally giggled. 'Daniel is fun, but I can see through him,' she linked arms as they walked towards Fran's room, 'and I am sure that he likes to gamble.'

'What makes you say that?'

'I took a sneaky look at his laptop, and he'd left it open on a betting site.'

'For gawd's sake, don't give him any money. You learned your lesson with Ross.'

'There's no fear of that and I haven't got any money.' Sally shrugged and followed Fran into her room. 'Ross wiped me out, and I'm trying to get back on my feet.'

They stopped and looked around. Fran's makeup was spread all over a dressing table. An animal-print scarf was curled like a snake on a chair, and clothes were littered around the room.

'We'd better get cracking,' Sally said, heaving Fran's canvas holdall from under the bed. 'If we hurry, there's still time for a swim before dinner.'

'Perfect,' Fran agreed and, pushing up her sleeves, set to with Sally.

There was little relief from the day's heat as guests assembled for dinner. The air was clammy, and even the tabby cat hadn't stirred from her bed beneath the lavender border. Waltho had prepared a refreshing aperitif, which Angelique served from a ladle dipped in a silver tureen and poured into 1930s cocktail glasses.

'These are attractive,' Bridgette said as she held up her glass and admired the art deco pattern.

'You won't get merry on such a small measure,' Fran replied as she downed her drink and held out her glass for a refill.

'Drinking vessels were much smaller years ago,' Bridgette noted. 'I have all my grandmother's glassware, and the sherry glasses are like thimbles.'

'They probably don't come out of the cupboard very often?'

'Never. I'd be pouring forever.'

'This drink is delicious.' Fran licked her lips.

'Waltho says it is called a Jacqueline. A cocktail made of white wine, grenadine and soda.'

'It's like pop; I could drink it all day.'

'Very refreshing on a summer's evening.' Bridgette ran a finger over the pretty cut-out pattern. 'Do you remember glasses called schooners?' she asked.

'Yes, I do,' Fran nodded, 'a schooner of Harvey's Bristol Cream in Yates' Wine Lodge at Christmas was my all-time favourite.'

'*What* was your favourite?' Sally appeared in a silky sheath that clung to the curves of her figure.

'You're too young to remember schooners,' Bridgette said.

Fran stared at Sally and realised that her friend couldn't be wearing more than a thong beneath the glimmering gown. How she wished that she could discard her own undies. Fran's Marks and Sparks bra for the bigger bust was chafing, her tummy-control briefs offered no relief from the heat, and her jumpsuit was like a roasting bag. Fran felt that if the temperature rose any further, she'd be renamed Frying Pan Fran, able to cook a fry-up on her face within seconds.

'Oh bugger,' Fran sighed as she saw Caroline step across the courtyard. Annoyingly, Caroline looked as cool as a block of ice in white linen culottes and a lacey cotton top. Fran watched her accept a drink from Angelique.

'Get one of these Jackies down you,' Fran told Sally, taking a glass from Angelique, 'it's lovely and thirst-quenching.'

'Ah, I vaguely remember *Jackie* magazine…' Bridgette had a far-off look.

'Oh, I used to love that weekly mag,' Fran nodded, 'there was always a photo of Cliff Richard on the cover, and I used to cut them out and pin him to my bedroom wall.' Fran was wistful. 'There was advice on boys, a problem page and tips on beauty too.'

'Beauty tips?' Bridgette raised an eyebrow.

Fran giggled. 'I'm hopeless with makeup. Sid says I look like a drag act some days, but he loves me all the same.'

'Well, I think you look great,' Brigette smiled.

'I wish I could join you both on this trip down memory

lane,' Sally said, 'but I think Daniel is about to call us for dinner.'

A bell rang, and Daniel appeared. He looked hot and frazzled, and Fran thought she could store her shopping in the bags beneath his eyes.

'Please, take your places,' Daniel said with a wave of his hand, waiting while guests made themselves comfortable. 'Tonight, we have prepared a meal using a method some of you may wish to learn,' he began. 'Sous-vide has been around for many years and is a great asset in professional kitchens but can be used domestically too.'

'Care to explain?' Bridgette asked.

'Indeed. The advantages of sous-vide are that it enables you to prepare dishes in advance and keep them for one or two days in a fridge, or freeze and reheat as required.' Daniel ran his fingers through hair that refused to be tamed by his Styling-For-A-Man's-Man-Gel. The muggy atmosphere caused his limp and wayward fringe to fall forward over his perspiring face. 'If you have a party,' he continued, 'by using this method, you will find there is less to do on the day.'

Jeanette and Pearl exchanged glances and nodded enthusiastically.

'In my restaurant, we use a professional vacuum-packed machine to seal in the food, which is then ready to go into a special water bath named a sous-vide.'

Ahmed asked, 'What are the benefits of cooking this way?'

'It is a slow cooking process which locks in the flavours, creating an intensity in the finished dish.' There was a murmur of approval as guests wondered what was coming next. 'So, our meal tonight has been prepared in this manner.' Daniel indicated that Tomas and Angelique serve the starters. 'We have been away from the kitchen all afternoon, and because Tomas and I prepared this in advance, it has allowed minimum preparation this evening.'

Everyone stared at the warm salad dish placed before them. Tiny lettuces with croutons and crumbled goat's cheese had been drizzled with olive oil and basil leaves. The combination was a hit with the guests.

'Can I learn to make this?' Ahmed stuck his fork into a crouton.

'But of course, Tomas is including an extra session for those who want to learn more about this method.'

'Warm salad, well I never.' Fran's eyes were wide as tangy goat's cheese melted in her mouth. 'It's the future,' she said.

The next course was poussin, and Daniel explained that the tiny chicken breast was gently cooked in the sous-vide bath while the legs were sauteed in goose fat. Adding the breast to the legs, he'd deglazed the pan with a splash of wine vinegar and seasoning. It was served with a lemon and black olive sauce, new potatoes and steamed baby carrots from the garden. Caroline's was the only plate that wasn't completely clean.

Daniel and Tomas received a round of applause as Angelique and Waltho tidied the table and bought out desserts.

'You can count me in for the sous-vide class,' Fran said as Waltho placed the next course before her. She dipped a long-handled spoon into a lavender-scented ice cream scooped into a glass flute. The top was decorated with tiny pieces of candied mint and lavender.

'This is amazing!' Fran looked around the table to see if anyone else was experiencing the taste sensation, too. 'I would never have chosen this flavour, but it's damn good.'

'In France, we call ice cream "glacé", and there are several types, depending on how they are made and the ingredients used,' Daniel said. 'We will be holding an extra class on ice cream before you leave. Please tell Angelique if you would like to take part.'

All hands shot up and Daniel laughed. 'That's everyone.'

Only one guest hadn't called out.

'Caroline, what about you?' Daniel asked.

'Yes, of course, and I'd like to learn how you make this?'

Caroline had barely touched her ice cream but held a tiny piece of candied lavender to her mouth and licked it hesitatingly. Then, placing her spoon beside a gold-rimmed side plate, Caroline looked at Waltho.

'Actually,' she asked in a clear voice, above the guest's chatter, 'I'd be very interested to know why there is lavender all over the house and garden?' Her eyes met Waltho's. 'Is the plant a favourite of yours?'

Chapter Sixteen

Caroline had been unable to sleep a wink. Without getting undressed, she'd paced her room, wondering how on earth she could repair the damage she'd done.

It wasn't the sound of Fran's snores that had kept her awake. Strangely, there wasn't a peep from next door, and the last Caroline had heard was on their return from Montmorillon, when she was trying to rest. Drawers had been opened and closed, and a wardrobe rattled, suggesting clothes were being removed from their hangers. She couldn't imagine what Fran had been up to. Perhaps rearranging the furniture and creating a mess to make it more like the lounge of Dunromin?

Caroline sighed.

Whatever Fran had been doing, right now it was blissfully quiet on the other side of the wall. But outside, the hoot of the owl had competed with a cacophonous chorus of croaking frogs and the high-pitched screech of a bat, and,

183

despite the earplugs she'd acquired from Angelique, Caroline had remained wide awake.

Over the years, Caroline had learned to live with little sleep. With one ear tuned to the front door and staircase and her eyes staring at her bedside clock, she'd lay awake for hours wondering where Stanley was and what he was getting up to. She knew that speechwriters kept unsociable hours, dependant on events in the House, but Stanley could put a tomcat to shame and would often creep in with the dawn to the sound of the milkman, who still delivered in affluent Kensington, rattling bottles as he made his rounds.

But the real reason for her insomnia was the question she'd posed to Waltho about lavender. She could have kicked herself. How could she have been so insensitive?

Biting her lip and clenching her fingers, yet again, she recalled the event that ended the evening. Why, oh why, hadn't she had the perception to ask her question privately? After all, she'd witnessed firsthand Waltho having a moment to himself in the garden, at night, as he wandered along the lavender path. Why hadn't she been more intuitive? Was she so blinded by her own problems that she failed to see problems in others?

Caroline hadn't known that such an innocent question would cause upset. She remembered how his dark skin paled when, trance-like, he'd pushed back his chair and disappeared from the courtyard.

Now, as she stood alone in her room, Caroline thought of the conversation that followed amongst the guests and could almost feel the electricity that had charged as they looked from one to the other.

Fran had been the first to speak.

Turning to Angelique, she'd softly asked, 'Is Waltho alright? Has something upset him?'

All eyes stared at Angelique who looked around. 'Waltho didn't want it discussed,' she said. 'He worried it might spoil your holiday.'

'What could possibly spoil such a wonderful week as this?' Bridgette frowned.

Angelique twisted the stem of her glass in her fingers. 'People in the village remember and have been very kind,' she said.

'Remember what?' Fran asked.

Angelique sighed. 'Waltho wasn't alone when he bought La Maison du Paradis. It had been a dream that he shared with his partner.'

'Partner?' Sally looked puzzled. 'I thought *you* were his partner?'

Angelique laughed. 'My goodness, no, Arletta is my partner. We live in the village, but she has taken our little boy, Florian, to visit family in Holland.'

'Then *where is* Waltho's partner?' Sally asked.

Angelique shifted in her chair and pulled at the beads at her throat. Not a sound was heard in the courtyard as hands holding glasses paused, bodies leaned in, and heads tilted to capture her softly spoken words.

'I'm afraid,' Angelique had whispered, 'that Lauren, Waltho's partner, is dead.'

Angelique's words echoed in Caroline's head as she stared out at the garden slowly appearing in the dawn light, and she wondered how on earth she could put things right with Waltho. But as her brain raced, she suddenly saw a figure heading to the pool.

It was Waltho!

Without pausing to check her appearance, nor pick up her bag, she flung open the door to her room and hurried down the stairs. As Caroline headed out to the garden, she knew what she had to do.

The night had been restless for Waltho and with only a few hours' sleep, he decided that an early swim would clear his mind and prepare him for the day. He was about to slip out of his robe and dive into the water, when he heard a voice calling out.

'Waltho, please, wait!'

It was Caroline. Surprised to see her, he noted her appearance was a little dishevelled. She was wearing the same dress she'd worn the night before.

'I must speak to you,' she said, her footsteps bringing her closer.

Waltho was puzzled and wondered if Caroline was unwell.

'Of course,' he replied and gestured to chairs beside a table. 'Are you alright?'

'I am so sorry to disturb you, but I … I must apologise,' Caroline stammered, nervously running her fingers through her hair.

'Why, what has happened?'

'The question I asked last night w… was insensitive, and I didn't mean to upset you.'

'You mean…' Waltho paused as though searching his memory. 'About the lavender in the garden?'

'Y… yes, I didn't know about L… Lauren.' Caroline looked away, unable to meet Waltho's eyes. 'Angelique told us,' she whispered.

'Oh, my dear.' Waltho shook his head. 'You haven't upset me, it's not your fault.'

'No, please,' Caroline held up her hand, 'don't be kind, I don't deserve it.'

Waltho sighed.

Staring at Caroline, he realised that she was more troubled than he'd originally thought. He resisted the urge to take her hand and reassure her that she'd done nothing wrong. But, fearing that she'd leave, he knew that he had to relieve her of this misunderstanding.

'Sometimes, a reminder of Lauren hits me so hard that I have to walk away.' Waltho turned to study the pool and his gaze lingered on the surface water. 'It's no one's fault, merely my own for not dealing with her death as I should.'

Caroline looked up. 'Do you want to talk about it?' she asked.

'Yes,' he quietly replied. 'Now, I think I do.'

Waltho told Caroline that he'd met Lauren while studying in London. 'I was wholly invested in my art and used to browse flea markets in my spare time, searching for inspiration,' he said.

'Is that where you met?' Caroline asked.

'Yes, Lauren lived in Notting Hill and had a stall on Portobello Market selling antiques and bric-a-brac. When I saw that she had an old paint-covered easel, I stopped to ask its history.' Wistfully, he smiled. 'She told me it had belonged to a school and was dated around the 1950s. If I wanted to buy it I'd have to take her out for dinner.'

So began their love affair.

Waltho explained that Lauren, who came from Provence, regularly coaxed a beaten-up old van, laden with stripped pine, Lloyd loom chairs, French trinkets and interesting objets d'art, along the autoroutes and onto a ferry to cross the Channel and offload on her Portobello stall. She sold to the cosmopolitan crowds who flocked in search of a bargain. He admitted that he was fascinated by the confident French woman who encouraged him to paint, even selling some of his work on her stall.

As their love deepened, he told Caroline that he enjoyed accompanying Lauren on her trips. 'I soon fell in love with France,' he said. 'I became fascinated by the antique fairs, where people thronged to grab a bargain and pour over jumble, sourced from forgotten farmhouses and abandoned chateaux.'

'It sounds magical.' Caroline was engrossed as he continued his story.

They ate in cafés where fiery salads were served with eggs and anchovy fillets, dressed with pitted green olives, thick balsamic and rich olive oil. Waltho tasted his first tapenade, the black butter of France, and learned how to spread it on freshly baked baguettes, as they sipped pastis and red wine.

'We planned our future together during those days.'

'But you had businesses in London?'

'Yes, I had a successful gallery and Lauren was an antique dealer. We thought we could have a gallery here and run various residential courses. So, we sold up and made enough to buy this property.' Waltho sat back and folded his arms.

Caroline sensed that he'd come to the end of his story.

'And of course, you know the rest,' Waltho concluded, sparing Caroline of further detail.

'Thank you for telling me,' Caroline said.

'Thank *you* for asking.'

Waltho's eyes were like dark pools and Caroline was mesmerised. *God, he's attractive!* No wonder Lauren had given her all to be with this man.

'Would it help if you talked too?' Waltho softly asked.

Caroline felt her breath become shallow in her chest and her heart hammering. Confiding her self-inflicted problems in this gorgeous man was the last thing she wanted to do. He'd think her completely incompetent if she told him of her failures.

Praying that she wasn't going to have a panic attack, Caroline thrust back her chair.

'N... no, thank you, I'm fine, really,' she stammered. 'As long as you're alright, that's all that matters.' She began to move away. 'I must get ready for class or I'll be late.'

Without waiting for Waltho's reply, Caroline willed her

feet to move swiftly. But as she reached the lavender path, an invisible pull made her stop. She turned and to her surprise saw that Waltho was staring at her.

He hadn't entered the pool.

Feeling overcome that he'd trusted her with his precious memory, Caroline fought the urge to tell him everything. But fearing she was being foolish, she hurried back to her room.

Chapter Seventeen

On a table in the shade on the terrace, Fran sat with Bridgette and Sally, tucking into her breakfast. The women were thoughtful as they remembered Angelique's revelations at dinner the previous evening.

'You could have knocked me down with a feather,' Fran said, shaking her head. 'It just shows how it does no good to jump to conclusions.'

'I was convinced that Angelique and Waltho were together.' Bridgette buttered a croissant. 'It never occurred to me that it wasn't the case.'

'It's not important who they partner; the saddest thing is that Waltho lost his greatest love.' Sally sipped a black coffee, cradling the cup with both hands.

'And now we know how Angelique came to work here,' Bridgette said. 'She was an estate agent who showed them around this house when Waltho and Lauren first came to Poutaloux-Beauvoir.'

'An agent immobilier,' Sally added, 'it was her job to do viewings on properties for sale.'

'It must have cost a fortune to do this place up.' Fran stated the obvious and reached for a slice of toast.

'Lauren planted lavender everywhere,' Bridgette said, remembering Angelique's explanation. 'She dressed in the colour and even wore the perfume.'

The three women fell silent. They remembered how Angelique explained that Lauren became unwell. Her cervical cancer was stage four. It had spread rapidly, and there was nothing the doctors could have done.

'Ghastly,' Bridgette muttered.

'Tragic.' Fran shook her head.

'But thank goodness Waltho carried on,' Bridgette said, 'and it appears to be his mission to make La Maison du Paradis his final love. In Lauren's name.'

Fran buttered more toast. 'I'm surprised he hasn't run art classes,' she said. 'Art must still be his passion.'

Sally reached out to top up her coffee. 'But Angelique says he hasn't been near his studio since Lauren died.'

'Such a waste,' the women all agreed as the morning sun rose over the garden, and another perfect day at La Maison du Paradis began.

Heat bounced from the terrace, and Fran fidgeted as her legs, encased in pink shorts, felt the warmth on her pale skin.

'I think it's time we made a move,' Sally glanced at her watch, 'class begins in ten minutes.'

'Pasta making.' Bridgette smiled. 'This should be fun.

I've never made it before; it's always from a supermarket in my kitchen.'

'Daniel says every decent chef should make their own pasta.' Fran eased to her feet. 'Let's go and see what sort of mess I can make of this session.' She reached for a lipstick to smooth pink gloss on her lips.

Bridgette marched ahead and smiled reassuringly. 'I'm sure you will be fine, Fran,' she said, 'and whatever concoction you create will be delicious at dinner tonight.'

After breakfast, guests assembled in the kitchen and sat around the table. Clean aprons lay on the table, and as folders were opened and notebooks produced, they heard Tomas say the day threatened to be hot again.

'You must drink,' he said, raising a glass of water. 'Please keep hydrated.'

'This looks interesting,' Fran commented to Ahmed as she picked up a recipe sheet and glanced at the ingredients. 'What do you think that is?' Fran pointed to a curious machine. Silver and square-shaped, it had a long handle and metal rollers.

'A pasta machine,' Ahmed replied. 'I've never dared to use one.'

'Nor me, I bulk-buy my pasta in Aldi. My Sid loves a good spag bol.'

Daniel came into the kitchen wearing a dazzling white chef's jacket. Despite the shadowy bags beneath his eyes, he was alert and charming as he greeted the guests. To everyone's delight, Waltho followed and, after taking a glass of water from Tomas, began to speak.

'Good morning,' he said brightly, 'I have good news and bad.'

'Oh heck,' Fran grimaced, 'I hope everything is alright?'

'Well, the bad news is that today, we are in for another hot morning.' Waltho paused as everyone groaned. 'But the weather forecast indicates that the air will become cooler, and there is even a possibility of light rain.'

'Hurrah!' Everyone cheered.

'I never thought I'd be cheering for rain.' Fran turned to Ahmed and held her hand to high-five.

'It would be most welcome,' Ahmed grinned.

'But back to today.' Waltho took a drink. 'Chef will teach you the rudiments of pasta making.' He looked around at the guests. 'The process is magical, as you are about to learn. Enjoy your morning, and we have a lovely surprise for you this afternoon,' he added, then disappeared into the garden.

'Good to see Waltho so cheery,' Fran whispered to Ahmed.

'Okay, everyone, listen up,' Daniel said. 'Before you begin any cookery session, you must set up the required equipment and prepare your components.'

The guests studied the range of utensils and ingredients that Tomas had laid out.

'This is called "mise en place", which means "everything in its place."' Daniel swept his hand over the table. 'It is thought that this practice started with the legendary chef, Auguste Escoffier, who pioneered French cuisine and the system of a modern brigade found in great kitchens globally.'

'I have his cookery book in my collection,' Ahmed added.

Daniel reached out and selected an egg. 'One egg for each person,' he said, then picked up a measure of flour, tipped it neatly onto the table and sprinkled it with salt. 'Break the egg in the centre and, using your fingers, knead it into the flour.'

The guests were fascinated as Daniel worked the dough into a smooth, workable ball. Next, he placed it to one side and carefully covered it with a damp cloth. 'Let the gluten relax for a while,' he said.

Fran thought that she was melting. Was it possible that the air was muggier than ever? She felt herself drift into a daydream as she stared at Daniel's covered dough ball and visualised it relaxing beneath the cloth, lounging on a sunbed, with dark glasses and a sunshade over its smooth round mound.

'Why do you need to do that?' Ahmed asked, stirring Fran from her daydream.

'A good question.' Daniel stared at a sleepy-faced Fran, 'I'm glad to see that *most* of you are paying attention. It will make the pasta more manageable as we roll it to the required thickness and shape.'

As Sally clicked away with her camera, capturing the initial stage of pasta making, Daniel and Tomas weighed flour for everyone and told the class to begin. A little while later, with their dough balls relaxed, the guests were split into groups, and Fran found herself alone. She watched as the groups gathered around pasta machines. With one guest guiding, another turning the handle and a third waiting to receive, they made sheets of pasta before cutting them into the desired shapes and placing them to dry.

'What about me?' Fran asked when Daniel turned to face her.

'I have something special for you. Follow me.' Daniel strolled ahead. He carried dough in a bowl.

Fran followed, tossing her dough ball from one hand to the other and wondered what the chef had in store. Sadly, it was becoming clear that Daniel didn't really like Fran. Perhaps he thought she fooled around too much? Now, she was alone in the adjacent kitchen with him and as Fran nervously scratched at the skin on her folded arms, she determined she would prove him wrong.

Daniel floured the table's surface, then, taking his dough, began twirling it with his fingers. 'Knead it like this,' he instructed.

With a rolling pin, he began to methodically roll, turning the ever-increasing shape as he worked. Fran hopped from one foot to the other and wondered what part she would play in this tutorial. It wasn't long before she found out.

Suddenly, Daniel folded his pasta and dumped it in the bowl. 'Now, I want you to do the same with yours until the pasta covers this table, and you can see your fingers through it.'

'Eh?' Fran looked puzzled.

'You will make a savoury pasta roll by spreading this sauce on your pasta.' He handed Fran a jar of mushroom and olive paste made during the steriliser class. 'You will roll your pasta and wrap it in a cloth, then place it in the steamer.' Daniel waved his hand towards a long-lidded container on the stove. 'You have the recipe in your folder.'

'Well, I'm not sure...'

'I am entrusting you with this, Fran, and I know you can do it.'

Fran was unaware that Daniel was determined to test her passion for cooking, and he'd singled her out for a difficult task. In his heart, he wanted to help her, but she'd have to prove that she was worth it.

Daniel made everything sound simple, and Fran nodded and ran her hot fingers over her apron. She resolved to make him proud.

'Yes, Chef,' she said as Daniel strolled away. Taking her dough and rolling pin, Fran began to sing and bounce on the balls of her feet as she floured the table. 'You ain't nothing but a hound dog...'

———

Some considerable time later, Fran was gasping.

The kitchen was like a furnace, her dough a sticky, gooey mess. Peeling it away from her perspiring hands, Fran thought she might cry. She had been so keen to impress Daniel and to make her dish the most successful of the day, but he'd left her alone in the kitchen with no idea how to remedy the situation, and she was lost for words and furious with the chef.

To make matters worse, everyone had completed their

dishes and gone for a pool dip with no notion that Fran was failing miserably.

She went over to the sink and washed her hands. While she was drying them, Fran noticed a small storage room at the back of the kitchen. Making sure that no one was about, she crept in.

The room was stacked with tinned goods and boxes, and appeared to double up as Daniel's office. Recipe sheets lay on a printer beside a black marker pen, and a laptop sat on a table. Fran was about to retreat when she noticed a clean white jacket hanging on the back of the door. On the front pocket, neat embroidery spelt out Daniel's name. Without pausing to think about her actions, Fran took the marker pen and, turning the jacket, began to draw.

Moments later, she was back in the kitchen, staring at her gooey dough and, still furious with Daniel, wondering what she could do with it.

'Need some help?' Like a knight in shining chef's wear, Tomas walked into the room. 'Quelle situation difficile,' he murmured and shook his head. 'You shouldn't be on your own, laisse moi aider.'

Whatever Tomas had said, Fran hadn't a clue. But the handsome young man smiled at her and offered to put things right as he pushed back his sleeves and cleared the table of Fran's catastrophe.

'Tomas, I think I love you,' Fran whispered as she watched him weigh out flour and hand her an egg.

'Mais bien sûr.' He shrugged. 'Now, we work together.'

Fran was mesmerised as her newly relaxed dough spread thinly over the table. She placed two fingers underneath and beamed at Tomas. 'Look!' she said. 'It's paper thin and perfect.'

'You are a great chef.' Tomas gave her a wink as he reached for a palette knife and showed her how to spread the filling.

Standing side by side, they rolled the dough into a textbook shape. Tomas sliced it into sections, then showed Fran how to wrap it in a cloth and place it in the steamer.

'Okay, it needs one hour,' he said, fiddling with his watch. 'Leave it with me, and you go and relax.'

Fran was about to throw her arms around Tomas to thank him, but Sally had come into the kitchen and, seeing her friend, Fran dusted off her hands.

'There you are!' Sally said. 'I've been sent to find you. Everyone thought you'd gone for a lie-down, but you weren't in your room.'

Fran was about to answer, but Tomas interrupted.

'I have been watching her cook,' he said. 'Elle est très bien.' Making a sign of approval, Tomas touched his fingers to his lips.

'Eh?' Fran looked anxious. 'In English, please, Tomas.'

Sally laughed, 'He says you are very good, and I don't doubt him if you've spent all this time making your pasta dish.'

'Well…'

'I hope we're going to sample it tonight,' Sally continued. 'I've made a total balls-up of my ravioli, but there's no doubt that Caroline's cannelloni will save the day.'

'Is it that good?' Fran asked.

Sally nodded. 'I thought Daniel was going to have an orgasm over it.'

Fran lowered her voice. 'Well, you'd know all about that,' she laughed.

'Come on, Waltho has arranged a mystery trip,' Sally said, wiping flour from Fran's cheek. 'Let's get you tidied up, and then we can enjoy the afternoon.'

'Are you coming too?' Fran asked Tomas.

But he shook his head and, reaching into a fridge, took a cold beer. 'No, I have the afternoon off and am babysitting a mushroom pasta.'

Unable to help herself, Fran stood on her toes and reached out to pull Tomas into a hug. 'You're my hero,' she said. Then, tossing her apron on the table, hurried to catch up with Sally. 'A mystery trip?' she asked, 'I like the sound of that!'

Chapter Eighteen

In the small town of Saint-Savin, in the shade of a dozen colourful umbrellas, chairs and tables were set out on the cobbled terrace of Martine Le Glacier. The pastel-painted shop displayed a glass-fronted cabinet beneath which a dozen ice creams were packed in frozen trays. The family-run business was headed up by Martine, who looked almost as old as the square's medieval buildings. Petit in stature, in a well-tailored dress, with simple shoes and neatly styled silver hair, her wrinkles and lines told the story of her years.

Waltho, who'd given his staff the afternoon off, had driven the minibus to Saint-Savin. Now, he shepherded everyone to sit at the café as he greeted the old lady with warmth and affection. He bent down as Martine took his face in her hands and ran calloused thumbs over his skin. Her eyes shone with adoration, and she nodded and accepted a kiss on both cheeks.

Turning away but holding Martine's hand, Waltho spoke to the guests.

'I hope you enjoy this indulgence,' he began and smiled at the old lady. 'Martine and her daughter are the proprietors, and they welcome you all.' Waltho felt Martine squeeze his hand. 'They use the freshest local ingredients, and I know you will be wowed by the creative options. I urge you to be adventurous in your choice.' Waltho added, 'Strawberry and pistachio is my favourite.'

Guests took turns to stand by the counter and order. Martine's daughter, a younger version of her mother, smiled as she scooped generous balls of soft creamy ice cream into vintage dishes and topped them with sauces and wafers.

Fran sank back in her cushioned seat as she dug a spoon into a hazelnut praline concoction. The dessert sat in an amethyst-fluted sundae bowl topped with caramel sauce and sprinkled with toasted pine nuts. 'Gawd, this is good,' Fran sighed with pleasure. 'It's cooling me down a treat.'

Ahmed sat beside Fran and licked his lips as he tasted avocado gelato, rippled with chocolate sauce. 'Most unusual but very excellent,' he said as he studied the contents of the old-fashioned soda fountain dish.

'Pineapple and coconut for me,' Sally said, taking a pretty cocktail umbrella from her pale lemon and vanilla white ice. 'Goodness, this is simply the best, and I want to take this dish home.' Sally stroked the gold band of her goblet and stared at the leaf and grape design etched into the glass. 'It's gorgeous.'

Bridgette bustled over to join the group. She held a long sundae dish that appeared to be piled high with toasted meringue. 'Baked Alaska!' she said and sat down. Patting her waistband, she announced, 'I decided when I got to seventy to hell with any diet; old age is a time for outrage, and if I want to eat everything I see, I shall.'

Plunging her spoon through the fluffy concoction, Bridgette dug into the sponge and raspberry ice cream.

Waltho decided to sit beside Caroline. He ate a strawberry and pistachio combination topped with fruit coulis. 'What did you choose?' he asked and sat forward to peer into Caroline's cornet-shaped porcelain cone.

'It's lemon and verbena glacé,' she replied, 'and very refreshing.'

Waltho was pleased to see that Caroline seemed at ease after their morning discussion, but he noted that she hardly ate a morsel, unlike everyone else.

Enjoying his ice cream, Waltho watched Martine move amongst the tables, fussing and encouraging guests to try more flavours, and he saw that many went back for another helping. He smiled as he watched Fran push her dish to one side to rub her belly and Bridgette lick a moustache of meringue from her lip.

Turning to Caroline, he said, 'I enjoyed our earlier chat. Thank you for listening.'

'Oh...'

Fearing that Caroline would begin to apologise again, Waltho interrupted. 'Talking about Lauren was very therapeutic for me.'

'They say that talking about love, whether lost or found, is always good for the soul,' Caroline replied.

Waltho wanted to question Caroline further, but before

he could continue, she pushed her dish aside and looked up at the sky.

'Is it me, or are those dark clouds?' Caroline asked.

Waltho stared too. 'The sun seems to have disappeared behind them, but it's still as hot as a furnace.' Pushing his chair back, Waltho stood. 'I must go and settle the bill.'

Moments later, having thanked Martine, Waltho addressed the guests.

'If everyone is ready,' he said, 'I'd like you to come with me to the church across the square.' He pointed to a sizeable pale building with a tall Gothic spire. 'Built in 1026, it is known as the Abbey of Saint-Savin sur Gartempe. A Romanesque Sistine Chapel with many beautiful eleventh- and twelfth-century murals that have been well preserved.'

Waltho walked ahead and the guests all followed.

'I think you will enjoy what you are about to see,' he said.

As the group made their way across the square, Caroline followed behind. How she'd longed to finish the delicious tart glacé, but she knew that sorbet was loaded with sugar. Touching the belt of her fitted dress, Caroline felt her hipbones and was satisfied that she'd controlled her desire. It didn't take much for Caroline to slip up, and if she gave in and ate everything that was placed before her, she knew that it would lead to a binge, and the scales would scream at her the next day. Stanley might have channelled his affection elsewhere, but he'd imbued her with the mantra that fat is foolish and being overweight unattractive.

She had no intention of letting bad habits return.

At the entrance to the Abbey, Caroline waited in the queue. Still hungry, she considered her upbringing as an only child in a terraced cottage in the Northeast mining village. With low wages, food was scarce for families with multiple children of all ages, who crowded around kitchen tables to pile cheap, stodgy food on their plates.

I've always felt in the minority, she thought as she stood alone and looked at the guests, happily chatting in groups as they waited.

Even at junior school, where kids wore hand-me-down clothes and second-hand shoes, Caroline was teased and tormented because they thought her name was posh. Her parents gave her whatever they could afford and did their best for their precious child, including feeding her with treats. When Caroline astounded everyone by gaining a place at university, she was topping the scales at an all-time weight, and the plus-size clothes that her mother made were tight.

Now at the front of the queue, Caroline shuddered at the memory as she was handed a guidebook.

'Are you alright, Caro?' Fran appeared and touched Caroline's arm. 'I thought I saw you shiver, not coming down with anything, I hope?' Fran tilted her head, her painted eyebrows drawn together.

Caroline wanted to reply that it was nothing that two hundred yards of space between them wouldn't solve. But instead, she replied, 'I'm fine, thank you, and I'm looking forward to peace and quiet in the abbey.'

'Must be the heat that makes her so unpleasant,' Bridgette said as she joined Fran and watched Caroline move away. 'The oppressive air is probably getting to her.'

'Maybe,' Fran agreed. 'We could all do with a drop of cool circulating to energise us.' She opened her guidebook and searched for the index. 'Now, where are these marvellous murals…'

In an alcove, away from the crowd, Caroline reached into a pocket to remove her phone and, glancing at the screen, noted no calls or messages. She felt her pulse begin to race, and acid rising in her stomach was making her feel nauseous. Her solicitor had promised to call by midweek and was already a day overdue. Did the delay mean news far worse than she'd expected? At any time, she would know the exact details of her divorce, the likely settlement and what she must juggle to begin her life again.

Caroline sighed. She wasn't hopeful.

Stanley's dishonesty would have permeated their finances as well as his extra-marital affairs. She'd hoped that this trip to France would take her mind off problems at home, but it seemed to be exacerbating them. It was impossible to concentrate on the classes and trips that had promised to be an excellent diversion.

With nervous fingers, Caroline turned her phone to silent and, gripping it tightly, followed everyone into the old building.

Inside the church, all eyes were drawn to the vaulted ceilings where pictural scenes of biblical narrative were depicted. Fran stood on the inner porch, her eyes wide and her jaw open as she stared at paintings of the Apocalypse in disturbing detail. As she stepped in, she noted images of the Passion of Christ surrounding scenes of martyrs.

Moving forward, Fran noticed a man lying flat on his back on a pew. Concerned for his well-being, she reached out to touch his foot.

'Are you alright, dear?' Fran asked.

The man jerked away and pointed to the ceiling. Fran realised he was studying drawings of Noah's Ark, which, her guidebook instructed, showed one end of the ark to be Roman and the other Viking.

'The animals went in two-by-two, hurrah, hurrah,' Fran sang. 'The elephant and the kangaroo...'

'Silence!' The man, angry and half-seated, pressed fingers to his lips, then lay back down to continue his study of the ceiling.

'Sorry,' Fran spluttered and hurried to catch up with Sally and Bridgette.

Standing near the crypt, Sally clicked away with her camera while Bridgette ran her fingers over wall cracks that appeared to have been plastered over.

'Such a shame,' Bridgette sighed. 'In trying to preserve the church, later restoration of the paintings has ruined the originals.'

'Someone must have had a sense of humour,' Fran grinned. 'Look at Eve, standing next to Adam – a beard has been painted on her face.' Fran pointed to the image. 'Eve looks like one of Snow White's helpers.'

'At least it's not as grim as this.' Sally sat on a bench and stared upwards. 'Poor Saint Savin,' she whispered, 'he was victim to iron fingers.'

'Eh?' Fran looked puzzled, but Sally's comment became clear as Fran saw a painting of a man hanging on a post. He'd been clawed to death with iron spikes.

The women looked at the murals, where the garish colours of the Tower of Babylon showed petrified expressions on the faces of those fleeing the devastation.

'Not the most cheerful of places, is it?' Fran said as they sat with their backs to the cold stone walls.

Suddenly, a flash of white-hot light and an enormous crack of lightning electrified the church. Blue and purple bolts zigzagged through the aisles. It was followed by a booming sound in the distance.

'What on earth?' Fran gripped Bridgette and Sally's hands.

Overhead hanging lights that had illuminated the building unexpectedly flickered and moments later went out, plunging those beneath into semi-darkness.

'I thought Waltho said there might be a drop of light rain?' Fran said as they heard sudden and intense rainfall ricochet off the stained-glass windows. 'It sounds like the wind is getting up,' she added as a howling sound came from the nave. 'Listen…' Fran gripped tighter. 'Is that Waltho calling us?'

They squinted through the semi-gloom to see Waltho appear. The remaining guests followed close behind.

'There you are,' Waltho said as he saw the friends grouped on the bench. 'Thank goodness you stayed in the church.'

'What's happening?' Fran asked as everyone settled on nearby pews.

'The guide in reception says that a storm has blown in, and at the moment, it is raging around the village.'

'It's very sudden,' Bridgette said, 'I didn't hear anything on the weather forecast today other than light rain.'

'Yes, that's what I heard,' Waltho agreed.

'I remember the storm of 1987,' Bridgette said, 'Hugo and I were staying with friends in Surrey when unexpected ferocious weather swept across the south.'

Waltho nodded. He, too, remembered weatherman Michael Fish famously declaring that there was nothing to worry about and the weather was calm. Hours later, a terrifying storm caused widespread havoc that transformed areas of the south of England for years to come.

'I am sure this will soon pass; it's quite safe here,' Waltho reassured everyone. 'We are in a church, after all.'

He didn't want to alarm his guests and searched for a distraction as rain battered the windows and the wind continued to howl. As his eyes fell on the torrid scenes of hell and damnation painted throughout the building, he determined to keep their eyes from wandering over the walls and ceilings.

Moving to stand before the guests, Waltho took a deep breath. 'Does anyone know how to play charades?' he asked.

Chapter Nineteen

The storm raged, and guests sat close together, listening to the torrential downpour pound against the church. Flashes of blue and white lightning intermittently illuminated the scenes depicted on the walls and ceiling, where the figures seemed to dance menacingly as each flash distorted the image further. Thunder, at times, was deafening as clouds crashed together to eliminate the heat that had dominated the skies for so long. Windows and doors rattled, and the wind whistled eerily like an unearthly cry of the lost souls above. Now and again, ghostly sounds came from the crypt as though ancient spirits were climbing over the cold marble graves below.

With the sudden drop in temperature, the guests were feeling the chill, and their flimsy clothes held no warmth. Despite the earlier heat, the church suddenly felt as cold as a tomb.

'How long do you think the storm will last?' Ahmed asked Waltho. He sat huddled between Jeanette and Pearl, his arms draped over their shoulders to share body heat and keep warm.

'I don't know,' Waltho replied, 'my phone isn't working. I don't have a signal.'

'All mobile networks are down,' the expats agreed as they stared at their screens and tapped in vain.

Waltho saw Caroline grip her phone to her chest. Standing, she rocked nervously from one foot to the other.

'Well, we must make do and mend,' Bridgette announced. 'Might I suggest that we pool our resources?'

'If you think it's necessary,' Waltho replied.

'Any water and snacks, place on a pew,' Bridgette instructed, 'and those who feel in need can tuck in.'

Waltho thought that Bridgette made a good point. Caroline was deathly pale in colour, and he wondered when she'd last eaten.

Ahmed produced a juice bottle, and the twins rummaged for two apples and a banana. At the same time, the expats emptied pockets of mints, chewing gum and a misshapen cereal bar.

Sally had a bag of macarons at the bottom of her tote bag. 'I'd forgotten about these,' she said as she examined the broken biscuit-like shapes.

Fran victoriously held up a large bag of sticky jelly babies that hadn't fared well in the heat. 'Anyone need a sugar hit?' she asked, passing the bag around. 'Caro, you're the colour of custard. Get your laughing gear around a couple of these.'

To Fran's surprise, Caroline reached out and unglued a sweet. Closing her eyes, she placed it in her mouth.

Bridgette dug deep into her rucksack and held up a flask of brandy. 'I always keep this handy in case of emergencies.' Unscrewing the lid, she took a long glug.

'It's quite spooky in here.' Sally looked around. 'Do you think there are any ghosts?' she asked. 'I love a good ghost story. Does anyone have one they can share?'

Waltho stood up. The last thing he needed was a party of pensioners scared out of their wits. 'I don't think that we need to hear...'

A sudden crash of thunder directly overhead halted Waltho. It shook the guests, and they shivered as the rain sounded heavier, battering against the roof. Eyes were wide as they looked up, and Fran's gaze fell on Noah's Ark. She wondered if he might have room for a few more as she studied Noah and the animals climbing aboard.

'What's that tower all about?' Sally asked as she adjusted a zoom lens and pointed it at the ceiling.

Bridgette, whose emergency brandy didn't seem to extend to anyone else, moved to the group's centre. 'The Tower of Babylon had a curse. The people built it for their own convenience, not their obedience to the will of God,' she said.

Jeanette and Pearl huddled closer to Ahmed and gazed at the ceiling. The expats nodded, and Caroline looked away.

'The people were doing their own thing, and not what God wished, and he felt it symbolised the arrogance of humans.'

'What do you mean?' Sally asked.

'Well, in my interpretation, God thought that humans

were seeking to be free of his influence; they thought they could waltz into heaven on their own, and they arrogantly built the tower out of inferior materials. Brick instead of stone and tar instead of mortar.'

Another crack of thunder resounded, and Ahmed gripped the twins. 'I hope I've done enough to get into heaven,' he anxiously muttered.

'So, they didn't use the durable materials that God had created,' Sally concurred.

'My thoughts exactly,' Bridgette took another slug of brandy. 'They didn't give glory to God, and what you see depicted in these paintings is the aftermath of the tower falling down.'

More clouds thundered as the guests studied the haunted eyes of those fleeing from the tower, and as the storm raged on, everyone felt a sense of unease.

'Do you think the tower's curse is manifesting inside the church?' Sally seemed intent on mischief-making.

'I really don't think that there is any such thing as a curse,' Waltho said. 'Perhaps we should change the subject and go back to my original suggestion of a game of charades?' He was determined to lighten the mood as he watched the seated group. However, Bridgette and Caroline were standing up. 'Caroline, why don't you start?' Waltho asked.

All eyes turned to Caroline.

Taking a step towards the group, Caroline suddenly seemed to falter. Reaching out blindly, she grappled with thin air. Before anyone could stop her, Caroline's knees had buckled, and her feet slid away as she tumbled.

Momentarily frozen, everyone stared at the unconscious body lying on the cold surface of an inscribed stone slab.

'It's the curse of the tower!' Sally exclaimed.

Caroline couldn't explain what had happened. One moment, she was watching Bridgette necking a flask of brandy while discussing the terror of the Tower of Babylon, and the next, she could hear Jeanette and Pearl conferring on the need to find a pulse and check Caroline's breathing.

Now, she realised she was lying on her back with her feet raised on Bridgette's rucksack, and Jeannette was loosening the belt at her waist. She could hear voices in the background and was aware of Waltho's concern.

'Do I need to find a doctor?' he asked.

'Pearl and I are trained nurses,' Jeanette replied. 'We both worked on the major trauma unit at the Royal United Hospital in Bath before we took early retirement to open our gift shop.'

'Is she alright?' Waltho sounded anxious.

'It looks like she's fainted. Stay calm,' Pearl assured as she checked Caroline's pulse. 'She's coming round, which is a good thing. Blood will be flowing to her brain in this position, and her body is recovering.'

'Checking for any cuts or bumps,' Jeanette said, her warm fingers gently feeling Caroline's head before touching her body. 'All fine,' Jeanette declared.

'I want to sit up.' Caroline struggled to pull her body into a sitting position.

'Feeling sick?' Jeanette asked. Quick as a flash, she upturned the Tilley hat from Bridgette's head and held it to Caroline's mouth.

'I say!' Aghast, Bridgette stamped her feet but was relieved when Caroline pushed the hat away.

Moments later, Caroline sat on a pew, a cereal bar in her hand as Jeanette held Ahmed's juice to her lips. 'Take a sip. It will do you good.'

'How is she?' Caroline heard Waltho ask. *Is he concerned for me?* She could almost sense his anxiety, and it felt strangely calming to know that he hovered nearby.

'Just a faint,' Jeanette said. 'Lack of food, I'd say, and she's probably dehydrated in all that heat, we'll need to keep an eye on her, but no harm done, I'm sure.'

'Thank goodness.' Waltho sounded relieved. 'Please, tell me if there is anything I can do.'

'Nothing while the storm continues. Let's wait for it to pass.'

Caroline looked up as Waltho moved away. She saw him turn, and their eyes met. For a moment, Caroline was paralysed. She had a peculiar feeling in her stomach and wondered if she would be sick. Someone called out for Waltho, and he waved a hand to show he'd heard. As he moved away, Waltho smiled, and for a moment, Caroline felt as though a glorious light had been turned on in the church and a heavenly chorus of angels were singing.

Was she hallucinating? But Waltho's smile was wide and his kindly eyes warm.

'Are you alright?' Jeanette touched Caroline's shoulder. 'You look like you've seen a ghost.'

Caroline didn't reply.

What she'd seen held no comparison to a ghost, and she longed to call Waltho back and have his reassuring presence beside her. But she knew he was keen to appease the situation and divert everyone's attention from gales, ghosts and a fainting woman. She watched him calm the guests and felt their eyes bearing down on her.

Turning away from the penetrating stares, Caroline was relieved that Jeanette and Pearl were beside her, not Fran, creating a fuss. She remembered the jelly baby she'd eaten, retrieved from the bottom of Fran's bag. It was probably contaminated from months of moulding away in the depths and, she thought with a grimace, could have been the cause of her complaint.

Waltho had revived his original suggestion of charades, and the guests were miming TV programmes. Caroline looked on in horror as Fran crouched down and crawled away on all fours. As she returned to the group, she poked out her tongue and began to pant.

'Rovers Return!' Ahmed shouted out excitedly. '*Coronation Street!*'

Caroline sighed as she bit into a broken macaron and tasted the soft, sweet filling.

'Why don't you put your head down?' Jeanette asked. She'd removed her cardigan and rolled it into a pillow. 'I'll wake you when the storm has passed.'

Caroline lay down on the pew, happy to be told what to do. She closed her eyes and counted images of beautiful chateaux with glorious gardens, fountains and lakes.

In moments, she was asleep.

As quickly as it had formed, the storm suddenly abated, and as Waltho and the guests stepped out of the church, they were stunned by the silence in the square. A surreal stillness had replaced the pounding wind and rain as though nature had taken a deep breath, allowing everything to settle. The dark, ominous haze had lifted, and the sky appeared bleached, milky white.

With relief, Waltho saw that the minibus was intact and parked where he'd left it on the cobbles. But to his alarm, the tables and chairs from Martine Le Glacier were scattered all over the square and the canopy above the pastel-painted shop, soaked from the rain, hung low and was dragging across the ground. Martine and her daughter stood in the doorway, wringing their hands as they stared at the carnage.

Waltho was torn. Instinctively, he wanted to run to the ice cream shop and ensure Martine was alright. But he felt a duty to his guests and needed to get them safely on the minibus and return them to La Maison du Paradis. Turning to the guests, he saw Bridgette, standing with hands placed firmly on her hips.

'Time to sort out this mise en place,' Bridgette called out, remembering Daniel's orderly working method. 'Might I suggest you toss your keys to Jeanette so she can settle Caroline onto the minibus?'

'Well, yes,' Waltho replied, 'but everyone else needs to...'

But Bridgette ignored his protest. Sloshing through

puddles in her hiking boots, she gathered the guests. 'It seems to me that Martine could do with a hand,' she began. 'If anyone doesn't feel up to it, you can wait on the bus.'

'You can't possibly.' Waltho was moving towards Bridgette, his hands held up in protest.

To his astonishment, the guests piled their bags into Pearl's outstretched arms and, rolling up sleeves and shaking back shoulders, moved as one to clear up the mess. Ahmed made it his mission to sort out the canopy and, hoisting Sally onto his shoulders, held firm as she reached up and threaded the canvas back into place.

The expats gathered all the chairs and soon had them neatly stacked by the shop as Bridgette commandeered Fran to help with the tables. Brushes appeared in the hands of villagers who'd come out to sweep up after the storm.

'There, that didn't take long,' Bridgette said a little while later, as she rubbed her palms together and cleaned mud from her shorts. Reaching into a pocket, she removed her flask and drained the last of the brandy.

The village of Saint-Savin slowly returned to normal, and Martine and her daughter embraced the guests. Their thanks were effusive and unrestrained. Everyone clambered aboard the minibus, and as Waltho drove away, arms went up, and hands waved as the villagers said their goodbyes. The phone signal had returned, and mobiles buzzed and bleeped.

Jeanette insisted that Caroline sit at the front alongside

Waltho. 'Sit upright and look out of the window so you don't feel faint again,' she'd instructed.

With hesitation, Caroline did as she was told. Suddenly, her phone rang and, in a panic, she dropped it on the floor.

Waltho had briefly taken his eyes off the road, and watched as Caroline scrambled to retrieve it.

'Hello, Hello?' Caroline gripped the mobile tightly.

Waltho heard Caroline speak and realised that the line was poor. Caroline had her phone on loudspeaker, still clutched to her ear. He had no intention of eavesdropping but was unable to give Caroline privacy.

But Caroline seemed unaware of being overheard and was intent on the conversation. 'Oh, I see, I didn't realise...' Caroline said. 'It's as bad as that... Yes, yes – I understand.'

Acknowledging the grave news, Waltho placed a steadying hand on Caroline's shoulder.

'Well, th— thank you for letting m me know.'

Ashen-faced, Caroline ended the call.

Removing his hand, and fearing Caroline was about to burst into tears, Waltho turned the radio on. He drummed his fingers to the music, noting Caroline stare vacantly out the window, her misty eyes fixed on the road ahead. Caroline didn't speak, but he could see her blink and realised that tears had formed in the corner of her eyes.

At a loss, Waltho remained silent. He felt helpless that he couldn't pull over and comfort her. It would alert all the guests to her difficulty, and he knew Caroline wouldn't want sympathy, or her difficulties exposed. But Waltho had heard every word of her conversation, and Caroline's problems suddenly fell into place.

Chapter Twenty

It was late when the guests returned to La Maison du Paradis. Buzzing with the day's excitement, instead of heading to their rooms, everyone gathered in the salon. With relief for their safety, Angelique arranged that Daniel and Tomas would prepare a meal for anyone who felt up to it.

The guests were spirited as they gathered, ready to accept a refreshing drink.

'That tastes good,' Fran said. She sipped her first glass of Kir Royale and held it up to study the bubbles in the chilled champagne.

'The berry sweetness in the Crème de Cassis is delicious,' Bridgette agreed. 'A drop of this would soon perk Caroline up. Has anyone seen her?'

'I saw the twins heading to her room; perhaps she's gone for a lie-down?'

'What she needs is a damn good dinner,' Bridgette replied.

'Fancy the twins being nurses.' Fran was reflective. 'That was lucky, wasn't it?'

'They came into their own and handled the situation perfectly,' Bridgette agreed, 'Waltho might have panicked.'

'I don't think so,' Fran said. 'He told me he is a trained first aider and took a course before opening classes to the public.'

'I do hope Caroline is alright.'

'She took a real tumble when she fell in the church, she was as white as a ghost.'

'The poor woman was clearly unwell.' Bridgette sighed.

'I wanted to assist, but the twins took over,' Fran said. 'Do you think we can do anything to help Caro feel better? Maybe write her a note with well wishes?' She looked thoughtful. 'I could offer her a squirt of my pillow spray to help her sleep.'

'The twins are here now, let's ask them.'

Bridgette watched Jeanette and Pearl enter the salon. They both took a drink from Angelique.

'How's the patient?' Bridgette called out.

'Caroline is fine,' Jeanette said. 'She assures us that she is simply feeling a little tired and will be as right as rain in the morning.'

'Oh, that's a relief.' Fran patted Bridgette's arm and smiled. 'Thank goodness she'll be back in class tomorrow.'

'We've suggested an early night, and Daniel has kindly offered to make up a tray with her dinner so that she doesn't miss out on a meal,' Pearl said.

'That would be a first.' Bridgette lowered her voice and, draining her glass, helped herself to a brandy. 'Now, where do you suppose we are going to dine tonight? The courtyard is full of puddles and out of the question.'

Perched on the sofa's edge, Sally reached out as Angelique offered top-ups. 'I hope we haven't got to change for dinner,' she said. 'I'm absolutely ravenous.'

Angelique smiled and reassured everyone that there was no need to change. Dinner would be served in Waltho's private sitting room, and they could all go through when they were ready.

'Blimey, I can't wait to see this,' Fran said, linking her arm through Sally's to follow everyone through the house.

'Do you think Lauren's ghost will be joining us?' Sally whispered.

'Oh, you and your ghosts.' Fran shook her head and smiled.

———

Waltho was in the kitchen, watching Daniel and Tomas finish the pasta creations the guests had made earlier in the day. Following the storm, the air, as though set free from a furnace, was cooler and moved playfully through the open door, relieving the humidity trapped within the rooms. Distinctly cooler, it had an energising effect on the chefs.

'We will lay everything on the table, and the guests can help themselves,' Daniel instructed. 'They may or may not be hungry and can pick and choose as they like.'

He garnished a tray of blushing penne pasta thickened with vodka and cream and tinged with a ruby-red paste that Ahmed had made from sun-dried tomatoes. Grating Parmigiano-Reggiano generously, he moved it to one side.

Tomas took a dish of rigatoni from the oven.

The twins had prepared the rigatoni, and the smell of spicy sausages and tangy goat's cheese was mouth-watering. Bridgette and Sally's linguine had been baked with basil and lemon-flavoured crab, and Daniel smiled and nodded his approval as he scattered chopped coriander over the surface. Tomas sauteed scallops to add to the expat's shrimp and artichoke fettuccine. In addition, he'd also put the finishing touches to a selection of delicious salads that included Caroline's apple, grape and pecan pasta.

'This is a feast,' Angelique said as she entered the kitchen. 'Just as well because everyone says they are hungry after their exploits today.'

'It will almost be midnight by the time we finish up,' Tomas sighed. 'Do you think you should suggest a later start tomorrow?' Hoping for a lie-in, Tomas had arranged to head off to the bar in the village after work.

'Let's see how things go,' Waltho suggested. 'Now, where is the tray for Caroline?'

Stooping to take a tray of ramekin dishes from the oven, Daniel began unloading miniature portions of all the dishes the guests had prepared. Angelique fiddled with a linen napkin containing silver cutlery and added a bud vase with a rose from the garden. Placing the ramekins on the tray, she covered the meal with a pretty lace cloth and was about to head off to Caroline's room.

'I'll take it,' Waltho said, 'I need to make sure she's alright.'

'Well, if you are sure.'

'I am,' Waltho replied. He gripped the handles of the tray. 'I won't be long, please do start without me.

In Waltho's sitting room, guests stood around and gazed at the lovely antiques that furnished the room. On one wall, a painting of Lauren was displayed against a trompe-l'oeil background of a lavender-filled garden.

'It's like a shrine,' Fran whispered to Sally as she stared and placed her hands on a velvet sofa upholstered in a classic French style.

'Wasn't she beautiful,' Sally replied as she gazed at the painting.

Swathed in purple silk, Lauren sat on a rustic rattan chair on a lavender-lined pathway while a cat nestled in her lap. Her smile was wide, as though amused to be posing for her portrait as she stroked the cat's glossy body.

Sally reached out to touch the painting. 'It's almost as real as a photograph,' she said, 'and the artist is so clever to surround the subject with the optical illusion of the garden.'

Fran nodded. 'I feel as though she is going to stand up and join us for dinner. Do you think Waltho painted the portrait?'

'Yes, there's no doubt. There is another painting of this style in the salon, and it's unsigned. It's such a shame she's no longer with us. She must have been a fascinating woman to have captured Waltho's heart. I wonder if he'll ever fall in love again?'

'It would be a waste if he doesn't,' Fran said, 'that man needs a good woman to share everything he's worked so hard to achieve.'

Sally's fingers traced the cat on Lauren's knee, 'This must be the old cat that wanders through the garden,' she said.

'Angelique says the cat is called Tabby and I think she sleeps in here.' Fran reached down and picked up a raggedy mouse amongst a pile of moth-eaten toys from the hollow of an old, frayed cushion. The fabric was worn and soft, and the mouse was missing its eyes. She turned when Angelique instructed that it was time to sit at the table.

Dinner was about to be served.

'Hurrah,' Bridgette commented as she pulled out a chair beside Ahmed. 'I am ravenous.'

'My stomach thinks my throat's been cut,' Fran said as she flicked a napkin onto her knee. She smiled at the twins, who sat beside the expats.

'What a gorgeous table,' Sally said as she pulled up a chair and stroked the reddish-brown mahogany, admiring the elegance and craftsmanship. 'It's huge and would fill the space in my little apartment.'

'Lauren had such good taste,' Bridgette added. 'Waltho's sitting room is as lovely as the rest of the house.' She looked around and admired the ambience of the room, comfortably furnished with shabby chic furniture. Waltho's reading glasses lay on the cover of Camille Claudel's biography, on a bamboo table next to an armchair facing the wall with Lauren's painting.

Tomas placed serving dishes on the table, and everyone's eyes were drawn to the mouth-watering display of pasta as they searched for the recipes they'd individually prepared.

Angelique tapped a spoon on the side of a glass.

'Before you begin to enjoy the wonderful dishes you created today,' she said, 'Chef has one more dish.'

The guests looked up as Daniel made an entrance. He wore a tall chef's hat, which matched his immaculate white jacket, and, in his hands, held a tray covered by a silver dome.

Daniel faced the guests to announce, 'Ladies and gentlemen, here we have a dish that I consider the most successful of the day.'

Guests glanced at the dishes already on the table to spot their own. With a gasp, Fran realised she couldn't see her pasta and that the dish Daniel carried must be hers.

'The pasta you are about to taste is flawless and beautifully worked and rolled to the consistency of tissue. It takes great skill to achieve this. The pasta embraces the mushroom filling and has been perfectly cooked.'

Daniel lifted the top of the dome with great drama and swept the tray in a circle before the guests' eyes. When he connected with Fran, he stopped. 'Fran, you are to be congratulated,' he said, 'you have been the best pupil today.'

Everyone applauded, and Fran flushed the colour of the blushing penne pasta.

'Oh, Chef, I don't know what to say… Really, I don't think I deserve…'

She was about to confess that the dish was entirely Tomas's work, but as she glanced at the young chef, he emphatically shook his head and winked. Everyone was congratulating Fran, including Tomas, who added that he was impressed that she'd stayed behind to perfect her pasta.

Daniel placed the dish down, and as Angelique passed plates, he sliced the pasta roll and poured a measure of mushroom and cognac cream with each serving.

'This is scrumptious,' Sally said as she tasted Fran's dish, 'so light and tasty.'

'To be commended,' Bridgette agreed.

The twins were nodding, and the expats raised their glasses. Ahmed closed his eyes and licked his lips, 'Made with love,' he said. 'Absolutely delicious.'

Fran was flustered. It wasn't in her nature to mislead, and she wondered how to remedy the situation. But, before she could mumble that it wasn't entirely her work and that Tomas had made most of the dish while Fran had merely sprinkled some flour, she saw that Daniel had turned his back to place the dome on a side table.

As he fussed about creating a space, the room suddenly became quiet.

Guest's eyes were drawn to the back of Daniel's jacket, and time seemed to stand still. Knives and forks were held mid-air, eyes wide as everyone studied a drawing on the clean white fabric.

'It's a cock and balls!' Sally whispered and almost spat

out her pasta. She bit on her lip to try and stop the laughter that was erupting in her throat.

Angelique, aware that the chef was about to be humiliated, was quick to divert attention. She clapped her hands as Daniel turned to face the guests.

'Now, please, you must try each other's dishes and discuss the methods used,' Angelique said.

Fran was mortified. She dipped her head low and forked food around her plate. Her appetite had disappeared, and she wondered what would happen when Daniel discovered that Fran had defaced his jacket with an obscenity.

Fran thought Daniel didn't like her, but he'd just called her his best pupil! She felt like a complete fraud. Would she be kicked off the course, and what would everyone think of her?

Her moment of madness had backfired.

Chapter Twenty-One

C aroline sat on the side of the bed in her room. She clenched her fingers into fists and tried to remember the techniques she'd learned to stave off anxiety. Nothing was working. No amount of deep breathing, holding her breath and slowly releasing would stop the pounding in her chest. Not only had she made a complete fool of herself by fainting in the church, but the news she'd been dreading had finally been delivered, and the impact felt like a knock-out blow.

She wondered what the other guests were thinking. Had they noticed she hardly ate in her determination to keep her figure and not gain a pound? If they did, they would say her fainting was the result of vanity. Were they all laughing behind her back? But these thoughts soon paled, and Caroline's anguish heightened when she remembered the phone call from her solicitor.

Unable to sit still, she rose and paced around the room. Finally, the truth was out. Months of worrying about whether she could survive her divorce and make a fresh start were over, and now she had her answer.

Stanley and Caroline were broke.

Their home had a massive mortgage, and Stanley owed money everywhere. He'd run up debts of thousands to wine suppliers, and money mysteriously disappeared each month. There were accounts she had no knowledge of, but with none in credit, they mattered little. The debts from her catering business had to be repaid. Making the company insolvent wouldn't help her credit rating, and if she was to survive, she had to protect it.

But Stanley seemed unconcerned when she called him, demanding to know where all the money had gone and what he intended to do.

'Get on with your life, Caro,' Stanley said, 'make a new start.' With no further comment, to her anger and frustration, he'd disconnected the call.

Reluctant to tell her but feeling obligated, her solicitor had added that Stanley, in Caroline's absence, had moved out of their home and was living with Celia Ackland.

Caroline gritted her teeth.

A headache was threatening, and she pressed her fingers to her forehead. The wretched Celia Ackland was loaded. Caroline knew that a windfall had fallen into her lap from her father's property portfolio, and Stanley's lack of funds wouldn't be of any concern. Having a lover with access to the House and Parliament parties was an opportunity not to be missed for the social climber, and Caroline imagined a wedding already in the pipeline. The date, no doubt imminent, following Stanley's divorce.

Caroline moved to the window.

What was she to do? The few thousand she'd have left after the house sale and debts repaid would hardly fund a property. She'd have to find somewhere to rent, and that meant a move she didn't want to make.

Should she call Leo? Perhaps her son would offer her the sofa in his studio apartment. But she knew it would never work. They weren't close before the divorce, and after, crowding his life wouldn't make things any better.

But Caroline couldn't think of Leo now, and as she stared at the moonlight, she realised that the storm had washed away the heat and humidity, leaving cooler, more comfortable air. The smell of damp earth and scents from the garden drifted up, intensified by the heavy rain's cleansing effect, and she could hear the familiar sound of an owl as it gave its long, loud hoot.

Had Caroline been in a better frame of mind, she would have enjoyed this fresh start, as though nature was reviving itself with optimism after weeks of drought and heat. But she was in no mood to appreciate the beauty beyond her window and her burden felt like a dead weight, bringing her down.

On the other side of Caroline's door, Waltho gently knocked. 'It's me,' he called out. 'Daniel has prepared a tray, and I'd like to bring it in.'

Waltho heard Caroline moving around the room and

imagined her anxiously straightening the bed and tidying a cushion.

'Just a moment,' Caroline replied.

Moments later, she opened the door.

Waltho placed the tray on a table. 'How are you feeling?' he asked.

'Much better, thank you.'

'You still look very pale.'

Waltho thought Caroline appeared tense. Her shoulders were hunched as she rubbed her arms and fidgeted with the collar of her blouse. He noticed worry lines creasing the skin on her forehead.

'Come and sit down,' he said, drawing back a chair.

As Caroline took a seat, Waltho decided that he would stay and perhaps encourage her to talk. A shared problem might lessen her anxiety. He sat, removed the cloth from the tray, and placed a plate before Caroline. Taking a spoon, he served individual portions of pasta.

'This is a selection of the dishes you all made earlier,' he said, adding a helping of her salad.

'I really don't think I can eat all this...' Caroline began as she stared at the mouth-watering food.

'Just try, take a little at a time.'

Waltho poured wine. Sitting back, he took a sip and studied Caroline as she robotically moved a spoon to her mouth. Deciding that he would talk to divert attention from the food, Waltho spoke of the day and the events that had so unexpectedly occurred.

'Madame Martine was so grateful to the guests,' he began, 'and while you were resting, everyone helped to restore the square after the storm had created such havoc.' He saw that Caroline was listening and was pleased to see she'd taken two mouthfuls of food. 'It was all so unexpected. The weather forecast hadn't predicted that rain with such force would sweep over the area so suddenly.'

Waltho knew he was waffling, but as Caroline continued to eat, he kept going.

'I hope it didn't spoil everyone's memories of the church, which is unique and the interior so rare and a privilege to see.' Waltho paused and took another sip of wine. 'But it was a good place to shelter and kept everyone safe while the downpour passed over.'

Waltho's voice, like velvet, was soothing and Caroline's shoulders slowly relaxed, the tension gently lifting. She wasn't conscious of his words, just the richness of his tone, like one of Stanley's fine aged wines. Steady, with an unhurried pace, as the words flowed smoothly.

Before realising what had happened, Caroline put down her spoon and pushed her plate away. To her astonishment, she saw that she'd eaten every scrap.

'Would you like more?' Waltho asked, 'I can ask Daniel to plate up another portion of the dishes.'

'Oh, good heavens, no!'

Caroline was shocked. She'd eaten more in one sitting than she'd had all week, and her stomach felt like it might burst. But the feeling was peculiar, and instead of rushing to the bathroom to force her fingers down her throat, she let the feeling of fullness settle.

'Please, drink some wine,' Waltho suggested, filling her glass.

Caroline did as she was told and savoured the delicious taste in the room's quiet. She glanced at the label on the bottle, and her eyes popped. It was a Château Margaux – one of Stanley's favourites. Leaning back in her chair, Caroline stared at Waltho. The cost of a bottle was exorbitant, and, as if reading her mind, Waltho smiled.

'You deserve something special after the day you've had,' he said.

Caroline drained her glass, and as she watched it being refilled, she felt like she would cry. 'I don't deserve anything,' she whispered.

She saw Waltho lean in.

'Would you like to talk about it?' he asked.

Caroline felt a lump in her throat.

Emotions welled up, and her eyes felt misty. What was it about this man that made her feel safe? Cocooned in the room, with only Waltho beside her, she felt tears tracing a path down her cheeks. Her chest heaved, and, unable to help herself, she placed her glass down and, burying her face in her hands, began to sob.

Waltho moved the tray to one side.

Edging his chair closer, he reached out and prayed that she wouldn't think he was taking advantage as he held Caroline's shoulders and pulled her into his arms.

Soundlessly, he gently rocked as Caroline's controlled demeanour crumbled. He felt her body shudder as her weeping filled the room. Closing his eyes, he remembered holding Lauren throughout the agony of her illness. But as he comforted Caroline, Waltho knew this wasn't about him or Lauren. Caroline was suffering, and he determined that he would help her.

If she allowed him.

'I know how you feel. I understand emotional pain,' Waltho spoke softly. 'You're not alone.'

After a while, Caroline's sobs eased. As Waltho opened his eyes, to his surprise, he realised that Lauren's cat was sitting on the floor, staring at him. Had she followed him into the room?

Tabby's gaze, clouded with the wisdom of years, was intent. The cat seemed to be saying, 'Not again?' Tattered ears with tufts of fur twitched as she caught the sounds of Caroline's distress.

Waltho remembered how Tabby kept a vigil by Lauren's side during those dark days, rarely leaving her room, nestling gently on her lap or beside Lauren on the bed, purring comfortingly to the touch of a hand.

Suddenly, Caroline trembled. 'Oh, God, I'm so s— sorry, I don't know what has come over me. It must be the wine.'

Waltho wondered if she would start crying again and reached into a pocket to hand her a handkerchief. 'Here,' he said kindly, 'wipe your eyes.'

'S— Stanley always has a clean white handkerchief,' Caroline stuttered. 'He insists on it.' She blotted her face and dabbed at her eyes.

'Your husband.'

'Y— yes.'

'Is he the cause of your problems?'

'W— well, yes, I'm afraid he is.'

Waltho handed Caroline her wine and, standing, moved

to the window. He closed the curtains and adjusted the angle of a lamp to diffuse light from Caroline's puffy face. Eyeballing Tabby, the cat didn't move.

Returning to his seat, Waltho sat and made a pyramid of his fingers, resting them on his chest. 'Why don't you start at the beginning,' he said, his voice gentle, 'and when you've finished, we might have found a way to sort through everything.'

Sometime later, Caroline lay on her bed and stared at the ceiling. A beam shone through a gap in the curtains, where the moon cast a silvery light. She felt drained and weary and could scarcely believe that she'd poured her heart out to Waltho and told him every sordid detail of her marriage to Stanley, her failed catering business, her divorce and even why she kept so slim.

She wondered if he would arrange for her to leave early in the morning, unable to face the hysterical guest who'd made such a fool of herself. But a little glimmer of light was dancing around on the ceiling, and as she watched the diamond-like facets, Caroline suddenly felt a ray of hope.

Waltho had spoken so wisely and acknowledged her situation.

'Far worse things happen in life,' he'd said. 'I'm not demeaning your problems, but I think these are problems that can be overcome.'

Caroline had sipped the delicious wine and listened intently. She almost held her breath as he continued.

'When life as you know it ends, another beckons if you are brave enough to step forward.' Waltho's voice was captivating and his amber eyes drew her in as she savoured each word. 'Once you decide what to do, you can go forward,' he said. 'At the moment, you are scared because you have no direction.'

He'd suggested that she sell what she could and, after debts repaid, with her divorce settlement, begin a completely new life. Waltho seemed to have the power to dispel her anxiety, and now, as she enjoyed the softness of the downy bed that embraced her, she felt a sense of calm.

To her amazement, the tabby cat lay beside her.

Caroline could hardly believe that she'd reached out a hand and was softly stroking the silky fur. She'd never liked cats and always thought she was allergic to them. Still, as she snuggled into the duvet, Caroline realised that Tabby hadn't caused any reaction and as the animal curled into the curve of her back, the rhythmic purr was strangely comforting and her rickety old body warm.

Caroline felt exhausted. But there was no need to visualise and count chateaux to help her sleep, and she felt sure she would drift off within moments. But how would she feel in the morning? Would all her fears return?

Shaking away nagging doubts, Caroline remembered Waltho's parting words, *'Sleep is the key that unlocks the door to a happy and healthier life.'*

In moments, with her eyes closed and a hint of a smile on her lips, Caroline was slumbering.

Chapter Twenty-Two

On Friday morning, La Maison du Paradis was bathed in a soft golden light as the sun rose over the French landscape. A slight chill felt welcome after weeks of heat and dry weather, and a hint of dew created freshness where tiny droplets of water glistened in the garden like mystic charms.

Up early and dressed in a robe, Fran sat on a bench and stared at the countryside. Tapping her slippers on the path, she fidgeted with the rings on her fingers. Fran's active mind was jumbled. In the night, she'd had a dream of Daniel attacking her with a knife and, as he gripped her throat, Fran shouted out, suddenly wide awake. Weary and anxious but unable to sleep, she'd got up.

Anxious of the day ahead, Fran felt sure that Daniel would have discovered her drawing and demanded she be booted off the course. Fran sighed and considered pre-empting the situation by coming clean about her antics. She could reason that Daniel had been vile when he left her alone with the pasta, struggling to comprehend a complicated recipe, which, without help, she would never master. But it was no excuse for her bad behaviour, and she shouldn't have done what she did.

'You are a silly old woman,' Fran said as she gazed at the tranquil surroundings. Then, determined to change the subject, she thought of the week's highlights.

One of her favourite outings was to the market in Chauvigny. Fran remembered the colourful shutters being flung open as café owners arranged tables and chairs on the perimeter of the cobblestone square. Like herself, they would be up early to welcome traders and shoppers with a café au lait or robust expresso. Fran wished she'd had time to stroll along the river Vienne, with its vast banks and leafy pathways. She loved to be beside the water and found it so relaxing. Being by the sea in Blackpool had always given her pleasure.

Sparrows were chirping, and Fran thought she could smell freshly baked bread. Someone was preparing breakfast, and she imagined Tomas or Angelique in the kitchen. She wondered if Daniel was awake but doubted that he'd risen early to help heat the oven for crusty baguettes and buttery croissants and prepare fresh fruit for breakfast bowls.

He was likely wrapped around Sally, snuggled down and sleeping off the excesses of another late night.

'Well, it's no good sitting here,' Fran told herself and, gripping the bench, turned to the house. Following the pathway, she shuffled in her fluffy slippers, reaching into her pocket for hair clips to pin escaping tendrils into a messy top knot. 'It's time to get dressed and face the music.'

With a heavy sigh, Fran headed towards her room.

After a surprisingly refreshing sleep, Waltho stood under the shower and turned the dial. Icy needles of water pelted his skin, and Waltho gasped, but as blood circulated, the cold shock soon focused his mind.

He hadn't expected to sleep so well.

Caroline's worries were niggling, and Angelique had informed him about the incident with Daniel's jacket. On top of this, he was undecided on what to do with the guests that afternoon and wondered if he should leave options open for them to decide.

Stepping out of the shower, he reached for a towel and rubbed briskly.

Waltho wondered how Caroline felt as a new day began; he hoped that her problems didn't seem impossible after their chat. He remembered holding her in his arms and realised he'd enjoyed the experience. Caroline's hair was soft as it brushed his hand, and her skin smelt of bergamot and citrus fruits, reminding him of the sun-kissed Mediterranean coast he'd visited for holidays with Lauren.

As he buttoned an Oxford shirt, he thought of the years since Lauren had gone. These were dark, dismal days where the future held no promise, hope of joy, or pleasure in living a singular life. But as he slipped his feet into loafers, he thought about something she'd whispered in her final hours.

'We as human beings need to believe that there is something better out there.'

Waltho paused to reflect.

Friends told him that only time would heal his pain, and there had been occasions when he never thought he'd get over Lauren's death. But strangely, in the last few days, he could feel the shoots of recovery. Perhaps having the house full of people gave him a purpose. But there was something he was uncertain of, and this involved Caroline. For some inexplicable reason, she tugged at his broken heart. Knowing hers was as shattered as his own, he felt a compelling urge to help put it back together again. If she could continue to talk to him, maybe they would find a way to ease her out of her problems.

It was time to stop thinking of himself. Time to stop dwelling in the past and wallowing in his own misery. Lauren would be furious if she thought he'd lost the will to enjoy life and make the best of what he was fortunate to have left.

'Take the word "I" out of your vocabulary,' she'd told him. 'By helping others, you'll learn to live again.'

Waltho entered his sitting room and opened the shutters to flood the room with light. The sun lit the painting of Lauren, and the glow caught a glint in her eyes. As she smiled, he caught his breath. Such was his feeling of love. Her gentle hands seemed to reach out, caress his face, and tell him everything was alright. *'It's time to move on,'* he heard her whisper.

Waltho wiped a tear from his eye and, after touching fingers to his lips, pressed them to Lauren's cheek. 'Thank you,' he replied.

Turning to a window, he looked out at the garden where he could see Fran hurrying along the path towards her room. She wore a vibrant purple robe and fluffy pink slippers, and Waltho smiled. If only everyone had such a generous heart like Fran. He knew that Fran had swapped accommodations with Sally to relieve Caroline of the sound of her snoring and that Sally now spent each night with Daniel.

He also knew that Fran was the likely culprit that had defaced Daniel's jacket, and Waltho chuckled. Daniel could be difficult and seemed to put Fran under pressure. Waltho wondered if it was Daniel's way of turning Fran into a decent chef in the limited time available. But, he reasoned, the guests were paying a decent amount to be in Daniel's company, and the least he could do was be civil.

Angelique knocked on the door.

'Come in,' Waltho called out, and as she crossed the room, he took hold of her shoulders and kissed her forehead. 'Good morning,' he said, 'it's a beautiful day out there.'

'Yes, it is, and the temperature will be pleasant too.' She placed a mug of coffee on the bamboo table and stood back. 'You look very chirpy. Is there something I should know?'

'For the first time in ages, it feels good to be alive.'

'Hallelujah!' Angelique exclaimed and clapped her hands. 'The magic of La Maison du Paradis is finally working.'

'Indeed,' Waltho nodded, 'there were times when I wondered if it ever would.'

'Well, whatever is happening, long may it last,' Angelique smiled. 'Now take your coffee and come and help me. The guests are up and about despite me thinking they'd want a late start after yesterday's exploits.'

'I'm on my way,' Waltho replied, and blowing a kiss to Lauren's portrait, he picked up his coffee and followed.

In the trees outside Daniel's room, the chirruping of birds had built into a crescendo, and the noisy warblers meant that sleep was no longer an option for Sally. As she eased into a sitting position and ran fingers through her mop of tousled pink hair, Sally thought of the man who slumbered beside her.

She was no fool and had soon sussed out Daniel's culpabilities.

The enormous ego that came from his celebrity status, she now knew, was a front that hid an anxious man. Reaching out to stroke his naked shoulder, she remembered that after a moonlight swim, they'd talked long into the night, and he'd been surprisingly candid.

Confiding in Sally, he'd told her about his background. It was something he said he'd never disclosed to anyone.

'Not even my agent,' Daniel said as he held Sally in his arms. 'My dad was a drunk and mother just as bad,' he told her. 'They were terrible parents, and I suppose the world should be grateful that they didn't have any more children.'

Sally wanted to tell Daniel not to be hard on himself, but she feared he might not continue if she butted in.

'I walked away from my parents many years ago. They're both dead now, and my memories of childhood will stay firmly in the past.'

'Were there no happy times?' she'd tentatively asked.

'Occasionally, when they were sober, but that was rare.'

'But you should be so proud of what you achieved, how you overcame your hurdles to do so much with your life.'

'I was determined not to be like them. I couldn't face living in poverty and seeing the harm that alcoholism can inflict.'

'It's a rags-to-riches tale and would make a brilliant story,' Sally insisted. 'If your agent got hold of it, you'd have a best-selling biography, another *Kitchen Confidential* and a Netflix deal.'

'No, you're wrong,' Daniel had laughed, 'the hospitality industry has many like me. I'm nothing special.'

But Sally thought Daniel *was* special. He was the most talented chef she'd met. She was aware that Fran thought he disliked her, and despite his tough approach, Sally felt that Daniel was doing all he could to help Fran on the path to achieving her dream.

Daniel had once had a dream too, which to his credit, he'd made come true.

For all his faults, she could sense that Daniel was fragile and gambling was a diversion. For Daniel, a win on the roulette wheel was a way to lift his spirits, away from the rigours of the kitchen and pressures of business. He gave little thought to the subsequent debts that often mounted when he lost. Daniel was his own worst enemy and when his gambling took over, his successful business suffered.

But Daniel's failures were issues she wasn't prepared to overcome. *Been there, done that!* Sally thought as she stroked his thick dark hair.

Last night, under the moon and stars of the silvery sky, the soft, silky water of the pool embraced their naked bodies. As they intertwined, Daniel surprised her. He'd whispered in Sally's ear that he wanted her to return to the Cotswolds and move into his home. They could get engaged if she wanted respectability.

Sally had almost laughed at the preposterous suggestion! Did he really imagine that she would throw in her lot with a man she hardly knew after only a few short days?

As she stared out at the milky blue sky where puffy white clouds drifted over the garden, Sally thought La Maison du Paradis was one of the most magical places she'd ever visited and she vowed to enjoy this brief fling. But at the end of the week, she would return with Romeo to her solo life.

As she'd swum with Daniel, he pressed her for an answer and luckily, she'd had no time to reply. A shadowy figure had appeared on the pathway, and moments later, they'd stared wide-eyed as Bridgette removed her robe and slid, naked, into the water at the other end of the pool.

'Don't mind me!' she'd called out, bare breasts bobbing, as she swished about in the shadows.

Now, as Daniel stirred and reached out to pull Sally into his arms, she giggled. Good old Bridgette! She'd saved Sally from coming up with a response. As Daniel's hands wandered lovingly over her body, Sally sighed with pleasure and silently thanked Bridgette, the naked swimmer.

———

It was with hesitant footsteps that Caroline walked into the salon for breakfast. Looking around the room, she saw that most guests had left. Only Jeanette and Pearl remained. Both had finished their coffee and stood to shake napkins free of croissant crumbs before folding the linen neatly and placing it on the table.

'Good morning,' Jeanette said.

'It's good to see you up and about,' Pearl smiled.

'I'm fine,' Caroline replied, 'but thank you both for everything you did for me yesterday. You were very kind.'

'It was nothing,' Jeanette waved a dismissive hand. 'After this heat, any of us might have had a funny turn.'

'Well, I had a wonderful sleep and now feel refreshed.'

'We're so pleased to hear that,' Jeanette smiled. 'The temperature is much more comfortable today, but the sun will still be hot, so don't forget to drink plenty of water and stay hydrated.'

'No more fainting!' Pearl wagged a finger.

Caroline resisted the urge to swat the finger. She'd had more than her share of finger-wagging from Stanley throughout her marriage.

'See you in class,' the twins called out and, linking arms, moved away.

Caroline wasn't hungry. She was still sated from the night before. Still, after promising Waltho that she would try to eat more, she poured a glass of juice and selected a pastry, then, taking a seat by the window, began to eat.

She looked up when she heard laughter and saw Fran, Sally and Bridgette on the path that led to the kitchen. Fran was holding court, waving her arms, and Sally and Bridgette shook their heads, chuckling at Fran's antics.

Caroline noted that Fran wore a hat to one side at an angle on her untidy hair. *A beret?* Caroline wondered. Why on earth would Fran wear such a hat?

With a Breton-style top above navy-blue cut-offs, Fran finished her outfit with a flashy display of gaudy costume jewellery.

She looks like she's going to a fancy-dress party, Caroline thought, pushing away the half-eaten pastry.

Studying the trio, Caroline wondered at the speed of their friendship.

In only a few short days, everyone on the course had bonded. Even Bridgette, grieving her Hugo, was part of the pack and openly admitted that she was touched by everyone's kindness. Caroline had never known friendship so quickly adopted, and she felt alone with worries never far from her mind.

Sighing, Caroline glanced at her watch. The class was about to start, and she'd better get a move on. Slipping her bag onto her shoulder and straightening the skirt of her dress, Caroline took a deep breath. Facing the guests was causing mild anxiety, and she wondered how everyone would react to all the fuss she'd created.

But most of all, she was fearful of seeing Waltho. Would he still be kind and caring in the cold light of day? Or would he take her discreetly to one side and suggest it might be better if she returned home as soon as possible to sort out her problems?

Caroline remembered the embrace as she'd sobbed on his shoulder.

Despite her despair, the strength that came from Waltho had been so comforting. With soft, rhythmic strokes on her back, his fingers were like a salve, soothing away her fears, and momentarily, she felt safe. Waltho's presence radiated reassurance that her problems were mere molehills, little bumps to be skipped over, not the mountains she felt she had to climb.

He seemed to understand the fragility of her emotional state.

But most of all, she'd felt a surge of emotion that had nothing to do with debts and divorce. Caroline's heart had pounded, and her tummy began to spin. Was it the considerable dinner she'd eaten or something more? The same feeling nudged from the past, and she remembered how she'd fallen in love with Stanley.

The touch of his hand, the feel of his skin, the warmth of his body...

'Stop it!' Caroline suddenly told herself. This was ridiculous. At sixty-one, about to turn sixty-two, with all her difficulties, there wasn't a hope that any man would find her attractive. She was tempted to return to her room and pack her bags, but the thought of additional travel costs stopped her.

Caroline couldn't afford more expense.

She left the salon and slowly walked along the path to the kitchen. Her heart was heavy despite the start of another glorious day and the beautiful surroundings. But, taking a deep breath and patting her churning stomach, she willed herself on.

'Another day in paradise,' she whispered.

Chapter Twenty-Three

I n the kitchen, with aprons in place and folders open, guests reached for pens and chattered as they waited for class to begin. Fran sat next to Bridgette and nervously flicked through the pages of her notebook. She hadn't confided in anyone about her drawing on Daniel's jacket, despite the whispers at breakfast and a chain reaction of shock and amusement amongst the guests. Instead, she'd kept quiet and changed the subject whenever it was discussed.

'I wonder who the culprit of the cartoon cock is?' Sally asked as she sat down.

'It could be anyone with a grudge; Daniel can be rude at times,' Bridgette replied.

'I think it's hilarious.' Sally readied her camera to catch images of the class and fiddled with the lens.

Fran didn't comment and feigned fascination as she watched Sally in her professional mode.

'Does Daniel know?' Bridgette asked.

'He hasn't a clue, and I have no intention of telling him,' Sally said as she adjusted the lens's focus to ensure the correct depth of field.

'I don't understand how he *doesn't* know?' Fran was puzzled and couldn't imagine how the chef had removed the jacket without seeing her artwork.

'Didn't you notice?' Sally turned her attention to Fran. 'As everyone was retiring, Angelique cleared the table.' Sally lowered her voice as she continued, 'She accidentally spilt Ahmed's tomato sauce on Daniel's sleeve.'

'Eh?' Fran was even more puzzled.

'Angelique insisted that Daniel remove his jacket immediately so she could attend to the stain.'

'Oh, I see.' Fran pursed her lips. She'd been so worried and barely noticed Angelique and Daniel leaving Waltho's sitting room together. She'd gone to bed before they came back.

'Angelique helped Daniel slip out of the offending garment before he had time to notice,' Sally explained.

'So he had no idea?'

'None,' Sally smiled. 'In fact, he was in a great mood, and we stayed up late, swimming in the moonlight.' Turning to Bridgette, she called out, 'Did you enjoy your swim?'

'First class,' Bridgette replied.

Sally turned back to Fran and nudged her arm. 'A penny for your thoughts? You seem far away.'

'Er, sorry. I was thinking...' Desperate to change the subject, Fran sat up and looked around. 'How lovely Bridgette's outfit is today.'

Bridgette was wearing a pantsuit patterned with bees, birds and colourful bougainvillaea. In her hair, she'd knotted a butterfly-decorated scarf.

Seeing their glances, Bridgette smoothed her hands over the vibrant fabric. 'I bought this ensemble as a guest speaker,' she proudly explained, 'on an Amazon River boat cruise deep in South America. I think it's rather fetching, don't you?'

'Fabulous.' Fran nodded and wondered what the local Amazonians thought of it.

'But you're treating us to French chic today,' Bridgette said as she studied Fran's get-up. 'I've never been brave enough to wear a beret, but seeing how attractive it looks on you, I might be tempted.'

'Sid chose it,' Fran said, glancing down at her Breton top and navy cut-offs. She touched a hand to her beret, adjusting the angle over one ear. 'He said that while in France, I must do my best to fit in.'

Sally focused her camera on the pair. She couldn't remember a French woman dressing like Fran and wondered where the outfit had come from. The horizontal lines on Fran's top did nothing to flatter her figure, and Bridgette's outfit resembled a botanical garden. But the pair had charisma and oozed fun.

'A photo, please,' Sally said, not wishing to miss an opportunity. 'Can you stand together and hold something that suggests "cookery" as you smile?'

When Caroline entered the kitchen, the first thing she saw was Bridgette's arm around Fran's shoulder and the pair beaming for Sally's camera. While Bridgette picked up a knife, Fran waved a whisk and a wooden spoon.

'Smile for the Sunday supplements!' Sally called out as she clicked away.

'This will put bums on seats for future courses.' Fran grinned.

Unnoticed, Caroline slid onto a chair at the end of the table.

Moments later, Daniel and Tomas came into the kitchen. Both carried covered trays.

'Good morning, how are we all?' Daniel asked. Not waiting for guests to reply, he began the class. 'Today is all about fish,' he said. 'With the fish and chip expert in residence, Fran may be telling *me* what to do.'

Caroline saw Fran flop back in her chair. A smile spread across her face. *She knows that her chip shop experience will help her sail through this class!* Caroline thought.

'But Chef,' Fran grinned, 'you can always teach an old dog new tricks.'

Caroline picked up a pen and focused. Fran's comment was debatable.

'I love fish!' Ahmed called out, his expression eager as he soaked up Daniel's words.

'Then you are in the right class,' Daniel acknowledged. 'Fish is good for you and very healthy to eat. You don't have to be an expert to prepare it, but you must know what to do.'

With a theatrical gesture, he held the cloths covering the

trays and revealed a mountain of uncooked fish. Guests oohed and aahed and sat forward to study the variety.

'Many people are squeamish when it comes to preparation.'

'I don't eat fish because of all the bones,' one of the expats said.

'Exactly.' Daniel turned to the person who'd spoken. 'If you prefer not to fillet and gut the fish yourself, ask your fishmonger to do this simple task.' He picked up a sea bass and held it high. 'First, you must check that the eyes are bright.'

From her seat on a stool, Fran looked puzzled. The eyes on the fish Daniel held were as dull and dead as a doornail, never to blink or wink again.

'Secondly,' he continued, 'look inside the gills, which should be pink.' Like a surgeon undergoing a procedure, he poked about with his knife to make his point. 'Then, smell the fish.' Daniel closed his eyes and ran his nose along the cold, scaley flesh.

Some of the guests recoiled.

'Fresh fish smells of the sea,' Daniel announced. He slapped the fish onto a marble slab and, taking a razor-sharp cleaver, chopped off the head and tail. With a long filleting knife, Daniel opened the belly and drew out the contents, tossing the bloody mass into a dish. He threw the gutted object to Tomas, who turned on a tap to clean the sea bass.

'Whatever you do, don't overcook fish. Cook it gently.' Daniel washed his bloody fingers. 'This isn't the 1950s, and no one boils fish anymore.'

'My mother used to boil cod bone dry then serve it with a lumpy parsley sauce,' Bridgette commented. 'It was hideous.'

Daniel ignored Bridgette. 'If you poach fish, remove the skin before serving,' he said. 'If you grill it, leave the skin on as it protects the flesh.' He took the fish from Tomas, returned it to the slab, sliced down the back, and started removing the spine. 'If you fry your fish, use butter and don't complicate the cooking.'

Fran was captivated as she watched Daniel prepare two fillets, taking a pair of tweezers to remove the last of the bones. There wasn't much that Daniel could tell her about the process of filleting and frying fish. She'd handled thousands over the years.

Phew! Fran thought as he meticulously plucked the tiny bones. Daniel hadn't referred to the jacket incident, and surely he *would* have mentioned it. Despite her fears, and to her relief, it looked like she'd got away with it.

Fran sat up and paid attention.

'If you insist on battering your fish, please use the best batter possible.' Daniel told the class. 'As we have an award-winning batter authority, this is a recipe Fran can share with the class.'

Fran folded her arms. There wasn't a cat in hell's chance that she would ever share her batter recipe. Like the French with their macarons, she'd never written down her secret, and only Sid knew the components of the best batter in Blackpool and beyond. Fish fryers throughout Lancashire had been vying for ingredient clues for years, and it was no wonder that Fran's Fish 'n' Chips had won medals at the annual National Fish & Chip Awards. Despite being offered considerable financial reward, she'd fought off local competition from the likes of Fry-Daddy in Fleetwood, The Codfather in Cleveleys, and the Laughing Lobster in Lytham. Fran wasn't about to divulge any details, no matter how many requests Daniel made.

'Sorry. No can do.' Fran was firm.

'Surely you can give us a hint?' Daniel had a menacing expression as he tilted his head.

Fran wondered if the chef was issuing a threat. Perhaps he *did* know about her artwork after all?

'Well…' Fran began, searching for a compromise. 'I always use expensive sparkling spa water to mix with the flour. That's the main tip I can give you.' She was lying through her teeth, but Daniel would never know. 'Add plenty of pepper, too,' she added.

'Perfect!' Daniel clapped his hands. 'Now, I want you to all take a fish, or a mollusc, and decide how you would like it to be served for dinner, and Tomas and I will help you create something spectacular.'

As the guests crowded around the fish, Sally turned to Fran. 'Do you really use spa water in your batter?' she asked.

'I'd have to kill you if I gave you the recipe,' Fran said and wriggled into her apron.

'Go on. You can tell me.'

'And see my secret in one of the Sundays?' Fran raised

her pencilled eyebrows. 'Every chippy in the country would be falling over themselves to buy a copy.'

'I promise I'll never tell.' Sally placed her hand across her heart.

'Very well, but this goes no further…' Fran looked over her shoulder and dipped her head to whisper. 'I use Corporation Pop.'

'Corporation Pop?'

'Aye, the Fylde Coast's finest.'

Sally laughed. 'Oh Fran. Tap water? That's hilarious. And you said to add plenty of pepper?'

'Pepper? Are you insane?' Fran's eyes were wide. 'The fish we serve has a delicate seasoning in the batter that I prepare myself. A secret I'll never disclose.'

Fran turned to the trays and realised they were almost empty. 'Looks like we're the last. Let's see what's left for us to work a miracle with.'

They moved towards the almost empty trays.

Sally frowned and pulled a face, 'What are these?' she asked, 'I'm not sure what to do. In fact, I don't even want to touch them.' She stepped back.

The elongated, torpedo-shaped body of two gelatinous objects lay lifeless on a tray. Fran leaned in to study their long tentacles and poked at the suckers with her finger.

'Are they squid?' Sally asked. She wrinkled her nose and folded her arms. 'I love to eat them, but I'm not sure about turning these into a plate of calamari?'

'No, lass, these are octopuses,' Fran breathed, 'they're molluscs; such beautiful creatures.' In awe, she touched the parrot-like beaks, which she knew were used to break open the shells of their prey. 'Did you know that they can see in colour?' she asked. 'And they are the masters of camouflage, able to blend into their surroundings.' Respectfully, Fran stroked the slippery skin. 'They change in pattern, dependant on their mood.'

'Goodness, how clever.' Sally's curiosity was piqued, and she reached for her camera and moved closer.

'Aye, these gorgeous creatures have three hearts, would you believe, and they live in oceans worldwide and are extremely intelligent.'

'What do you mean?'

'Well, they can learn and solve problems and are skilled hunters. They expel water through a syphon.' Fran pointed to a small funnel on the body of the creature. 'It allows them to swim, crawl, and even fly for short distances.'

'How do you know so much about them?' Sally asked.

'It's not just marine biologists who are fascinated by the species. Sid and I have all sorts of fish chalked up on our menu – whatever we can source from our supplier in Fleetwood. It mostly comes from the North Atlantic.'

'Goodness, there's much more to fish and chips than I imagined,' Sally said.

'You better believe it, and don't get me started on the best variety of potatoes for chips and the perfect oil for frying.'

'No wonder you've been so successful.'

'We won't be very successful with this lot if we don't get a move on,' Fran replied. 'Here, grab hold of this.'

'Ugh,' Sally said as Fran passed her an octopus.

'I forgot to mention something,' Fran added as they

returned to the table to decide what to make. She stroked her octopus. 'These little creatures reproduce just once in their life. The females lay thousands of eggs and take great care to waft water over the eggs to give their babies oxygen.'

'Sounds like a lot of hard work.'

'It is.' Fran smiled. 'Good job, you're not an octopus.'

'Why do you say that?'

'Because not long after the female octopus reproduces, she dies.'

Chapter Twenty-Four

To her relief, Caroline managed to avoid many of the guests during the morning. Although delighted to see Caroline, they were busy with their recipes and didn't stop for discussions on her well-being.

Just my presence in class probably answers their questions, Caroline thought as she chose a monkfish from the selection and carried it to the table where she was paired with Ahmed. Caroline was pleased to work with Ahmed, who discreetly whispered that he hoped she felt better.

They'd listened when Tomas demonstrated the knack of making fish stock. Now, everyone was intent on preparing a knock-out dish for dinner, focusing on the finer points of fish preparation and perfecting their recipes with the help of both chefs. As the expats mastered a bouillabaisse, the twins learned how to bake a bass in sea salt crust. Bridgette had a salt cod puree recipe and planned to serve it with a gratin of carp.

Fran and Sally were working in the adjacent kitchen.

Caroline could hear their laughter and wondered if their conversation included gossip about Caroline's collapse the previous day.

'I remember a chef on the TV show *Saturday Kitchen*,' Ahmed announced. He was staring at the monkfish, and, adjusting his spectacles, continued, 'The chef made a monkfish dish by wrapping it in nettles and I think there was some sort of pesto-based filling.' He picked up a pencil and contemplated a recipe.

'That sounds interesting and somewhat different,' Caroline commented, 'shall we try it?'

'I'm not sure we'd find any nettles, but I know there is basil in the garden, which we could use for the pesto.' Ahmed's face lit up. 'Shall I go and have a look?'

'Yes, that's a good idea, and while you do that, I'll look through the recipe books and see if there are any other suggestions for cooking monkfish.'

Caroline watched Ahmed take a bowl and almost skip past the open door to the garden. She wandered over to the dresser and began searching through the fascinating collection of cookery books. She recognised many top chefs whose works were stacked neatly in the culinary library, and her fingers moved over hardcovers by Delia, Jamie, Nigella, Gordon and Heston.

A tome by Paul Bocuse lay alongside Julia Child's *Mastering the Art of French Cookery*.

But her eyes were drawn to a tiny book entitled *Whistler's Mother's Cookbook*. Caroline recognised the cover. It was of the well-known painting of the artist's mother, Anna McNeill Whistler, and Caroline was intrigued.

'You've found one of my favourite books,' a voice behind her quietly spoke.

Caroline felt her heart lurch and, turning the book in her hand, spun around to see Waltho. 'Oh, have I?' she asked.

'Yes, it's a collection of books and letters from James Whistler's estate, including a manuscript of recipes, which his mother kept,' Waltho explained, pointing to the book. 'He called it her bible, and this edition was printed almost fifty years ago.'

'It looks interesting.' Caroline flicked through the pages to stare at sketches by the artist alongside recipes and excerpts from his mother's letters.

'It's a fascinating account of the Whistler household in the mid-nineteenth century when they lived in America, Russia and Britain.'

'A glimpse of Victorian housekeeping,' Caroline said.

'And of Mrs Whistler and her famous son's interest in food.'

'Where did you find it?'

'I didn't.' Waltho shrugged. 'Lauren had it in a collection.'

Caroline was instantly reminded of her outpourings the previous evening at the mention of Lauren's name. Now, feeling acutely embarrassed, she knew she had to apologise.

Caroline glanced over Waltho's shoulder to ensure they weren't overheard.

'I am so sorry about last night,' she began, 'I can't imagine what came over me to make such a fool of myself and burden you with my stupid blubbering.'

Before Waltho could interrupt, Caroline stumbled on.

'I understand you probably want me to leave because I can't be such a responsibility. After all, I fainted in the church and put everyone out, and then you wasted so much of your time listening to me drone on and on.'

'Caroline,' Waltho sighed and took her arm. 'Stop it.'

Biting her lip, she looked up. 'I really do understand if you want me to…'

'Please.' Waltho's grip was firmer 'You have nothing to apologise for.'

'But I…'

He dipped his head to look into her eyes. 'There is no need to express regret. I am humbled that you shared your difficulties and trusted me.'

'Well…'

'All that matters is that you enjoy your time here and maybe take stock of your situation to find a way to cope with your problems.' Waltho was smiling. 'Please know I will do whatever I can to help you.'

Caroline thought she might burst into tears.

She couldn't ever remember anyone being so kind, and Waltho's words were so gentle and soothing that it was all she could do not to reach up and kiss his wonderful face and wrap herself in his arms.

Shocked by her thoughts, she stepped back. *Am I crazy?* There wasn't a prayer that Waltho would look at anyone like her. He'd aim for a much younger model if he ever got over Lauren. She knew she was too old, and her financial position was dire. No man in his right mind would give her a second glance.

'Are you alright?' Waltho asked. 'Can I get you a drink, some coffee perhaps or water?'

'No… No, thank you, I'm fine.'

Caroline knew that she sounded curt, and she could have kicked herself. Really, she had to apologise again, but as she was about to thank Waltho for his kindness, Ahmed came running into the kitchen. When he saw Caroline, she could see that he was elated.

'Look!' Ahmed called out. 'I didn't think I would find any in such a perfect garden, but I've a whole bowl full!'

'What has he found?' Waltho looked puzzled.

'Nettles.' Caroline suddenly smiled.

'Nettles?'

'Yes, he has a recipe in his head that he wants us to try, and it looks like he's found a bunch of nettles in your perfect garden.'

Waltho threw back his head and laughed, and Caroline found that she was laughing, too. The feeling was unexpected. As her laughter subsided, she wiped a happy tear from the corner of her eye.

'Not such a perfect garden, then.' Waltho grinned.

Unexpectedly, Caroline remembered a snide comment that Stanley had made about her failed catering business. 'You're not so *perfect* after all,' he'd said.

Turning to Waltho, Caroline said, 'Who needs perfect?'

The morning class stretched on, and when everyone completed the finishing touches to their dishes, they gathered around the table to sip coffee and eat cake while listening to Daniel demonstrate different methods of meringue making.

Caroline sat beside the expats and stared at the slice of honey cake on her plate.

Mindful of Waltho's encouragement to eat more, she took a dainty pastry fork and cut a slither. A gentle awakening of her senses made her aware of the delicate flavours of lavender, chestnut and thyme, and she was surprised by her emotional response.

The cake was beyond delicious; it was pure heaven, and she had to have the recipe. Tomas had made the cake and used honey from a local vendor at the market in Chauvigny. If there had been time, Caroline would have gone to find the beekeeper who produced such an excellent product.

On the other side of the table, Fran sat beside Sally and drank her coffee. She'd finished her cake and considered another slice as she watched Daniel whip up a froth with egg whites.

As the chef worked away, Fran glanced at Caroline. She was amazed that her plate was empty, and Caroline had taken a second helping of the honey cake.

Fran nudged Sally. 'Look,' she whispered, 'Caroline is eating cake!'

'So she is,' Sally replied and peered over her mug. 'That must be a first.'

'Whip your camera out and capture it.'

'Better not; she might stab me in the eye with her cake fork.'

'I think it's great, perhaps she's feeling a bit better?' Fran whispered. 'I do hope so. I feel anxious for her as she always seems to have the worry of the world on her shoulders.'

'Is there anything that we can do that might help?'

'I'm going to try and include her in our conversations,' Fran said. 'Let's make an effort to be friendly and sit with her later and have a nice chat.'

As Caroline ate her cake and was about to fork another mouthful, she realised that Fran and Sally were talking about her. She wondered what they had found to gossip about now. But before she could worry further, Waltho came into the kitchen and, finding a chair, sat beside her.

'That looks good,' he said as Angelique silently handed him a coffee and passed him a plate. 'Honey cake, my favourite.'

'It's delicious,' Caroline agreed.

'How's the class?' Waltho whispered.

'Perfect, we're learning all about meringues.'

They listened to Daniel explain the versatility of meringues and how they could be used in many recipes. He told them that he would demonstrate a dacquoise using French meringue, and then Tomas would help everyone master the Swiss and Italian meringue process.

Ahmed held up his hand. 'Is dacquoise a nut meringue?' he asked.

'Very good, yes, it is,' Daniel replied, 'and I shall be using almonds from the macaron shop in Montmorillon.' He weighed out sugar and flour. 'A dacquoise is a layered cake,' Daniel told the class, 'and it is very popular throughout France, originating in Aquitaine.'

'Are you using fresh eggs?' Ahmed asked.

'Another good question,' Daniel smiled. 'Older eggs have thinner whites and are easier to whip, creating a fluffier meringue, but they are less stable. For a firm meringue, use fresh eggs at room temperature.'

Fran studied the concoction that was coming together under Daniel's skilful hands.

As he piped three neat circles onto a tray, she remembered a domestic science class at school. The teacher, Miss Foulkes, had been formidable, and Fran, prone to misbehaviour, often spent the lesson sitting in a corner with her face to the wall,

'Fran, are you listening?' Daniel called out.

'Er, yes, Chef, I'm on it,' Fran snapped to attention.

'Excellent, because *you* will make Italian meringues, and I expect an outstanding result.'

'Rats,' Fran sighed. 'Chef knows they're the hardest,' she murmured to Sally, 'you have to use a thermometer and get the temperature of melted sugar absolutely right.'

'Don't worry, I'll help,' Sally encouraged.

Daniel placed his dacquoise in the oven and set a timer and, like a TV cookery show clip, Tomas produced one they'd made earlier. Taking a spatula, Daniel spun the meringues on a rotating stand. He skilfully sandwiched almond-flavoured Chantilly cream on the layers, which he stacked and covered with the same.

He finished the cake by sprinkling finely chopped

almonds around the sides and piping a pretty pattern on the top with melted chocolate.

'Voila!' Daniel announced, pushing his creation forward for the class to admire.

Waltho stood and draining his coffee, licked cake crumbs from his lips. 'Forgive me, Daniel,' Waltho interrupted, 'but before guests begin making their meringues, I want to ask if there is anything they would particularly like to do this afternoon?'

'I'd like to relax,' Bridgette said.

'I'd like to stretch my legs.' Ahmed joined in. 'A walk would be agreeable,'

'The weather is sunny, and it would be lovely to go out.' Sally fiddled with her camera, checking the shots she'd taken that morning.

'We enjoyed the picnic by the river,' the twins said, 'it was such a delightful afternoon.'

The expats agreed with the twins and thought a game of cards and a bottle of wine in a shady riverside spot sounded marvellous.

'I could have a walk if we go to the river again.' Ahmed nodded.

'And I could snooze on a blanket.' Bridgette smiled.

Waltho turned to Fran. 'What would you like to do?' he asked.

'A picnic by the river sounds good,' Fran agreed.

Turning to Caroline, Waltho raised his eyebrows.

'Yes, that suits me,' Caroline said.

'Excellent,' Waltho said. 'Angelique, Tomas – can this be arranged?'

Assured that a picnic could be prepared while the guests finished the class, everyone agreed to meet later.

'I think I'll take my cozzie,' Fran said to Sally as she separated eggs into bowls.

'The river might be too high after all the rain.' Sally measured sugar into a pan and searched for a thermometer.

'If that's the case, I'll just have a paddle.'

But little did Fran know, as she whipped her egg whites into perfect peaks and Sally drizzled hot sugar syrup over them, that the river expedition would include more than a gentle paddle.

Chapter Twenty-Five

After their meringue-making lesson, the guests were treated to an ice cream demonstration. Showcasing ingredients that included thick cream, sugar, vanilla and flavourings, Daniel captured his audience's attention when he introduced the star of the show.

'An ice cream machine is a good investment, and enables you to produce the perfect consistency with minimum effort,' Daniel explained. 'This is accomplished by keeping everything well-chilled, and it is important to use fresh, high-fat dairy to achieve a luxurious texture.'

He asked everyone to suggest flavourings and nodded as choices were called out. When the ice cream reached the desired consistency, he spooned portions into individual bowls and invited the guests to add their own flavourings.

Fran stirred chocolate chips and mint essence into her ice cream, and Sally added Malibu and coconut. Bridgette scattered rum-soaked raisins and added extra rum. Daniel flinched when he tasted Ahmed's curried banana glacé but praised him for being adventurous, then told Caroline that her strawberry and black pepper was very good.

As guests made notes, Daniel concluded with tips on storage and serving suggestions, pairing their flavours with complementary desserts and beverages.

'Now, if there are no further questions,' Daniel said looking around the class, 'please gather your belongings and assemble in ten minutes. Tomas is waiting with the minibus to take you out for the afternoon.'

Waltho and Angelique travelled ahead of the guests and when they arrived in the village of Poutaloux-Beauvoir, Waltho parked his Citroën by the bridge. It was a pleasantly warm afternoon, with temperatures returning to normal for the time of year and, heading to the shady spot that had served them well last time, the pair made several trips from the car with baskets, chairs and blankets. Erecting a table, they set out chilled bottles of rosé wine and sealed boxes of bread, cheese and meats, alongside fruit and cake.

'The river is high,' Angelique commented as she folded cutlery into napkins. She wore bright, baggy harem pants with a smocked waist, a cotton vest and a long overshirt. Her hair hung in plaited braids, threaded with coloured beads. 'You must warn the guests not to go near the edge. It may be slippery from all the rain.'

'I will,' Waltho replied. 'The ground is still a little damp, but we have plenty of blankets with waterproof backing.'

Angelique stopped to study Waltho. Smartly dressed as

always, he hummed as he worked. She held her head to one side, and her expression was puzzled as she watched him unfold chairs and plump-up cushions.

'You're very cheery,' Angelique said. 'Has something happened to lift your spirits?'

Waltho stopped what he was doing and looked at his friend.

'As ever, you are a most perceptive person,' Waltho began. 'I don't know what's happened, but I think I am finally accepting that life goes on, after death.'

'Your anger is lifting?'

'Yes, perhaps it is.'

'And Lauren?'

'I felt for so long that she'd abandoned me,' he sighed. 'I recognise that I was so enraged, left alone to cope in a world that together, we'd worked so hard to create.'

'And this has changed?' Angelique was curious.

'I feel that I can connect with her now. When I look at her painting in my room, it's as though she's smiling.' Waltho paused. 'The angst in her eyes isn't there.'

Angelique nodded. 'Maybe she was always smiling, but it was your own angst that you saw,' she replied. 'Comfort in coping with the loss of your soulmate may be from believing that you still have a connection.' She shrugged. 'The anger that fuelled the flames must have gone if your memories of her smile are good.'

'I can't describe it,' Waltho said. 'Whether it's because the house is fully operational and I have a purpose or maybe it is being amongst people again?' He looked perplexed. 'But my heart is lighter.'

'Don't feel guilty that you are here, and Lauren is not.' Angelique picked up a bottle. 'As you say, life goes on, and so should we.' She poured wine into two glasses and smiled as she handed one to Waltho. 'Hey, do you remember what John Lennon said?'

'Life is what happens when you're busy making other plans!' they both chorused and began to laugh.

Waltho reached for his phone and, tapping the keys, blue-toothed it to a speaker.

Angelique started to dance as the bars of a song by the Beatles struck up. Holding her glass high, she threw back her head. 'Oh, I get by with a little help from my friends,' she sang and, grinning, pointed at Waltho. 'You'll get by with a little help from your friends.' Taking his hand, she encouraged him to dance, and as his feet moved and body swayed, Waltho closed his eyes and began to sing, too.

The guests trooped out of the minibus and, forming a snaking line, walked through the village towards the bridge that arched over the river Vienne. The twins admired baskets of blossoms and window boxes planted with herbs as Bridgette waved at locals going into a bakery.

Fran stopped to press her nose to the window to stare at the patisserie section.

'Come on.' Sally took Fran's arm. 'I'm sure there will be plenty of pastries at the picnic.'

'I hope so,' Fran replied, 'the honey cake has given me a craving for something sweet.'

Fran was wearing pink shorts to the knee and a matching T-shirt, and her tote bag, slung across her body, was bulging with a beach towel. A visor perched on her head above giant sunshades bore the slogan, *Shady Lady*.

In contrast, Sally wore a tiny halter-neck dress that left little to the imagination.

Bridgette waved at a group of children in a playground. Turning to Sally, she said, 'My handkerchief is bigger than your dress!' Dressed in her regulation walking gear of khaki shorts, Aertex shirt and hiking boots, Bridgette's Tilley hat was strapped firmly under her chin. The children giggled as she strode past.

'You're only jealous,' Sally called out to Bridgette.

'Yes, I am, absolutely,' Bridgette replied, 'I haven't worn anything so brief since the Big Bopper's music had me jiving around to "Chantilly Lace".' Bridgette swung her arms, 'It was all tiny tops and layers of skirt in those days, and I loved it.'

'Chantilly lace and a pretty face,' Fran started to sing, 'and a ponytail a hanging down!'

As they reached the bridge, guests joined in with Fran, and their hands clapped in rhythm.

'That wiggle in the walk and giggle in the talk,' sang Ahmed and the expats as they danced over the cobbles.

The twins and Sally circled and called out, 'Makes the world go round!'

At the back of the group, Caroline slowed down.

The strap of her sandal had slipped, and she reached out to adjust it. She realised that wearing walking trainers would have been sensible, but she'd have to make do. At least she felt comfortable in her white linen dress.

Caroline looked up, and when she saw Fran, she could scarcely believe she was making such an example of herself in front of the villagers. Whatever must they think of the ridiculously dressed English woman who looked like a blancmange on legs as she wobbled around, singing to Bridgette's out-of-tune whistling?

Caroline was surprised, too, at the twins and the expats, who clearly didn't object to making a fool of themselves. She noticed that Tomas and Daniel had hung back and, despite smiling, didn't join in. Ahmed had the sense to restrain himself, but as the guests stood by the steps down to the riverbank, she was dismayed that the dentist had taken Sally by the hand to jive.

'Please don't throw her over your shoulder,' Caroline muttered. She imagined Sally's minuscule skirt hoisted up to reveal nothing but a thong.

They'd all be arrested if they carried on like this.

Stop being so critical! the monkey on Caroline's shoulder unexpectedly whispered.

Caroline took a deep breath and slowly exhaled. She had to learn to relax and let life carry on around her. How would she ever sort her problems out if she was always so tense?

Wondering where Waltho and Angelique had gotten to, Caroline paused to peer over the bridge's wall. She could hardly believe her eyes. In a hollow dip, beside the picnic table, chairs and blankets, the pair were dancing too!

Caroline wondered if she could slip away and get back

on the bus or even find a café to quietly sit until it was time to leave. But before she could make a discreet exit, Fran sashayed over and held out her hands.

'Come and dance, Caro,' Fran laughed.

'No, thanks.' Caroline snatched her hands back.

'Oops, I'm sorry.' Fran stopped and removed her sunglasses. She looked sheepish. 'I didn't mean to upset you,' she said. 'Can I walk with you to the picnic? We could sit together and have a chat?'

'Well, yes, I suppose so.' Caroline was hesitant but, with no options, found herself alongside Fran.

'I seem to upset you,' Fran began. 'I don't mean to. I know I am loud and always pitch in without thinking, but the last thing I'd ever intend is to offend.'

Caroline stopped and stared at Fran. The woman was offering an apology! But before Caroline could reply, Fran was bumbling on.

'I think we come from opposite worlds,' Fran reasoned, 'and I'm sorry if I have done anything that makes you unhappy or you think inappropriate. Please know it hasn't been intentional.'

'But...' Caroline was suddenly lost for words.

Pausing by the steps, Fran said, 'You see, I am just an ordinary Lancashire lass who hasn't travelled far and knows little about life outside Blackpool. You come from London and I'm sure you must be sophisticated and worldly and live a very different life to me.' Fran continued to humble herself with apologies.

As Caroline stared at Fran's earnest face, she digested her words, remembering her own modest background, where she'd grown up with little money in a mining village with parents whom Caroline had shamefully hardly seen after her marriage to Stanley. Now, here was Fran, who, unlike herself, was happy with her lot, financially comfortable, successful in business, in a loving relationship, and *she* was apologising!

Caroline was mortified. What a dreadful snob she'd been. No wonder she never formed close friendships.

'Oh Fran, please don't apologise.' Caroline felt an urge to reach out and touch Fran's arm. 'It is me who should be apologising to you. I've been such a stuffed shirt.'

'Stuffed shirt? That's a new one.' Fran laughed, but as she looked into Caroline's eyes, she saw that they held the weight of unspoken sorrow.

'Oh, lass…' Fran whispered, 'whatever troubles you?'

'D… Do you think we might start again?'

Fran sensed Caroline's anxiety, and suddenly, as though a silent language had passed between them, she understood the sadness in her eyes.

Instinctively, the two women reached out and linked arms.

'Sh— should we go and join the picnic?' Caroline asked.

'Good idea. Steady as you go down the steps,' she said, gripping Caroline tightly, 'we don't want any casualties this afternoon.'

As Fran and Caroline reached the others, Caroline's phone began to ring, and she reached into her pocket. Her eyes were wide as she stared at the screen.

'I'm sorry, but I must take this call,' Caroline said.

'Aye, of course, I'll grab us both a chair.' Fran nodded.

As Caroline moved away, gripping the phone to her ear, Fran flopped down on a chair beside Sally. She placed her bag on an empty seat.

'Save that one for Caro,' Fran said.

The Beatles were still playing on Waltho's speaker, and Fran noticed that Bridgette had stretched out on her back on a nearby rug, her hat covering her face. Ahmed was chatting to the twins, and the expats had begun to play cards.

'I poured a drink for you.' Sally held up a glass of wine. 'How did your chat with Caroline go?'

'I think there might be a breakthrough.' Fran smiled. After seeing Caroline's sadness and sensing her distress, Fran felt protective and decided, for now, not to say more.

Sipping her drink, she stared at Sally. 'You look tired,' she said. 'Have you been burning the midnight oil?'

'A bit. After our exertions in the pool, skinny dipping at midnight in the moonlight. I have no idea what time we eventually got to bed.'

'Skinny dipping?' Fran raised a heavily pencilled eyebrow. She visualised Daniel's top-to-toe tan and grinned.

Sid always had lines. Despite ruddy brown arms and a conker-coloured face in the summer, his body was pure white where his vest and shorts were worn, matched by the line of his socks. Sunshine and Sid's hidden bits were never destined to meet. Fran, on the other hand, enjoyed wearing a bikini. After all, she thought, brown flesh looked better than the milky-blue colour that seemed to tinge her ageing flesh.

'What about you?' Fran asked Sally. 'Do you enjoy swimming without your kit?'

But before Sally could reply, a muffled voice piped up, 'Can't beat it. Naturism is marvellous.'

Fran turned to stare at Bridgette, who lay with her hands linked over her chest. The Tilley hat covered her face, and it quivered as she spoke.

'Bridgette enjoys skinny dipping,' Sally smiled.

'I whip my kit off at every opportunity,' Bridgette said. 'Took to it later in life, and Hugo soon got the hang of things.'

Fran did a double take. She stared incredulously and imagined Hugo and Bridgette in the buff, at their manor house, as naked as the birds and bees.

'But how?' Fran asked, wondering how pensioners suddenly took to wandering around stark naked.

'I went on a spa break and met a man named Norman,' Bridgette sighed. 'He taught me the benefits and I've never looked back.'

'I see.' Fran frowned. She didn't see at all and couldn't imagine Sid and Norman the Naturist hitting it off.

'I might join Sally and Daniel again for another midnight dip,' Bridgette said, and with a yawn, turned on her side. In moments, her snores told everyone that she was sound asleep.

'Well, I never.' Fran giggled. 'Never judge a book by its cover.'

'Or Bridgette by her botanical pantsuit.' Sally giggled too. She held her wine and closed her eyes. 'Hasn't this been a heavenly week?'

'Yes, it has, I've loved every moment,' Fran said. 'Even the storm in the church was exciting, and I felt it bonded us all together.'

'Caroline is the only person who hasn't bonded with everyone.'

'I know,' Fran sighed. 'I thought she disapproved of me, but hopefully that might change.'

'But why would she disapprove?'

'It could be my clothes, my face, my snores, my laugh... Everything about me, in fact.'

'Oh Fran, you mustn't feel that way.' Sally sat up and touched Fran's arm. 'You're a wonderful person with a huge heart,' she said. 'Perhaps Caroline has troubles she doesn't want to share, and they make her grumpy.'

'Aye, well, that may be so.'

Angelique was circulating with wine, and Sally held out her empty glass.

'Not for me,' Fran said, 'I'll fall asleep if I have another.' She looked around to see if lunch was ready, but everyone was still enjoying a drink and appetisers.

Ahmed was delighting in a sing-song with the twins. As Fran listened, she considered their repertoire of Beatles songs impressive. The expats were still engrossed in their card game while Waltho, Daniel and Tomas sat in chairs, beers in hand, deep in discussion, putting world politics to rights.

Fran couldn't see Caroline and wondered where she'd got to. Now might be a good time to continue their chat. Feeling restless, she placed her empty glass down and stretched her arms.

'I think I might have a stroll to look at the river after all that rain,' Fran said to Sally. 'Why don't you join Bridgette and have forty winks? You look like you need it.'

'I might just do that.' Sally yawned. 'The sun is making me drowsy.' Sally closed her eyes. 'Enjoy your walk, and don't get lost.'

Chapter Twenty-Six

Fran toyed with the notion of taking her towel and having a paddle. But seeing that the river was still high, left her bag beside Sally and, adjusting her visor, put her hands in her pockets and strolled away. As she searched for Caroline, she'd take a few pictures for Sid so he could see the countryside. Fran began her river walk and was pleased she'd worn her trainers with a grippy sole. The grass was damp underfoot, and she could easily misplace her footing if she wasn't careful.

How green everything was, Fran thought. After weeks of hot, dry weather, the parched land, after the storm, had absorbed nature's nectar and magically bought back lush fields and blossoming hedgerows. Strolling through a meadow of wildflowers, she whipped out her phone to take a photo. Grinning into the lens, she took a selfie and then clicked several shots of weeping willow trees that dipped into the water.

A heron, as still as a statue, stood on the riverbank, and

Fran stopped to eyeball the bird. Unfazed by her presence, the elegant creature stretched its long neck, scanning the water for prey. Deciding to take flight, the heron spread its wings, and Fran marvelled at the display of power and grace.

'By heck,' she breathed, 'we don't see many like you in Blackpool.'

She thought of the squawking gulls plaguing visitors who sat on deckchairs eating fish and chips. One unguarded move with a plastic fork and their fish supper was gone.

Fran plodded on.

The river, which had been tranquil and meandering on their last picnic, surged along in a raging torrent, and she could see where the force of the stormwater had carved into the earth. No longer the clear, sparkling stream, it was muddy and brown, carrying debris in the current.

'I certainly won't be paddling today,' Fran said, wondering where Caro had got to as she watched water gush over rocks and boulders, creating whirlpools.

Her phone began to ring, and glancing at the screen, Fran smiled when she saw that Sid was calling. Looking for somewhere to perch, Fran chose a tree stump close to the water and made herself comfortable.

'Hello, gorgeous!' she said, 'Oh, I'm so happy to hear your voice.'

Caroline, too, had chosen to walk by the river, deciding that she needed a few moments to collect her thoughts. To her surprise, the phone call had been from Leo.

'Hello Mum,' Leo had begun, 'are you still in France?'

'Yes, I return after the weekend.'

Initially hesitant, Leo told Caroline he'd spoken to his father and had the gist of the divorce. 'He's not given me all the details, but it sounds like he's left you in quite a mess.'

Caroline listened, letting her son ramble on.

'I realise now that Dad has been an absolute shit over the years, and I am sorry that I never stood up for you,' Leo concluded.

As Caroline reached a bend, she stopped by a picturesque bridge.

What a day it was for revelations: first Fran with an apology and now Leo! She was touched that Leo had offered the sofa bed in his studio, should she need it, and he would take her out for lunch as soon as she got home.

Caroline wondered how she could fix things with Fran and decided that she should swallow her pride and make every effort as soon as she returned to the picnic. After all, a friendship with Fran might spark. A fluttery feeling in her stomach made Caroline shiver, and she wondered if it was the first ray of hope.

An old stone cottage with a clay-tiled roof nestled beside the bridge, and as she studied it, Caroline wondered who lived in the almost derelict building and if it had been flooded during the storm. Would she end up in such a property if her funds failed to stretch to something more suitable? Despite being run-down, having a home so close to nature would be a beautiful spot. During her walk she'd admired the weeping willows and wildflowers and had even seen a heron. She marvelled at the sight of the giant bird, its eyes keenly focused on the water's surface, ever watchful for the slightest movement that might be his next meal.

Caroline felt far away from London, from the hustle and bustle of busy Kensington streets, where no one stopped to speak, their eyes glued to the screen of a mobile, ignoring human contact as they hurried to fill their lives with the day-to-day details of forgettable experiences.

But I mustn't be so bitter, she thought. *I'm so wrapped up in myself that I never stop to think about anyone or anything but me.*

Stepping over a fallen branch, Caroline thought of Waltho.

The man was not only kind, he was solid and stable and his words had been comforting as he considered her problems. Caroline wondered if she *was* making a mountain out of a molehill. After all, she was fit and healthy, and, as Waltho had suggested, nothing could stop her from walking out of her life.

But why was she so scared?

Caroline would have some capital – not a lot, but something at least, and it was unlikely that Stanley would want much from the house. Waltho had suggested selling a few bits and pieces, which might make more money. She'd collected some good antiques over the years; she could pay off the business debts and let her old life go. What was the point of trying to adhere to a time when she'd been unhappy?

The next day was her birthday, and although Caroline wouldn't acknowledge another year, she considered herself young enough to find a job. These days, with the state of the economy, she read in the papers that many sixty-somethings, through necessity, carried on working. Perhaps she could be helpful somewhere? It would depend on how much she'd need to make ends meet. Her state pension wouldn't kick in for another four years, and her solicitor had told her not to expect much of a share from Stanley's private pensions, most of which had been cashed in.

As Caroline continued walking, the fluttering feeling returned. Was she having an epiphany? This week had suddenly become an enlightening experience, and Waltho's comments on her circumstances were beginning to change her views. Instead of being so angry with people, she knew she must take everyone at face value and treat them respectfully.

Especially Fran. Caroline had been perfectly horrible to the woman, and given that Fran had made the first move, she must make amends.

She thought about the time they had left at La Maison du Paradis. It had gone quickly, and tomorrow would be the last day. The programme of events had mentioned a meal in a local restaurant, and Caroline brightened. She wouldn't tell anyone about her birthday, but she could at least raise a glass to herself. And, as Waltho recommended, making a decision would help her to feel more optimistic.

La Maison du Paradis had worked its magic over the last few hours. How much lighter she felt!

Caroline stopped by the water's edge to listen to birdsong and watch beams of sunlight cast patterns on the trees as they shone through a canopy of leaves. The sun caressed her face like a warm, soothing hand, and she closed her eyes. Taking a deep breath of the fresh, clean air, she filled her lungs and relaxed as she slowly exhaled.

The tension in her shoulders was lifting.

Suddenly, Caroline became aware of activity nearby. She opened her eyes to see a heron land on the opposite bank. But the river was fast flowing, and the creature began beating its grey-feathered wings, unable to wade gracefully through the shallows in search of prey. With up and down strokes, the heron glided effortlessly into the sky as if in slow motion. In awe, Caroline stepped back to marvel at the sight as the vast bird overshadowed her.

But suddenly, the damp surface beneath her feet gave way, and Caroline felt herself sliding down the bank.

'Oh hell!' she cried out as her sandal caught on bramble, the strap loosening as it released her foot. She grabbed handfuls of damp grass to try and stop her fall, but her body was sliding on the muddy earth.

Adrenaline surged as her heart raced, and panic took hold.

'HELP!' Caroline screamed as mud squished beneath her hands and feet, coating her clothing and skin. It was impossible to control her fall or stop her descent. As the rushing river filled her ears and she saw the churning water get closer, Caroline let out one long, desperate scream. 'HELP! I CAN'T SWIM!'

Fran finished chatting with Sid and placed her phone in her pocket. Smiling with pleasure, she plodded on and thought about their conversation. He'd asked if Fran had learned enough to get their new venture off the ground. After considering his question, Fran replied that being in a creative atmosphere had given her the necessary enthusiasm. She'd never learn all she needed to know in a week but would take inspiration from some of the recipes she'd mastered and return home with a renewed eagerness to learn more. Fran had assured her husband that she would do her best to ensure that his dream came true, and together, they could begin planning for all the changes in the coming months.

Fran looked around. She couldn't see Caroline and wondered if she'd returned to the picnic while Fran was chatting to Sid.

But suddenly, out of the blue, she thought she heard a cry.

Fran cocked her head to one side, wondering if it was an animal. But the sound seemed human, and the blood-curdling scream that followed made Fran realise it was a desperate cry for help.

'Oh, my gawd!' Fran shouted and looked around, but there was no one to turn to. Should she return and alert the others? If she did, it might be too late.

'Damn, damn, damn!' Fran muttered and, unaware that she'd dropped her phone, whipped off her visor and sunglasses and began to run.

Fran's eyes searched the riverbank, and she hadn't gone very far when she saw a jewelled white sandal peek out from a bramble. It was partially covered in mud, and to Fran's horror, she recognised Caroline's footwear.

'CARO!' Fran screamed out in desperation. 'CARO! WHERE ARE YOU?' Fran's eyes scanned the muddy waters as the river roared alongside.

Where the hell *was* Caro? There was no sign of her clinging to the bank or struggling against the current. Fran's feet were now immersed, and it was all she could do not to plunge in, but her lifeguard training told her to assess the danger while searching the surface.

'Oh, shite!' Fran suddenly said.

She could see a pale arm and a blonde head flailing about no more than ten metres ahead. 'Here goes!' Fran's heart pounded as she calculated her next move and waded in without thinking further. 'HANG ON CARO! I'M COMING!'

Time seemed to slow.

The coldness of the water enveloped Fran, and as the current dragged her along, she fought against it with every ounce of strength. In seconds, she was next to Caroline, and her lungs screamed for air as she reached out to grab the drowning woman.

'GOTCHA!' Fran shouted, pulling her close, entwining their bodies in a desperate embrace. Their eyes locked, and Fran saw the fear in Caroline's eyes. Fran stood firm, grateful for the stony floor and thankful that her trainers didn't slip. She had to get Caroline out of the water and fast!

'M... My f... foot!' Caroline's voice was weak, and as Fran tugged, she realised that something was pinning Caroline to the riverbed.

'I've got you, hang on!'

Fran closed her mouth and plunged under the water, her hands laddering down Caroline's body until she found a foot. The remaining sandal was locked beneath a stone. Fran's lungs felt like they were about to burst, and without letting go of Caroline, she resurfaced, took a huge breath and then plunged down again. Seconds later, she felt the leather give as she wrenched the sandal off. But the action abruptly released Caroline, and before Fran could steady her footing, the pair were tugged by the river's relentless grip.

'IT'S OKAY!' Fran yelled as they were dragged downstream. She knew she had to hold tight and let the water take them. Battling hard to cradle Caroline's head and stop her from drowning, Fran stretched her neck and felt the sinews scream. She would not give in! Battling on, inch by inch, with all her might, Fran rounded a bend in the river. With a brute force that Fran didn't know she possessed, she eased them both to the bank's edge, where a huge boulder lay ahead.

Seconds later, they crashed against it.

Gasping for breath, Fran found her footing and dragged Caroline to the side, where stones and rocks created a slimy, wet, welcoming surface. Caroline, lying prone, was shivering, her eyes filled with disbelief. Soaked and exhausted, Fran sat back against the rock, allowing herself a moment of relief.

'We did it, Caro,' Fran whispered, 'we fought the battle and won.'

Caroline stared at her selfless rescuer, who had risked everything to save her. She was lightheaded as Fran's face blurred before her. 'Th— thank you,' Caroline whispered as she lost consciousness. 'Thank you, Fran.'

Chapter Twenty-Seven

Waltho wandered amongst the guests as lunch was served. He topped up glasses and offered baskets of bread and individual savoury quiches while encouraging everyone to help themselves to the excellent picnic Daniel and Tomas had prepared. The table was abundant with ham, sausage, pâté and a selection of charcuterie. Famous cheeses included comté, brie and camembert. Waltho noticed that Ahmed had chosen a chocolate éclair and appeared to enjoy the sweet treat so much that he reached out to select another.

'How strange,' Waltho said to Angelique, as he looked around and did a head count, 'Fran isn't here, and she's usually first to the table. I am certain that she wouldn't want to miss out on an éclair.'

He noted that Ahmed was sitting with the expats, Daniel and Sally were cosied up on a rug, and Bridgette was chatting with the twins.

'Caroline is missing too,' Angelique said. 'I saw them

both setting off individually for a walk, but I thought they would have been back by now.'

Waltho had a sudden feeling of discomfort. 'Which way did they go?' he asked.

'Downriver, but don't panic, they can't have got far, and Fran's food compass will soon bring her back,' Angelique assured Waltho, then went to help Tomas serve a fresh fruit salad.

But Waltho *was* worried. It was unlike his guests to disappear from the others, and, deciding that he'd better find out where they'd got to, he waved to Angelique and pointed to the pathway.

In return, Angelique nodded her head.

As he walked, Waltho called out. 'Fran, are you there? Caroline, can you hear me?' He wondered if they'd decided to make up and be friends and, for a moment, imagined the women sitting by the riverbank, sorting their differences, pledging to stop falling out.

Waltho hadn't gone far when he saw something pink on the path ahead. Getting closer, he made out the words, *Shady Lady*, on the peak of a visor. 'That's Fran's,' he uttered. Reaching down, he noticed a pair of oversized gaudy sunglasses, which lay in the grass nearby, alongside a mobile phone in a pink case. Scooping the objects into his pockets, Waltho called out, 'Fran! FRAN! CAN YOU HEAR ME?'

Waltho felt his muscles tense. Something was wrong.

Walking faster, he searched around, raking over the pathway and combing the riverbank. A flash of white caught his attention, and Waltho stopped. A white sandal was caught in a clump of brambles. As he got closer, Waltho's heart lurched. It was clear from the indentation in the mud that something or someone had slid down the bank and must have entered the water. 'Oh, no...' he whispered in horror.

Waltho took flight. He ran as fast as he could, scouring the river for signs of anything that could tell him where Fran and Caroline might be.

'FRAN! CAROLINE!' he called out in his urgency.

Rounding a bend, Waltho saw a massive boulder on a shingled shore ahead. He rubbed his eyes and tried to focus on what appeared to be a bundle of clothes close by. A pink mass was huddled by a muddy brown lump, and as he got closer, he realised it was Fran! Oh, God, was that Caroline she was holding onto?

'FRAN! FRAN!' he yelled and slid down the bank.

'By heck, you look like Superman coming to the rescue!'

Waltho heard Fran call out and saw her watching him hurtle over the stones.

'Are you alright?' Waltho almost screamed, such was his anxiety.

But Fran reached out to pat his arm. 'Aye, don't panic,' she said. 'I'm as right as rain, but poor old Caro here has had a bit of a shock.'

Fran looked far from alright. Soaking wet, her clothes were covered in mud and debris. Her mascara had run, her lipstick was smudged and her hair was plastered to her face.

'Is she breathing?' Waltho turned his attention to Caroline, his hands reaching out to lift her sodden hair from her face. He felt for a pulse and was relieved to find one.

'I... I'm alright...' Caroline suddenly whispered. 'Don't worry about me.'

'Oh, thank God!' Waltho felt tears in his eyes, and it was all he could do not to scoop Caroline into his arms and hug her tightly.

'I think she could do with a blanket,' Fran said. 'She looks to be shivering, it will be the shock.'

'Oh yes ... of course!' Waltho reached for his phone and punched in Angelique's number. 'There's been an accident,' he hurriedly said, 'bring blankets and the first aid kit and tell the twins they're needed. Follow the river path until you come to a bend. We're on a shingle beach below.'

Satisfied that help was coming, Waltho asked Fran, 'Is anything broken? Do you hurt anywhere?'

'No, there's nothing wrong with me that one of Bridgette's brandies won't put right and maybe one of those fancy éclairs that I saw Tomas making.' She pulled a damp twig from her hair. 'Caro, here, needs all of your attention.'

Caroline was struggling to sit up. 'Fran saved my life,' she whispered. 'I... I would have drowned if she hadn't found me.'

Waltho had no idea what had happened, but it was fast becoming apparent that he had a hero on his hands. He remembered Caroline couldn't swim and knew Fran must have plunged in to save her. Instinctively, he reached out to hug Fran.

'Aw, be off with you,' Fran said as Waltho enveloped her. 'Caro would have made it to the bank alright.'

'No ... no...' Caroline shook her head, and Waltho turned. 'My foot was stuck, and I was d— drowning. Fran dived down to release it.' She choked back a sob. 'I c— can't imagine how she m— managed,' she said and began to cry.

Without realising his actions, Waltho scooped Caroline into his arms. His grip was firm, but his touch was gentle as he stroked her face and soothed. 'Shush, it's okay, you're safe now.'

Despite the smell of mud and river, a familiar trace of bergamot and citrus was in her hair. Waltho felt an overwhelming urge to protect this woman, who was suffering through so much.

'Look out,' Fran called out, 'the cavalry is here!'

The trio turned to see Bridgette hurtling ahead. Her rucksack bounced as she ran, and she held one hand to her head to stop her Tilley hat from flying off. Ahmed had an armful of towels, and the expats carried blankets from the picnic. Sally and Daniel, laden with cushions, sprinted beside the twins, who were both red in the face but determined to keep up. They carried a first aid kit from the minibus. Angelique was the first to scramble down the bank, followed by Tomas.

'My God,' Angelique breathed as she bent down to study the victims, 'what on earth has happened here?'

'Caroline is cold. Do you have the blankets?' Waltho asked.

'Here they are.' The expats bundled the blankets around Caroline as Sally tucked supportive cushions into place.

Tomas reached Fran's side and wrapped his arm around her shoulder.

'Est-ce que tu vas bien?' he asked. 'Vos vêtements sont trempés.' His eyes were wide as he stared at her soaked clothing. With his free hand, he grabbed a towel from Ahmed.

Fran sighed with pleasure. She hadn't a clue what Tomas had said, but with the young man's arm around her shoulder, she dabbed at her face with the towel before making a turban around her hair. 'Oh, it's lovely to have a warm body so close,' she said.

'Let us through.' The twins, gasping for breath, eased the guests away. 'How long were you in the water?'

'Caroline longer than me,' Fran said, 'but it can't have been many minutes.'

'She's very pale,' Jeanette said. She knelt beside Caroline and reached for her wrist. 'Her pulse is quite rapid too.'

Pearl sat on a cushion and began to check Fran. She discovered no broken bones, nausea or weakness and seemed satisfied that Fran was faring well after her ordeal.

'I think we'd be well advised to get Caroline to a doctor,' Jeanette said.

'N... No,' Caroline stuttered. 'I'm fine, r... really.'

'It's best to be on the safe side.' Jeanette turned to Waltho. 'Can this be arranged?'

Waltho held his phone in his hand. 'I've spoken to the local doctor, and he is meeting us at La Maison du Paradis,' he said. 'It's quicker than trying to find us here.'

Everyone gathered around and shook their heads in wonder as the story of Caroline's rescue became clear.

'Would a drop of something medicinal help?' Bridgette asked and held out her flask. She had a slither of apple poking from her shirt, and as she tugged it out, a grape popped out too. 'Delicious fruit salad, shame I upended it in the haste.' Bridgette began to munch.

'No, nothing to drink or eat, not until they've seen the doctor.' Jeanette was brisk. 'They may need surgery and I don't want either being sick.'

Fran suddenly sat up, *'Surgery?'* She shrugged out of her blanket and grabbed the flask from Bridgette's hand. 'There's nowt wrong with me,' she said, taking a hefty slug of the brandy. 'By heck, that'll do the trick,' she grinned as the fiery liquid warmed her throat.

'Do you think you can stand?' Jeanette asked.

'I'm good to go,' Fran replied and, with the help of Tomas, eased to her feet. 'I'll not be swimming back, though.'

'I'll take care of Caroline,' Waltho said. Wrapping a blanket securely around her body, he carefully lifted her into his arms and carried her away from the river.

'There's your hero,' Fran whispered to Sally.

'It's surprising how one finds a superhuman strength in a crisis,' Sally said. She took Fran's arm with Tomas and helped her ascend from the shingle shore. 'You're the hero of the hour and are truly amazing,' Sally continued as they began their walk back. 'If it wasn't for your actions, I don't think Caroline would have made it.'

'You must swim so strong,' Tomas added.

'Try a dip in the Irish Sea in Blackpool on a windy day.' Fran laughed. 'It makes this river look like a trickling tap.'

Angelique and Daniel had gone ahead and packed the picnic away. By the time everyone was seated on the minibus, colour was returning to Caroline's face. Angelique and Sally held up towels to let Caroline slip out of her muddy, wet clothes. Now, she wore Angelique's long overshirt beneath a warm blanket.

In a partially shaded spot by the bus, Fran stripped off her soaked clothing and now stood in Bridgette's spare shorts and shirt.

'I always carry a spare set,' Bridgette said as she lowered the towel shielding Fran. 'Can't say that khaki is your colour, my dear, and you might need a belt with the shorts.' Bridgette whipped off the belt at her waist and handed it to Fran to gather the gaping shorts that refused to meet over Fran's bulging tummy.

Caroline sat at the front of the bus beside Waltho. 'I really am fine,' she insisted, 'please don't go to any trouble finding a doctor.'

'Shush.' Waltho held up a finger. 'You will do as you're told.'

In truth, Waltho felt responsible and privately berated himself for allowing the guests to wander off independently. The situation could have been fatal had Fran not acted so speedily, and the thought troubled him deeply.

The guests were subdued as Tomas took the wheel and began the journey back. Everyone stared out of the windows as the bus drove over the bridge and the river came into view. Whoever would have thought that a stretch of water that seemed so innocent only a few days before had become such a source of danger?

Sitting on an aisle seat next to Bridgette, Fran looked around. She was dismayed to see frowning faces. This incident mustn't ruin the holiday, she thought, after such a wonderful week. It would be wretched to let it spoil things. Taking to her feet, she gripped the seat backs and decided to cheer everyone up.

'Now then, Ahmed,' she said, 'how about you lead us in a chorus of the song that had you jiving with Sally?' Fran nodded pointedly at the dentist and pumped her hands, indicating that they should liven things up.

Ahmed, momentarily confused, soon understood. 'Chantilly lace and a pretty face,' he started to sing, 'and a ponytail a hanging down!'

The atmosphere suddenly brightened as they left the little village and guests joined in with Ahmed and Fran, clapping their hands in rhythm.

'That wiggle in the walk and giggle in the talk,' the expats sang loudly.

'Makes the world go round!' Sally and the twins called out.

And as Fran walked up and down the aisle, she smiled at the surrounding faces. 'The world continues to go round,' she said, 'and in our little world, thankfully, all is well.'

Chapter Twenty-Eight

Caroline lay on her bed and closed her eyes. Following a hot shower, she agreed to see the doctor, who assured her that she was in good health after her ordeal. He told her she was very fortunate. The river was notoriously dangerous, especially after a storm, and only last year had claimed the life of an elderly man who'd lived in a cottage by the bridge, close to their picnic location. Like Caroline, the old man had slipped into the river but, with no one to rescue him, had drowned.

Caroline remembered the cottage with the clay-tiled roof. What a horrible way for a life to end. No wonder the building was derelict now.

Caroline asked the doctor if he'd seen Fran. He told her that the hero of the hour had refused any consultation and, after finishing her friend's flask of brandy, had eaten three chocolate éclairs and gone to her room for a soak in a hot bath.

'Tout un personage,' the doctor smiled, 'you were lucky that such an excellent swimmer got to you in time.'

Caroline thanked the doctor as he left.

'Make sure that you rest,' he called out and closed the door.

Caroline settled back against the pillows. Her fingers stroked the cotton sheets, and she thought how lucky she was to be back in the comfort of this lovely room and not a dead weight on the bottom of the riverbed.

Suddenly, the cat sprang up from the side of the bed and landed beside Caroline. 'Goodness, where have you come from?'

Tabby was slowly circling. She purred as her paws pounded the bed to build a comfortable nest, and their mutual stare confirmed that the other's presence was welcome.

Caroline stroked the cat's soft, sagging tummy. After a while, she said, 'It's no good. I can't lie here indulging myself in your company when there is something I must do.'

Gently easing the sheet away, Caroline moved Tabby to the centre of the bed. She felt sure that Waltho would be here at any moment, and knowing that their conversation would involve his insistence that she rest, she hurried to dress, eager to be on her way.

Caroline slipped out of her room and crept along the corridor. Taking the stairs, she avoided seeing anyone as she went out of the main door to cross the garden. Sally appeared from the accommodation at the back of the house, and Caroline hung back until Sally made her way into the central kitchen.

'This must be Fran's room,' she thought as she recognised a muddy pink T-shirt and trousers draped over patio chairs beside a door.

Tentatively knocking, Caroline stood back. There was no reply, and she wondered if Fran was sleeping. Reaching out to knock again, she heard a voice yell that the door wasn't locked and to come in.

Conquering her hesitancy, Caroline turned the handle and stepped in.

Fran was in her bathroom, luxuriating in a bath filled with lavender-smelling bubbles, thoughtfully provided by Sally alongside a cup of hot tea, two painkillers and a chocolate éclair. Sally, who'd just left, said she would keep any visitors at bay and that Fran was to enjoy a bit of 'me time'.

Fran longed for an hour or so of peace to give her time to relax, soak her weary body, and recover from the afternoon ordeal. She was loath to admit that the rescue had taken it out of her. Her neck ached, and her sore muscles indicated that lifesaving in one's sixties wasn't such a good idea. She hadn't told Sid about her escapade and decided it might be best left until she got home.

Swallowing the painkillers, Fran took a sip of tea and bit into the éclair. But a tapping noise alerted her, and Fran cocked her head to one side. There was someone at the door. A repeated knock meant that the person wasn't going to go away.

Frustrated, Fran sat up and called out. 'It's open!' She took a last bite of the éclair, savouring the sweet sensation, then puffed out her cheeks and heaved herself out of the water, grabbing the sides of the bath.

'Rats...' Fran mumbled as she wrapped a turban-style towel around her head and thrust her arms into a gown. 'That's messed up my "me time".'

To her surprise, when Fran stepped out of the bathroom she saw Caroline.

'Caro,' she said. 'Oh, heck, sorry ... sorry, I mean Caroline,' Fran garbled. 'I know that you don't like me calling you Caro.'

'You can call me anything you like,' Caroline replied, 'grumpy old woman, pain in the arse, someone who should know better than to go walking close to a raging river.'

'Well, never mind all that,' Fran said, bustling about moving items from a chair. 'Sit yourself down and tell me how you are and what the doctor said?'

Fran saw Caroline move a bag of jelly babies perched on the chair's arm.

'I'm fine, thank you,' Caroline said, 'the doctor told me that I am extremely lucky, and if it wasn't for your heroic effort in saving me, I would be floating downstream with the Grim Reaper.'

'Oh, it was nothing. I'm sure you'd have reached the bank on your own.' Fran was dismissive as she plopped herself on the bed.

'But you know that's not true.' Caroline was adamant.

'You plunged into the water to reach me without stopping to think about your own safety. My foot was caught, and you somehow managed to untangle it.' Tears were welling in her eyes. 'Despite the danger to yourself, you held on and kept me afloat while all the time you were searching for a way to get us out of the current.'

Fran felt weary and wasn't sure how to respond.

The last thing she wanted was to be praised when she'd only done what anyone would have done under the circumstances. Her turban had fallen to one side, and as wisps of wet hair trailed onto her neck, Fran shivered, and her hand began to shake. Her lips were dry, and as she poked out her tongue to lick them, she found a large dollop of cream at the corner of her mouth.

'Fran, are you alright?'

Fran was suddenly feeling quite unwell and she felt Caroline touch her arm.

'You're as pale as a ghost,' Caroline added.

Had the enormity of what Fran had done hit home and was shock setting in?

'Aye, r... right as r... rain,' Fran muttered, her teeth beginning to chatter.

'Let's get your hair dry and get you into something warm.'

As Fran gave in, Caroline, energised by purposeful activity, came to life. Swinging into action, she ignored Fran's protests. After drying her hair and removing her damp robe, she found a pair of cosy pyjamas. Tucking Fran into bed, Caroline moved around the room, tidied away stray clothes and items that Fran had haphazardly discarded and went into the bathroom to do the same.

Boiling a kettle, Caroline made a warm drink and sat beside Fran as she drank it. Taking a deep breath, Caroline bit on her lip and then began.

'Not only do I owe you my life,' she said, 'but where do I begin to apologise for how I've treated you? My behaviour has been unforgivable.'

'No, lass, you don't have to do that.' Fran smiled.

The warm drink had done the trick, and the painkillers had kicked in. Her fingers had stopped shaking, and the aches in her body were melting away. Fran was beginning to perk up.

'I'm not everyone's cup of tea,' Fran said, 'so you can be forgiven for not taking to my northern ways.'

'But I can't be forgiven,' Caroline insisted, 'I had no right to be so rude to you all week.' Caroline reached out to take Fran's hand. 'I have been an absolute cow and am truly sorry.'

'Well, your apology is accepted, even though you don't need to.' Fran put her mug on a table beside the bed. 'But you can do something for me,' she said.

'Anything, please tell me what you'd like me to do.' Caroline glanced around the room, wondering if Fran wanted a cardigan or, perhaps, she needed to brush her hair.

'Tell me why you can't swim, what is troubling you and why you never eat.'

Startled, Caroline blinked. She hadn't expected so many questions out of the blue. Randomly picking up Fran's mug,

Caroline paused to stroke the smooth porcelain, then put it down again.

'Please don't think I'm being nosy, but I'm worried about you,' Fran said softly.

For the second time since entering the room, Caroline felt tears prick in her eyes. Someone else was worried about her. First Waltho, and now Fran. But could she really confide in Fran? What would she think of her when she learned the extent of Caroline's troubles?

'A problem shared is a problem halved,' Fran said.

'I... I'm not sure where to start.'

Fran reached out and plumped up a pillow beside her. 'When you don't know what to do, there's only one option.' She patted the place beside her. 'And that's to start at the beginning.'

Slowly, Caroline sat down. She placed her elbows on her knees and covered her face with her hands. 'You'll hate me when you realise what a failure I am,' Caroline muttered.

'We all fall and fail at times,' Fran soothed, 'but the secret is to get back up again. Failure is just a stepping stone along life's pathway.'

'H... Have you ever fallen?' Caroline looked up and stared at Fran. Fran who was fearless, confident and strong.

'More times than you'll ever imagine.' Fran reached out to take Caroline's hand again. She thought of the babies she'd lost and the times she'd not wanted to go on. Her lethargy each time and how poor Sid, struggling to cope himself, had laboured with the business on his own. Grief had woven in and out of their marriage, but somehow, Fran thought, she'd found an inner strength to bounce back. There was no reason Caroline couldn't bounce back, too.

'Now tell me all about it, and then we can plan to put it right. You're not on your own now.'

As Fran's warm fingers reassuringly wrapped around Caroline's, she saw her take a deep breath. Could Caroline become a friend? An unlikely alliance of two middle-aged women?

There was only one way to find out.

Waltho and Sally could hardly believe their eyes when, a little while later, they gently tapped on the door of Fran's room. To their delight, they were greeted by the sight of Fran and Caroline, sitting up in bed, smiling from ear to ear and laughing their heads off.

'Fran's been telling me about some of the strange requests she gets from customers in her fish and chip shop,' Caroline said. She dabbed her eyes and gently nudged Fran. 'Tell them about the time you were asked to batter a beer mat.'

'I mustn't gossip,' Fran chuckled, 'but it is safe to say that the husband of the lady who requested that particular delicacy for his supper doesn't spend so much time in the pub these days.'

'I can't tell you how relieved I am to see you both in such good spirits,' Waltho said.

'Talking of spirits.' Fran nudged Caroline 'Do you think

it's time to shake a leg and venture downstairs for a livener?'

'Why not,' Caroline agreed. 'I'm hungry too and if I remember, there are some interesting fish dishes on the menu tonight.'

'We were wondering if you felt up to joining everyone,' Waltho said. 'Daniel and Tomas have delayed the meal, and although it is very late, all the guests agreed to wait and see how you were both feeling, but it looks like we can go ahead.'

'That would be grand,' Fran replied and slid out of the bed. 'Give me five minutes to get my slap on.'

'Would it be alright if I tidied myself up here too?' Caroline asked Fran.

'Of course, help yourself, Caro.' Fran beamed.

Waltho and Sally exchanged bemused glances and Waltho left the room.

'Well, you two seem to be nicely acquainted at last,' Sally said and sat down in an armchair. She folded her arms and watched as Fran and Caroline made ready to go down to dinner. 'And to think,' she added, 'it's only taken a week.'

Chapter Twenty-Nine

As the first light broke over the French countryside, Fran began her morning stroll. She felt a gentle glow as she looked up to see that the sky still had the cool shades of a pre-dawn rhubarb pink and blue. Birds were beginning to twitter, and the vast field of sunflowers stretching beyond the garden appeared like a thousand cheerful faces, smiling and nodding as she strode by.

'Good morning, sunny sunflowers!' Fran called out as the slender stems bent and swayed, their golden petals radiating energy and joy. 'My last day in paradise,' she said as the soft, dry earth crunched beneath her fluffy slippers. With her hands in the pockets of her robe, Fran closed her eyes and held her face to the sun. 'By heck, Sid,' she mused, 'this has been a cracking week. You were so wise to send me to this magical place.'

Fran thought of the things she'd learned and the recipes she would aim to perfect when she got home to Dunromin. Sid's dream of a fancy restaurant might become a reality.

After her initial doubts, and her week in France, Fran felt rejuvenated. Maybe she *could* produce a menu to attract Lancashire folks to Blackpool.

As she walked back to the house, she thought of the company she'd enjoyed. They were a lovely group, and Fran hoped everyone would keep in touch with news of their newly acquired cookery skills.

Most surprising had been her blossoming friendship with Caroline.

Fran had never dreamt that the ice queen she'd encountered all week would break down and pour out her troubles. It had taken a near-death experience to shatter Caroline's frosty manner. But, as the gloves came off and Caroline began to melt, Fran was saddened by Caroline's problems.

Still, Fran thought as she paused by a bench, Caroline's difficulties could ultimately be overcome, and if there was any way she could help, she intended to step up and get stuck in. Fran thought of her spare bedroom at Dunromin with its plumped-up cushions, pink quilted bedspread and lacey net curtains. Hardly Kensington style, but Caroline was welcome to stay if she needed space and a bed.

The tabby cat appeared and wrapped its ageing body around Fran's legs. Like a slow-starting motor, Tabby's purr stuttered and juddered to a happy crescendo as Fran stroked her soft fur.

'I'd best be getting back,' Fran said, tickling Tabby's chin. 'It's our last day of learning, and Waltho says we have a surprise tonight.'

Turning away from the garden and, together with Tabby, Fran made her way to her room.

Caroline stood on her balcony and held onto the rail. She'd slept like a log, and as the new day dawned, she felt as though a great weight had been lifted from her shoulders. Years of pent-up frustration and months of anxiety had melted in the last twenty-four hours, and having poured out her heart to Waltho and Fran, Caroline knew that she could face her future and sort out her problems, no matter how dark the days ahead might be.

She looked out to the swimming pool, where sunlight reflecting on the surface created light and shadow. It looked so inviting. Unlike the raging river she'd encountered the day before. Caroline imagined swimming in the refreshing water and wondered if she would ever have the confidence to learn.

A cool breeze caressed her skin, and as she wrapped her silky gown tighter, Caroline thought about Stanley. Was he sitting in bed with a breakfast tray on his knee while Celia sat nearby, slathering her face in expensive cream? Had Stanley placed his size tens so firmly in the indulgent lifestyle on offer that he was now set for life? Caroline assumed that his position was permanent, and Stanley didn't give a moment's thought to the wife he'd tossed so casually to one side when a better offer had come knocking on his door.

But there was little point in wasting any more energy on

Stanley. From now on, she had to focus on herself. She turned from the railing and sat down. Taking a glass of water, Caroline sipped slowly. The air was scented with sweet flowers, and as she stared out to the field of sunflowers, she saw Fran strolling along a path with Tabby by her side.

Dear Fran. When Caroline was in need, Fran was a friend indeed.

Caroline hated herself for being so vile to the woman who had never retaliated or taken umbrage when she'd been on the receiving end of Caroline's sharp tongue. The previous evening, with kindness and consideration, she'd patiently listened to Caroline's problems and made her realise that there was nothing that Caroline couldn't overcome. All that, on top of saving her life.

Caroline smiled as a butterfly landed on a vase of blossom.

She studied the delicate wings, and her thoughts turned to Waltho. What a wonderful host he'd been. Despite his pain being brought to the surface, Waltho had done everything possible to ensure the guests were well looked after. Caroline watched the butterfly continue its weightless ballet. In a confined environment, her personal problems had been exposed. But instead of being rebuffed or rejected, the guests, too, had reached out, and their closeness had been like a warm, welcoming blanket, wrapping itself securely around her with unspoken understanding and love.

At dinner the previous evening, she'd received hugs from everyone and words of encouragement. Somehow, they seemed to understand her problems when Caroline made a speech, thanking Fran for saving her life. Caroline explained that her week had been burdensome as she faced divorce and an uncertain financial future. Her near-death experience was a wake-up call. It was time to be kinder to herself and, most of all, to everyone around her. Caroline apologised if she'd upset anyone and hoped they could forgive her. As she reached for the heart-shaped box of chocolates that Ahmed had gifted, she removed the ribbon and encouraged everyone to indulge.

When Waltho took the box, their eyes met, and Caroline felt a strange tingling sensation. Now, she stared at the beautiful butterfly, alight on the blossom, and remembered the fluttering feeling in her stomach akin to the butterfly's wings. Her heart had begun to beat faster as Waltho's hand brushed her own, and his smile almost made her gasp. Hints of gold had flickered in his amber eyes, and it was all she could do not to reach out and kiss his handsome face.

Caroline sighed.

Somehow, she'd pulled herself together and torn her eyes away from the host. It was ludicrous to feel such emotion for someone she hardly knew. It was even more ridiculous to contemplate that any such feeling might be reciprocal. Waltho had been kind to his guest, a listening ear when needed. It was a kindness he proffered to anyone staying under his roof.

Caroline stood and, gripping the water glass, took a lingering look at the garden then went into her room to prepare for the day ahead.

Sally sat up in bed and reached for her laptop. The week was drawing to a close, and she needed to finish gathering all the information for her articles. Daniel had risen a few moments ago, muttering that he had a task in the kitchen.

'Keep the bed warm,' he'd pleaded, 'I won't be long.'

Despite Daniel's almost hourly suggestion that she return to the Cotswolds with him at the end of the course, Sally had work to do. Prioritising her career over his ridiculous request, she collated her notes.

All in all, the week had been successful, and as her thoughts settled into working boxes, she remembered dinner the previous evening. Despite the late hour, everyone had been in good spirits, especially when Fran and Caroline appeared, and it became clear that their differences were overcome. Many guests had tears in their eyes as Caroline gave a speech of thanks and told them of her troubles. Sally was deeply moved to see how everyone bonded and offered accommodation should Caroline need it and help to find a job, assuring her that it was never too late for change and to become what *she* wanted to be.

In one short week, friendships that might last for the remaining years of their lives had been forged. Sally, fingers paused over her keyboard, was thoughtful. Could she capture the unique experience in an article?

La Maison du Paradis was a recipe for success. Add all the right ingredients, no matter how strange, and bind them together. Et voila! What have you got?

With eyes alight, Sally frantically began to type.

Waltho rose early and, after his cold shower, hurriedly dressed. From the moment he opened his eyes, he knew he had a sudden and essential task. Hurrying through the silent house, Waltho went to a building adjacent to the staff accommodation.

Pushing a pile of old bicycles to one side and taking a key from his pocket, Waltho unlocked the aged stable door, where a horseshoe had been nailed above the framework. The door creaked on rusty hinges, and stepping into the gloom, he felt the weight of centuries ooze from the weathered stone walls. Sunbeams filtered through murky windows, and light flooded in as he opened shutters. Cobwebs dangled from the rafters, and a delicate lace brushed his face as he moved around in the gloom.

In this old stable, where horses had been the heartbeat of daily life and history whispered through the timeworn walls, Lauren had commandeered the space for her partner and insisted that Waltho use it as his studio.

Bunches of dried lavender hung from beams. Dusty and frail from two years of neglect, the dried-up blossoms dissipated as Waltho tore them down. A battered oak table was covered with boxes of paint, and glazed pots held an assortment of brushes, and stacked around the room and covered in dust sheets lay canvasses of every size. Reaching down, Waltho peeled back dustsheets, his eyes scanning the paintings beneath.

In the centre of the room stood an easel. It was covered

with a length of cloth. Waltho could almost hear a ghostly sigh as he tentatively held the edges.

'It's time...' Lauren whispered.

Taking a deep breath, Waltho gripped the edge and drew the cloth away from the easel. Beneath stood a large, blank canvas.

'Yes, my love,' he said, staring at the canvas, 'It's time,' he whispered softly, and in moments, Waltho began to paint.

Chapter Thirty

At breakfast, Angelique announced that guests could choose how they wanted to spend their last day. She informed them that Daniel and Tomas were available in the kitchen to give one-to-one tuition to anyone who wanted an extra lesson. Angelique also explained that a nearby street market that day, in the village of Poutaloux-Beauvoir, included vendors selling antiques and bric-a-brac. She'd received an invitation from one of the expats, and anyone who'd like to have coffee and cake at their home and perhaps participate in a game of boules was most welcome. She added that evening dinner would be a celebratory occasion at a surprise location.

'By heck, I'm not sure what to do,' Fran said as she finished a pain au chocolat. 'I'd like to know more about sous vide cooking, but the market and boules sound like fun too.'

'I'm up to my ears with cooking,' Bridgette commented. 'I noticed a collection of bicycles by an old stable at the back of the house,' she said. 'I might commandeer one and cycle into Poutaloux-Beauvoir. Anyone care to join me?'

Ahmed and the twins raised their hands, and to everyone's surprise, Caroline said she'd like to join them, too.

'Looks like you'll be Billy-no-mates in the kitchen.' Sally turned to Fran. She ran her fingers through her tousled pink mop. 'I'm going to sort my hair out, which will take at least an hour.'

'Do you think Daniel will put up with me alone?'

'Of course, he will,' Sally smiled, 'but when you've finished, why don't we take Romeo and catch up with the others?'

Fran pushed her chair back. 'Sounds like a plan,' she replied.

A short while later, she stood with Sally and watched the cycling group set off. Teetering about on ancient rickety bikes, Bridgette rang her bell and peddled ahead, her Tilley hat rammed tight and baggy shorts billowing. The twins hoisted their skirts and wobbled into Bridgette's slipstream while Ahmed and Caroline brought up the rear.

Fran returned to the house, and to her surprise, Daniel was warm in his greeting as she stepped into the kitchen. With only one class participant, he'd dismissed Tomas and now sat at the table, indicating that Fran sit opposite.

'I know you wish to open a fine dining restaurant,'

Daniel said, studying Fran. Flicking his quiff of hair away from his forehead, he asked, 'You will be the main cook?'

'Well … that's Sid's dream,' Fran faltered. 'I'm not sure that I'm up to fine dining, but I intend to do my best.'

'At the start of the week, I would have thought it impossible, but having seen your progress, I want to help you.'

Fran was puzzled.

How could Daniel assist her, and why was the chef being benevolent? Had he been struck by the kindness that had swept over Caroline in the last twenty-four hours? Or had Sally softened the man with her sexual prowess? Fran considered that whatever it was, she was eager to hear him out and reached for her notebook and pen.

———

A little while later, Fran was bewildered as she wandered from the kitchen to meet Sally, who stood beside Romeo, tying a silk scarf over her neatly styled hair.

'You seem to be in a daze,' Sally said and raised an eyebrow before placing sunglasses on her nose. 'Are you experiencing a Daniel Douglas De Beers overload?' she asked.

'I think there's a strong possibility I'm about to,' Fran muttered.

She opened Romeo's passenger door and climbed in. Still taken aback, she settled her rear on the soft leather upholstery, reached for the seat belt and fastened it over her tummy.

Sally hit the accelerator pedal, and as they roared off, she realised that she hadn't a clue what Fran was mumbling about and decided not to pursue it. It was their last day, and with any luck, she'd grab photos at the market to complete her information gathering.

'Vive la France!' Sally called out as they raced through the gates of La Maison du Paradis.

'Aye,' Fran agreed, 'whatever that means.'

———————————

The day had been a success, and a happy group of guests boarded the minibus to take them to dinner that evening. Waltho was beaming as he assisted everyone to their seats.

'You look lovely,' Waltho said, steadying Caroline's elbow as she ascended the steps.

Caroline had caught the sun as she wandered the street market, marvelling at the mountain of bric-a-brac piled high under stalls draped in multi-coloured canvas. Waltho noticed a hint of bronzer, which complemented her tan and a light makeup application, including rose-coloured lipstick. As though a magic wand had been waved, Caroline, dazzling in peach silk and smiling, looked like a different woman to the pale, pompous figure who'd sat anxiously throughout the course.

And here comes the fairy who waved the wand, he thought as Fran followed behind Caroline and grabbed Waltho's hand.

Decked out in a long animal print dress wrapped at the waist, Fran had fashioned a matching turban on her head and added glitzy jewellery.

'Room for a little one?' Fran asked. 'My word, Waltho, you look like James Bond in that get-up,' she added, stopping to admire Waltho's beautifully cut suit. She plopped a kiss on his cheek. 'Gawd, you smell gorgeous! Good enough to eat.'

With a cheeky wink, she followed Caroline onto the minibus.

Ahmed and Bridgette came next. Besuited and booted, Ahmed cut a dash in pale cream linen. Bridgette resembled a forest glade with swathes of foliage-patterned fabric draped around her body, held in place with a leather belt. The twins wore matching dresses with puff sleeves and a tulip hem, and Sally followed in barely more than a whisp of pink silk, styled with shoestring straps tied into bows on her shoulders.

Angelique, resplendent in a rainbow-coloured kaftan and sparkling beads, sat at the front while Waltho slipped in behind the wheel.

'And we're off!' Fran called out as the minibus gathered speed and sped along the road leading out of the village.

As the guests travelled, the light began to fade along the narrow roads, and tall trees created an overhead canopy that allowed glimpses of a starlit sky. Occasional windows were aglow in distant houses dotted amongst a patchwork of fields bathed in the soft moonlight, and after a few kilometres, they turned off, passing through acres of vines that led to the driveway of an imposing chateau.

'Oh, my goodness!' Caroline breathed. 'I imagine beautiful chateaux at night and count them to help me sleep, and now, we are going to be dining in one.'

Remembering that it was her birthday that day, Caroline thought this location was the perfect place for her silent celebration.

The entrance to the chateau was marked by a grand wrought-iron gate, and Waltho guided the minibus along a driveway bordered by ancient shrubs. Centuries of history rose before them as the guests stared at imposing turrets and stone facades that had stood the test of time. In a courtyard, a cascade of silvery water danced in a floodlit fountain where a uniformed host welcomed them. He guided the guests up steps that led into a foyer, and they gazed at antique tapestries and opulent furniture.

'I've never seen anything like it.' Fran held Caroline's arm to walk across a marbled hallway. 'I feel like I've stepped back in time.'

'Angelique told me this is where Tomas works,' Caroline said as they stood in a salon and accepted a glass of champagne with myrtle berry liqueur. 'It has an excellent restaurant, and I understand he took a week's holiday to work alongside Daniel.'

They were led into the dining room, where a crystal chandelier cast an inviting glow above a table set with silver and glassware. Luxurious drapes lined tall windows. Portraits of the chateau's predecessors gazed down at the guests, arrogant and aloof, as though challenging the visitor's right to dine there.

'It's a bit spooky,' Fran said as flames flickered from

candles, casting shadows in ornate mirrors dotted around the room. She sat beside Bridgette, and a waiter flicked out a napkin and placed it on her knee.

'A chateau has many hidden doorways and passages,' Bridgette commented.

'What for?' Fran was goggle-eyed.

'To allow discreet movement from one room to another. Always useful if one is conducting an affair.'

Fran's mouth slackened in surprise, and she imagined Bridgette's shenanigans over the years.

'Who knows what capers the residents of this beautiful old building have enjoyed?' Bridgette said.

When their starters arrived Fran tasted a delicate amuse-bouche, and as she bit into truffle-infused pâté served on crisp wafers, she sighed with delight.

Caroline pierced a perfectly seared scallop drizzled with a citrus reduction. 'This is divine,' she said.

'I'm so pleased to see you enjoying food.' Fran patted Caroline's hand.

'I keep thinking of everything I missed this week,' Caroline admitted when a creamy vichyssoise, garnished with chives, came next.

Fran saw Ahmed hold up a heavy silver spoon and heard him call out, 'Almost as good as your bean soup!'

The main course arrived with drama as the head chef of the chateau was followed by Daniel and Tomas. The chefs presented filet mignon on a silver platter and flamed it in brandy. The glow glinted on razor-sharp knives as the chefs sliced the tender beef.

Hot from assisting in the kitchen, Daniel mopped his

brow with the back of his hand and flicked his wayward quiff under his hat. 'SOS,' he said to Tomas, who placed portions of beef onto gold-edged plates and added a rich brown sauce.

'Sauce on the side,' Fran grinned knowledgeably at Daniel's culinary term. 'Oh, doesn't Tomas look grand in his finery,' she added, waving at the young man.

Bridgette pierced white asparagus with her fork. 'It looks like a Roman candle,' she said and bit into the tender stem, then licked garlicky butter from her lips.

Wine was served to complement the dishes, and now artisanal cheeses followed, presented on long wooden boards representing flavours of the region. Fran chose a creamy brie while Ahmed took a pungent Chabichou du Poitou. He spread it on thinly sliced bread and drizzled the cheese with honey.

'Magnifique!' Ahmed exclaimed and closed his eyes. When he opened them, he offered the cheese to Caroline.

Caroline remembered the smelly lump Ahmed had purchased in the market and marvelled at his taste buds. 'What the hell.' She laughed and took a bite. But her eyes bulged as the overpowering lactic taste hit the back of her throat.

'Here, have a slurp of this.' Fran held out a glass of Pineau des Charentes and nodded as the sweet pudding wine soothed Caroline's palate.

A classic tarte tatin ended the meal, and guests, stomachs bulging, found room for caramelised apples surrounded by a buttery crust and a quenelle of velvety vanilla bean ice cream.

'I can't believe I've eaten so much,' Caroline confessed, falling back onto a soft upholstered chaise in the drawing room. 'What a memorable meal,' she said.

'The perfect way to end the week,' Fran added and flopped beside her.

Having photographed each course as it arrived, Sally had produced her camera and now flicked through her digital library.

'Have you gathered everything you need for your articles?' Ahmed asked as he stood behind Sally's chair and leaned in to study her work.

'More than enough,' Sally replied. 'I will be writing about this week for some time to come.'

Bridgette sat beside a fireplace, where logs crackled in a vast grate. Staring into the flames, she cradled a brandy. 'I do hope that we all meet up again. I would love to have you all come and stay at the manor.'

'We've never been to Lancashire.' The twins nodded. 'We'd like to see your interesting gardens.'

'And I would enjoy revisiting Bath,' Bridgette replied.

'My partner and I would be honoured to host you all at our home,' Ahmed added, 'I will make many of the dishes I've prepared this week.'

'Always room with us, here in France,' the expats called out, 'and we will beat you again at boules!'

Fran rolled her eyes. Earlier, after enjoying coffee and cakes at the home of one of the expats, she'd agreed to join in with the game. Now, everyone laughed as they remembered Fran trying her hand. She'd found it impossible to keep her feet together in the designated circle.

When she tossed her metal ball into the air, aiming for the cochonnet, or 'jack' as Fran knew it, she'd almost decapitated Bridgette, who'd thrown herself, nose down, on the grass.

'What about you?' Bridgette asked Sally. 'Will you join in with our reunions?'

'You bet.' Sally grinned. 'There is a story in each of you, and I promise to keep in touch.'

'Everyone is very welcome in Blackpool to come and try my fish and chips,' Fran said, 'and should our dreams come true, you must come to our fancy restaurant.'

The guests turned to Caroline, keen to press her on her future.

Ahmed posed the question they all wanted an answer to. 'Caroline,' he began, 'your life will change when you leave here, and we all wish you the best.' He paused. 'But will you remember us?'

Caroline felt Fran squeeze her hand.

'This week has been life-changing for me,' Caroline said and looked at the faces reflected in the glow of the fire. 'With your help, I have found the confidence to face my problems, and I hope with all my heart that we keep in touch.'

She looked up to see Waltho staring at her.

The butterfly dance began in her tummy, and Caroline fought the urge to rise to her feet and fling her arms around him. Here stood the man who'd given her confidence and, together with Fran, helped her face up to her problems. But she knew Waltho wouldn't reciprocate in anything more than a friendship. A man like that would never entertain romance with an ageing failure.

Before Caroline had time to continue, Waltho suddenly held up his hand.

'Ladies and gentlemen,' he began, 'as this extraordinary week draws to a close, I feel that the occasion calls for a few words.'

Chapter Thirty-One

B ridgette settled back in her chair and took a swig of her drink. 'A speech, excellent,' she said as Waltho stepped into the centre of the room.

'I trust that your days at La Maison du Paradis have been fruitful,' Waltho began, 'and that you leave here with many happy memories.'

'Hear, hear!' Bridgette agreed.

'I hope you have prospered from this experience and will try something new at home.' Waltho's eyes scanned the guests. 'Or, like me ... you have found the enthusiasm to do something that gives you great pleasure.'

'Had sex been on the menu, I would concur.' Bridgette sipped more brandy.

Waltho smiled. 'This week, you have given me the zest to return to my passion, which some of you know is to paint.'

'Oh, how wonderful!' Fran gripped her hands together.

'After Lauren died, I never thought I would stand at an

easel and pick up a brush again.' Waltho shrugged. 'But I have spent all day in my studio, and although it is unfinished, I would like you to see the result of my efforts.'

He turned to a large canvas and, revealing it slowly, held it up.

'Oh, I say...' Bridgette gasped.

Depicted in oils, Waltho had captured the guests gathered around the long oak table. Using artistic licence, he'd placed sunflowers to circle the cameo scene. Laughing and chatting amiably, guests leaned into one another, and others raised a glass. Although unfinished, each could discern their own caricature.

'My word.' Bridgette laughed. 'You've taken years off me!'

'I think I look most handsome,' Ahmed preened.

'I take it that I'm the pink blob in the shimmering jumpsuit?' Sally giggled.

'It's inspired,' Caroline spoke quietly, almost overcome that Waltho had included her, too. 'Lauren would be so proud,' she added.

'It is, as yet, unfinished. I have never worked so quickly, but I will ensure you all receive an image of the final work.'

Everyone applauded.

'Now it falls to me to thank my helpers this week,' Waltho continued. 'Please put your hands together for the ever-efficient Angelique, without whom none of this would have been possible.'

Angelique stepped forward, radiant in the firelight. 'It has been my pleasure,' she said, accepting thanks from all the guests.

'And what would we have done without Tomas?' Waltho asked.

Fran leapt to her feet to clap loudly for the young chef.

'Tomas leaves us tonight to return to his work here, at this chateau, and I am sure you will all wish him well for his future.'

More applause resounded as Tomas took a bow.

'But today is a special day for one of you,' Waltho said.

Heads turned to see Daniel enter the room. He carried a large, elaborately decorated cake where several candles burned.

'Please join us in wishing Caroline a happy birthday!'

'Oh, you dark horse.' Fran nudged Caroline.

Caroline shook her head in disbelief and stared at the beautiful cake crafted with sugar paste sunflowers.

'Make a wish!' Ahmed called out as Caroline blew out the candles.

When Caroline opened her eyes, her gaze was met by Waltho's.

'How did you know it was my birthday?' she asked.

'I have everyone's passport details,' he replied. 'It's a legal requirement.'

'Ah, of course.'

'I hope you don't mind. I realised during the day that you hadn't told anyone, and I wanted to respect your wishes, but as it's the last night…'

'It's wonderful, really. I can't tell you how much it means.' Caroline smiled. 'The cake is like sunshine. Everyone must have a slice.'

The guests sang *Happy Birthday* and raised their glasses

to toast Caroline with champagne, and Waltho finished his speech.

'My final thanks are to Daniel,' he said, 'I hope you have lasting memories of his talent. A round of applause, please, for our celebrity chef.'

Guests clapped, and some took to their feet as Daniel took a bow.

'Thank you... Merci,' Daniel said. 'My friends, it has been my honour. You have been quick to learn, and the results of your efforts have been outstanding.' Daniel looked at the smiling faces. 'I am confident you will cook like pros from now on.'

He raised his glass, but his expression suddenly changed, and he furrowed his brow as though deep in thought.

'However,' Daniel said, 'there is one exception.' He turned to stare at Fran. 'One group member has given me much to think about this week.'

Fran shrank back. Daniel's eyes were like daggers, and they bore into her suddenly beating heart. 'Oh, heck,' she said, reaching for Caroline's arm. 'I think I'm in trouble.'

Daniel suddenly spun around and, placing his hands on his hips, displayed Fran's drawing on the back of his jacket.

Guests gasped, and the twin's hands flew to their mouths.

'It's curtains for me,' Fran said, closing her eyes. She waited for firm hands on her shoulders to boot her from the room.

But to the astonishment of the onlookers, Daniel began to laugh.

'Fran,' Daniel said, 'I have a gift for you.'

He held up a chef's jacket, and Fran could see her name embroidered in bright blue stitching on the pocket. But as Daniel slowly turned it around, Fran's heart threatened to bounce out of her body.

'Oh, heck, he's finally going to get his own back,' she whispered and closed her eyes.

Suddenly, everyone applauded, and Ahmed called, 'Three cheers!'

As Fran opened her eyes to stare at the jacket, she could hardly believe the words written on the reverse in matching bright blue stitching:

STAR PUPIL

'Congratulations,' Daniel beamed. 'I award you this prestigious jacket to acknowledge your hard work throughout the course.'

'Oh… No… I really, d— don't deserve it,' Fran stumbled over her words. 'I should never have defaced your jacket; it was such a rotten thing.'

'On the contrary, I deserved it.' Daniel handed the jacket to Fran. 'I have been tough on you, but it was my test to see if you would rise to the challenge, and you did.'

Speechless, Fran gripped the jacket.

'And I have one more announcement,' Daniel said.

'You've become engaged to Sally?' Bridgette asked.

'Sadly, no, although I would like to.' Daniel looked at Sally and sighed. 'My other news is that I have asked Fran to join me at my restaurant to work a stage alongside me and my team.'

'Is she going to be performing in a theatre?' Bridgette was puzzled.

'No.' Daniel laughed. 'It is from the French word "Stagiaire", which means to become an apprentice or trainee.'

'Ah.' Bridgette nodded. 'You mean an unpaid internship.'

'Kind of, but it allows a student chef to hone their skills with hands-on experience, and will help Fran in her determination to open a fine-dining restaurant,' Daniel added.

'Well, I think it is marvellous and hats off to you, Chef, for your generosity.' Bridgette was enthusiastic but cautiously added, 'She's sure to be a handful.'

Everyone rushed forward to congratulate Fran.

'I hope I don't let Daniel down,' Fran said, still clinging to her jacket.

Sally, who'd captured the scene with multiple photos, wrapped her arm around Fran's shoulder, and their eyes met. 'You really will become a star,' she said, 'and I will be with you all the way, helping to promote your business.'

Caroline, who'd observed everyone's enthusiasm, wanted to add some of her own.

'Sally is quite right,' Caroline said, 'and I am in awe of the amount of work you are about to undertake, but if I could have one wish from this week, it would be to see your star become Michelin.'

'Oh heck.' Fran shook her head. 'Now you really are

dreaming. There must have been something in all that wine,' he laughed. 'Fran's Fish 'n' Chips are one thing, but Michelin stars are the stuff of dreams and just pie in the sky for a modest cook like me.'

Waltho stepped forward. He held a bottle of champagne in his hand. 'We all need to have a dream, Fran,' Waltho said, 'without our dreams, we could never make them come true.' Turning back to the guests, he began to refill glasses.

In the beautiful, intimate room, in the glow of firelight and warm flickering candles, where shadows danced on the walls and ceiling, Fran was mesmerised. The formal portraits of the chateau's predecessors appeared softened, their eyes wide, almost moving from side to side as though tracking the guests' movements, and Fran imagined their ghosts coming out to play.

She thought of Waltho's speech and shook her head in wonder. He'd repeated the very words that Sid had spoken throughout their married life.

Now, Fran studied the guests. Relaxed and happy, conversation lively, they were chatting, making more memories of the week, and she wondered what *their* dreams held.

Bridgette sat ruddy-faced by the fire, glass gripped in her hand. Would she gain confidence and embrace the new friends she so sorely needed? And what of Sally? Dear sweet Sally, whose pretty eyes sparkled and lit up the room.

Fran hoped that Sally would soften and allow herself to love.

Then there was Caroline.

Caroline, who, like a butterfly, had remarkably metamorphosed in the last two days. Fran stared at the woman who'd come out of her self-imposed chrysalis to face challenging times ahead. 'How I hope that we become friends,' Fran whispered.

She saw Caroline turn to Waltho, and all at once, their eyes met.

At that moment, Fran thought she felt an electric current surge through the room, and she quivered. She blinked rapidly and shook her head. Was that a shimmering aura that had suddenly enveloped the pair?

'Well, I never...' Fran was in awe. Were the faces in the portraits now smiling, and were there mystical bees and butterflies fluttering around Caroline and Waltho's heads?

Fran thought of Caroline blowing out her birthday candles and hoped that the birthday girl had made a wish. Holding her precious jacket close, Fran felt embraced in a spiritual hug and closing her eyes, she whispered...

'The magic of La Maison du Paradis.'

Chapter Thirty-Two

The dreamlike week at La Maison du Paradis was ending and the natural alarm clock of birdsong woke Caroline. She rose from her bed. Stretching out her arms, she stepped on the lime-washed floorboards and walked slowly to the window to open it wide.

As the scents of the early morning dew-dappled garden enveloped her, she closed her eyes. Now, it was time to go home and face the music.

By the end of the day, she would be back in Kensington, alone in the house she'd shared with Stanley for all their married life. But instead of the anxiety that had gripped her in the first days of her holiday in France, Caroline felt a flutter of hope. The road ahead didn't appear as difficult and now, she had someone to talk to. For Caroline had no doubt that her friendship with Fran would flourish.

Caroline opened her eyes and gazed out at the sunflowers.

Despite her optimism, there was a sadness that tugged

at her heart and that was Waltho. How she longed to stay in his beautiful home and spend time in his company. It was as though Waltho had reawakened a passion she'd forgotten and never hoped to experience again.

What would it be like to be loved by a man like Waltho, she wondered?

But it was something she would never know and it was pointless to contemplate such thoughts. Soon, another class would arrive and Waltho would play host to a new set of guests. One day, she imagined, someone would walk through his door and he'd lose his heart again. The perfect person, beautiful, clever and capable. So unlike herself.

Suddenly, Caroline was eager to pack her case and be on her way. It was painful to stay any longer. But first, she must say goodbye to her new friends.

———————

Fran was flustered. She'd overslept, and now, after Angelique had knocked loudly on her door, she rushed to sling clothes into her holdall, heave it onto her shoulder and catch the minibus waiting to take her to the airport.

'Gawd, I'm late,' Fran muttered.

Dressing hurriedly in her orange slacks and a matching T-shirt, she took a last look at her room. There wasn't time to straighten the bed or tidy the bathroom. Taking twenty euros from her purse, she left it on the dressing table for the lovely lady in housekeeping.

Sorry to be such a slob, Fran scribbled on paper torn from her notebook.

Shielding her eyes, Fran ran across the gravel and breathed a sigh of relief when Tomas came forward to take her bag.

'It's okay, we wait for you,' he said, packing the holdall onto the minibus.

'You missed breakfast,' Angelique said. 'I heard you snoring and let you sleep in. You have a long day ahead.'

Fran wished that Angelique hadn't been so generous. Useless without a hearty start to the day, Fran rubbed her stomach as hunger pains began to bite.

'But Tomas has made provisions for you to enjoy on your journey.' Angelique handed Fran a perfectly packed parcel of delicacies.

'Oh, you darlin', I could kiss you.' Without further ado, Fran grabbed hold of Tomas and smacked her lips on his cheek.

'I will miss you…' Tomas laughed. 'But good luck in your new endeavour.'

'I will miss you too,' Fran replied.

The twins were waiting beside the minibus. In matching cardigans and comfortable cotton trousers, they said their goodbyes. Ahmed, standing alongside, was returning home by train, and soon, a taxi would take him to the station in Poitiers.

Bridgette marched over, followed by Waltho carrying her cases. 'Where's Caroline?' she demanded as she searched the departing faces.

'Here I am!' Caroline called out.

Clutching a hat to her head, Caroline tugged on the handle of her case.

A car pulled up, tooting its horn and the expats, here to say their farewells, bundled out.

'Has anyone seen Sally?' Fran asked anxiously, wondering if Sally was still in bed. She didn't want to leave without saying goodbye.

'There she is.' Bridgette pointed. 'It looks like she has a valet.'

All eyes turned as Sally walked confidently towards them. In her wake, Daniel, loaded with cases, made his way to Romeo.

'By heck, am I seeing what I hope I am seeing?' Fran asked.

'I'm giving him a lift, that's all,' Sally said. 'Don't read anything into it. There's space in Romeo, and it will be company for me on the journey.'

Fran held out her arms. 'Come and stay with me and Sid soon,' she said with a hug.

'Try keeping me away.'

As guests bound for the airport piled on the minibus, Tomas started the engine.

Waltho stood beside Caroline and held out his hand.

'Good luck,' he said and gripped her fingers. 'I hope that all goes well, will you let me know?'

Caroline couldn't find words to express how she felt. With the guests bustling around them and Angelique announcing that to catch their flights, Tomas needed to go, she found herself tongue-tied. But Waltho's hand clenched hers firmly, his eyes heartfelt.

'Thank you,' Caroline whispered. 'Thank you.' That was

all she could say and there were tears in her eyes as she turned away.

Fran sat behind Tomas. Her eyes were searching and she crossed her fingers as she watched Caroline and Waltho say goodbye. 'Oh, no.' Fran sighed as Caroline pulled her hand from Waltho's grip. Fran thought she saw Waltho shake his head as Caroline boarded the minibus.

'I must have misread the signals.' Fran was bemused. 'Rats,' she sighed with frustration. 'There's a romance that's slipped away.'

Tomas started the engine, and with the airport-bound guests safely aboard, hands began to wave. Ahmed climbed into his taxi, waving too, as the vehicles started to move. Romeo sprang to life, and Sally, sunglasses in place and her silky scarf shimmering, smiled as Daniel strapped himself in, and they followed behind. The expats, tooting their horn, joined the end of the convoy as it progressed towards the gates.

'Goodbye!' Everyone called out. 'Safe travels! Keep in touch!'

Waltho felt Angelique's presence beside him. He placed his arm on her shoulder, and together, they watched the vehicles disappear from the grounds of La Maison du

Paradis. Suddenly, everywhere was quiet and still, as though the beating heart of the house had paused.

As the dust on the driveway began to settle, Tabby appeared. She flicked her tail and sauntered over to Waltho, where she wrapped her creaking body around his legs.

'What now?' Waltho turned to Angelique.

Angelique disengaged his arm and turned to face Waltho. 'Now,' she began, 'you embrace all the good from this week. The French Cookery School has been a success.'

'I hope so.'

'Best of all,' Angelique smiled, 'you're painting again.'

'It's a bonus,' he agreed.

'Life is like the theatre,' Angelique said, 'a stage for us to act out our lives. When one drama finishes, we stand in the wings, waiting for the curtains to open on a new performance.'

Waltho stared at Angelique. Was she right?

'Let's celebrate with coffee and cake, to more success!' Angelique called out and disappeared into the kitchen.

Waltho scooped Tabby into his arms. He thought of the question he asked himself only a week ago. Had that day, with the opening of the cookery school, marked the first day of the rest of his life?

As he strolled along the lavender-lined pathway, he realised that it might well have done.

The darkness of losing Lauren had lifted, and he was enjoying his home. His studio had come to life, and he felt inspired by ideas for future paintings. But, Waltho pondered, had cookery been the right thing to do? Would he feel happier if he ran painting courses and followed his true passion?

Waltho thought of Caroline.

Unknowingly, Caroline had contributed to his recovery, and he wished that there was some way he could contribute to hers. As she'd climbed onto the minibus, he'd been aware of an unspoken bond between them, but it felt like it had broken away when she'd pulled her hand from his fingers. Shaking his head, he'd wanted to call out and implore her to stay.

Waltho sighed, but that was foolish. Caroline had a new life to engineer, and who knew what her future held?

He'd reached the pool, and Tabby slid from his arms. She jumped on a chair and curled up happily. The confident cat knew what she wanted from life. As Waltho stroked her fur, Tabby stared at the hesitating man.

'*Of course...*' Waltho whispered and began to smile as comprehension suddenly dawned.

The stage curtains had parted, and a new show was about to begin!

Chapter Thirty-Three

Twelve months later

Headlines:

The Lancashire Evening Post
Fran's Finest Fare Soars to Success!

The Caterer
Blackpool Couple Take Top Award

Sunday Times Top 100
A Brand-New Entry from Blackpool

Michelin Menus
It's stars all the way for Fran & Sid!

Sally sat at her laptop and flicked through her ever-increasing press file for Fran's Finest Fare. The sparkling new foodie haunt was gathering awards and, in all her years of writing food-related articles for the hospitality industry, Sally had never known an eating establishment to gain such recognition in so short a time.

The press was lapping it up, and the pocket rocket that was Fran teamed with Sid's determination, had seen plans swing into action on the day Fran returned from France.

Leaving Sid, who'd already begun work on revamping their café, Fran had headed south to roll up her sleeves and work as hard as she could at Daniel's restaurant. After giving her all in the busy kitchen for six solid weeks, Fran and Daniel devised a suitable menu, and she returned to Blackpool to set everything up.

Sally stared at her files. Her favourite article from her time at La Maison du Paradis was the feature in the Sunday supplement. She opened the four-page spread, and her eyes danced over the words. The editor loved the setting and characters and Sally giggled as she stared at the kitchen image of Fran, dressed in a Breton top and beret, alongside botanical-clad Bridgette, waving wooden spoons and whisks. Group photos showed the guests enjoying themselves in the glorious French surroundings, and the section describing Daniel's talents was interspersed with images of the smiling chef.

As Sally closed the article, she felt familiar hands gently touch her shoulders.

'*You* should receive an award for these amazing articles.'

She nestled close to the face that leaned in to kiss her.

'Never has my restaurant been so profitable,' Daniel said, wrapping his arms around Sally.

Sally caressed Daniels's fingers and closed her eyes.

How her life had changed in the last year! The road trip with Daniel had been the catalyst when a strike by ferry companies delayed their journey. After a night in Orleans, they spent a morning wandering around museums and parks before travelling to St Malo, where they'd enjoyed two days and nights, enjoying the beach, eating seafood and drinking wine.

'You make my heart sing,' Daniel told her as they watched the sun set over the sea. 'I am so happy when I'm with you.'

Daniel was excellent company, and Sally slowly began to relax. It wasn't just about sex anymore. After all, how could she spend so much time with him if they didn't get on?

Daniel insisted she stay overnight at his home when they arrived in England. 'Stay for one night, and, if you like it, stay more,' he said.

There was no pressure on her and no financial demands. Sally was showered with gifts and good food, and in Daniel's home, while he was working, she could quietly get on with her job. For a few short weeks, Sally had Fran for company during the limited free hours Fran spent away from the kitchen.

'You haven't been gambling since I came here,' Sally said to Daniel as they tramped through lanes of autumn leaves.

'I have no need for diversions,' he replied, 'you are my habit now.'

As autumn turned into winter and winter turned to

spring, with a strong woman by his side and a loving partner in his bed, Daniel was like a dog with two tails, and with Sally taking over PR, his business was booming. She only returned to her apartment to collect her things.

Sally closed her laptop as sunshine shone through an open window on the dazzling diamond that dominated the finger of her left hand. Like Waltho's Tabby, Sally preened and almost purred as she stared at her engagement ring.

'Our romance began at La Maison du Paradis,' she said with a wistful smile, 'and it really was paradise.'

'I can't wait for the celebration,' Daniel said, kissing her neck again. 'Are we all packed?'

'Wrapped, packed and Romeo is ready,' Sally replied. Softly stroking Daniel's face, she hugged her fiancée.

Chapter Thirty-Four

On a warm summer day in the middle of July, a gentle breeze whispered through the trees at La Maison du Paradis. The ornate gates, adorned with blooming wisteria, were open, and a noticeboard, perched on an old painted-splattered easel, welcomed guests. Waltho removed his sunglasses to study the wording and, with a satisfied nod, began to walk.

Passing rustic tubs brimming with a kaleidoscope of colour, he moved slowly along the driveway. When his gaze swivelled to the house, he stopped. La Maison du Paradis stood tall and proud, with shutters flung back and doors open wide, and Waltho felt the centuries-old stones ooze with romance and mystery.

It was the perfect setting for a celebration.

In the courtyard, beneath a newly extended gazebo, Waltho watched Angelique and Arletta. Centralised arrangements of flowers surrounded by tall, pillared candles stood on tables draped in white linen, and

Angelique fussed at the sweet-smelling roses, tweaking wildflowers into place. Arletta tied sprigs of fresh lavender to napkin rings and placed them on silver-edged place settings beside sparkling crystal.

A little boy dressed in navy dungarees and polished leather sandals ran excitedly through the tables.

'Fabien!' Angelique said. 'Be careful, please.'

Waltho picked up a sunflower-bordered place card to admire the elegant print. 'You did a good job of these,' he told Arletta.

He watched as Fabien ran into the garden to the swimming pool, where sunlight dappled the surface, rippling the water like a million tiny diamonds under the azure blue sky. Fabien zigzagged along the lavender-lined pathway, to a red carpet which formed a petal-lined aisle to an area prepared for a ceremony.

Waltho hurried to reach the boy. Taking his hand, they stood on the manicured lawn. Flanked on either side stood rows of empty wooden chairs tied with pretty bows, facing a sizeable arbor. It was threaded with ivy and trailing white ribbons. Sunflowers wove through the greenery amongst eucalyptus leaves and wisps of delicate ferns.

Fabien tipped his head to one side, his little face puzzled. 'Uncle Waltho,' he said, 'why have the birds stopped singing?'

Waltho looked up to see birds gathered on branches perched high. Fabien was right. Not a sound could be heard from the trees, and the air felt heavy with anticipation of an impending event.

'Like us, they are excited,' Waltho replied.

'Are they holding their breath? I do that sometimes when I want something good to happen.'

'Don't worry.' Waltho smiled and scooped the child into his arms. 'Soon, they will be singing.'

'Is the party going to start?' Fabien asked.

Waltho took one last look around and stroked the top of Fabien's head, satisfied that all was in order. 'Yes, little one,' he said, 'a magical summer wedding is about to begin.'

In the kitchen, Caroline stood at the table and, picking up a clipboard, studied a lengthy list and called out items to Tomas, who circled around her.

'Oui, all in order,' he replied, checking cloth-covered food and opening fridges and cooler boxes to delve deep inside. 'Everything is ready.'

'Then, there's just time for a cool drink before I get changed.' She smiled and patted Tomas on the shoulder. 'You're a star. We couldn't have done this without you.'

'Does that "we" include me?' a voice called out, and Fran appeared, looking frazzled.

'It's been a team effort,' Caroline said. 'How's your mushroom pasta?'

'It will feed five hundred,' Fran said and wiped a hand across her brow.

Tomas grinned. 'Daniel will be proud of you both,' he said, and with a wave left the kitchen.

'Come and sit with me and drink a cordial.' Caroline

reached for Fran's arm. Leading her out, they sat companionably on the garden swing.

'Is it really a year since you were here?' Caroline asked.

'It is, and I can't believe all that's happened.'

'I don't know how you do it – where do you get your energy from?'

'Sid calls me his battery-operated bunny. The more I work, the more charged up I get, and despite my age, I've never felt so well.' Fran cradled her cordial and sighed a happy sigh.

'I'm so thrilled at your success. Fran's Finest Fare is a credit to you both, and you've put Blackpool on the foodie map.' Caroline turned to Fran. 'Your dreams really have come true.'

'I know, me and Sid can hardly believe it. But your story is the one that needs telling,' Fran said. 'Just look at you, you're glowing and that bit of extra weight really suits you.'

Caroline laughed. 'The pounds have piled on and I really don't care.'

'I know we chat on the phone,' Fran continued, 'but now that I'm here, I want you to tell me all the gory details of the past year.'

Caroline glanced at her watch. 'You can have an edited version, will that do?'

Fran smiled and settled more comfortably. 'Aye, lass, it will have to.'

After her journey from France, when Caroline returned to Kensington, she'd found the house dark and empty. A *For Sale* board had appeared in the front garden and she hurried inside to turn on all the lights to see exactly what Stanley had left behind.

It wasn't very much.

Shockingly, he'd removed most of the furniture, and several antiques that she'd been hoping to sell had disappeared too. Ornaments that held any worth had vanished and paintings had been removed from the walls. Other than a worthless print or two, any artwork of value had gone.

'You rotter,' Caroline cursed as she threw open cupboards and wardrobes. All her best linen and china had been taken. 'How quickly you must have worked,' she angrily hissed, marvelling at Stanley's ability to suddenly get off his rotund rear and clean her out. No doubt he was salvaging as much as he could to pay for debts he'd probably kept hidden from both Caroline and the wretched Celia Ackland.

Unsurprisingly, his wine cellar was empty too.

'What a mess,' Caroline cried as she sat on her bed, 'what on earth am I to do?'

She had no energy to call Stanley and rant and rave, it would serve no purpose and making threats through a solicitor would only incur cost.

As Caroline waited for the house to sell, and as days turned into weeks, she gathered her clothes and sourcing out second-hand agencies, began to sell off her designer wardrobe. Studying vacancies for jobs, she even went out on interview – but knowing that it was unlikely that anyone would employ an ageing housewife whose only experience was a failed catering business, Caroline's desperation increased.

When Waltho rang, she ignored his calls, speaking to him only by text.

All okay, she'd texted him. *House going through. Got a couple of interviews.*

How could she admit that things were so grim? If he knew the truth, he'd only turn away, besides which, he'd told her he was painting again and life in France was good. The last thing he needed were her unsolvable problems.

Leo was kind, he invited Caroline to lunch and told her to try not to worry. 'Dad has treated you terribly,' he'd said, 'you must tell your solicitor.' But Caroline didn't want to burden her son with her problems, so kept their conversation light.

In the long days and worrying nights, Fran was Caroline's saviour.

No matter how tired, or how much work Fran had to do, she regularly called and her chats were uplifting and warm. On the pretence of asking for advice, Fran sent food deliveries, asking Caroline to try the products and feedback, for Fran's Finest Fare.

Sally too, kept in touch, as did Bridgette, both asking Caroline to come and stay.

But Caroline was sliding, and knew she wouldn't be good company, even if she could afford the train fare. The hope and optimism she'd felt in her last few days at La

Maison du Paradis had faded, along with her wishes and dreams.

'So what suddenly changed?' Fran asked. She pushed her foot on the ground and rocked the swing gently. 'You left before the house sold, and it was very sudden.'

Caroline sipped her cordial. The sun was warm on her face, and smiling, she closed her eyes. 'It was a call from Waltho that changed my life,' she said.

'Whatever did he say?'

'He must have borrowed a phone because I didn't recognise the number and thinking it might be news of a job, I answered.'

'And was it?'

'Well, yes.' Caroline said, 'I was shocked at first and couldn't speak when he asked me not to hang up.'

'But what did he say?'

'He told me he was in a pickle; he'd decided to run a painting course, which had filled very quickly. Some of the students were residential, and he had no one to cook or care for them.'

'Where was Angelique?'

'With her family in Holland.'

'And Tomas?'

'Working at the chateau with no holidays left.'

'What about the housekeeping lady?'

'Her husband was ill and she was caring for him.'

'Oh, he was in a pickle alright.' Fran nodded.

'Waltho said he would fund my travel and pay me if I could help him. He asked me to take a leap of faith.'

'A big leap but too good an offer to turn down.'

'Yes, in the end it was.' Caroline turned to Fran. 'I came to La Maison du Paradis and never returned.'

'Hallelujah!' Fran waved her hands in the air.

Caroline stood up. 'I can't believe that you came here to help with all the food preparations for the wedding,' she said, 'I couldn't have managed without you.'

'Ah, nonsense.' Fran brushed Caroline's comments away. 'What are friends for, eh?'

'You are the best friend I've ever had.'

'Well, I'm not much of a friend if I let you turn up at Sally and Daniel's wedding in that mucky old chef's jacket.' Fran took hold of Caroline's arm. 'There's a bride to be that needs a hand and we must get glammed up, we can't let the happy couple down.'

Caroline and Fran entered the house to get ready as puffy white clouds drifted high above the garden. Suddenly, silhouetted against a backdrop of blue, the soft coo of nature could be heard above the beating of wings, and as the sunlight caught their feathers, the birds began to sing.

Chapter Thirty-Five

W altho stood by the arbor in the garden and checked his watch. Everything was going to plan. The guests would assemble any moment, and Daniel and Sally would enjoy their bespoke ceremony. As non-residents of France, a legal ceremony, with only the couple in attendance, had taken place the previous week at a register office in Cheltenham, and today was the official celebration for Daniel and Sally to enjoy with their guests.

The calm before the storm, Waltho thought. But this happy storm would bring a day of joy, a bringing together of friends and the union of a couple very much in love.

Waltho looked at his surroundings and felt his heart swell with pride. All he'd dreamt of with Lauren had been achieved. He'd created a home, a business, and an environment that welcomed guests to learn while enjoying a holiday. The past year, he'd hosted folk from far-flung corners who enjoyed painting and cookery courses and, judging from their favourable reviews, found new friends and the perfect holiday at La Maison du Paradis.

Now, with so much romance in the air, Waltho thought of Caroline.

She'd weathered her own storm in the aftermath of her setbacks. Gone was the pale, uncertain woman he'd met off the flight bringing her back to France. Nervous, but with a sense of purpose from feeling needed, Caroline had embraced the workload that awaited her and Waltho had willingly let her take over the day-to-day running of the house. Guests loved her cooking and were rapturous over the meals she prepared while enjoying the comfortable ambience of the house under Caroline's housekeeping regime. Allowing Waltho time to paint, Caroline even took charge of the bookings, and courses soon filled, as guests recommended La Maison du Paradis. Her return to London was never discussed, and given responsibility, time and space, Caroline's protective shell was broken, and she blossomed.

Early one morning, during his daily swim, Caroline surprised Waltho by appearing at the pool. 'Will you teach me?' she'd asked. Slipping out of her robe, she'd tentatively reached out and took Waltho's hand as he guided her into the water.

'Don't be scared,' he said as he felt her body tremble and remembered her plight when she'd fallen in the river. Waltho knew it took great courage, but to his surprise, Caroline was soon swimming into his arms.

'I did it,' she whispered in awe, 'I *can* swim.'

As their eyes met, Waltho punched the air, and they both laughed.

In the time that they'd worked together, they'd formed a bond, and with Caroline's newfound space to build her confidence and discover that she *could* run a successful business, the woman had transformed. Here, in the pool, when Waltho wrapped his arms around Caroline, she melted into his grip, and, at last, their lips and kisses were as loving and long as their embrace.

The stage was set, Waltho thought as he walked back to the house, with a new performance about to begin.

A string quartet had struck up in the courtyard, and glasses clinked above a happy hum of conversation as Angelique and Arletta served champagne. The many friends of Daniel and Sally, who'd travelled for the wedding, joined with cookery school guests who'd returned to celebrate too.

Soft classical music played, and Tomas, who'd been designated to assist, announced that it was time for everyone to take their seats. As Waltho disappeared into the house, Tomas led the procession to the garden.

Angelique and Arletta held Fabien's hand and took their place. Sally's mother, who'd arrived the previous day, wore an enormous hat and perched on the front row, next to her husband.

Smart in a suit with an accompanying animal print bow tie, Sid sat with Bridgette, who'd gone to town in florals and ribbons that blended well with the arbor.

'I can't see a damn thing for that woman's hat,' Bridgette complained.

Caroline had invited Leo for a holiday and, delighted to be included in the wedding party, he sat with the expats, enjoying their company. With a twin on each arm, Ahmed and his partner walked down the carpeted aisle to assist Jeanette and Pearl, both elegant in turquoise and pearl outfits, to their seats.

Daniel stood at the end of the aisle and watched everyone's arrival. In a cream linen suit with a small sunflower in his lapel, he smiled eagerly at the guests.

Reaching his side, Tomas whispered, 'Ça va, Chef?'

'Never better,' Daniel replied.

The quartet had left the courtyard and now came into the garden. As guests heard Stevie Wonder's 'Isn't She Lovely', they took to their feet and turned to see the bride. Dressed in an ankle-length flowing lace gown and a pretty diamond tiara in her hair, she carried a bouquet of daisies and sunflowers.

Sally looked stunning, and guests gasped. With Waltho by her side, she linked his arm, and her smile was as radiant as the surroundings.

Behind them came Fran and Caroline. The bridesmaids carried smaller, matching bouquets and wore pale lemon dresses that swirled at the knee. Caroline's shining hair was pinned back with flowers, and Fran had an animal print scrunchie knotting her mop into a neat coil.

As Fran passed Sid, she gave him a wink.

Daniel shook Waltho's hand and reached out to Sally. 'You look beautiful,' he said.

The celebrant started the service, and the couple said their vows. Cheers could be heard as far as the village when they were pronounced man and wife, and the post-ceremony celebrations began. Caroline's menu, a gourmet feast, was a hit with everyone and served by waiting staff from the chateau against the picturesque backdrop of the garden.

'I couldn't have managed without the help of Tomas and Fran,' Caroline insisted during speeches, as glasses were raised to thank them for their efforts.

'Don't forget that I'm the star pupil!' Fran called out and, together with Tomas, took a bow.

As the sun began to set, and the sky became a palette of pastel pinks and golden orange, the lights of twinkling lanterns weaved a soft glow on the faces of the guests, creating a magical atmosphere that embraced the oncoming night. With tables moved back, the courtyard was transformed into a dance floor, and the newlyweds shared their first dance, surrounded by the warmth and affection of their friends.

Guests took to the floor, and Sid held his hand for Fran to join him. 'Come on, my pocket rocket,' he said, and she moved happily into his arms.

'Ladies, will you join us?' Ahmed and his partner asked Jeanette and Pearl, and they led the twins in a sophisticated waltz.

Angelique and Arletta held hands and danced in circles with Fabien. At the same time, Tomas stood and, straightening his lapels, reached out to Bridgette.

'Will you dance? Tomas asked.

Bridgette, who'd been enjoying Waltho's finest brandy, rose unsteadily to her feet. 'Who's asking?' she demanded.

'Moi, Tomas, I'm asking.'

'Then, I'm dancing.' Bridgette grinned and, gripping tightly, whirled Tomas onto the floor.

In a corner of the courtyard, Caroline sat and watched the wedding guests. Relaxed and mellowed by food and fine wine, she felt happier than she could ever remember. Her own wedding day had been a hurried affair where, bundled into an uncomfortable, tightly fitting dress, she'd witnessed Stanley drinking himself into a stupor.

If only she'd known it was a sign of times to come.

Who would have thought all those years ago that she'd begin another life in France? She could never have imagined meeting new friends and finding a job that she loved in later life. This had been a journey worth taking, and her cookery holiday a blessing in disguise. When she'd returned to London, and Waltho telephoned and asked her to take a leap of faith, little did she know it would be the best decision she'd ever make.

Caroline looked up. A female singer had joined the musicians, and the words to a love song floated in the balmy evening air.

Crossing the courtyard, Caroline saw Waltho.

How handsome he looked. This kind and generous man who'd allowed her to begin a new life. As he came forward, Waltho stretched out his hands and, moving slowly, Caroline slid into his arms, and as she stared into his amber eyes, she felt a sudden rush of emotion. Caroline no longer felt vulnerable and afraid. Life with Waltho had given her a strong sense of connection, and he accepted all her flaws and celebrated her strengths. La Maison du Paradis had enriched her life in countless ways, and Caroline felt like pinching herself to ensure this wasn't a dream.

Waltho searched for Caroline and when he found her, he paused momentarily to drink in the woman before him and thought how beautiful she looked. Her hair, longer and loosely styled, shone, and the pale lemon of her dress delicately complimented her lightly tanned skin. Lines of anxiety crossing her brow had lifted in the last few months, and Caroline was radiant.

He remembered again the question he'd posed when he'd opened his home to visitors a year ago. Would the opening of the French Cookery School mark the first day of the rest of his life?

A breeze, gentle yet persistent, whispered through the warm night air. Shrouded in the veil of darkness, it felt almost ghostly. Suddenly, a tendril of mist rose before him, and the scent of lavender filled the air.

Waltho caught his breath. For a moment, Lauren's face appeared ethereal, smiling with approval. But, in the blink of an eye, she was gone.

Waltho held out his hands and felt Caroline slide into his

arms. Their eyes met, and when she lay her head on his shoulder, he felt her lips brush his ear.

'Will you marry me?' Caroline whispered.

Waltho sighed with happiness. At last, the rest of his life had finally begun.

Acknowledgments

Dear Reader,

I am indebted to you for taking the time to read The French Cookery School. For those of you who have enjoyed my previous novels, thank you for enabling me to fulfil a lifelong dream and write on.

This story was motivated by a week I spent in France many years ago on a press trip to a gorgeous old farmhouse on the edge of the Charente. As a media agent representing celebrity chefs, I was invited by the host, the exceptional chef, Valentina Harris, to attend alongside notable journalists and experience the cookery course that Valentina and her helpers were instigating. It was a magical time, and I fell in love with the house named Le Touvent, overlooking the Dordogne Valley, which had been the former boyhood home of the late President Mitterrand. In the years that followed, I always remembered the magic of Le Touvent, and I knew the venue would make an excellent fictional base for a novel. On a return visit to France, I decided to set the story in the Vienne district in central-western France, and my research proved fruitful as I found many interesting places to take my characters to. I thank Valentina Harris for her hospitality and kindness, which inspired this novel.

Huge thanks to Lorella Belli, my talented agent. My work is in safe hands.

Charlotte Ledger, Bonnie Macleod, and the team at One More Chapter have gone the extra mile to ensure that this novel receives the best attention. I am deeply grateful to them, especially Bonnie, for her hard work and insightful editing.

Writing about older characters embracing their later years has given me a new lease on life. I am so fortunate to walk this path with my partner, Eric. He is always supportive, and his encouragement never flounders. We met later in life, and may our time together continue for many years. It is never too late to take a leap of faith and live your dream. My mother always told me, 'The time to be happy is now…' How right she was.

Happy reading, lovely readers. Do get in touch. I would love to hear from you.

Warmest wishes,

Caroline xx

ONE MORE CHAPTER

YOUR NUMBER ONE STOP

FOR PAGETURNING BOOKS

The author and One More Chapter would like to thank everyone
who contributed to the publication of this story...

Analytics
Abigail Fryer
Maria Osa

Audio
Fionnuala Barrett
Ciara Briggs

Contracts
Sasha Duszynska
Lewis

Design
Lucy Bennett
Fiona Greenway
Liane Payne
Dean Russell

Digital Sales
Hannah Lismore
Emily Scorer

Editorial
Kate Elton
Dushi Horti
Arsalan Isa
Charlotte Ledger
Bonnie Macleod
Laura McCallen
Jennie Rothwell
Caroline Scott-
Bowden

Harper360
Emily Gerbner
Jean Marie Kelly
Emma Sullivan
Sophia Walker

International Sales
Bethan Moore

Marketing & Publicity
Chloe Cummings
Emma Petfield

Operations
Melissa Okusanya
Hannah Stamp

Production
Emily Chan
Denis Manson
Simon Moore
Francesca Tuzzeo

Rights
Rachel McCarron
Hany Sheikh
Mohamed
Zoe Shine

**The HarperCollins
Distribution Team**

**The HarperCollins
Finance & Royalties
Team**

**The HarperCollins
Legal Team**

**The HarperCollins
Technology Team**

Trade Marketing
Ben Hurd

UK Sales
Laura Carpenter
Isabel Coburn
Jay Cochrane
Sabina Lewis
Holly Martin
Erin White
Harriet Williams
Leah Woods

**And every other
essential link in the
chain from delivery
drivers to booksellers
to librarians and
beyond!**

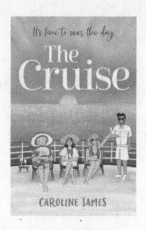

Three women.
One widowed.
One unmarried.
One almost divorced.
All aged 63, but not ready to give up on life!

Leaving behind the heartache, guilt and disappointment of their real lives, three friends decide that now they're in their sixties, it's time they finally did something for themselves!

Swapping Christmas turkeys and BBC reruns for crystal waters, white sandy beaches and smooth golden rum, Anne, Jane and Kath throw caution (and tradition) to the wind as they set sail on a luxury two-week Christmas cruise around the Caribbean. Will the three friends find the comfort and joy they seek aboard the Diamond Star?

Available now in paperback, eBook, and audio!

What happens at the spa stays at the spa

The Spa Break

CAROLINE JAMES

A weekend at the spa will leave four old friends with a whole lot more than they'd bargained for...

The glossy brochure promised a serene experience of total tranquillity and rejuvenation, but what best friends Bridgette, Emily, Serena and Marjory get is a weekend that upends their lives!

There for a girls' weekend to celebrate Bridgette's impending seventieth birthday, the spa soon has these spicy sexagenarians realising that there are unexpected benefits to age and experience, and that over the hill certainly doesn't mean out of the game...in any respect...

Available now in paperback and eBook!

ONE MORE CHAPTER

One More Chapter is an
award-winning global
division of HarperCollins.

Subscribe to our newsletter to get our
latest eBook deals and stay up to date
with all our new releases!

signup.harpercollins.co.uk/
join/signup-omc

Meet the team at
www.onemorechapter.com

Follow us!

 @OneMoreChapter_
 @OneMoreChapter
@onemorechapterhc

Do you write unputdownable fiction?
We love to hear from new voices.
Find out how to submit your novel at
www.onemorechapter.com/submissions